Acknowledgements

The section of this fictitious novel concerning some of the punishments inflicted on the girls trapped in enforced prostitution was based on true life experiences as recalled by those who were rescued/escaped and have now moved on with their lives.

My gratitude goes to those girls who sadly must remain nameless, for sharing their stories with me.

Thank you also to Kelly for her inspired suggestion for a suitable title

And finally to my wonderful wife Ellie, whom I can never thank enough, not only for her love and encouragement but also for proof reading, wise advice and suggested changes.

Ken Fryer

Born in London in 1951. Ken Fryer first began writing poetry in the latter half of the sixties; with limited success in being published he turned his talent towards writing lyrics of which he has since penned over two hundred titles. He took a break from the mid seventies to concentrate on his commercial activities. He resumed his first love of writing with a collection of short stories based on his observation of people, their relationships and subconscious traits. This was followed by a play for radio. He is also the author of several works of non-fiction relating to English medieval history. He is married and lives in a small Georgian market town in Bedfordshire, England.

ISBN: 978-1-84944-004-2

British Library Cataloguing in Publication Data.
A catalogue record for this book is available from the British Library.

Published by UKUnpublished

UKUnpublished
.CO.UK

www.ukunpublished.co.uk
info@ukunpublished.co.uk

A
LIFE LESS
KNOWN

By

Ken Fryer

PROLOGUE

The day started with frost and fog patches. It was a cold day, although apparently there were sunny periods. The temperature inside the overworked, understaffed maternity wing remained constant. The fourteenth day of February: the day I was born. Me. Rebecca Tanner. Not that I remember anything about it, but apparently my mother Madge had a rough time giving birth to me, and she reminded me of it often during my childhood, usually accompanying her reminders by hitting me for some reason or other and when she wasn't then *he* was.

He, of course, was Victor – my step-dad, or "Sergeant Bloody Major Wilson!" as she used to call him during their frequent rows. Not that he ever was a sergeant major. He never joined any of the services; he just like to swagger about in his highly polished work boots as though he was on a parade ground. He was also a typical bully, good for hitting women and kids but would run a mile if another man challenged him, even though he was built like the proverbial brick out-house. But whatever he was, whilst they couldn't afford a lot of things, he always made sure we had a roof over our heads and food on the table. Mum had married Victor shortly after her divorce from my real dad and promptly had our surnames changed from Tanner to Wilson.

My mother always felt, and acted as though they were a cut above other people. Why, I have no idea, because when they went full-blown into one of their rows, which normally ended with his hand coming down heavily on her, they certainly sounded or acted no differently to me than our neighbours. Ours was a working class street in a lower class area, far too common for anyone to have any social pretensions, but I suppose that's the thing about any working class area: the people who want to better themselves and get out can do so, and those who are happy to wallow in the mire, along with those who accept that this is going to be their lot in life, can make themselves comfortable and get on with it!

There were always the kids of certain families that I was told not to mix with, which of course were always the ones I found myself hanging out with the most. Between my step dad and my stepbrother, testosterone ruled in our house, so I grew up very much a tomboy. But that wasn't me, that wasn't the real Rebecca, or Becky or Becks as I was normally referred to, depending on the mood of the moment. No, I wanted the same as other girls…the fairytale romance, the dream wedding to my prince and of course the happily-ever-after bit, but I had to show a hard exterior, had to act tough because it was expected.

I had one sister, Ruth, who was just fifteen months older than me. We were close-ish but we had our own friends and basically we did our own thing. In most ways she was the complete opposite to me.

Our stepbrother completed the sibling line-up. Christened Albert, but known to all as Alby. He had the same build as my step-dad but, unlike him, Alby was a vicious bastard to anyone who crossed him. His own mother had died when he was only a few months old. She had been one of my mother's closest friends and so the story goes, with the absence of any other family, she became like a surrogate mother to Alby and a lover to Victor, which is probably what drove my real dad to drink!

Alby was four years older then me, and hated me from the word go, and as I grew from a toddler to an infant, and into a junior so I reciprocated those feelings. Alby was also the apple of both Victor's and my mother's eyes. They acted towards him as though the sun shone out of his every orifice. He could do no wrong as far as they were concerned, whilst I was always told that I'd bring them nothing but trouble and shame. I suppose being told that on a regular basis became a factor in the moulding of my personality and also preordained my life. I was certainly a rebel in that I wouldn't take shit from anyone. At the age of thirteen I dyed my hair from dark brown to jet-black and followed the Goth fashion. I completed my look with bright red lipstick and matching nail-varnish. Whereas my brother Alby took after my step dad in stature, Ruth and I had inherited my mum's genes and were of a slim, well-toned build and, like my mum, we were also lucky in that we could eat almost anything without gaining any extra ounces.

I never knew my real dad; he left shortly after I was born, but from what mum said he was just a no-good drunk. He certainly never bothered with me or Ruth, not a card, or letter, or phone call or anything while we were growing up. He was just a no-good waster, but as far as I was concerned it was his loss. Even now mum hated him with a passion but I think that was more to do with the fact that shortly after the divorce she lost possession of their beautiful big house due to the debts they'd both run up.

My best friend was a Jewish girl called Hannah Isaacs. Hannah had developed physically quite early and was of a more solid build. She quickly became, and had remained my role model. She was who I wanted to be like, even though my true persona was, well, chickenshit really! Hannah and I had met on our first day at primary school at the tender age of five and had remained firm friends from that day on. We were inseparable. My sister Ruth used to mock us and say she was surprised we hadn't become joined at the hip. But we didn't care, we were happy in one another's company, and as we grew up and entered into our teenage years we confided our dreams, desires and aspirations to each other.

Hannah was just twelve days older than me, but in my eyes she was a woman of the world and she had a confidence about her that made people take notice of anything she had to say. She could handle herself in a fight, so she never took any lip from other girls; she wasn't backward in giving boys a taste of her fist either, if they stepped out of line. Like me, Hannah was also a rebel; she had dyed her hair red and complimented it with black lipstick and nail polish. Neither of us fancied the Doc Martin fashion so we would wear trainers, big chunky black ones. The hidden truth of course was that Hannah was my role model; she was everything that I knew I was expected to be, hard and tough! And so I acted and displayed myself as a carbon copy of her.

Hannah was also sexually active and had been for some time, but it was on her terms and when she wanted it. For me it was different. I suppose deep inside I was still a little girl and in the back of my mind I still carried the fairytale fantasy of finding my prince, who would take me gently and lovingly into womanhood as our lives entered that blissful realm of happily ever after. But no! My passage into womanhood was more of a frenzied lustful assault by Paul Tyler, one of my step-brother's drunken friends, when I was fifteen years old. Admittedly I had fancied Paul for quite a while and one particular Saturday evening he turned up at a party at Hannah's house, when her parents were away for the weekend.

We'd all consumed copious amounts of alcohol, and some of the boys were passing around pills. None of us really knew what they were, but what the hell, we were young and this was our time!

As the evening drew on, couples were beginning to get it on together. Hannah had already picked out the boy she was going to screw and she quickly disappeared into her bedroom with him. Inside me was a combination of drink, pills and a desire to be on a par with Hannah. I spotted Paul who was standing by the living room door, shaking his head to the beat of the music, in between swigging from a half bottle of Hannah's dad's brandy he'd discovered. I took a deep breath and moved hazily towards him, he smiled at me as his eyes instantly fell to my tits. I grabbed his crotch firmly but gently and whispered to him, "There's a spare bedroom upstairs. If you've got a condom and fancy fucking me, we could use it."

His jaw almost dropped open with either shock or surprise. He ran his fingers up my arm as a leer spread across his face, and at that same split second I felt a strong cold shiver across my shoulders. I quickly pulled my arm away as the realisation hit me that I'd taken my bravado too far. I turned away and he followed me obediently upstairs into Becky's parents' bedroom. No sooner had the bedroom door closed behind us then he was on me like an animal…and it hurt! His hands gripped my breasts through my tee shirt as though he was kneading dough; he quickly pulled my shirt up over my head and as my unclipped bra fell to the floor I felt a sudden shudder of vulnerable fear. I felt the coldness of the room skimming over my now naked breasts. His lips closed over my nipple and, as I felt him sucking hard, it irritated me and I wanted to put my nails to my nipple and scratch it off. I closed my eyes as he pushed me back onto the bed and thrust his hand between my legs. The little muscles in my eyelids clamped them shut while I desperately tried to conjure up images of every fit boy from every boy band I could recall. I bit my lip…a little too hard as he pushed into me, against my dryness and I tasted the smear of blood in my mouth.

I blotted out his grunts. I wanted to believe it was really a cute boy gently loving me, but no – his rancid breath nauseated me as I felt him thrusting into me, faster, harder and then in that same split second I felt his warm gush as he relieved himself into me. He grunted again as he gave a final thrust and then rolled off me.

He pulled a cigarette out of the packet and lit it, inhaling and sucking hard on the filter; the glowing end of it seemed to burn down quite a way. He exhaled the smoke partly through his nostrils, the remainder through his mouth. I waited for him to speak but he said nothing. He left his cigarette balancing on the edge of the bedside table while he lifted the brandy bottle he'd brought with him and he took a long swig. The smoke gave an almost hypnotic dance as it floated towards the ceiling and for a moment I was mesmerised by it… but as he was bending down to pull up his jeans, he broke wind loudly, which snapped me out of my daydream. My eyes fell upon the sweat stains on his shirt and as the whiff of his fart reached me I felt his vile seed trickling out of me: the bastard hadn't used a condom!

Putting my hand under my crotch to catch it, I rushed into the en-suite bathroom, slamming and locking the door behind me. I felt dirty and contaminated. I just wanted to scrub myself clean, but how do you scrub your insides? Then an even more terrifying thought entered my head. What if I was pregnant? A chill returned to my body and I felt that I should cry – almost that it was expected of me to cry, but I couldn't have produced a tear if my life had depended on it. I just felt cold and detached.

I don't know how long I stayed in the bathroom. It probably wasn't as long as it seemed. When I came out Paul was sitting in a chair by the dressing table. A hand mirror was laying face up with a razor blade beside it; he had drawn out a couple of lines of cocaine and as I approached the bed to collect my underwear he rolled a new crisp twenty pound note into a tube and ran it along one of the white lines, inhaling it into his nostril. When he reached the end of the line he stopped and sniffed a couple of times. "Fuck, that's good stuff…d'you want some?"

I shook my head. "No thanks…a few pills, a lot of booze, but that's about my limit…why didn't you use a condom you bastard?"

He grinned smugly. "I don't like 'em…anyway, you're on the pill - what's your problem?"

"The problem, you fucking arsehole, is that I'm *not* on the pill. F'rall I know now I could be pregnant. You really are a useless tosser…." As I spoke I could both see and sense an anger building up in him, spreading through his arteries, consuming him and evolving into a rage. I instinctively edged back.

As the rage released itself within him he jumped up out of the chair and grabbed my wrist, twisting it. I didn't move or struggle; the atmosphere quickly became thick and heavy with his menacing overtones. I felt the colour draining from my face as his words spat at me. "Shut it, unless you want some of this…!" He held his fist held tightly against my cheek bone as he continued his rant. "D'you want me to teach you a fuckin' lesson, you dirty slag? If you are pregnant it's because you've fucked all and sundry, so don't try pinning it onto me, okay!"

I said nothing; my eyes just looked up at him with pure hatred. The snarl on his face remained, and I didn't need to be a mind reader to know he was contemplating whether or not to hit me. Thankfully he thought better of it and turned away. "Yeah, well, I got things to do, and I don't need no slag like you giving me grief, so you better jus' shut it, right!"

I watched in silence as he walked out, slamming the door behind him. The tension remained within the room and could feel my fingers tightening into a fist. I determined that he was going to be hurt for that…and hurt badly. But then I felt the tears fill my eyes and run down my cheeks. I had an almost uncontrollable urge to hurt someone, to inflict pain on someone the way it had been inflicted on me, almost as though it would somehow alleviate the pain inside me. I went back downstairs; Paul had left. I went into the living room and turned the music up loud. A CD was playing American rap music. I couldn't make out any of the words, but I hadn't turned the volume up to listen to it; I needed the noise to scream at me, to drown out my thoughts…

I didn't see much of Paul Tyler after that. He was apparently scared shitless that I'd tell my brother and, as much as Alby had no time for me, I was still family and he would have had no compunction in maiming anyone who in his eyes had violated his sister. The only good news was that two days afterwards my period came and I couldn't remember ever feeling so grateful.

Around this time both Hannah and I spent more time playing truant rather than attending school. I mean neither of us had any interest in it anyway. We were later told that apparently one of the teachers was overheard saying how much they appreciated the absence of our disruptive influence in the classroom!

We occupied our days sampling boys, booze, and drugs, in no particular order. We quickly learned the finer art of shoplifting, mostly from the high street fashion chains, and within a short time we were stealing anything and everything we could lay our hands on. We even tried petty burglary, but I was uncomfortable with that. Not for any moral reason; I just felt exposed and vulnerable while doing it. Alby had always said it was a mug's game. He claimed he'd known too many people getting nicked and going away and for what…a few pounds if they were lucky. So Hannah came up with the idea that we'd check out some suitable targets to turn over and then persuade a couple of mugs to do our thieving for us. We would of course take a percentage of whatever they took as our commission.

Our street cred was rising quite fast during this time, so there was never a shortage of mugs that wanted to impress us and who were willing to do our every bidding. If any of them ever tried to stitch us up by withholding our percentage, then they had Hannah to answer to and believe me, those days no one wanted a confrontation with Hannah!

My parents had never really shown or expressed any love for me; certainly not in the way I'd seen other parents act towards their kids. As a result they were never really concerned with how late I stayed out each night, so another one of the activities Hannah and I carried out quite successfully was mugging drunks. We'd wait outside a selected pub until a suitable drunk staggered out, follow him at a safe distance until he entered a side street or darkened area and then mug him. Our normal procedure would be just to rush at him from behind and club him with a length of wood; they usually collapsed after the third or fourth strike, and then we'd strip their pockets clean and leg it away, in case some busybody had seen something and decided to call the police. Each of these nights' work was quite successful.

Quite soon we had enough of these different earners to ensure we didn't have to fuss too much about finding a job after finally leaving school and, yeah, our later teenage years were pretty good.

Chapter 1

Becky

Today was my birthday. I'd reached twenty-one years of age, and I was already bored with this key-of-the-door crap. Come on, I'd had one of those since I was twelve! The previous night I'd dumped my boyfriend of the previous eight months: Darren, or Dopey Darren as I thought of him. I'd made sure he gave me my birthday present first though – a gold necklace pendant with matching stud earrings in the shape of a Chinese letter. I hadn't a clue which one it was, but it looked quite cool. Anyway he liked to spend money on me, and all it cost me was occasionally to allow his hands to wander up under my top. Shit, I didn't even have to take my bra off!

Looks-wise, I suppose I was in pretty good shape. Quite tall, slim and taut, shoulder-length black, bouncy hair, full lips and – as told by previous boyfriends – my body was sexy and hot, with a hot arse and tits to die for.

Hannah and I were doing all right with our little business. I wouldn't exactly call us a regular pair of Fagins, but income from our percentages was coming in on a nice and steady basis. We were also fencing the more luxurious items that our mugs were stealing, which added considerably to our income and, thanks to the skills of one of Hannah's boyfriends, we were also introduced to the art of stealing the occasional car to order; nothing special, just average family saloons, delivered after dark to a back street garage or lock-up. We knew we were never going to earn a fortune from it, but it was a good supply of additional pocket money. Anyway, on the times we did it, it livened up and put a nice gloss on the evening.

We kept our feet on the ground; we knew we were nothing more than a couple of kids hustling for a living but it was our belief that, despite being female, we deserved respect, and in the long run we intended to go for gold. Our message was simple: fuck with us and you'll end up worse off – and that was certainly true where the local low-life was concerned.

One particular piece of scum called Kevin Crestwell thought he could move in on us. It was one Saturday night and Hannah and I were out clubbing. We'd had quite a bit to drink and – like most of the clubbers – we were pilled-up. We were in the club's outer corridor, making our way back from the ladies when he cornered us.

Kevin was of a stocky build with close-cropped hair and one of those silly goatee beards; he had a round, chubby face that became more flushed in relation to his input of alcohol. Kevin ran a little team of about five thugs; mostly into petty crime, smuggling fags and booze from across the channel, with occasional ram raiding and violence for hire.

He approached us holding a bottle of lager. "Hello you two. I've been meaning to have a little chat with you..." he took a swig from his bottle, swallowed his drink and then burped loudly. I felt myself stiffen warily.

Hannah was looking at him with nervous eyes. "Why, whatcha got in mind?" she replied cautiously.

"Dunno yet – but...just want you to know that I'm open to offers ... and I'm not talking about the occasional blow-job!" He gave a drunken laugh, as he undressed us with his eyes.

"As she just said, whatcha got in mind, 'cos to be honest you're just pissin' me off at the moment!" My tone and expression showed exactly the level of contempt I had for him. I knew he was a dangerous man to upset, but he needed to know that we weren't going to just roll over and become his bitches.

"Give me a couple of monkeys a week for starters then we'll sort something out."

"We can't afford that," I stated defiantly.

"Look, if you want a quiet life then pay up. Look at it this way: you can't afford not to pay me. Just up your game a little bit, then when the money starts coming in regular you won't even miss it. Besides, I can do you favours ... we can scratch each others' crotches as it were, and believe me I'll be worth every penny."

Hannah sneered at him with contempt. "You smarmy bastard! You put your 'ands anywhere near me and I'll cut your fuckin' throat..."

"Let me give you a piece of free advice," he said menacingly. "Learn from other people, people who know their way around, people that can help you. You don't impress me with your hard talk, it's just bollocks ... now, are we doing business or what?"

Hannah and I understood each other's train of thought. She flashed me her look, the one that said, 'Let's do the bastard!' She smiled at him and said, "I think he could be useful to us Becky ... yes, I definitely think a grand a week could turn out to be a worthwhile investment."

"He doesn't come across as someone who just talks a lot of shit," I added.

Kevin had the look of a man who was about to enjoy a sex sandwich, but as he stepped forward to embrace us, Hannah quickly snatched a fire extinguisher off the wall and slammed it hard into his face, breaking his nose with the impact, and as he staggered backwards she moved in after him and smashed it into his face again. Kevin instantly fell to the ground, his face bloodied and swollen; he was gasping for air through his mouth, which was quickly filling with the blood erupting from his nose. He was making gurgling sounds as though he was choking; it was obvious he wouldn't be giving anybody any grief for a while.

Hannah stood over him and spoke quietly. "If you as much as raise an eyebrow to either Becky, me, our operation or anybody who works for us, I'm

gonna cut your head off and send it to your mummy, d'you understand?" She
swung her foot and caught him squarely between his legs.

I started pulling her away. "Come on, that's enough!" We headed
towards an illuminated emergency exit. Both the doors swung open forcefully as
we burst through them, and we ran into a nearby alley, that brought us out by a
takeaway restaurant, which at that particular moment appeared to be having its
busy period, with clubbers stopping off on their way home. We slowed to a
normal walk as we passed the shop front then began running again. As we turned
into a side road Becky stopped and leaned on a parked car for support; she was
out of breath.

"Stuff this for a laugh!" she gasped. "I've had it…I ain't running
anymore!"

For the next few days we were both apprehensive, knowing that at any
moment Kevin Crestwell's response could come crashing around us, but there
was nothing, just whispers about what he intended doing to us – or more
specifically Hannah – but words had never hurt anyone. The important thing was
that he left our little business and us alone. Money continued to come in at a
steady rate and, little by little, I realised that all the things Hannah had spoken
about were actually going to happen.

Things on the family front had not improved in any way, shape or form.
I had completely stopped talking to my step dad; in fact I refused to even
acknowledge his existence. He was just a no-good, lying tosser and a bully as far
as I was concerned. Equally I despised my mother. Not that there had ever been
any closeness between us, but I just resented her for all the times she'd hit me,
from my time as a toddler through to shortly after my fourteenth birthday, when I
hit her back. I think in her own way she probably loved me but just didn't know
how to show it. For all I knew, maybe that's why my real dad had turned to
drink. Although I must admit: the thought had crossed my mind on more than
one occasion to wonder if they'd been given the wrong baby in hospital.

My sister Ruth had done well for herself. She'd left school with an
armful of qualifications and gone straight into university, and having completed
that with flying colours she was now working for a large American conglomerate
in the city. A degree wasn't the only thing she brought home from University;
she also discovered she was quite partial to swinging the other way. Not that she
was the out and out butch type. In fact she was feminine and incredibly beautiful,
but she liked women as much as the boys did. Still, she kept her preferences
discreet and I was probably the only one in the family who knew.

My stepbrother Alby had firmly established himself within the criminal
society and was raking in the money. Not that it was ever doubted that he
wouldn't do well for himself. He was, and had always been his own man and had
no intention of surrendering any part of himself to anyone else. He was a

survivor and ensured he remained on top of others by brutalising to achieve his aims, regardless of whether it was a much-needed requirement or just a whim. Alby always got what he wanted; he had a strong personality and certainly didn't suffer fools very gladly.

He was now a part-owner of a popular snooker hall, which was also known among a certain clientele for its after hours drinking and no limit gambling. A couple of years earlier Alby had sussed out the place and its potential and offered Tony the Greek, the owner, just a few hundred pounds for a half share, whilst also offering to bring respectability and profit to the place. Tony wasn't impressed and suggested Alby should walk away to avoid a slapping. That night Tony's house was torched while his wife and kids were inside. Oh, they escaped okay but the message wasn't lost on Tony. This was followed up by Tony's beloved Mercedes being torched right outside the club, then his staff starting phoning in sick. Fights also broke out in the club, which led to a decline in business. Tony quickly sent a message to Alby that he had probably acted hastily and upon reflection would be honoured to have Alby join him as an equal business partner. I later heard that my brother had given him just a few thousand pounds for his half share, claiming he didn't want to be accused of being a slag and taking it for nothing, whilst at the same time hammering home the message that it was now Alby's club.

The place where we tended to hang out most, which Hannah called our base, was the 'Lucky Eight' coffee bar, so called because the owners, Bob and Marcie, had bought it some years before following a win on the football pools; apparently they were in a pools syndicate that selected the only eight score draws of that Saturday's games. Nobody knew how much their share of the winnings had come to. It obviously hadn't been enough for them to give up work completely, but enough for them to buy a high street café outright and rename it. The current state of the place showed that whatever money they'd had had obviously dried up over the years, or else they were extremely stingy with it; it was a wonder they had any customers considering the state of the décor; what was left of the last paint job was now flaking away. The tables were the laminated type and bolted to the floor, the chairs were tubular metal with plastic seating and backs. The lino was worn down into scrappy holes by the endless trail of customers from its heyday as a bright coffee-cum-snack house, to its now decaying throes attracting an occasional clientele of the odd market trader, lorry driver and homeless beggars. We had been using it for quite some time, mainly because it was a place to meet, chat and just hang out, where we weren't disturbed and I honestly believe they appreciated our regular patronage; even if we did just drink soft drinks and feed the juke box, we certainly gave the place a lively atmosphere. More importantly, however, we could discuss our – or at least Hannah's dreams of a criminal business enterprise and, of course, hold court to our lackeys.

Life carried on sweetly for us. The weeks turned into months, which turned into seasons, and suddenly a year had passed, then we were well into the following year. Becky and I had decided to move in together; both sets of our parents were becoming a drag, so we rented a three bedroomed flat. The rooms were exceptionally large and its location was ideal for us, and it also gave us an opportunity to spend some of the money we had been earning on furnishing it.

It was around this time that I started seeing a new face around. He used the café a fair bit, but I'd also bump into him in different pubs, clubs, even when just strolling around the market; his name was Danny Dolan. He had piercing eyes, which were constantly alert, darting in all directions like a hawk looking for prey and he was extremely fit – in fact I'd go one better and say he was absolutely gorgeous! I must admit I felt a little disappointed that he didn't seem to show much interest in me.

He didn't exactly come across as the stereotype womaniser either. I mean, Danny would often be seen with a pretty girl, he'd lavish gifts on them and treat them like princesses, and on the times I'd seen him out on these dates, he came across as being really attentive to them. Then suddenly, after a couple of months, the relationship would end and Danny would revert to being a loner. I wouldn't say Danny was well known in the area but enough people knew him to endorse his credentials. He was by trade a professional pick pocket and confidence trickster, commonly known as a grifter. They said he was one of the best, a natural talent and if he'd only shown an interest, I certainly wouldn't have objected to his fingers dipping into me!

As time went on, the money really started rolling in and life was good for us. One day Hannah surprised me by saying that we needed to have a legit business, move some of our money through the books; cover our backs in case the Old Bill started to get busy and stick their noses in to what we were doing. I agreed, not because it was something I'd also thought of, but because I knew Hannah had already made her mind up and it was her way of telling me what we were going to do, as opposed to opening it up for discussion.

Two Turkish brothers ran quite a successful mini-cab business nearby. Apparently one of them had been discovered screwing the other one's wife and all hell had let loose, with both of them now threatening to kill each other. Hannah went along to see the brother's uncle, who was trying to mediate between them, and made him a very attractive offer to put to the warring brothers: to buy the business on a straight cash deal. The offer was accepted and Hannah became the legal and registered owner of the business. I was a bit disappointed that I wasn't included as a joint proprietor, but I suppose she was the brain behind the business and I was the passenger, although she never treated me as such. She put in a guy called Lew Parker to run it. Lew was a tall and skinny streak of piss. We knew he had a perverted side to him, but as long as it didn't interfere with business, we didn't ask too many questions. Well, what the hell … after all, it takes all types.

The money continued to roll in and although we could easily have afforded to buy a bigger, better flat, we didn't want to draw any attention to ourselves. One particular day Hannah and I were holding court at the café. Hannah was sitting at a table and I was standing behind her, having just returned from the cesspit commonly known as the ladies' toilet. A girl called Sarah Mulden came into the cafe with two of her friends. Sarah was about a year older than us. She was known for being mouthy and had a bit of a reputation for being hard. She certainly came across as someone full of attitude and was under the impression she was something special. We just thought of her as a slag! She ran a group of girls who called themselves masseurs, but were actually just very low level call girls. Sarah's other speciality was breaking and entering, demanding money with menaces and general mugging, but unfortunately all her victims were disabled people, pensioners, in fact anyone who couldn't fight back and the added highlight for her was any opportunity to inflict a barrage of unrelenting violence upon her victims. Whilst I would have been happy to have nothing to do with her, Hannah viewed all business as business, and had recently muscled in and taken over the massage agency, whilst still leaving Sarah to run it on her behalf.

"I want a word with you…" Sarah said aggressively to Hannah.

"Okay, sit down and talk to me with a bit of civility and I just might listen to what you've got to say!" Hannah replied sternly.

Sarah remained standing with her hands on her hips in a stance of defiance. "I don't like splitting my earnings with you. I take all the risks – while you do sweet FA and take a big wedge of it, so there's gonna be nothing coming across!"

There was a tense silence for a moment as she finished speaking and the two of them just glared at each other. I felt slightly apprehensive, not knowing what our next move would be. My eyes quickly darted around looking for anything I could use as a weapon if it all developed into a free-for-all.

Hannah looked up at her and smiled. "Real tough girl aren't you? But you've got it wrong there darling; I do actually do something – I allow you to do a job in what is now my agency and then I take my due percentage, and if you ever try to intimidate me again in public…" her tone changed "…I'll cut your fuckin' throat out…you piece of shite!"

For the first time Sarah looked unsure of herself. "You think you got it pretty much your own way don'tcha?"

"As long as we understand one another darling, there won't be any problems. Now, you run along and send one of your monkeys back with my money…"

"I might just come back myself with a shooter in me hand!" Sarah's bravado no longer impressed anyone.

Hannah offered a loose shrug. "Like I said, real tough girl aren't you, but remember I ain't no defenceless pensioner, so if you try to stitch me up or try to front me again, I'll fucking crucify you and that's a promise!"

"Yeah but unless you can keep it, it's just words innit!" Sarah spat back; her confidence at fronting Hannah was clearly waning.

"Don't you worry girl! I can keep it alright!" Hannah replied while maintaining a fixed stare. Sarah gave her the finger and walked out, leaving her two friends standing there. Hannah looked at each of them in turn. "If you've got something in mind, let's have it now or else you can fuck off as well!"

The two girls left without speaking. We could see them through the large picture window of the café standing talking outside. Sarah was gesticulating with her arms. She was known as a vindictive woman and whilst there was no doubt that we would get our money, I also wondered what else would be coming our way courtesy of Sarah Mulden, all of which suggested nothing was settled.

Suddenly a voice spoke to me, breaking the tense silence; it was Danny. I hadn't noticed him come into the café.

"D'you want a cappuccino?"

As I turned and faced him, his eyes dropped to my tits; my nipples had just as suddenly become quite prominent. What was it about this man that had this effect on my body?

"What?" was all I could think of to say and in hindsight it sounded quite pathetic.

"Cappuccino. I asked if you would like a cappuccino?"

"Oh, yeah, I s'pose so…" I tried to sound cool and not show my surprise at being asked.

As Danny turned and walked up to the counter to order it, Hannah looked up at me. "She's doing my fucking brain in. I think she's gonna need hurting to teach her a lesson."

"Yeah I fink so," I replied half-heartedly. My attention was on Danny, now sitting at a table near the counter waiting for the coffees, which with my impatience seemed as though they would never arrive.

"She's had some nice little blags out of me…some nice earners…" Hannah was still wound up about Sarah. I briefly wondered whether she would suggest we pay her a visit and slap her back into line, and then just as quickly dismissed the thoughts, as I noticed that the coffees had been served to Danny at his table and that was where my full attention now lay.

As I came alongside his table he gestured to the cappuccino. "Yeah, cheers," I said casually as I sat opposite him. "D'you mind me sitting here or is it true that you enjoy your own solitary company?"

He gave a wry smile at my humour. "I'm not actually that aloof. A lot of people bore me senseless, so I'd rather not invest time in being with them…"

"What about me…do I bore you?" I gave him what I hoped was my most seductive smile as I turned my spoon over and over in my cup playing with the froth.

"No, you intrigue me. You're somebody that I'd really like to get to know but I'm afraid I may not be in your league."

"Are you taking the piss?" My eyes flashed up at him.

"No! No, I really mean it…to me you are an incredible sexy lady and you could probably have your pick of any man. If I asked you out, you'd probably just laugh at me."

"I ain't sure about you," I said suspiciously. "You come across as someone who could charm the birds out of the trees and you're giving me all this fanny about not having the confidence to ask me out…naw, you're just piss taking…" I stood up. "Thanks for the coffee, but no thanks…"

"Becky, please let's start again. Can I take you for a meal, tomorrow evening…somewhere nice where we can just talk…?"

Something in his voice sounded sincere. "Okay, I'll meet you outside, here, at eight o'clock sharp, but I warn you now, don't fuck with me!"

"No, I promise I would never do that."

I picked up the coffee cup and returned to where Hannah was sitting. As I sat down next to her she said, "What was all that about?"

"He's taking me out for a meal tomorrow night, somewhere nice, he reckons," I said with a smug smile.

"Well, it's about bloody time; you've been wanting to shag him for I don't know how long!"

The following day about lunchtime young Mary Lester came into the café. We always referred to her as 'Young Mary,' even though she was the same age as us. She was perfectly formed, with all the right curves and, yeah, beautiful, but she was short and because of her height she really did look about ten years younger. I actually had a lot of time for her, even though she had an annoying habit of starting almost every sentence with, "Well…"

Hannah called her over to our table and gestured to her to sit with us; we'd always got on in a good way so she had no qualms about joining us.

"You been a bit flash with the cash recently…what you done, had it off on the lottery or something?" Hannah asked.

"Naw, I been getting some hush money from old Mr Singh at the corner shop."

"What's going on there then…and how'd it start?" Hannah questioned, her mind instantly honing in to a possible earner.

"Well … I went to buy my little brother one of those left-over boxed Easter eggs; you know the ones that give a free action figure with it…well they only had the one…"

"And…?" Hannah snapped irritably.

"Well … it was on the top shelf, an' 'cos I'm short I couldn't reach it, so old Mr Singh comes out from behind the counter, stands behind me and reaches up for it, then as he's doing that he starts rubbing himself against me…"

"What did you do?" I interrupted, with my face screwed up in disgust.

"Nuffin'. I could feel the dirty old perv was getting himself horny, so I wiggled me arse a bit to tease him…"

"Then what?"

"Well … he passed me the box and said I could have it for being a good girl, then he said that he usually shut the shop for a couple of hours in the afternoon and if I wanted to come back then…well I could help myself to some more treats…"

"So what did you say?"

"I told him I'd be more interested in money than sweets, and he said that wasn't a problem and we could easily come to an arrangement."

"WHAT! Ah c'mon Mary, please tell me you didn't…?"

"I went back the next afternoon and we went into his little back storeroom."

"What'd the perv do to ya?" Hannah had an almost mocking smile on her face as she spoke.

"Well he felt me up for a bit, then he asked me to give him a hand job…it didn't take him long, then he gave me fifty quid out of the till, threw a handful of chocolate bars into a bag, then let me out of the side door…"

"And you've done this a couple of times?" she asked incredulously.

"Yeah, why not? It's easy money." Mary spoke with an almost childlike innocence.

"You going back again?" I could see Hannah's mind working overtime as she spoke.

Mary shrugged a shoulder casually. "Probably, one last time…once I've done the cash…but I'm gonna tell him my dad's getting suspicious and call a halt to it."

"I want you to go back, and I want you to write down the dates, the times and exactly what you do with him…better still, you write it that he makes you do these things…which reminds me, have you got a camera phone?"

"Yeah, course!" Mary answered almost indignantly.

"Good, try and get me some pictures with it."

"That sounds a bit pervy as well. What d'you want all that for?" Mary asked in surprise.

"Let's just say it's an insurance policy for you…I just want to ensure you're safe, that's all…" Hannah said in a non-committal manner.

"I will be safe; I shall stop going."

"Please do this one thing for me, and it's not just for you. Think about all the other little girls he could grab."

"Yeah, alright, I'll see what I can do."

"Good girl...anyway, unless there was something else, I've got some things I need to discuss with Becks. Oh, and one last thing: let me be the one that tells him you won't be going back?" Hannah watched in silence as Mary left the café, a twenty three year old girl with the physique of a mature twelve year old. As the door closed behind her, Hannah turned to me. "I think we could earn some money, putting a bit of extortion on old Mr Singh."

"I dunno. I think we gotta feel our way around a little bit first. I mean, Mary's alright, but she can be a bit neurotic at times," I replied warily

"Yeah, fair comment, but let's wait and see what she turns up with." Her tone and gesture told me she was only paying me lip service. Hannah had already made up her mind.

That evening I made a special effort to look my best. I had butterflies in my stomach as I showered and put on my makeup. I was determined to dress to kill, and if the evening turned into a disaster, at least he would see what he'd lost.

I arrived at the café at five minutes past eight. Danny was sitting in his car, waiting. He gave a little wave as I approached. I didn't walk any faster; I couldn't – I was wearing heels, and I never wore heels. I hated heels! I walked ladylike and with dignity; I was determined I wouldn't stumble and end up in a heap on the floor. Danny started the car as I climbed in next to him, then he leaned over and kissed me on the lips; I didn't pull away.

He engaged the car into gear and smoothly pulled away. "I've booked us a table at that new restaurant, 'Chuzzles'," he said as the car increased its speed.

"Yeah, I've heard of that. It's a pricey gaff though. Are you alright for dosh?" I asked in surprise.

"I told you, I messed up yesterday...so I'm going to do this properly."

"Okay, it's your money, but it's only fair to warn you, I've got no interest in all this lovey-dovey shit, alright?"

"Yeah, of course, and my smile isn't because I'm mocking you in any way, I just admire your openness in everything."

Small talk occupied the rest of the journey. Upon arrival Danny parked the car in a side road opposite the restaurant and as we climbed out of the car, I realised for the first time that he was actually wearing a suit and, well, to be honest I quite fancied eating him up whole right there and then.

The interior of the restaurant was certainly classy and reeked of expense. I didn't understand a lot of the things on the menu and I certainly wasn't going to ask the stuck up waiter what they were, so I settled for melon as a starter, followed by roasted chicken slivers on top of a potato salad dressed in a light vinaigrette – at least I understood it and knew what I would be getting! For dessert I settled on a chocolate truffle cake with a very light whipped cream, and I most certainly had no complaints about that. Danny had also ordered a very nice wine, which complimented the meal and slid down easily, but was also quite potent. I could certainly feel I'd had something to drink. I also felt that I'd had the most fantastic and enjoyable evening in company that I certainly wanted more of.

Danny was about to get the waiter's attention for the bill when another man came across to our table and shook hands with him. He was prosperous looking in a well cut business suit and he was introduced to me purely as Doug. I didn't pay him much attention. He didn't look like much to me, just another straight, but I did notice – albeit briefly – that Danny was overly respectful to him.

During the drive back I rested my hand on the top of his leg. It seemed the most natural thing to do and, as we got nearer to home, Danny said, "D'you want to go to a club, or straight home, or of course you're more than welcome to finish the evening off with a coffee at my place. I've been told I make a pretty mean instant coffee."

"Yeah, I've never seen where you live…this is where I find out if you are really a slob at home!" I laughed.

"I can assure you that my place is on a par with that restaurant we've just been to," he answered.

"What, full of tables and people sitting around eating?" I joked back at him.

"Okay, you win that round, but you'll soon see…we're here now."

The car came to a gentle halt outside a row of terraced houses. "Have you got the whole house?" I asked.

"Naw, just the upstairs. The landlord converted it into two flats, but at least each of us got our own front door."

He was right: he did make good coffee. We talked and laughed and it felt as though we'd known each other for years. However, the preliminaries were now over.

I leaned back against the coolness of the stretch-leathered sofa as he snuggled in closer. "Mm," was my only response as he gently stroked my hair. I ran my tongue over my lips and closed my eyes as he moved his face closer to mine. I felt his breath on my face for just a few nano seconds before he kissed me. Our lips together, lips so soft, equally arousing erotic senses, waking them to a potential passionate encounter. As our lips parted I quickly drew in air. The lips returned, this time with urgency, and my mouth gave itself to him as his tongue gently and nervously entered and explored. I felt alive with excitement; I could feel my heart pounding so hard that I thought it would burst out of my chest. His lips parted, hovered above mine, then slowly brushed against my cheek and down to my neck. He began a series of small kisses as his lips drew circles on my neck. I felt electrified, as though my whole body was about to shudder in sheer ecstasy. The lips moved to the side of my face, brushing tiny kisses en route, then to my ear. I felt his tongue lap at my ear lobe then gently nibble it before drawing it into his warm mouth. I had melted, I had no resistance and as his lips joined back to mine with an unmistakable urgency, I was completely submissive to him. My skin tingled and I had to bite my lip to stop myself from screaming out in sheer pleasure.

His hand automatically reached for my breast, and he traced his fingers around my nipple through my top, circling repetitively as my nipple responded by swelling slightly as it sent little electric shivers through me. His lips met with mine again; this time our tongues met and investigated each other. His hand meanwhile moved to my outer thigh and pushed my tiny skirt upwards as his hand moved up under it...my legs parted, allowing him access as though they had been pre-programmed to his touch.

"D'you want to move this to the bedroom?" he whispered with an urgency of his need into my ear.

"Oh, yes please," was the only possible answer.

We hastily moved into his bedroom, Danny removing his clothes as he went. I stepped out of my skirt and pulled my top clear over my head. I moved one hand behind my back and unclipped my bra, allowing the puppies to roam free, and I just laid back on the bed with my arms up above my head, offering myself completely submissively to him.

I awoke early the next morning … or it could have been several mornings later; I'd lost track of time. I knew that I'd been taken to paradise and that part of me was still orbiting the stratosphere waiting to return to earth. I felt a slight chill on my shoulders and quickly covered myself with the duvet. Danny was sleeping deeply and peacefully, as was his entitlement; he had given an outstanding performance and was quite rightly exhausted.

While I did actually feel far too tired to crawl out of bed, I knew I had things to do. I walked to the bathroom in a daze with one eye open. I saw that Danny had a shower over the bath but no shower curtain, but what the hell – it wasn't my place. I stood in the bath and let the hot water cascade over me. I noticed the dried out remains of a bar of soap on the side of the bath so I used that to freshen myself. I couldn't find any clean towels, and the ones he had on the towel rail looked as though they had been there for at least six months so as I hadn't washed my hair, I decided to let my body dry naturally. I walked back into the bedroom and pulled on my underwear.

"Hello you," a voice said from beneath the duvet.

"Good morning lover, so you're awake at last?"

"Mmm, what time is it?"

"It's definitely time you was up; I'm just about to leave…I was looking for the keys to steal your car."

"Are you going to finish dressing first?"

"No I'm going to give your neighbours a thrill."

"If you wait a while, I'll give you a lift home."

"Okay…" I casually folded my arms and watched as he stepped into his boxers. "Isn't it around this time when you're suppose to say you had a fantastic time and would really like to see me again?"

"Ah, yes…I was going to get round to that."

"I'll assume that's a no then!" I hesitated only briefly. "Don't worry yourself, the relief was appreciated but I wasn't looking for anything other than a one night stand…"

He zipped up his jeans and came across to me. "Becks, please listen to me." He took both my hands in his and held them tightly.

I shrugged my shoulders. "Look Danny, you were something to pass the time and that's all…don't try reading something into it that isn't there!" Inside I felt completely drained. I felt the bottom had dropped out of my world, but I was determined he would never see it.

"Becky, you're the one who's reading it wrong…you didn't give me a chance to explain fully …"

"Leave it out Danny…I told yer, I ain't been laid for a long time and I was getting ratty. I needed a shag and you were available, that's all there is to it…the meal was a bonus…thank you, but that's it! 'Nuff said, alright?" I gave him a glare that said 'you're pissing me off!' then turned away and finished dressing.

The atmosphere was tense as he drove me home and no words were exchanged. At the Lucky-Eight café, he pulled over but kept the engine running. As I opened the car door he rested his hand on my arm; I felt myself becoming agitated with him.

"Yeah, I'm alright, leave it…" I purposely wouldn't look at him as I spoke. Inside I felt emotional and I could find no rational reason for it. For fuck's sake I'd been on one date and yet my insides were churning as though it was a ten-year relationship that was ending. I shook my arm free from his hand, which was still resting on it.

Eventually he spoke: "Becky, I've got to go away for two or three weeks … the man in the restaurant who spoke to us, it's to do with him…he's a major face and he's got a scam going on a mark in Manchester, and if I don't go he'll cut my fingers off and probably smash my knee caps for good measure. I can't tell you any more…God knows I've told you too much already, but please Becky, I really do want to see you again." He put his hand back on my arm, but this time his gesture was calming. For some stupid reason my thoughts jumped to the car engine and how gently it was idling. I quickly snapped out of my reverie and then taking a deep breath I looked into his eyes.

"You're not fucking with me are you?" I said it almost submissively.

"Eh? No, for fuck's sake Becks, I'm not gonna use the love word, but you know what I'm saying…"

"What, after one date?" I gave a snort of false laughter.

"You gonna tell me you don't feel nothing?" His words came out soft and sincere. He was looking at me, waiting for an answer.

"Alright, you were more than just a fuck, but that's all yer getting from me!" I remained aloof despite every instinct screaming at me to throw my arms around his neck and to tell him I was actually falling for him in a big way and I'd wait for him forever if needed. Well … maybe three weeks!

"I'll come and see you when I get back and…we're good, yeah?" His hand squeezed my arm in affection.

I looked at him and our eyes met. In Danny's eyes I could see vulnerability; his face resembled a little lost puppy that was desperate to please. I gave him a smile. "If you don't come and see me the instant you're back, then take it as read that I'll fucking track you down…you bastard" I leaned forward and kissed him firmly and most passionately on the lips, then got out of the car and walked into the Lucky-Eight without looking back, although my ears were honed to the sound of his car's engine as it pulled away.

Once in the café I looked around for Hannah. I saw her sitting at a corner table, deep in conversation with Marion and Pete Perkins, a local brother and sister act. The rumour was they were the result of a couple of generations of inbreeding. Whether it was true or not I have no idea but the gene pool was certainly empty at the time they were conceived. Marion was muscular and a confirmed man-hating lesbian whilst her brother Pete had probably eroded what few brain cells he had by sniffing not only glue, but also any potent substance he could lay his hands on. They made their living through intimidation and menace and were a part of what was now becoming Hannah's team. I wasn't too fussed; after all she was the driving force, the brains, the organiser and the one a lot of people feared. I was quite happy to go along as a passenger. I was still part of her inner circle, and whilst it was unsaid between us, she seemed to slot into the role of the caring big sister I never felt I had.

As I approached their table the three of them were looking at me. Marion mumbled something, which caused Pete to giggle.

"What?" I asked defiantly.

"Nuffink," Hannah answered.

"Yes there is, you were all staring at me!" I felt myself quickly becoming apprehensive.

"Naw, it's nothing, don't worry about it."

"How d'you feel…relieved?" Pete asked before attempting to stifle a very childish giggle.

"What are you talking about, you gormless fucking moron?" I spat back.

"All right, pack it in…" Hannah said angrily. "I jokingly said to Marion that you might come in bandy-legged as you were looking to get yourself laid. It was meant humorously."

"Oh, fucking brilliant! What, my private life's now public knowledge?"

"Well did you get laid or not?" Pete giggled again like a stupid schoolboy.

"Pete, the subject is closed. Now tell me what part of that you don't understand." Hannah spoke without looking at him, but her tone was enough and the silly grin left his face. He stood up without speaking and went over to a fruit machine, while fumbling in his pocket for some loose change. Hannah looked up at me, a smile breaking across her face. "You didn't come home last night and you look radiantly happy; I take it your wish came true and you got laid?"

"I smiled back at her, "Yeah, all night long."

"Dirty, lucky bitch…" she replied with a beaming smile but the moment was interrupted by a loud clatter of crockery breaking in the small kitchen as either Bob or Marcie had dropped a stack of plates.

Chapter 2

John Tanner

John Tanner sat alone in the living room of his flat. His hand lightly held an empty whisky tumbler as he rested it on the wide arm of the leather armchair in which he had been reclining. His mind brought back images of people and events from the many years that had passed by in his life. A lot of water had passed under the bridge. A succession of lovers had come and gone; some had lingered longer than others but they were no different from old colleagues, both living and dead. All of them now just faces from the past; ghosts without the ability to haunt.

He felt scornful of his life, bitter that things had never seemed to work out in his favour. During the early nineteen-eighties his wife Madge had divorced him because of his heavy drinking; she had kept their four-bedroomed house on the outskirts of London, along with their two daughters and her lover. A lover he had been aware she'd had for a number of years. Madge remained embittered towards him and had taken every opportunity to poison his daughters' minds against their father. She had quickly married her lover and actively promoted his role as stepfather and hence Tanner's contact with his daughters became sparse and sporadic. Tanner now regretted the fact that during his daughters' childhood years he'd forgotten their birthdays, had never quite got around to buying and sending Christmas presents, and now the girls were adults they reciprocated by ignoring his existence.

Twenty years earlier, while working for the security services, he had foiled a terrorist plot: a threat to explode a crudely devised atomic bomb in London's square mile in an attempt to blackmail the Government. He, John Tanner had saved the day, saved the country, saved countless lives, but it was deemed too sensitive, too horrifying to make public and so it was buried away under the Official Secrets Act and his reward was a trip to Buckingham Palace to receive the OBE and promotion to a cushy desk job. All of which meant nothing…just bullshit, the equivalent to a pat on the head for being a good boy and remembering his manners.

As John Tanner had aged he had ensured he kept both his mind and body alert and fit, but his intuition nagged him that something wasn't right. It wasn't with the job and it wasn't his health. It was something he couldn't quite put his finger on…and along with this instinctive knowledge he also knew there was a huge something missing from his life.

Tanner gave a deep sigh and stared at the walls around him. He had been sitting there for two and a half hours and yet it felt as though it was only seconds. His mind jumped forward to more recent events. His job bored him rigid, he detested the young so-called super-graduates on their fast-track career paths and they in turn treated him with contempt. Only days before Tanner had submitted his request for early retirement from the security services. He replayed the scene in his head …

Upon receiving the written request, Sebastian Toakes, Tanner's section head who was renown for his officiousness, had requested him to attend a meeting in his office. Toakes rose from behind his desk as John Tanner entered, and offered his hand, which felt as limp as a wet rag as Tanner shook it. He gestured to a chair, and then returned to his own; he looked at Tanner thoughtfully for a while before leaning back in his chair. Tanner looked at the vast clutter of papers on the desk between them; he had personally never liked working in a clutter.

Toakes held up the retirement request then dropped it onto a space on his desk. "I can't say I'm surprised to have received this, John. You've given good service to the department but these last few years you seem to have deliberately ostracised yourself from your colleagues. You should know better than anyone that the secret of survival here is all about rubbing shoulders with the right people, and yet you go out of your way to alienate them!"

"Yeah, well, my horoscope told me to stay away from pompous pricks so I feel ignoring them is a step in the right direction."

"Yes, that about sums you up Tanner…unfortunately I have to ask you this question. Are you sure?"

"Absofuckinlutely." Tanner fixed him with a gaze, holding it defiantly, not wanting to be the first to look away. Toakes drew in breath as though he was about to say something when his desk phone rang.

The meeting was over but even Tanner was surprised at the alacrity with which his request was accepted and processed. They wanted him out as much as he wanted to be out!

Chapter 3

Becky

It was early afternoon, later the following week when I arrived at the Lucky-Eight café. Hannah was sitting at our usual table with Marion, and as I drew nearer to them, Hannah slid a large envelope across the table towards me. "Here, have a look at this, it'll gross you out."

"Why, what is it?"

"A few pictures of our sweet little Mary with Mr Singh's cock in her hand, amongst other places…"

"EWWW! No thank you!" I quickly slid the envelope back towards her. Both of them laughed at my reaction, but with Marion it seemed more of a half-mocking tone. I ignored it and looked directly at Hannah as I sat down opposite her. "To be honest, I'm a bit worried…"

"About what?" she asked.

"About this whole…"

Before I could finish, Marion butted in. "Look at the fucking pictures Becky. The man is sick. He should be grateful we're just gonna take some of his money…if I had my way we'd be cutting his balls off and ramming them down the sicko's throat!"

Hannah made a patting motion with her hand, "Yeah, yeah, let's just keep it down…I don't like it any more than you do, Becks, but this is our profession, it's what we do; we find mugs and we take money from them…tell me, have I let you down before?"

"No…no, I'm sorry it's just me, I'm having an off day."

"Perhaps you should stay here, and I'll just take Marion with me."

"No, don't be silly…I'll be alright." The three of us left the café and climbed into Marion's battered Renault, the interior of which had certainly seen better days. Hannah travelled in the front, while I sat amongst the filth and litter in the back.

As we arrived at the shop, Mr Singh was taking in an outside display rack prior to his customary habit of shutting the shop for a few hours. Hannah walked in first, followed by Marion and then me. Marion stood by Hannah's side at the counter, I stood by the door, ready to slide the bolt across to ensure we weren't disturbed by a last minute shopper. As Mr Singh returned behind his counter to serve them Hannah withdrew the envelope and placed it on the shop counter in front of him. He looked puzzled; he picked up the envelope, tipping out the photographs, and as they landed face up on the counter he looked up at Hannah in horror.

"Mmm, nice looking girl, she must be, what, all of twelve?" Hannah said, her voice laced with sarcasm.

Marion gave a disapproving tut. "So inappropriate, don't you think?" The man's face turned crimson with a mixture of rage and embarrassment; he actually looked a prime candidate for a heart attack.

"So, what have you to say for yourself?" Hannah asked with apparent disinterest. "I guess we'll just have to pass them on to the police..."

"And social services...'cos I believe you've got kids yourself?" Marion added.

"No, don't, please don't, not that please, no!" His voice was a dead giveaway; he was now putty in Hannah's hands. He seemed to be close to hysteria: fidgety, moving his weight from one leg to the other. From his shaking hands I could see that his fingernails had been bitten down to the quick, almost a visible symbol of the fear of discovery of the sordid secret he'd been living with.

Hannah pursed her lips, and then paused as though it would give her words greater effect. "I suppose we could come to an agreement ... but it will be expensive. I mean, there's little Mary's therapy treatment, and that doesn't come cheap. Then of course there's my own conscience. I mean I'll have to do some serious shopping to get the horrific images of those pictures out of my head."

"How much?" Mr Singh's voice was barely a whisper.

"What...? What are you going on about? Are you putting a proposition to me?" Hannah replied casually.

"Yes I s'pose I am," he said vaguely.

"Look, don't do me any favours, darlin'. I'm quite happy to give these photos, along with young Mary's written account of the things you made her do, to the police...and maybe a copy to the local newspapers..."

"Okay, you bitch, just tell me how much you want, but please stop torturing me. I didn't mean it to happen, it just happened, and while I know it's no excuse, she was fully compliant with everything that happened. Some of the things she even initiated."

"You sick bastard! Okay, I want two grand a week, and if you piss me about, even once then it doubles to four!"

"I can't afford that sort of money..."

"It's your choice, pal – I really don't give a monkey's either way..."

"But don't you see...you'll bankrupt me!"

"As I said...it's not my problem."

Mr Singh rubbed his forehead in dismay. "Okay, okay, I'll pay...please now just go, my wife is due here any moment!"

Hannah indicated Marion. "My friend here will visit you every Monday and you'll have the money ready for her, do you understand?"

"No, I insist on paying the money directly to you, and only you. If too many people know, then soon everyone will know. I must insist that it's only you that I pay."

Hannah knew she was holding the winning hand but also realised that blackmail victims in a state of high anxiety needed to be handled carefully and as this was her first major achievement in blackmailing, she decided to loosen the noose slightly. "Okay, that's not a problem…well at the moment it's not a problem. I'll see you on Monday morning." As she turned I slid open the bolt and opened the door. Marion was first out, and as Hannah reached the door she turned back towards Mr Singh. "Oh, and you can keep those photos…I've got copies of all of them!"

As we drove back, Hannah turned around to face me. "See? Told ya! It wasn't 'ard, was it?"

I gave her a faint smile.

"I still say we should have beaten seven shades of shit out of him first, the dirty pervert!" Marion said angrily. I wondered if her outburst was related to her own incestuous upbringing. I opened my mouth to answer but a feeling inside…not intuition but very brief waves of uncertainty surging through me causing a slight chill across my shoulders…made me close my mouth. I casually folded my arms and spent the remainder of the short trip listening to Hannah giving instruction to Marion about Sarah Mulden who had, in her eyes, stepped out of line again and this time needed a good slapping.

The next two weeks just seemed to fly pass, and this evening I was meeting Danny. Although we'd only had the one date, I hadn't been able to get him out of my thoughts, which in a nice-cum-irritating sort of way had been bit distracting, but the truth was, I really had missed him. He phoned and asked me to meet him in The Lamb's Coat, one of the pubs in town; he said he just had a tiny bit of business to take care of and then the evening was ours.

I took a taxi to the pub he mentioned. I wasn't comfortable with having to meet him there; it was a known haunt for a lot of the east European migrants who were now coming over and working here. It was also an infamous red-light district, where sadly a large number of teenage street prostitutes plied their trade. Rumour had it that some of the rougher elements considered any woman seen walking alone as fair game. When my taxi pulled up outside the pub, I paid the driver and asked him to wait for a couple of minutes while I checked that my boyfriend was inside. He took my money and looked at me as though I was the lowest form of life, then quickly checked his mirrors, and without as much as a second glance, he pulled away. As I saw him look in his rear view mirror at me I gave him the finger, then turned and entered the pub.

Thankfully Danny was there, standing at the bar talking to two guys. One of them looked in his mid-thirties; the other one looked more like he was either in his late forties or early fifties. As I approached them Danny had just moved his pint glass from his mouth, and the froth had left a small moustache across his upper lip. He looked at me and smiled before he wiped the back of his hand across his mouth. The instant I arrived beside him I threw my arms around his head and pulled him to me. My eyes closed as our lips met. There was no mistaking the sincerity and passion of his kiss and even though we were in a pub and I was aware of the other regulars cheering, jeering and taunting us, I didn't care; he was my new man and I wanted to stamp my ownership on him.

I was then introduced to the two men Danny had been talking to; the older one was called Andrei and the younger one Costi. They seemed quite friendly and both bought me a drink. Costi was particularly attentive, and I was waiting for Danny to show a sign of slight jealousy, but he didn't seem the least bit worried about it. He and Andrei were talking quietly to one another and although with the general noise in the pub, I couldn't actually hear what they were saying, the atmosphere was becoming just a tad too tense for my liking. Just then Andrei put his arm around my shoulder. I immediately shrugged it off; one thing I couldn't stand was being touched with familiarity by someone I'd just met – and most certainly when it wasn't welcomed.

Andrei said something to Danny in what I assumed was Romanian. I had no idea what it was but it certainly added to the tension building between them. All of a sudden it seemed as though the entire bar had gone silent, a scary deadly silence. Suddenly, and without warning, Danny smashed his fist into Andrei's face. The next moment I was aware of Costi standing behind me; he reached round and put his hands over my breasts, squeezing them as though he was doing me a favour, while whispering in my ear just how he would look after me and take care of me. I kicked my heel backwards, catching him on the ankle.

"Get your fuckin' hands off me, you piece of chickenshit!" As I broke free and turned to face him I kicked out at his balls, only it was more of a girly kick and I ended up hurting my own toes.

Danny grabbed my arm and pulled me along behind him out of the pub. I was fully expecting the place to erupt, but all I could hear was a burst of laughter from the other drinkers in there. We walked quickly to the end of the road where there was a mini-cab office and, as luck would have it, there was an available car parked outside. Danny told the driver the name of a restaurant up West and then, giving a deep sigh, sank back in the seat next to me. As the mini-cab made its way through the traffic, we both sat in silence, I suppose neither of us really wanting to be the first to speak and neither of us knowing what to say apart from the obvious. I didn't feel I should ask him what had happened in the pub. I knew enough to know there are some questions you don't ask, the same as I wouldn't expect him to ask questions about things Hannah and I were involved in.

"Are you okay?" He spoke casually, and without looking at me.

I shrugged in that gesture that says, "Yeah, whatever." I was trying to appear cool but curiosity was burning inside me. "So, d'ya wanna talk about it?"

"Nothing really to talk about. It was Andrei, he just sort of freaked out!"

"To be honest Danny, I didn't hear what was said between you two, and I don't wanna know, but it was actually you that hit him!"

"Let's just say we had a business deal which suddenly went pear shaped and leave at that shall we?" In the next instant he was full of apologies, promising to make it up to me, and adding that tonight it would be champagne all the way. Little did he realise that all I really wanted to do was to hold him in my arms and carry on from where we'd left off after our last date.

We arrived at the restaurant. Danny, so I discovered had apparently pre-booked us a table, and I wondered what other surprises he had in store for me. The restaurant was one of those frequented by celebrities; okay, not the A-list movie celebrities but certainly the ones you saw regularly on the TV soaps and shows. I must admit, during the early part of the evening I didn't take much too notice of what Danny was saying; my eyes kept darting around to see who was entering and whether I recognised them, but I soon became bored with that and settled down to enjoy the experience of excellent food, superb wine and good conversation. But even that eluded me. Danny held my hand and told me how much he had missed me, then gave me a gold bracelet with my initial etched into it. It was nice, and some girls may have been overwhelmed by it, but I actually looked upon it as being a bit tacky. However I accepted it graciously and put it on my wrist and cooed about how lovely it looked.

Then the bombshell came; he told me he hadn't been able to get me out of his mind, that the whole time he'd been away he'd been desperate to get back to see me and believed that he was falling head over heels for me, adding that he had never fallen in love in such a big way before, that he felt completely consumed by me, and how blissfully happy he felt knowing I was in his life. In fact it was everything a girl would want to hear, but, certainly not on the second date! I've had boys tell me they are in love after half a dozen dates but I assumed that was just a boy thing. This was something altogether different, almost creepy and I felt it was said in a cold, emotionless way, like an actor who'd repeated his well-rehearsed lines so well and so often that they were delivered without feeling. I didn't exactly have alarm bells ringing in my head, but my instincts told me to keep Danny at arm's length until I was able to think through whatever it was my instincts were warning me about. He poured two glasses of wine, passed one to me, and we held them up to one another.

"To us." He mouthed the words as, in unison, we lifted the glasses to our lips and while he swallowed the contents, I took only a couple of sips. I picked at my meal and ended up leaving most of it untouched on my plate. I assumed Danny had picked up my vibes but that he was sensibly refraining from too much inquiring as to what was wrong.

As we left the restaurant, Danny put his arm around my waist and we walked slowly towards the main taxi rank. The short cut was through a couple of dark narrow streets and as we walked into the semi darkness we didn't give it a second thought. Suddenly I stopped dead.

"What's wrong?" asked Danny, this time with a tone of genuine concern.

"I don't know, I just suddenly got an awful feeling," I said.

"Hello Danny Boy." A voice came abruptly from the darkness ahead of us. Three silhouettes approached us. Danny instinctively pushed me to one side. "Oh don't worry, your working girls are of no interest to us, but you've got some dues to pay, old son, and we're here to settle it up!" The three silhouettes were now partly visible, the glow from the distant neon lights making their appearances even more menacing.

"What's going on Danny?" I asked without taking my eyes off the three men.

"Stay out of it Becky, these three wankers are fucking psychos…" Before he could finish, a flying boot caught him full in the chest and threw him back against a wall. The three men moved in towards him, one either side and, one centre, who again lashed out with his boot, this time catching Danny on the inside of his kneecap. I watched him stumble as his leg gave way. The wall behind him steadied him, but I knew that if he went down, that would be the end of him, and as much as every instinct within me screamed out, urging me to pick up a brick, anything, and bring it down on one of their heads, I knew that I couldn't, even though it was three against one. I knew that if I helped in any way he would always be known, as the guy who relied on a woman to fight his battles and Danny would despise me for the rest of his life. We were only a few steps from a busy street, visible to people passing by and yet nobody made any attempt to intervene.

The men's fists were finding their target in rapid succession. Danny must have known that he'd be finished if he fell to the floor and thankfully from somewhere he found a surge of adrenalin; his fists flew out ferociously, a repetitive motion dispensing pain and injury to the faces of its recipients. Two of the men were now on the floor with blood spurting from the open splits across their swollen faces. The third member, not wanting to experience the same volume of pain, decided to run away. I went quickly to Danny's side and helped him to remain upright; his own face was severely bruised and one of his eyes was almost closed due to the swelling. As he put his arm around my shoulder I supported him around his waist, and then helped him back onto the main street, in the hope I could flag down a passing taxi. One of the men on the floor had rolled onto his stomach and was attempting to lift himself up. Almost in panic I kicked him hard in his ribs, causing him to crumple face down again onto the pavement. All that was on my mind was that the man who had run off could at any moment return team-handed and poor Danny would, without doubt, be beaten to death.

I thought about taking him to our flat, but I knew that Hannah would want to know chapter and verse on everything that had happened, and although I wasn't answerable to her, I really wasn't in the mood for giving either explanations or excuses. The taxi dropped us at Danny's flat. As he held on to me, I slipped my hand into his trouser pocket and retrieved his door key. Once inside I led him to the basin in the bathroom, turned on the tap and held his knuckles under the cold running water. He flinched slightly as the initial cascade of water stung him where the skin had split. I tenderly dabbed his knuckles dry. I found a clean-ish looking tea-towel in his kitchen, tore it in half lengthways and then gently bandaged his hands with it. His face was too sore to be touched so I led him into his bedroom and as he found a comfortable position to lay, I cradled his head in my lap, remembering all the stories I'd heard how you should not let anyone go to sleep following a blow to the head. But there was no way I was going to wake him, so I stayed awake watching him sleep, as if I was his personal guardian angel.

As my consciousness returned I had a sensation that I was falling and in that same split-second I awoke with a jolt. The light in the bedroom was still on but I knew I'd been asleep. I threw a look at the clock on his bedside table: 7.10am. I'd been asleep for a few hours sitting in an upright position and my body felt stiff and locked. I couldn't feel my left leg, as I'd sat with it tucked under me and now the numbness gave it almost a macabre sensation like swollen dead meat, or rather how I imagined a dead body would feel to the touch. I sat rubbing my leg for a while, until the blood was circulating fully again and it began to almost feel almost normal.

I gently lifted Danny's head and slid my lap from under it. My bladder was full and I knew if I didn't move quickly I'd be giving him a waterbed. I couldn't find any soap and was trying to wash my hands under the tap when I caught sight of myself in the mirror. I looked a mess, my make-up seemed to be smeared everywhere. With his remaining shower gel and water I soon looked presentable again and I walked quietly back into the bedroom and sat on the edge of the bed. I retrieved a brush from my handbag and began running it through my hair. I was re-living the previous night's events in my head, when I had a sensation that somebody was watching me. As I turned, I saw that Danny had perched himself up on one arm and was looking at me intently; it made me feel uncomfortable, as though he had been reading my thoughts and feelings.

"Are you okay about last night?" he asked cautiously.

"What, you mean that appalling crime that happened just off a busy street in a nation's capital?" I shrugged philosophically, despite the sickening churning feeling I felt inside about somebody I cared about being subjected to that level of violence. I was also aware of my own credibility, so there was no way I'd let him see it that it had got through to me. I acted casually, as though it was an everyday occurrence, as though I couldn't give a rat's arse either way.

"Just promise me something will you?" he said, smiling.

"Depends on what it is you want."

"Well, next time you get an awful feeling, can you give me a little bit more notice than last night's thirty seconds?"

"Why, is there going to be a next time?"

"If I could see into the future, I'd be picking this week's winning lottery numbers." As he spoke he reached across to the bedside table, opened the small drawer under it and removed a steel knuckle duster.

"Yeah, I'm beginning to wish I'd brought mine with me." My tone was loaded with sarcasm. "I think you need to go away for a while Danny…and it might be sensible to make it a long while…"

He raised his eyebrows as though in surprise. "Oh, come off it Becks, everyone knows what you did to Kevin Crestwell with that fire extinguisher…so don't tell me you're sensitive to seeing a slapping!"

I continued brushing my hair and said nothing; I saw no reason to correct him that it was actually Hannah who gave Crestwell his dues.

"Yeah, whatever," I sighed disinterestedly. I heard rain, a light rain gently starting its rhythm as it pattered against the window. "Anyway, I'm gonna make a move before that gets any heavier," nodding towards the window.

"I'll give you a lift."

"No it's alright, I need some air. Anyway, I've got a few bits to get on the way home."

"Yeah, but you're not alright are you?"

"Do us a favour and leave it, eh Danny? I tell you what – take me out tonight and make a fuss of me…I think I deserve that."

"Consider it sorted. I'll pick you up about seven-ish."

"Yeah, okay…bye." I blew him a kiss as I left…I also left the tacky bracelet that he had given me on his bedside table.

Chapter 4

John Tanner

John Tanner's farewell drink-cum-leaving do – if you could call it that – wasn't exactly a riotous affair and was as he'd expected; pretty much exclusive, with just two colleagues in attendance: Ernie Palmer and Maureen Dickins. Ernie was around the same age as Tanner and, like him, had spent the last fifteen years as a desk-jockey. But whereas Tanner was outspoken, Ernie kept his thoughts to himself and had the good sense to keep his head down. In his trademark cardigan, he gave out a strong image of being someone you could trust, cosy and unthreatening, somebody who wanted no more than the proverbial pipe and slippers. In reality Ernie Palmer was an experienced MI5 man through and through, and John Tanner's closest friend.

Maureen worked for a different branch of the Security Service to both Tanner and Ernie, but she was one of the few people for whom Tanner held the utmost respect. She was ice cool, competent, reliable and in Tanner's eyes a true professional; she was also respected as a Section Head of her own department, which was no easy task for a woman, considering that apart from these last ten years or so, she had been a female competing in an almost exclusively male world.

Whilst John Tanner had never made any secret of how he couldn't abide his younger and lower-ranked colleagues along with his fast-tracked, degree-carrying superiors, he'd never given any thought to what they actually thought of him. Now, with their notable absence, it brought home the sharp realisation of just how little those people actually thought of him, or more to the point, the likelihood of the contempt they held for him, both of which gave him slightly more than a pang of hurt.

Earlier in the afternoon a small gaggle of colleagues, Ernie and Maureen included, had gathered around his desk for his presentation of an outsized 'Good Luck, We'll Miss You' leaving card, which contained names that meant nothing to him writing good luck messages.

Sebastian Toakes said a few words, with more than a hint of insincerity, in appreciation of Tanner's loyal service and added just how much the service had changed in a positive sense since the time Tanner had first joined the department. He then threw in a barb of how the majority of longer-serving operatives had welcomed and embraced new standards and procedures.

Tanner's thoughts drifted. If he had wanted confirmation that he had made the correct decision this was it, a classic example of just how bloody minded the department and Section managers had become, especially with the politically correct doctrines that had now become mandatory within all government departments. The faces of previous section heads floated across his mind's eye; one by one the senior commanders who had favoured Tanner during his time there had either moved on with promotion or taken their pension and had embraced a wealthy retirement.

His thoughts were suddenly returned to the present by the sound of clapping. Toakes was presenting him with a small closed folder: his leaving gift. Tanner smiled for everyone's benefit and graciously accepted the folder. On opening it, he found inside a fanned-out display, a small wad of vouchers, to be used at any of the main participating Garden Centres which were listed on the inside of the folder – vouchers to a total value of one hundred and fifteen pounds. Tanner smiled and thanked them all; he decided against telling them that he actually lived in a flat with no garden, not even a window box.

Everybody had been informed by email of the leaving piss-up, which was now almost mandatory when anyone from the department either left, transferred, had a birthday or a baby, and on this occasion it would be starting at 5.30pm in the Three Kings pub, before moving on for the obligatory pub crawl, but as Tanner entered the pub at 5.45pm just Ernie and Maureen were present. There were a few faces that he thought might have put in an appearance but their absence again just confirmed the opinion he'd always had of them: petty and bloody minded. He hoped the look of disappointment didn't express itself too obviously on his face. As he approached the table where they were sitting, Ernie held up his glass.

"Well, here's to you Tanner…hope it all works out for you."

"Yeah, cheers Ernie." Tanner drained the whiskey tumbler, already waiting on the table for him, in one go.

"So, any regrets?" Maureen asked as she sipped her drink.

"No, I think this…" Tanner moved his head gesturing their lack of company "…just about sums it up. If anything, I should have done it ten, fifteen years ago."

"Have you given any thought to what you're going to do?" Ernie asked.

"I dare say something will come and knock on my door, so I'm not in any great hurry to go out looking for it." They continued in general gossip and small talk, as each of them bought a couple more rounds of drinks.

"I shall have to leave shortly; I have to visit my husband in hospital," Maureen said with almost a tinge of regret.

"How is Roger?" asked both men in unison.

"He's being kept alive with the aid of machines and drugs…he's terminal, he has no quality of life, he doesn't even know who I am most of the time…" She paused in a momentary act of composure "…but they say it could happen at any time now…"

"I'm really sorry, I'm…"

Maureen waved her hand in a dismissive gesture. "It's okay, we both fell out of love a long time ago. He spent far too much time in other women's beds…I turned a blind eye at the time, mostly for the sake of the children, but once they had grown up and married off and it was just us in the house, we were like two strangers…as to why I go and see him every night, well…I don't know why…I just feel that I should." Tanner glanced across at Ernie as he raised his eyebrows with a look of surprise. Rising, Maureen offered her hand across the table. "Well, if you stay in our line of work and you need anything…just ask; you know my number."

Tanner looked her in the eyes as he shook it. "Thanks I appreciate it."

Both men watched as she as she rose from the table: a beautiful, refined woman in her early fifties and yet with the air of a woman twenty years younger. Elegant in her movements and, almost as though she were modelling on a catwalk, she moved gracefully towards the far side of the pub towards the green neon light displaying the exit sign.

"A lot of men would give their right arm for a piece of that," Ernie said with a sigh, indicating he was resigned to the fact it would never be him.

"Yeah, Roger was a bloody fool…but the man just couldn't keep it in his pants."

"Mind you, she was married to the job anyway…maybe he had to look elsewhere for it?"

"That's not like you Ernie…you sound almost resentful."

"No, not at all…but you've got to admit, she is a bit of an ice maiden!"

"Yeah, but she's been a good mate to me over the years and that means something."

"Fair comment…but this is your evening, so tell me: what are you going to do with yourself?"

"Well tonight, I'm going to get three-parts-pissed, then stop off somewhere for a curry, then go home and sleep it off!"

"Yeah, sounds civilised…tell you what, I'll start the ball rolling by getting the next round of drinks."

Chapter 5

Becky

As was now becoming the norm whenever I woke up with Danny beside me, I felt happy, relaxed knew that I was probably displaying the silliest of grins. We'd spent the previous evening in his flat watching movies. I'd shoplifted a couple of DVDs from the garage shop while Danny was paying for his petrol; he teased me that I should have stolen some popcorn as well. He had a bottle of whisky so we cleared most of that, popped a few pills and then indulged in what I can only describe as sexual bliss.

It was now mid-morning and I had arranged to meet Marion for an afternoon's shoplifting for clothes. I'd already showered and was standing in front of his bathroom mirror fixing my make-up, my jeans half unzipped and in just my bra.

Danny had just stepped out of the shower and was towelling himself dry. He reached out and began stroking my hair, then dropped his towel and stood behind me, his fingers gently massaging my shoulder blades. I felt him close behind me, as his hips rotated against me. His fingers now played at the base of my neck, sending goose bumps down my arms and bringing all my senses alive. I felt his breath, warm and reassuring as he nibbled my earlobe. He nimbly unclipped my bra then moved his hand around me, reaching for my breast, his other hand moving down across my stomach; the anticipation of its destination sent a shiver of pleasure through me.

"Are you okay?" he whispered.

I turned around and faced him and put a finger to his lips. "Don't speak." I looked down at his hardness; it was looking up at me as though it had its own personality, trying to catch my attention. I looked back up at Danny: God, how I loved him! I couldn't think of anything I wouldn't do for him if he asked. "I think we need to do something about him," I said saucily as my fingers playfully wiggled his shaft.

In what seemed to be no more than an instant we were back on his bed, my legs wrapped tightly around him, feeling his warmth inside me and, as he brought each wave of pleasure within me, so my emotions were completely consumed with love for him.

It was well after the pre-arranged lunchtime. I was having a drink with Marion and her stupid brother Pete in a pub close to what used to be the old docklands. We were laughing and talking about nothing in particular when I became aware of a girl sitting at a table across the room, close to the entrance to the ladies' toilets. Her face was vaguely familiar but I couldn't recall from where I knew her. There was something about her that kept drawing my gaze towards her; she had the look of someone who either had been, or could be, very beautiful – well, perhaps with a make-over! She looked about the same age as me although the wear and tear on her face made her look a lot older. She had heavy lines etched deeply around her eyes and mouth; her eyes looked hollow and dead, which I put down to too many late nights partying and she was more than likely a dope and coke enthusiast. She was sitting with two men; both of them had their backs to me. She kept looking across at me. She gave no body language, but at the times our eyes met she quickly flashed them towards the ladies' loo, as though indicating I should look in that direction or maybe even go there. It was obvious she was trying to be discreet and the fact her face seemed familiar intrigued me. The next time our eyes met and, as before, she flashed hers towards the ladies', I nodded and stood up.

"I'm off to the loo…" I said, looking at neither Marion nor Pete.

"Hang on, let me drain this and I'll join yer," Marion answered, lifting her pint glass to her lips.

"If I wait for you there'll be a puddle on the floor…tell you what, you get another round in," I said humorously, and as I moved from the table, I noticed the girl who had been looking at me whispering something to one of the men at her table; he nodded and she stood up and entered the ladies loo, holding the door open as I walked in behind her. We walked down the one flight of stairs and in through another door to the ladies' toilets.

She stopped, turned around to face me and gently grabbed my arm. "Please…!"

"Sorry darling, I'm straight alright!" I interrupted her before she could finish and then at that same instant I realised who she was and why her face had been familiar.

"No, I'm not trying to pick you up…I saw you a while back at the Lambs Coat with Danny…"

"Yeah, that's right, we're going out together…an' I remember you, you're Laura Walsh. You went out with him for a while and then you dumped him…he told me just what a bitch you had been to him."

"No! No, it wasn't like that at all! He's lying to you! He tricked me…he sold me to one of those two men I'm with – it's what he does. He gets you to fall in love with him and then suddenly you find yourself with strangers, in a strange house and there's no escape…"

"Bullshit! Danny told me you took him for all his money and then when he had nothing left to spend on you, you dumped him!"

She shook her head as I spoke. "No…no, you'll have to believe what you want, but please promise me you won't tell him I've tried to warn you…but I am telling the truth; he put me up as security to pay off his gambling debts and now the guys I'm with say that the debt's now with me. I can't afford the three thousand quid they want so I'm forced to work as a prostitute to pay back the debt…only I never see any money, they claim it goes on my expenses…"

"Fuck off! I've never heard anything so ludicrous in all my life!"

Suddenly, the door to the ladies toilet flew open and one of the men she had been sitting with filled the doorway. He yelled something to her – I couldn't understand what was said; it was in some sort of Slavic language, but the look of fear on her face haunted me for hours afterwards. He grabbed her by the wrist, twisting it, and dragged her back into the bar.

By the time I'd washed my hands and got back to the bar, they had gone, and obviously in a rush, as all three of them had left their drinks half finished on the table.

I didn't believe what Laura had said about Danny; he'd already told me about some of her off-the-wall lies. But that look of fear on her face was a genuine fear. I now felt too distracted to go shoplifting with Marion, so I made a flimsy excuse and left.

When I arrived back at our flat Hannah was sitting on the toilet seat with her foot resting on the edge of the bath, painting her toenails.

"Hi," I mumbled as I passed the open bathroom, completely preoccupied.

"You alright?"

"Yeah," I replied half-heartedly.

"Are you sure?"

"Yes! What do you want, written confirmation?"

"Oh pardon me for fucking asking," she replied sarcastically.

"What?" I snapped.

"What is your fucking problem Becky?"

"I don't have one...or at least I didn't until I came home!"

Hannah stormed out of the bathroom to where I was standing with my hands on my hips in our living room. "You listen to me lady. I asked you a simple question okay! You've been acting quite weird lately and now you're giving me all this bitch with attitude crap, so what the fuck's going on?"

"Oh... I'm sorry, I've just got things on my mind that's all." My apology was genuine; Hannah was after all, my best and closest friend.

"What things...you're not pregnant are you?"

"No I am not, I've got more sense than that, thank you...they're just things, it's nothing."

"Obviously it is something or you wouldn't be so tetchy."

"I am not tetchy!" I replied indignantly.

"So tell me, what is it?"

"It's just something someone said about Danny, that's all."

"You're getting yourself all loved up with him ain't cha?"

"No, I like him and we care about each other..."

"So what was it you heard?" She butted in before I'd finished. "Is he putting it about or something?"

"It's more of a something."

"Okay, I'm listening, so tell me."

"Danny used to go out with a girl called Laura Walsh…"

"Yeah, I know…" she butted in again, "…and the last I heard of her she was one of Kevin Crestwell's bitches and I also heard that she was snorting his coke just as fast as he could shovel it up her nose."

"Well… an' I know this is going to sound crazy, and I didn't believe her when she told me but…"

"Oh for heaven's sake, just say it will you!" Hannah snapped irritably.

"She claimed that she didn't break up with Danny but that he sold her as debt for three grand and now she has to work as a prossie."

"Bullshit…I reckon she's been sniffin' the glue bag as well," Hannah scoffed disbelievingly.

"We were standing in the ladies and she reckoned she was having to have sex with all these punters just to pay the guy back his three grand, then while she's telling me, the guy suddenly bursts in and drags her out. She begged me not to tell anyone what she'd said."

"Oh Becky, you really are naïve at times, she's giving you all this bull and then saying don't tell anyone I've told you…well if it was true she should've been screaming the fucking place down!"

"Yeah, I suppose you're right, it was the look on her face. I can't describe it, but it made her sound genuine, if you know what I mean."

"Let me give you a more realistic scenario: the bloke was probably doing a deal and she was carrying his gear. He can't complete the sale because she's busy talking to you in the karsey, so he's pissed with her and drags her out."

"D'you know, you're right…I don't know why I let it get to me. I must be losing it."

"Naw, you're just loved up with your precious Danny." She held her arms out wide and we had a best friends hug.

The following Monday afternoon I was sitting running a brush through my hair. Hannah hadn't long been back from her regular meeting with Mr Singh; she was now clattering about in the kitchen.

"Oh shit!" Hannah exclaimed.

"What's wrong?" I called out.

"I meant to get a jar of coffee when I was at Singh's…completely went out of my head."

"I'm gonna nip out in a bit to get something from the chemist – I'll pick up a jar while I'm out."

"Ah cheers, Becks…if I don't get my regular shot of caffeine, I think I'll be climbing the walls."

I wasn't gone for more than thirty to forty minutes and when I arrived back at the flat, two police cars were parked outside and a policeman was standing by the side of one of the cars talking into his radio. Although having pairs of police cars wasn't unusual for this area, for some reason I felt a sudden spasm of anxiety, complete with a feeling of nausea churning in my stomach.

As I entered our flat, a tall man in a tweed jacket and brown lightly chequered trousers was standing by the window in our living room. Hannah was sitting in an armchair. Inside the room two uniformed WPCs were standing either side of the living room door, almost like a guard of honour. I entered the room; the two women looked me up and down and give the impression they were about to each grab one of my arms.

"Ah good, you're home…that will save us the trouble of having to pick you up, but I shouldn't think being picked up on the street is something you two are quite unused to!"

"What's going on?" I felt more indignant that they were in the flat, than at his insinuation.

"This is DS PRICK…he gets his jollies by harassing innocent people." Hannah stared at him defiantly as she emphasised his name.

"My name is PRI...ACK. Detective Sergeant Priack."

"Yeah, well, you'll always be a prick to me!" Hannah retorted. "…and you can leave her alone, she's just my housekeeper!"

"'Fraid not…" Priack said with a smug smile. "She's well involved, I've got no doubt about that."

Hannah flashed me a look that said '*distance yourself*' and I certainly didn't need telling twice. "What is it – something concerning me?" I inquired vaguely as though butter wouldn't melt in my mouth.

"Oh yes, I'm hearing a lot of verbals about you two."

His manner, tone of voice and unyielding expression would, I'm sure after a while, either wear you down completely or bore you to death. He spoke with an authority, which almost made you feel as though you should stand upright in his presence, his manner reminiscent of our old deputy headmaster.

Our deputy head also had a presence that initially commanded respect, but once we got used to him we considered him to be no more than a class 'A' prick. I remembered how he would approach us girls from behind as we were walking along the school corridor and as he came alongside us, he would gently pat us on the back and ask us silly questions like, "Hello, how are you getting on?" while all he was really interested in was if he could feel a bra strap! A few months after we'd left the school, an announcement was made that he had decided to take early retirement. The rumour mill was that he had tried squeezing the breast of one of the more developed girls, who had promptly complained to her form teacher. The school governors had managed to hush things up on the proviso that he left the school immediately. I'd also heard that some months later he'd hanged himself, although that may have just been wishful thinking…………

I quickly snapped out of my thoughts; something had obviously happened. I had no idea what this DC Prick or Priack or whatever, had just said to Becky but she had her defiant expression on and she was glaring at him with her lip curled. I know she was close to hitting him and was using the last of her restraint to keep herself in check.

"Well I couldn't give a flying fart one way or the other!" she screamed at him.

"Well you were certainly seen and we've got a witness." His tone was adamant.

"Yeah, well, I got rights; I ain't done nuffink wrong, alright!" Hannah spat the words arrogantly.

"Of course you haven't – you probably also go to charm school?" he replied sarcastically. "We've got more than enough on you two..." he said brusquely "...and all your little mates, all petty thieves together, you all think you're something special, but trust me, you're all just scum...just pieces of shit on my boots!"

"Oh well, that's a relief! But tell me, you must feel better now you've got that off your chest," Hannah answered with a smirk.

DS Priack frowned; he looked at the two WPCs and nodded, then looked back at Hannah. "Hannah Isaacs, you do not have to say anything, but it may harm your defence if you do not mention when questioned something which you later rely on in court. Anything you do say may be given in evidence."

Hannah raised her shoulders in a disinterested shrug. "On the advice of my solicitor, I have no comment to make at this time."

"And do you have a solicitor?" he asked almost wearily.

"No, but if I did I'm sure that's what he would tell me!"

The DS nodded solemnly and gave a sigh, a sigh that said: 'I've heard it all before.'

"You can get yourself a mouthpiece to speak for you or you can have one appointed..." he then looked across at the two uniforms. "Cuff her and take her to the station."

The policeman from outside came into the flat and along with one of the WPCs led Hannah out. Tears quickly appeared and stung my eyes; I wiped them quickly, but not quickly enough.

"Don't shed any tears over that one...she'll only involve you in more trouble than you're into now." He tried to speak kindly as though he was concerned for me.

"Involved in what?" I growled at him.

"Okay, have it your own way...we'll do it by the book." He turned to the WPC, who had remained. "Take her in as well for questioning. I'm sure she'll feel differently once she's been charged and processed."

Before I realised what was happening, my arms were behind my back and I was being led outside and into the remaining police car.

Everything had moved so quickly and now I was alone in a police cell. There was a narrow benched seat attached to the wall; in the corner was a stainless steel toilet with no seat-lid and there would certainly be no privacy for anyone using it as it was clearly visible from the spy hole in the cell door. At that moment the spy hole opened and I knew straight away it was DS Priack. I heard the lock turning and he stepped into the cell, pulling the door to after him.

"You're looking a bit anxious…" His tone wasn't actually mocking, but it seemed to be leaning that way.

"I thought you weren't allowed to interrogate me in my cell, and aren't I supposed to have my brief present?" I sat perch-like on the bench. My hair fell across my face but I made no attempt to move it.

"This is informal, just between the two of us. I'm hoping that after our little talk you can go home and all charges against you can be dropped … which I'm sure you'll agree is the preferred outcome?"

I casually folded my arms, and then unfolded them. "You called me a slapper when we were at the flat."

"A lot of girls your age are resorting to prostitution and petty crime in order to…be cool…make money, I don't know why they do it…"

"That's what you think I do, is it?"

"Why don't you tell me what you do instead? I'm sure it would be more informative than my guesses."

"Go to hell!"

" I'm afraid I can't help you there; you see your flatmate, Hannah Isaacs, has been charged with blackmail, intimidation, demanding money with menaces … oh, the list just goes on and on, and you are in the frame with her, right up to your neck."

He was arrogant, but his claim against me was a giveaway that he had nothing on me, otherwise by now I would also have been charged and processed. He was bullshitting me!

"What do you want?" I had a mixture of emotions churning around inside me. I was worried about Hannah, yet I was relieved about me and I was also quite frightened about the future.

"Perhaps you can tell me some things about your brother. I hear his little firm is quite busy these days," said Priack suddenly, in that 'I'm your kindly uncle' tone.

"I have absolutely no idea what he does, or more importantly, what he's currently doing. We both hate each other; in fact we don't even acknowledge the other's existence."

"That's a shame. You see, we recently detained a number of people on suspicion of drug trafficking and money laundering. We also seized…shall we just say an unspecified amount of cash during these raids. During the questioning, your brother's name came up almost constantly."

"Yeah, like I said, he's a stepbrother. We don't like each other and we never see each other. I probably wouldn't even recognise him if I bumped into him."

"You've got to give me something, Becky; if I'm going to wipe the slate clean for you, then I need something to make it worthwhile…"

"What are you after – a blow job or something? You dirty old bastard!"

"There's an old saying. Time is money, but knowledge is power, and information is that knowledge. There is a vast criminal community out there and a lot of the time I've got no idea what they're planning. You give me information as to what's happening on the streets, and I'll turn a blind eye to your little activities. It's a win-win scenario."

"Like I said, I'd really like to help you but I don't know anyone or anything!"

"I can smell crap Becky, but okay, we'll play it your way. You have a very good standard of living, yet you don't appear to have a job, so what do you do for a living?"

"I'm a housekeeper. I clean the house, I wash up … you know, that sort of thing."

"So how much do you get paid for being a…a housekeeper?"

"I don't actually get a wage as such; I get to live in the flat for free, along with my food and the occasional pocket money. I mean, I'm not one of those people who sponge off the state, if that's what you think."

"What I think ……well, for starters I think you are talking a load of bollocks."

"Yeah, whatever."

"You think you're a very clever lady, but listen to me when I tell you, you're not! We will break you, the same as we have others before you and no doubt those who follow you."

"Yes sir, no sir, shall I suck your cock sir?" I sat back and crossed my arms, smiling to myself. I heard the cell door close, the lock slam home and he was gone.

About an hour later the duty sergeant came in and I was released without charge.

I honestly expected Hannah to get bail when she went in front of the magistrates, but the police opposed it on the grounds that the charges were too serious. It was also believed that she would attempt to intimidate witnesses. The magistrate agreed and Hannah was put on remand. She was held in an open prison, just on the outskirts of London. Danny drove me out to see her. I was her first visitor; I took her in a change of clothes and a few comforts. She gave a relieved look when she saw that I'd arrived. Her eyes looked tired and sad; she also looked as though she'd lost a bit of weight. She was very bitter. It was her first experience of being confined and she didn't like it.

"Oh well, at least on remand you can have visitors whenever you want…" I said, trying to lift her mood.

"Yeah, fuckin' great. What about my loss of freedom? Who's gonna watch the business?"

"We'll tick over until you get out…I mean, what's the worst that can happen? You'll have to do a bit of community service. Anyway, the papers are full of people being let out of prison, so they're hardly likely to bang you up are they?"

"You keep a tight rein on 'em, especially Marion…something about her ain't right. I don't know what but I don't trust her!"

"Your hearing is in four weeks. Marion said she'd make sure that any witnesses they've got tucked away will have a sudden change of heart."

"Yeah, as I say, I've got a feeling in me water about her, but listen, I want you to go and see Marcie at the Lucky-Eight. Tell her I said she's to give you the letter…don't ask anything now, the letter will explain everything."

"You know the old bill turned the flat over…made a right mess…they did it when I wasn't there so I've got no idea what they took."

"I bet that was DS Prick…that arsehole's got it right in for me…and you should see the wanker they've given me for a brief; he's about as good as a fart in a thunderstorm!"

Tears started filling my eyes. She was closer to me than any mother or sister could ever be…and I was powerless to help her."

"Oh don't start all that weeping crap Becks, I need you to be strong…"

"I'm sorry…it's just seeing you in here and not being able to do anything."

"Well we both knew that along with success comes risk and danger and that was our thrill. Some slag has set me up, but we'll sort that when I get out of here."

The journey home was in silence; I was in no mood for talking and besides, my thoughts were analysing everything Hannah had said.

The following day I spoke to Marcie at the café, and she gave me the letter. I sat alone at one of the tables and opened it, quite cautiously. I didn't know either what I was expecting or what to expect.

Becky,

You're reading this so I'm either banged up or worse.

You're going to need money. Ask Marcie about our arrangement, she will show you what I mean. I normally pay her £50 per week, make sure you keep up the payments and don't tell anyone, especially Danny!

It will all become clear after you've spoken to Marcie.

Be brave and stop bloody crying

Love you
Hannah. xx

There were two keys in the envelope, and as I was looking at them I raised my head and saw Danny entering the café. I quickly slipped the keys into my jeans pocket, and stuffed the letter into my handbag.

"Hi Babe, what you up to?" he said as he sat opposite me at the table.

"Oh y'know, this and that…nothing special."

"I wondered if you, um…fancied coming to the flat. I've got some booze, I've just scored a few pills and I'm as horny as hell."

I moved my hand across the table and squeezed his. "I'm sorry babe, I'm not really in the mood…" and at that moment I felt a yawn coming on. It was one of those that you just can't hold back; the muscles in my face took over and suddenly my mouth was open, drawing in air. I covered my mouth with my hand and apologised but he said nothing…I'm not sure if he even noticed. He raised his eyebrows with either disappointment or surprise appearing on his face.

"Ah c'mon Becks I really fancy getting stoned."

"No Danny, I didn't sleep well last night. Hannah was on my mind…I'm worried about her…"

"Oh s'cuse me I'm sure, I thought I was your boyfriend!" He spoke like a spoilt kid.

"Danny, she's my best friend…it's only natural that I'd be worried about her…how can you have a problem with that?"

"I've got no problem with her, it's with, y'know…going without…jest 'cos she's banged up."

"Danny I can't believe you're being so fucking heartless…I'm actually really upset at her predicament!"

"So, I've got to become a born again virgin, jest cos that silly cow got caught?"

"No, but sometimes you've got to think of my feelings as well…I'm not going to be at your beck and call every time you feel horny."

"So what are you telling me…you're dumping me?" As he spoke, an expression of pain appeared on his face.

"No Danny. Oh, darling … I love you, I wouldn't dump you! Can't you see that I'm just emotionally upset at the moment?" Once again I felt tears sting my eyes. "Just go Danny…I'll come round to the flat later, and I'll make it up to you, I promise."

He rose and walked out without looking at me or even saying a word. I waited for him to go and also composed myself, then went to the counter and showed Marcie the letter she'd been holding from Hannah.

"You alright? Your eyes look bruised."

"Yeah, I'm fine … it's just where I've been rubbing them."

"It's none of my business Becky, but you watch yourself with that one!"

"Oh Danny's alright…I can handle him."

"Yeah, well, like I say it's none of my business." She lifted a flap in the counter for me to step through. "Go through to the back. There's an office…filing cabinet, third drawer down…cabinet's locked." With that she turned around, closed the flap and began wiping the chipped Formica surface of the counter.

A small room-cum-office at the back of the café was in a worse condition then the main area of the café. I reached into my jeans and removed the keys. I tried them both; the second one unlocked the filing cabinet. I pulled out the third drawer, it contained two attaché cases, the type salesmen use. I pulled one out and tried the other key. It opened, and what a surprise – it was filled with used notes. Tens, twenties even a wad of fifties … I couldn't even begin to imagine how much was there. I peeled off three fifties and a couple of hundred in tens and twenties. I then locked the case and returned it to the cabinet, ensuring that was also locked. I gave the three fifties to Marcie and asked her to give me the nod when the next payment was due.

I needed to de-stress and a long soak in the bath seemed the ideal start to calm my nerves. I returned to the flat and soon afterwards, as my body was immersed in hot water laced with lavender oils, I felt the tension flowing out of me. I lay soaking until I felt a slight chill in the water. I let out some of the bath water and topped up with hot, but after a while, as the water temperature again lowered, I thought about the wrinkly skin syndrome and decided it was time to get out. Wrapping myself in a warm fluffy bath towel, I daydreamed about being in one of those resorts where you paid to be completely pampered for the day. I then thought about Danny and how upset he'd looked at the café earlier. I sprayed myself with my favourite perfume, put on my sexiest clothes and phoned for a mini-cab. My man wanted loving and that's exactly what he was going to get.

The weeks flew by and the date of Hannah's hearing soon arrived. I hadn't seen much of Marion in the last couple of weeks; in fact I hadn't seen much of any of the regular crew. It was almost as though they had been lifted off the face of the earth. Danny had been most attentive to me, almost to the point where it felt like he was living in my pocket. I just put it down to his having a guilty conscience over his tantrum and because he was also head over heels in love with me.

Unfortunately he had further business in Manchester so couldn't be with me in court, but I didn't mind; I fully expected to be going home with Hannah after the hearing. I was in the upper public gallery; I had a good seat with a good view.

DS Priack was also there, talking to a uniformed policeman as I went into the gallery. He looked up at me but I took no notice and completely ignored him as I passed by.

The hearing started. The case against Hannah wasn't presented in a way that I'd expected; it was being presented as something a lot more serious. They had the dates that Hannah had personally collected the money from old Mr Singh, exactly how much had been collected on those dates and the total collected.

Mr Singh took the stand. He stated that Hannah and two other girls, who he could not identify, entered his shop and showed him pictures of a young girl being sexually assaulted. He claimed the perpetrator was not he, and that none of the pictures actually showed a clear view of the male person's face and the penis that was shown on the photographs was not his. He added that this had been confirmed by medical examination, to the satisfaction of the police.

My mind desperately tried to conjure up the images on the photos. I hadn't taken that much notice of the detail, and I'd automatically assumed it was Singh, because Mary had said it was. We'd all given just a mere glimpse at the face on the photo.

Mr Singh continued that he had pointed this out to the accused but she said the local vigilantes wouldn't worry about a small thing like that and would be only too happy to burn his shop down, and probably while he and his family were still in it. She also threatened to ensure his own Asian community was aware of the paedophile tendencies of one of their own!

Mary Lester then took the stand. Her evidence was that Hannah had forced her to engage in sexual acts with an elderly Asian man while she photographed it. Hannah yelled across the court at her: "You lying bitch, it's a fucking lie!"

I saw her brief quickly turn and instruct her to be quiet as her eyes flashed a look of hatred across at Mary.

Mary continued that Hannah had written down dates and times that she was supposed to have been assaulted by Mr Singh, including very explicit details, and had ordered her to copy it out in her own handwriting. Mary added that she was crying as she copied it, crying with fear of the threats Hannah had made against her if she should ever dare to tell anyone the truth. I wanted to stand up and call out that she was lying, but of course that would then put me firmly in the frame.

Hannah couldn't contain her rage. "You two-faced lying slag, I'm gonna rip your fucking throat out!" The district judge was visibly annoyed at her outburst and this time warned her that should any further outbursts occur, she would be removed.

Mary started to cry and really played up to her little girl image. She said that she now felt her life had been ruined and corrupted by Hannah Isaacs.

Next on the stand was Marian, who stated she was also threatened and frightened by Hannah into accompanying her and having to watch while she physically assaulted people … usually senior citizens who couldn't defend themselves. She then gave almost a catalogue of fictitious incidents that Hannah was supposed to have been personally involved in. As she spoke, her eyes were trained on somebody at the back of the court, but I couldn't see who it was.

Then the biggest surprise of all: Sarah Mulden appeared and claimed she was forced through fear to steal from people's homes and from empty offices and to give the proceeds to Hannah. She also claimed she lived in fear of Hannah's violence and was on anti depressants because of it. I didn't expect anything different from that lying slag, as there was no love lost between her and Hannah, but to turn grass, especially when it was a pack of lies, really gob-smacked me!

Two other girls, whom I'd never seen before, then followed one another on the stand and claimed they had been forced by Hannah to work as prostitutes under the guise of working for a masseur agency. Lie after lie painted Hannah as being an evil manipulative thug, living on the proceeds of prostitution and crime. DS Priack then claimed that a quantity of cocaine and hashish, along with a number of Ecstasy tablets, had been discovered during a search of the defendant's home. He added that although they were Class A, illegal drugs, they had been unable to establish if they were for personal use or if the defendant was a dealer, although he believed it was the latter, at which point Hannah's brief raised an objection that the detective's belief was speculative. DS Priack then gave a list of other offences that Hannah was supposed to have been involved in and asked for them to be taken in consideration.

Hannah's brief said very little to defend her or even try for leniency.

The judge summed up against Hannah. He gave her a lecture on her lack of self-control in his court, her reckless intimidation of innocent people, and her gratuitous lust for violence …. and sentenced her to seven years.

Hannah said nothing but as she was taken out of court, she suddenly looked very scared; her usual air of confidence had vanished and I saw she had tears in her eyes. I knew the next seven years would be a daunting prospect for her and I felt helpless at not being able to help or to be with her or even to give her a last hug.

I took a taxi back to the flat. My mind was in turmoil. Hannah had been well and truly set up. The lies, the so-called friends…but who was behind it? Somebody had to be pulling the strings. The police? The thought entered my head and was just as quickly dismissed. DS Priack had lied about the drugs, but he certainly didn't hold that much sway over the likes of Mary, Marian and Sarah, and Mr Singh certainly couldn't have been behind it. No, it was somebody else, somebody with a lot of clout who needed Hannah to disappear conveniently! I thought about how strange it would be, not having Hannah in my daily routine. She'd been part of my life for so long. I played various scenarios in my head, mostly 'what ifs' regarding the future. I was really depressed by the time I arrived back at the flat. I told myself to be positive; it wasn't as though she'd gone forever, and if she kept her nose clean she could possibly be tagged and out in less than half that time.

That evening I went to Danny's flat but I wasn't good company at all. I was withdrawn and sullen and it was quite evident that Danny was walking on eggshells around me. I decided to go back to my own flat and have a long soak in the bath, followed by an early night; at least then my mood wouldn't spoil his evening.

After a couple of days I noticed that people were avoiding me like the plague. All the old crew seemed to have disappeared into thin air. Acquaintances seemed to steer well clear of me, and if I visited any of them, they certainly went out of their way to make me feel unwelcome! I was beginning to feel quite sorry for myself. The only person who hadn't changed towards me was Marcie at the café, but then she was the same with everyone.

About a week later, it was mid morning and I had just returned to the flat from yet another pointless shopping trip alone. Moments after I closed the door, there was a knocking on it; DS Priack had decided to pay me a visit.

He came in alone with his usual solemn expression. He started off with some niceties, asking me how I was, what my plans were…etc. I wasn't in the mood for his crap so I just told him straight, "If you've come to arrest me then just do it, otherwise fuck off and leave me alone or I'm gonna be putting in a formal complaint of harassment!"

He hesitated slightly, then told me that Hannah had been taken to hospital the day before with horrific facial injuries after being slashed with an improvised blade by another inmate at the prison. He said she had received a total of 38 stitches to her face and mouth, along with treatment to wounds on her wrists and hands, which she'd received as she tried to defend herself.

A tiny tear rolled out of the corner of my eye and trickled down my face. It came home to me just how selfish I'd been, thinking only about myself while poor Hannah was locked away and at the mercy of psychos. My bottom lip trembled and I took deep breaths to compose myself. I fanned myself as his words echoed again in my head. The DS pulled a tissue from the box on our coffee table and handed it to me.

I spent the rest of the day moping about, my head filled with images of Hannah, with her poor face slashed to pieces. By late afternoon my eyes felt sore as though I'd cried continuously for weeks. The pain in my head was building, with nowhere for the pressure to escape. I felt the need to swallow, but my throat felt closed, crusty. I filled a glass with water and sipped slowly. It eased my throat but my head was still pulsating with the pain of trauma. I decided I needed fresh air, and settled on a brisk walk along the High Street.

A car pulled in just ahead of me. The front passenger window slowly slid down as I drew level; I immediately recognised both the driver and the front passenger: Paul Tyler and Kevin Crestwell – and I certainly didn't want to talk to either of them.

"Hello Becky, long time no see." That was Crestwell, with his arm almost hanging out of the front passenger window, leering at me. "Paul here was telling us how he once gave you a good seeing to, and you were really up for it. I quite fancy giving you one as well...unless you'd prefer Paul to do you again; you know...a little trip down memory lane. Naw, I reckon what you really want is the pair of us to service you...yeah, you'd like that wouldn't you?"

I ignored him, leaned down slightly so I could see Paul Tyler who was seated behind the steering wheel with the most stupid grin on his face.

"What are you doing, telling people you gave me a good seeing to, you little prick? You couldn't even see to the time of day!" I promptly turned around and walked into the first shop behind me, which luckily was a girly boutique.

As I entered the shop doorway I could hear Crestwell's voice calling after me: "Becks, I was only kidding! C'mon, I'll give you a lift home...stop acting like a spoilt kid, Becky...come on!"

A woman who was leaving the shop had obviously heard him calling out, and looked at me as though I was just a petulant teenager throwing a tantrum. My heart was beating fast, very fast. I was frightened. Without Hannah I suddenly felt very vulnerable. My bravado had evaporated; I was like a little girl lost! I needed to get to Danny, the one person I knew who would look after me. Thankfully, Kevin Crestwell hadn't followed me into the shop, and I watched through the window as their car pulled away from the kerb and sped off. I waited a few moments to ensure he wasn't just pulling around the corner, then quickly left the shop and returned to the flat, the place where I felt safe.

Chapter 6

John Tanner

John Tanner was into the fifth week of his retirement. He'd received two job offers to work as a security consultant but he'd turned them both down flat. The thought of working with a new set of pompous pricks and prickesses did little to inspire him.

A wave of envy came across him for the men who had nurtured hobbies and looked forward to retirement to be able to give full attention to their joy. But try as he might, he couldn't think of anything he would want to dedicate his spare time to.

He had never allowed anyone to get close to him emotionally so whilst he had many acquaintances, his actual friends he could count on one hand and still have fingers left over. He'd always enjoyed reading, and history was his favourite subject. He had a small number of lady friends, although again he'd always kept them at arms length emotionally. He treated them lavishly when he took them out and he ensure he took care of their needs in the bedroom, but away from that he knew he was a cold fish.

As his mind pondered his current situation, he realised that loneliness was the price he had to pay for the last twenty odd years of emotional detachment.

Tanner's thoughts went blank. He stared at the walls around him; the seconds really did seem like hours. He glanced out of his flat window, looking up at the sky, a cold grey sky with drizzling rain. "So this is what I'm going to be reduced to?" He gave a deep sigh and shook his head as his thoughts bordered on despair. He gave another sigh and then snapped himself out of his morbid drifting. There had to be something he could do, something to which he could turn his talents. He delved into his thoughts again looking, hoping for an inspiration. Memoirs. A lot of retired operatives wrote their memoirs…but as quickly as he thought of it, he decided against it; it would open far too many old wounds. Wounds that were better left buried in the sands of time.

He felt restless and irritated by his boredom. "Come on, there's got to be something…anything…please!" He spoke to the empty room. The sound of his doorbell broke his thought pattern, and he frowned as he stood up and made his way to open the front door of his flat.

Chapter 7

Becky

I couldn't get hold of Danny on his mobile. I left voice messages for him to call me, but he didn't call and of course I couldn't be sure he actually got them. I went to his flat but there was no answer.

I decided to visit my sister Ruth. She hadn't long moved into a house with a couple of work colleagues. It was one of those moments you hear about, when whatever shit the world drops on you, your family are always there for you. Not that I would have wanted to do the daughter-mumsy thing with Madge.

On second thoughts, I wasn't even interested in seeing Madge again. Every childhood memory of her was where she was hitting me. Childhood scenes were always remembered through tear-streaked eyes. As for my step-dad and stepbrother – well, they weren't even blood related and they were both arseholes in my book. No, Ruth was the only one I'd got…I actually started wondering what my real dad was like. I assumed he might already be dead by now. Madge always said he was a no good alcoholic…maybe I took after him and that Madge had been right when she declared that I'd never amount to anything.

It was actually good seeing Ruth again. We'd both changed in many ways, both grown up. I gave her a whitewashed version of things Hannah and I had been up to; told her about the court case, the stitch-up. She started to give me the older sister lecture about learning a lesson from what had happened to Hannah, did I want to end up in prison, it wasn't too late to change my ways etc.

I decided to change the subject, so I told her all about Danny. I probably painted it a little rosier than it was between us, because suddenly she was talking about weddings and asking about where we would live. I let her ramble on; I figured no harm would be done by not bursting her bubble. As she was talking I suddenly realised I was actually now dependent on Danny – not in any financial way, but certainly emotionally. He'd unknowingly filled the void left by Hannah. I realised I was missing him – God, how much I missed him! – and at that same moment I received a text from him, saying he'd just got back to his flat and asking if everything was all right. It was the trigger that sent a surge of happiness through me, and I said to myself, 'Oh my darling Danny, everything is all right now, everything is perfect.' Ruth phoned for a mini-cab for me, we had a sisterly hug and I went back to my flat to shower and change…to see my man.

I arrived at Danny's just after eight. His face lit up when he saw me. "Wow, Becks, you look a million dollars!"

"What, just a million…after all the trouble I've gone to?" I teased as I leaned forward for a kiss.

"You're right, I'll book us a table somewhere nice, then have a quick shower…I dare say you could probably do with cheering up." He punched a number into his mobile and I heard him book a table for two. While he was having his shower, his comment suddenly came to mind, that I could probably do with cheering up. It seemed a strange thing to say, considering I hadn't said anything to him about my experience with Kevin Crestwell. Perhaps he was referring to the text and voice messages I'd left on his mobile.

We went back to Chuzzles restaurant, the place of our first date; it had since gained a reputation as an eatery for the very well heeled clientele. I looked around at how it had changed since the last time we had eaten there. There were fewer tables than before, giving diners more privacy. The menu showed that prices had gone up by around a third. But the place absolutely shouted elegance.

While we were looking through the menu, I caught sight of another diner.

"Oh shit!"

"What's the matter?" asked Danny.

"Over there…it's my stepbrother."

"What? Alby Wilson…your stepbrother?"

"Yeah…he's an arsehole."

"Maybe, but that's not something many people would want to say to his face."

"I don't want to look in case he sees me…who's he with?" I hid my face behind the menu.

"An elderly guy in a suit and a couple of…mm, hot young foxes…"

"Well, feel free if you want to go and join them!" I retorted indignantly.

"Why on earth would I want to do that, when I've got the hottest fox of all sitting beside me?"

"You're too smooth for your own good sometimes, Danny Dolan," I giggled as I climbed off my high horse.

As Danny gave our order to the waiter, I looked across to where Alby was sitting. He was oblivious to fellow diners and anyway, the worst Alby could do to me was to ignore me, and that's how I felt about him so I pushed him from my mind.

While we were eating our starters, Danny hesitated, and then said tentatively, "We've been going out together for a while now; how far do you see it going?"

"As you brought the subject up…how far do *you* see it going?" I answered suspiciously and with a hint of dread.

"I'd like it to be permanent…I don't want to be old before I have kids…"

"Whoa, one step at a time… are you proposing to me?" I could feel a smile spreading across my face.

"Yes and no...obviously at some time in the future I'd like us to become legally permanent, but for now I just want to know if we've both got the same vision?"

"Oh, I can safely say yes, on both counts," I answered with a mixture of nervousness and excitement.

He moved his hand across the table and squeezed mine. "I do love you Becky."

"I love you too Danny."

He let go of my hand as the waiter cleared our empty dishes...within moments another waiter was placing our main course in front of us. As we enjoyed the meal, I glanced across to where Alby was sitting; two other men had joined them at their table. One of the men appeared familiar. I'd seen the face before, but I couldn't place where...then I remembered: it was here on my first date with Danny; he'd introduced me to him. I couldn't remember his name but I could certainly remember just how respectful Danny was to him, almost to the point of being fearful.

The man had now stood up. Whatever he was saying to Alby, he undoubtedly had an air of menace about him. Not in a violent way, more in a calm, chilling, terrifying sort of way. Alby didn't seem in the least bit bothered by whatever the man was saying.

I thought about the sort of man Alby had become. He'd now completely ousted Tony the Greek and had changed the snooker hall into a members' only club for high rollers, city types with more money than sense. His club now catered for almost every weakness and carnal desire: food, drink, drugs, and sex – everything was available at a price, with discretion assured. The city boys lapped it up and the money rolled in. The club actually had a waiting list for membership.

I nudged Danny. "There's your friend over there," I said nodding in the direction of Alby's table.

"Oh shit, don't let him see us!" he exclaimed, almost in shock.

"Isn't this a repeat of what I said earlier?" I mocked gently.

"The difference is Becky, where your stepbrother is just a vicious thug, Doug Mann is a completely different breed. He has a one-track mind; making money is all that matters to him. People are unimportant; he wouldn't think twice about killing anyone if he thought there was a few pounds in it for him!"

"Who's the other man with him?" I asked.

"That's Ray. He doesn't look much but believe me, he's solid muscle, and he's one of Doug's right hand men."

Both men left the restaurant. Whatever had been said between them and Alby, it had been said in a low key. I shouldn't think anyone else sitting around them was even aware a disagreement had taken place. Danny appeared to be agitated, and this time I moved my hand across the table and squeezed his. "Hey, they're gone now...don't let it spoil what has been a wonderful evening."

He gave me a half smile. "Yeah, you're right, I'm sorry."

We'd finished our meal; I was looking at the dessert menu, trying to decide whether I really fancied one, or if it was a case of my eyes being bigger than my belly.

"Oh fuck, no!"

"What's wrong?" I looked up at Danny in surprise at his loud outburst. He was staring at the entrance to the restaurant. A man had just entered and had made his way towards Alby's table. The man had long black curly hair that bounced on his shoulders, a black triangle beard and moustache.

"What is he, a look-alike of King Charles the First or something?" I joked.

"That's Tony, and believe me, only those in people in Doug's most inner circle would ever dare to mock him. A vicious little fucker if ever there was one. He's very loyal to Doug."

"What's actually going on here Danny? It seems to have become a roll call of the local undesirables!" I was beginning to feel uncomfortable.

The man arrived at Alby's table, and I saw Alby beckon him to sit next to him.

As Danny and I sat there watching, Tony suddenly reached into his coat pocket and produced a pistol, then without a further word he leaned forward, pressed the barrel downwards on the top of Alby's kneecap and fired. I saw Alby's mouth open, knew he was emitting a sickening scream, but I heard nothing. Everything seemed surreal to not only me, but also to most of the people there, who appeared not to believe what had happened. Tony casually stood up, pocketed the pistol and ambled towards the restaurant door. Danny grabbed my arm and pulled me to my feet then, keeping a firm grip on my arm, moved through the swing doors leading to the kitchen area and out through the rear door and into the alleyway behind.

We ran until we came to the main street, and by luck a black cab was passing; Danny waved it down and we both climbed inside. I was partly in shock and partly fired up with adrenalin. The cab dropped us at Danny's flat. As he fished in his pockets for his door key, I put my arms around his neck and pulled him to me. He wrapped both his arms around me and we kissed for what must have been five minutes. When we came up for air, I breathed in appreciation. "No one kisses like you," I panted lightly.

"I love your lips, they taste of wine…a fine wine." He licked them again, tasting me.

We quickly made our way upstairs into his flat and into the bedroom. He pulled me closer to him, running his fingers along my arm, while staring into my eyes, almost as though he was expecting a reaction. I was puzzled as to why…I mean we had sex at every opportunity, the man was insatiable and he knew my body intimately, inside and out!

His lips moved slowly until they joined mine, like suction cups, while his tongue swirled and explored my mouth; his hands moved under my top, his fingers caressing my back and in an instant I felt my breasts sag slightly as he unclipped my bra. I locked my arms behind his head, keeping his face stuck onto mine, my eyes firmly closed. I felt myself drifting, floating into a sea of sensuality and from within the cavern of our locked mouths, I released a murmur, almost as a confirmation that he was hitting all the right buttons in all the right order, and as I melted into him I just knew that every nerve end in my body was going to experience paradise before gently floating back to earth.

I never did bother to visit Alby afterwards, or even to enquire as to how he was, mainly because I didn't care, especially as he'd never given a toss about me anyway, so I figured it would be a bit hypocritical to start doing the caring sister bit. Ruth went to see him but he wasn't interested in seeing her, which also justified my decision. I had no idea or interest in what Madge and Victor thought of it all, although knowing Madge she was probably running around like a headless chicken, acting as though she was the victim; she wouldn't have been able to stomach the thought of someone else being the centre of attention.

Danny had had to go back to Manchester again on business. He'd stayed longer up there this time. He phoned to say one of his business deals had gone a bit pear shaped and he couldn't leave until he'd sorted it. I had to admit, I was really curious, but I didn't ask and he didn't elaborate.

A few days later, when he did return, he was very much a different Danny. He had none of his usual bounce; he was distant and preoccupied as though he had the worries of the world on his shoulders.

That evening we walked to our local pub, which was really crowded and overly loud even for us, so we didn't get much chance to talk. On the way home he was still very subdued and distracted. I just couldn't take anymore; I assumed he had found someone else.

"Danny you're acting very sussy. I know you said your business deal went tits up, but we've been going out together now for more than a few months and I want you to tell me straight: are you at it with someone else?"

"Eh? What?"

"Well, since you got back you just haven't seemed your usual self; you've hardly spoken and you haven't paid any attention to me or to anything I've been saying…"

"No! Of course I'm not messing about with anyone…I love you …"
Before he finished speaking I put my arms around him and told him that I loved him, but he just gave a sigh and a sad sort of smile. Anger then screamed through my brain … stuff this! He's screwing someone else … I don't need this shit! I turned away in a huff. In a second he was behind me, pulling me to him, his lips nuzzling against my neck. "I'm sorry…mmm, I missed you." His hands moved

up under my top, cupping around my breasts and squeezing them gently. I closed my eyes and let my head drop back on his shoulder, enjoying the desire building up slowly inside me. We arrived back at his flat and I anticipated my stud making love to me for the entire night and hopefully for most of the following morning.

We did make love but there was no passion. I don't even think his heartbeat increased, and it was over very quickly – far too quickly in fact. I left his bed and headed for the shower. I felt sticky, used and for some reason disgusted with myself. As the hot water hit me with force, I felt I wanted to stay under it, as though I could wash away what had just happened, and what *had* happened was that I had just woken up to the fact that my boyfriend didn't actually love me or care for me; he just wanted me around for sex, to supply a convenient relief for him. I thought back through our relationship and it had been a continuous sex romp, with breaks in between for meals in high-class restaurants, which was probably my payment!

I stepped out of the shower, wrapped a towel around me and walked back into the bedroom. Danny was sitting on the edge of the bed, his face buried in the palms of his hands.

"What's the matter with you then?" I tried to convey a tone, which implied: 'I don't give a flying fuck about you!'

Danny raised his head from his hands, cleared his throat, hesitated, and then spoke. "Becks, I've got to tell you something…"

"Don't bother…'cos I'm not fucking interested, alright!" I felt my bottom lip curl in anger as I spat the words at him. He reached out to grab me, but I shook my arm away.

"Becks, I'm in a lot of trouble. The reason I've been in Manchester is…well, let's just say I had some business that was going to make me – us – a lot of money and the reason I say *us* is because when it came in I was going to ask you about us getting married and perhaps getting that dream we spoke about…"

I gave a sneer. "Yeah, right, whatever Danny!" My words were loaded with venom.

"Please Becky, listen to me…" He started to sob gently, which quickly turned into full-blown tears; my man was genuinely crying, and seeing him perched on the edge of the bed crying, pulled at my heart. I quickly moved and knelt beside him.

"Danny darling, tell me what it is."

"I used somebody else's money to set up a scam, only before the payoff the mark got wind of it, shut everything down tight and pulled out…"

"Did he get the police in?" I asked.

"No, it might have been better if he had…" He looked me straight in the eye, his piercing eyes, which were normally flitting in all directions, were now just sad, vulnerable and watery. "The man who financed it wants his money back. He knows I haven't got that sort of dosh, so he's given me another job to do. An easy job, one I can do with my eyes shut…"

"So what's the problem?" I whispered.

"He wants security, in case I do a runner." At this point he dropped his gaze to the floor.

"How much is it? I've got some money put by; I can probably get the money and pay him off," I offered as my mind thought about the briefcase in the filing cabinet.

"The deal was for three quarters of a million pounds…have you got that sort of savings?" he asked with a wearied sigh.

"No…but my God, Danny, just what were you involved in?"

"I was securing our future, Becky, so that we wouldn't have to scrimp and save every penny we earn just to survive."

"What security is he after?"

"You, Becky…he wants to hold you for two days until I've done my part of the deal."

"What … they asked for me personally?"

"No, they said my wife, my kids or my girlfriend…even my mother, as long as it was somebody who is so important to me that they know I won't welch on the deal. You are the most important person in the world to me, Becks. You're my future, and you're my every happiness…"

"Yeah, okay, enough with the slush…what happens if I say no?" I was very uncomfortable with the scenario in my head.

"I owe the money to Doug Mann and you saw what he did to your stepbrother." He started rubbing his eyes with the back of his hands, making them look red and sore. I moved his hands away and kissed his eyes.

"It's okay, we can sort it," I whispered tenderly as though I was comforting an infant.

"Oh please Becks, I don't want to be crippled…" He squeezed my hand as he pleaded, "I promise you, when it's over we'll make serious plans for our future."

"Danny, I'm scared shitless…but I'll do it for you. Just promise me that they won't hurt me."

"I guarantee it…" He breathed a loud sigh of relief. "Oh Becky, I will never be able to explain what this means to me…I'll make the call now and tell them." I dressed quickly and we spent the next hour saying very little but cuddled up closely in each other's arms.

The sound of a car's horn outside snapped us both out of our personal trains of thought. Danny held my hand and led the way to his front door. As he opened the door, I had the biggest shock of my life and what I saw petrified me. Outside the door were Kevin Crestwell and Paul Tyler! There was a third man sitting in the back of the car but I couldn't make out who it was.

"What are these arseholes doing here?" I spoke to no one in particular.

"They work for Doug Mann now, as do most people these days!" Danny said, trying to reassure me.

We moved towards the car and as we stood by the rear door Crestwell opened the boot. "Get in!" he said with a sneer.

"Fuck off, I'm not getting in there for anybody!"

"Please Becks, please…do it for me. I just want this thing to be over." Danny's voice pleaded and I really did think he was going to burst into tears again.

"You bastard Danny…you'd better come and get me quickly…'cos you owe me big time!" I looked at each of the men with contempt, then I climbed into the boot of their car and before curling up in the foetal position, I called out one last time, "I'm relying on you Danny! Just do what you've got to do and then come and get me!"

Seconds before I was plunged into a claustrophobic blackness I heard Kevin Crestwell's laugh and then the cruelty in his voice: "I'm gonna enjoy taming that bitch!" That was the point when an almighty fear gripped me as my eyes suddenly opened to the realization that I had just delivered myself without any struggle to what were probably two of the most obnoxious lowlifes on the planet! The car pulled away with a jolt and it was deliberately thrown around corners, ensuring they were causing the maximum discomfort for me.

The journey seemed like an eternity. I could hear them laughing inside the car, especially after any sudden breaking or turning a corner at speed. One of them had a high-pitched, almost hysterical laugh. I shook my head from side to side; my eyes were dry, too dry, my lips wanted to tremble but they were taut with anger. I wanted to hate Danny, but part of me also wanted to believe that even at this very moment he was frantically trying to get me back. My mind replayed the moments before we left the flat. Danny had kissed me and given me a look that said, 'I love you more than life itself' and then the sweetest smile.

Eventually the car came to a stop. A deliberate, sudden stop; my body felt bruised and sore, my back was aching and I could feel a cramp starting in my legs. I was also aware that I was cold; a deep penetrating cold that made its way through to my bones. I heard them get out of the car and waited for the boot lid to open. Instead, one of them banged their hand on it – the sound amplified around my ears. "We're leaving you there for a while Becky…all part of your training! Don't waste your breath calling out; you're in one of our lock-ups!" I heard them laughing as they walked away until their voices grew faint and then no more…

The cold seemed to hit harder now; the cramp also quickly took hold, which was really painful but I couldn't move … after a while I couldn't feel the pain; I couldn't feel my limbs…just a deep penetrating cold and shivering. I quickly lost all sense of time, but suddenly I felt a warmth and then a horror as I realised it was my bladder emptying and as the wetness soaked my jeans so the warm pee quickly chilled, causing more discomfort along with the humiliating knowledge that I, a grown woman, had just peed herself. Coupled with the agony of my cramped position and the coldness seeped deep into my bones, I wanted to cry; I wanted the comfort of sobbing to release my fears and wretchedness. But no, my eyes remained dry...dry with fear. My instincts told me I was about to die. My breathing became a fast panting. My heartbeat felt painful. Faster. Louder. I felt suffocated. I needed air ... I needed to move ... my limbs had become rigid, as though rigor mortis had already set in. Then I heard a voice from deep inside my subconscious, screaming out at me: 'No, this is bollocks! This isn't fucking happening. Calm down ... relax ... breathe normally ... stop the panic taking control,' and in the cold darkness I slowly gained the edge over my nightmare.

As my breathing returned to normal, I heard voices, voices coming closer and then laughter...a feeling of dread came over me as I recognised the voices as belonging to Crestwell and Tyler. A hand thumped the top of the boot lid; the sound of the deep thud amplified again within the boot area, and continued echoing in my brain. I heard the sound of keys and suddenly the boot lid sprung open, the two men shining torches into my face and causing a temporary blindness. I felt myself being lifted out and stood on the ground. My legs were immobile and I instantly crashed to the ground. Both men laughed and as one of them picked me up and threw me over his shoulder, his hand slipped between my thighs and felt the wetness of my jeans. I heard more bellows of laughter and I knew they were making fun of me. A hand patted my arse amidst more laughter, but I couldn't make sense of what they were saying. Then the darkness of the night turned blacker, a hood was placed over my head; the slime bags wanted to make sure I had no idea where I was.

I could sense we had entered a house and the jolting, as I was taken upstairs added to the pain in my legs and back. We entered a room, and the hood was removed. I could see it was a small room. He took me towards the bed and stood me on my feet with my arms slung over his shoulder. I could feel his fingers grappling at the button at the front of my jeans, and after fumbling for a while; I felt my jeans slide slowly down my legs ... my cold, damp legs ... until they were lying at my feet.

It was as though I was watching a movie. It wasn't me; it was somebody else. I felt detached from my body. I could feel what he was doing but my whole body was paralysed with cold and cramp. The idea of hypothermia, maybe a mild form, entered my head; I'd read of lorry drivers dying as they slept in their cabs due to extreme cold. I tried speaking, but I could only manage a slurred speech, which came out as garbled rubbish. He sat me on the bed and knelt in front of me, and I recognised the face of Kevin Crestwell, who was grinning broadly, ear to ear, as he untied my trainers and removed them along with my jeans and knickers. He pulled my T-shirt up over my head and discarded it, then he unclipped and removed my bra.

"Wow!" he said as my breasts stood out proudly. "Oh yes, hot, hot, hot!" he muttered softly. I felt myself getting angry inside, but there was nothing I could do. I couldn't talk coherently and I couldn't move myself. He had stripped me completely and I was now at his mercy. My only hope was that I could gain control of my limbs before he had a chance to rape me.

Paul Tyler entered the room, along with another man, an older man who I instantly recognised as Andrei, the man Danny had hit that night at the Lambs Coat pub. All three men stood gawking at my naked body. Kevin Crestwell moved back to the side of the bed. Then he smiled, the smile of a psychopath.

"I have been looking forward to this," he said as he sat on the bed beside me. "Becky! Becky! Becky!" he whispered up close to my face. I wanted to scream back at him, to claw his face with my nails but I couldn't move. He shook me a little and I flopped like a rag doll. His hands started exploring me. "Oh yes, very nice!" he said giving a running commentary to the other two men who were watching, as though I was the main event. He stepped back and began loosening the belt of his trousers and pulling down his zip. He said nothing but I knew I was about to be raped.

He climbed between my legs and lowered himself onto me. He was hurting me. I couldn't believe the pain searing through my lower body. I'm sure the look on my face must have told him the agony I was experiencing, but he continued thrusting and then suddenly moaned, and collapsed on top of me kissing my neck. "That was so good," he whispered. "Mmm … yes, baby," he moaned again and I felt him pull out of me.

As he moved away from the bed, Andrei approached and pulled down his trousers. He climbed on top on me … my eyes filled with tears from the realisation of the imminence of my being gang-raped. I felt Andrei's weight and then he was inside me, raping me. "Ah yes," he sneered lustfully as he thrust into me, grunting with each motion, while I could only lie there completely distraught, completely helpless at the mercy of these lowlifes, scum from the very bowels of a cesspit.

After he'd finished and moved away I began to feel the use of my limbs again; in an ironic sort of way, it was as though the body heat from these scum had warmed my body. I saw Paul Tyler move towards me. "Hello Babe, I've been looking forward to this for a long time!" he sneered. I felt my bottom lip drop and my eyes welled with tears. I again felt helpless and terrified.

"Oh no," I moaned. "Please don't, please no!"

He ignored me and, like the others, climbed on top of me, his hands pawing me. I struggled, I felt repulsed, this creature that smelled of beer, sweat and vomit felt heavy on me. He held my breasts in the palms of his hands and kneaded them roughly, as though they weren't part of a human being. Like the others before him, he raped me, giving a running commentary as he did so, then suddenly with his face flushed with desire, he kissed me, his lips pressed hard against mine as his tongue, sliding between them, plunged deep into my mouth. I made a sound low in my throat, as his repulsive breath was exhaled into my mouth, my hands pushed against his shoulders as the nausea inside me built up into a gag. He pulled his face away. I gasped at the stale air that the room had to offer and the nausea subsided. His hand came down heavily and slapped the side of my face, then he pinned my arms to the mattress and as tears began to roll down my cheeks, he began a jerking spasm as he reached his climax.

I awoke, what could have been either moments or hours later, with my face wet and with tears blurring my vision, but I had regained full use of my limbs. I jumped up and off the bed and scrambled to find my clothes and cover myself with the small protection they could offer me. The bastards had taken them all except my trainers, which I assumed they had forgotten. I grabbed them and hid them under the bed, squirreling away what was mine. I tried the door but it was locked from the outside. I still felt cold so I snuggled under the dirty duvet, desperate to find some warmth.

I looked around the room. There was a bed, a small oblong shaped window that was firmly locked and which had metal bars fixed to the outside. It was certainly no good as an escape route. There was a chair next to my bed and over by the wall a small narrow three-drawer chest. Each of the drawers was empty. A single overhead naked light bulb illuminated the room. I started to feel sick as a rising panic began to take hold of me. I was also aware that I was close to exhaustion due to the extremities and the repeated violation to which my body and mind had been subjected.

After a while I composed myself and just sat in a trance. A lot of the time my mind was just blank, as though it was protecting me by not fully absorbing what had happened. The sound of the stairs creaking outside as someone made their way upstairs snapped me out of my trance. The bedroom door opened and it was Andrei.

"Ah you're awake…"

I sneered at him with contempt and before he could finish, I screamed at him. "I'm going to report you for rape! You abused me, you gang raped me like a pack of wild animals, only animals wouldn't do something like that…you are nothing but scum, fucking scum, d'you hear me?"

"Are you finished?" he asked softly.

"For the moment!" I spat back at him.

He approached the bed and with lightening speed the back of his hand slapped me across the side of my face. He grabbed my hair and pulled me off the bed. I frantically tried to hold on to the duvet, as though it would offer me some protection.

"Listen to me!" he screamed. "I own you! I have bought you! You belong to me, do you understand?"

"Fuck you…you pathetic piece of shit!" was all I could think of to say; my mind still hadn't fully absorbed his words. His hand came down again across my face; then he pulled me upright and landed me a kidney punch, causing my knees to buckle.

"You will work as a prostitute to cover the money that has been paid for you. You will be raped and beaten everyday until you submit, do you understand?"

I felt helpless, completely helpless and trapped at the mercy of this sadistic sicko.

"I said … do you understand?" He waited, but I didn't say anything. "Do you understand?" he asked again, a little more firmly, and this time he also yanked my hair to emphasise his point.

I gave a faint, "Yes."

"That's it, now say it again, but this time a bit louder, not in a whisper."

"Yes, yes, fucking yes … are you happy now?" I sobbed.

"It's okay, no one will hurt you if you are a good girl and work hard…" He pulled my hair, tipping my head backwards; his free hand moved to his crotch and began pulling down his zip. "You know you have the most soft, luscious lips," he said, and then grabbed my head, holding it firmly as he thrust his hips towards it. I screamed inwardly to myself: 'Be strong, don't give in…resist…resist…' and then I heard a familiar click and felt a sharp piercing pain at the side of my eye and fear took over. It was the point of a blade. He was holding it against my face. To say I was absolutely terrified would be a gross understatement, and as tears formed and stung my eyes, my lips fell open …..

As soon as he had finished he turned and walked out of the room, locking the door behind him. I lay back on the bed and closed my eyes. I sensed the walls closing in on me, my skin felt clammy; the floor was rising upward, pressing me against the ceiling, crushing the life from me. There was no air to breathe, my body was overheating, I wanted to claw at my throat with my hands as though that would make breathing easier; my stomach started churning, I felt bile in my throat…and then the vomit erupted. I gave no concern to where it went or what it covered; my body went into spasm as my stomach retched in its urgency to eject its contents. To be honest I didn't want to feel anything; I just wanted to shut myself away in a little cell inside my head until I could wake up from this nightmare. But intuition told me this was only the beginning, and approximately ten to fifteen minutes later that intuition was confirmed. The bedroom door opened and Costi entered with a facial expression of a predator about to devour his prey. He unbuckled his belt and pulled down his zip allowing his chinos to fall to his ankles. I could see he was commando and highly aroused.

"I've just heard how you pleasured Andrei…I want you to pleasure me the same way, but first I want you to beg me to allow you to please me!" I stood up facing him and ran my tongue over my lips provocatively. He stood in front of me, legs apart with his hands behind his back awaiting his treat and boy, did I let him have it! I kicked out straight between his legs with such velocity that I'm sure he could have worn his balls as earrings. He crumpled to the floor, emitting a loud grunting sound. This was my chance to escape. I ran to the door … I didn't care that I was naked. I glanced back as I walked out through the door. Costi was kneeling on the floor, his body heaving as though he was about to vomit.

I ran quickly down the stairs. I knew that if I could just make it to the street I could draw attention to myself; a naked woman in the street screaming should have been more than enough to arouse suspicion and hopefully …. rescue. I reached the bottom of the stairs. To the left I could see the front door at the end of a long passage.

I was almost there. I reached out for the handle … then suddenly I was yanked backwards by my hair. I twisted around, trying to break free. I saw Paul Tyler's face, glaring at me. He grabbed my shoulder. My whole body was pumped full of adrenalin, and I tried to lash out with my arms but he was too strong for me; he was dragging me back towards the stairs!

Another pair of hands grabbed my arms, and I heard Kevin Crestwell's voice. "Get the bitch upstairs!" I was dragged very roughly up the stairs and thrown unceremoniously back into the bedroom. Costi was no longer there. I could hear movement and voices outside the door. Something was about to happen and at the same moment that the thought entered my head, the bedroom door opened and Kevin, Paul and Andrei burst in brandishing leather straps, like wide belts but without the buckles. The three of them stood around me and began whipping me with the straps. Welts began appearing on my body.

After a while they stopped, but it wasn't over; they dragged me to the bathroom and plunged me into a bath of near-icy cold water. One of them grabbed the top of my head and pushed it down, submerging me completely. I thrashed my arms, my legs, but I couldn't break free. I knew my lungs were about to burst; my mouth was about to open automatically, beyond my control. I knew I was going to die…

Suddenly I was being pulled up out of the bath. I desperately grasped at anything that I could hold on to, to stop myself going back in, but found nothing. I opened my mouth to scream but all I did was to gasp in air … I was voiceless, as though I had never had any vocal cords.

I sensed being dragged back into the bedroom, and again I was thrown onto the floor. The men left, slamming the door behind them. I was shivering, not only due to the cold but also through fear! Sheer fear, something I had never experienced in my whole life.

Without any warning the door burst open again and the three men rushed in and once more started whipping me with the leather straps. It hurt even more this time, and my cold, wet skin began to open in small splits as the welts opened up. Then, just as quickly as it started, they stopped and left the room. I lay on the floor where they left me and cried inconsolably. I cried for my mum – I wanted her to come and scoop me up and take me somewhere safe and make everything better. The door was flung open again and I was dragged out. My vocal cords were working again, and I screamed, "No! No! Please, no…!" I was taken back to the bathroom and as before plunged into the icy cold water. I was on my back looking up, my vision blurred by the water; one of them held my legs up high, ensuring my head stayed underwater. The other two each pulled and held one of my arms. This was it: they intended to drown me. I could do nothing, as though I had no limbs. My head, shoulders and upper body were completely submerged. A pain in my chest intensified, becoming unbearable, my lungs at bursting point. I'd lost the will to struggle and felt I may as well open my mouth and allow the cold water to enter my lungs, to finally end this torture…

The person holding my legs dropped them without warning; my arms were freed. It felt as though they were pulling my hair out by the roots, but no, they were pulling me up out of the bath, completely out of the bath. As before, I was dragged back to the bedroom and thrown onto the floor.

"Please, no more…!" I cried out, begging. "I'll do it, I'll do whatever you want…but please, no more bath…no more beatings…!"

I heard the three of them laugh, and then the voice of Kevin Crestwell. "Trust me, this is going to be the best experience in your life Becks!" The laughter continued and they went, leaving me coiled on the floor like a sodden rag doll. I pulled the duvet off the bed and wrapped it around me. I was cold, damp, my teeth had begun chattering and I was scared shitless of what might happen to me.

I heard the door gently open and cowed in fear, afraid to look up. The voice was different – a girl's voice.

"Hello I'm Harvinda, but you can call me Harvey."

I looked up; she was young, probably around nineteen or twenty, and looked of Indian origin. Her make up was a bit over the top, but there was no mistaking her beauty. She was wearing a flowery, gypsy-style skirt and a white blouse. She was carrying a tray. It suddenly dawned on me that I hadn't eaten. I tried hard to recall when I had last eaten, and as I did so I started to feel giddy, but I wasn't sure if it was an actual symptom because I hadn't eaten, or the aftershock of my ordeal in the bathroom.

"I've been told to come and make sure you look nice," she said as she approached me.

"I just want to be left alone," I sighed, my throat and eyes feeling red raw due to all my screaming and crying.

"No, you must, you have to always be ready. If they see you without make up, they will use the strap on you. You have to always look nice."

"Look nice for who?" I asked.

"The customers of course…and if they complain about you, then you'll be beaten with the strap!" I sensed the same fear in her voice that I knew I had in mine.

She moved the duvet and touched my shoulder. "You're too cold. I will run you a warm bath and fix your hair while you soak. You cannot stay like that – you will catch pneumonia…" She spoke in a calm gentle way, like a little girl playing house with her dolls.

"Can I have some food?" I asked as my tummy rumbled.

"I have sandwiches for you now, but for the future, you are not allowed to eat if you don't make money," she answered in an almost matter-of-fact fashion.

"What else happens if I don't make money?"

"You will be put in a bath of ice-cold water and beaten and possibly worse…" Her voice trailed off in sadness.

"What do you mean by *possibly worse?*"

"I was one of three girls who were all brought here at the same time. I was the feisty one; I tried standing up to them and now I have a disfigured leg. The older one, Andrei, he switched on an electric iron and when it was hot he held it against my leg. He did this in front of the other girls as a lesson and as I was lying on the floor screaming, they beat me."

"Oh my God…!"

"Yes, and they will beat me again if I don't get you looking nice, so no more talking!"

She was like a surrogate mum. She even tested the bathwater with her elbow, and as I soaked in the bath, every part of my body absorbed the warmth from the water as it penetrated and chased the chill from out of my bones, whilst Harvey gently washed not only my hair, but also my battered body.

I thought of Danny, and of his promise that I would be safe. I had trusted him; how could he betray me? How could anyone sell another human being? I mean, I know they did it in Roman times, but this was the fucking twenty first century! Only a couple of days ago he had told me how much he loved me. He had even described the picture in his head of us as a married couple with a kid. I remembered teasing him that we'd have to adopt, as there was no way I was going to have a baby growing inside me, contorting and stretching my body into a hideous shape. That's when he had said that his dream was to have six kids… then turned the tables and began teasing how he'd still love me when I become misshapen and homely after having all his children. He had started tickling me and we had collapsed in laughter and spent the rest of the afternoon making love. No… no … Danny wouldn't do this to me. You just didn't sell off the person that you wanted to spend the rest of your life with…wait, what was I thinking about…you didn't sell people, period.

I got out of the bath and dried myself. Harvey watched me and then took me back to the bedroom.

She hadn't fixed my hair the way I liked it, but I didn't care. She applied moisturiser to my face, neck and shoulders, then thick foundation which concealed the puffiness around my eyes. Then she did my eyes and lips. The final look was far too overdone for my taste. She gave me an oversized tee shirt and said that was all I was to wear when we had no customers, then gave me a skirt similar to her own and a silk slip-on top with a plunging vee at the front emphasing my cleavage; this was to be worn during business hours.

"Harvey…" I asked nervously, "…apart from the obvious…what actually happens?"

"Men, all expecting sex. One will be brought to your room, come in, do whatever he wants, then he goes out and shortly afterwards another one comes in…"

"But that's horrific…it's like a conveyor belt!" I felt horrified at the thought!

Harvinda's eyes became vacant, and as I looked at her, it was hard to imagine she was someone's daughter, that she was once a little princess to proud parents.

"I had sex with 10 men on the first day they put me to work…" she continued. "…and now I don't even bother to count..." She paused in thought before carrying on. "Weekends are the worst; groups of young men who have far too much money, who spend their evenings drinking and just want to finish their night off with a shag, or else I have to perform sex acts on them and they treat me like a sub-human piece of meat…because a piece of meat doesn't have feelings does it?" She was struggling to hold her emotions in as she continued. "Sometimes I've asked the customers to help me, to just phone my parents and tell them where I am, but they just laugh at me and I have to be careful they don't complain. Kevin has threatened that if I cause any more trouble, they will inject me with drugs, they will make me dependent on them…that's what they do, you know."

At that point the door opened, and Andrei stood there. He looked me up and down, then looked at Harvey and nodded, indicating she should leave. He waited for her to go then stared at me, his eyes cold.

"I have customers for you. You will keep them happy or I will cripple you. There are no more warnings for you. If you cause me trouble you will disappear forever, do you understand?"

"Yes!" I spoke abruptly but not through any defiance; it was a mixture of fear and the knowledge that I had no other options. He looked me up and down again, his face showing absolutely no trace of emotion and then he went out.

Later, the first of three clients was brought to me, and from that point on, I was servicing ten to fifteen men a day. Their faces always remained shadowy. I lived in fear of the cold bath punishment and so I ensured the punters were happy, and whilst Harvey's words, *'You are not allowed to eat if you don't make money,'* still rang in my ears, there were frequent times that I wasn't fed, because in Kevin Crestwell's words, they didn't want me to become fat!

All too soon I lost all track of time. I wasn't allowed out of the house, and I had no idea if I'd been there for two weeks or two months!

Chapter 8

John Tanner

"Madge?" The pitch of Tanner's voice rose to an incredulous tone as he answered the door and gazed upon his visitor. The girl in front of him could have been his ex wife.

"No, Ruth."

"Ruth...Ruth? You mean my daughter Ruth?"

"Oh, you do remember you have daughters, then?"

"Yes...look, I'm sorry, I'm confused...yes, of course I know I have two daughters ... I just didn't expect to meet one of them after all these years...No, wait...look, this is coming out all wrong ... please, come in." Tanner stepped back, holding the door open for Ruth to enter. As she walked in, her eyes scanned the interior critically while Tanner's eyes scrutinised her. She was brunette, good-looking, and elegantly dressed.

"Can I get you a coffee or anything?" The offer wasn't made so much in politeness, but more to give Tanner a chance to decide how he felt. He couldn't decide if he felt pleased, or embarrassed, or annoyed at this sudden intrusion.

"Coffee please, white with no sugar." She spoke as though she was speaking to a waiter, no eye contact and with more than an air of detachment.

"Okay, I'll just be a couple of moments. Please, sit down ... make yourself comfortable." As Tanner moved into his kitchen, his mind worked overtime. It was a surreal situation; a ghost from the past ... no, it was more than a ghost; it was a guilty conscience long ago buried that had arisen and returned to haunt him. He switched on the electric kettle and took two mugs from the kitchen cupboard; he paused for a moment then replaced them and chose two china cups with matching saucers. He was momentarily grateful to whichever one of his ex lady friends it was who had refused to drink out of a mug and had left a few pieces of matching china for those occasional times when she stopped over. The thought of a biscuit entered his head, but he had never been a great biscuit eater, so any that he did have in his cupboard were probably going to be well past their sell-by date.

He used a small tray to take the coffees back into the living room. Ruth was sitting in his armchair, her body language defensive. She had built a huge emotional barrier around herself. Tanner knew that whatever the reason was for her appearance out of the blue, it wasn't going to be an affectionate daddy and daughter reunion. He placed her coffee on a small wine table next to her armchair and then sat on the sofa opposite her. He hesitated briefly before speaking.

"I have to be honest, Ruth, I don't know what to say...but you obviously found me for a reason and you have a purpose for coming to see me

…" He paused again, this time for longer. "…It will probably be best for you to say your piece and then we can take it from there." He smiled, hoping to ease the frosty atmosphere between them.

"Okay, let me start by saying you really are the last person on earth I wanted to have any contact with."

"Yes, I can understand your reasons for feeling that way…"

"Perhaps you would allow me the courtesy to finish what I am saying, before you interrupt." She spoke down to him as though he was the lowest form of life.

"I'm sorry, please carry on."

"I have a sister. You may remember your other daughter, Rebecca? She has gone missing and I believe she may be in some kind of trouble…"

"I'm going to interrupt you here Ruth. When you say 'missing,' do you mean she's run away or that she's just disappeared?"

"I believe she's being held somewhere against her will."

As she sat there, Tanner saw a tear suddenly appear in her eye. He glanced down at her hands; she was making a wringing motion with them as they rested in her lap. In his eyes she suddenly looked small and vulnerable, like a child. He thought she was going to cry with a full flood of tears; he could see she was struggling to hold it back.

"Ruth, tell me why you think that." He spoke gently, his years of interrogation experience kicked in and he switched onto autopilot.

"A lot of people have written Becky off as being a bad lot, but I know that she isn't, and I'm not just saying that because she is my sister…" She stopped at that point and sipped at her coffee. As Tanner listened he noted that whilst she was emotionally upset, she remained articulate and coherent as she spoke. Her gaze dropped down to the coffee cup she was now cradling with both hands in her lap. "Becky had fallen in with, and was very much influenced by a girl called Hannah Isaacs. This girl really is a bad lot and…well, as was to be expected, she is currently serving a lengthy prison sentence. I had hoped that without this influence Becky would have been able to sort her life out…"

"Can you be more specific when you say *influenced*…in what way?" Tanner interrupted.

"Crime. She isn't a dyke, if that's what you're thinking. Not that it's any of your business, but that is more my preference." The coldness had returned to her voice.

"I'm sorry, I wasn't inferring…"

"I'm sure you weren't…shall we continue? Shortly before she went missing, Becky came to see me. She said she'd met a wonderful boy who was definitely her Mr Right; she was expecting him to propose, and I as her big sister was obviously quite excited for her. But then…nothing, it was as though she disappeared off the face of the earth."

"You haven't said one thing that could be interpreted as potentially sinister." Tanner held her gaze for a while, trying to read her facial expression; she gave nothing away. He watched as she replaced her coffee cup onto the saucer and back on the small wine table, and then in an act of high anxiety began to push her open palms along her thighs and then clenched them into little tight fists, her small white hands becoming whiter as her anguish intensified.

"After a couple of weeks, I went around to her flat and discovered new tenants had recently moved in. I contacted her landlord to inquire if there was a forwarding address. He said he'd received a typed letter giving immediate notice. When he went to the flat, it had been completely cleared out. He added that he'd kept the deposit in lieu of notice."

"But that's still not sinister; she may have moved in with her boyfriend?"

"That's what I thought. All I had was his name: Danny Dolan. I tried to track him down and … what do I find? He's got himself another girlfriend, and when I asked him where Becky was he just shrugged his shoulders and said that she'd dumped him and he hadn't seen her since!"

"But surely that sounds quite plausible ... doesn't it?"

"No! She wouldn't dump him; she was too much in love."

"But what if she discovered that he'd been cheating on her with this new girlfriend. Couldn't she have been pissed off enough to dump him?"

"That's what the police said…"

"Whom did you speak to?"

"When?"

"You mentioned the police…you have reported her missing to the police haven't you?"

"Oh, I don't remember his name; I've probably got it on some papers he gave me."

"What did he say to you?"

"Nothing. Absolutely bugger all. He was condescending and told me she'd probably turn up in a day or two."

"Why did you come to see me?"

"I had hoped you may have been interested enough in your daughter to help me find her!"

"That's an unfair comment, Ruth. I don't know her, the same as I don't know you, and you haven't said one thing that even remotely suggests she is in any danger or being held against her will."

"Mum was right; you really are an uncaring bastard…"

"If you've come here just to have a pop at me, then fine, get it off your chest – I deserve it."

"I didn't come here for that. Becky used to use a café called the Lucky Eight. The woman who owns it told me that she'd tried to warn Becky about Danny Dolan. Apparently his girlfriends frequently go missing after a couple of months of, shall we say, intense involvement."

"Maybe he's one of those chaps who can't keep it in his trousers. Perhaps they find out he's putting it about and dump him and then maybe it's...I don't know ... embarrassment, shame, call it whatever, but possibly they don't want to face people for a while?"

"Why are you being so negative about this?"

"I'm not negative. I have to look at the facts, coldly and logically."

"Then I've wasted my time haven't I?"

"No you haven't...you certainly haven't, and I'm not uncaring."

"Mum still hates you and I think she'll hold a grudge against you for the rest of her life. She's said a lot of bad things about you..."

"It was along time ago, and I certainly don't want to get into a backstabbing session now."

"It's hard for us not to side with mum. After all, you didn't want to see us and all we ever wanted was to hear from you. A card would have been something. How hard is it to send a postcard?"

"It's easy to look back now and point a finger, but at the time there were circumstances."

"Utter rubbish ... you just didn't want to know us as a family, as *your* family!"

"How did you find me?" Tanner asked, changing the subject.

"Purely by accident...or fate, depends on what you believe." She held his gaze as she continued. "When we were kids, mum had a large framed picture on the wall, it was of a house in the middle of a field and everything was covered in snow. I always loved that picture and when I moved out of the house, mum said I could take it. I believe it was originally yours?"

Tanner nodded, although in truth he couldn't remember it.

"Anyway, during the move the picture frame became damaged...well completely broke actually, but at the back of the picture was an old letter; it looked as though it had been used to pack out the frame...it was a letter that had been sent to you, years ago, from the Inland Revenue and, whilst most of the type had faded, your National Insurance number was still visible. I have a friend who works for the Inland Revenue and although it wasn't easy, she managed to find an address for you."

"How did you know I still lived in London?"

"I didn't, but I had to start somewhere. I wasn't even sure if you were still alive; mum had told us you were an alcoholic."

"I was drinking heavily yes, but I was never an alcoholic...that was over twenty years ago, at that time I wasn't at a good place in my life. After the divorce I re-evaluated, sorted myself out and moved on, as they say."

"She said you were once a policeman but they threw you out."

"I worked for Her Majesty's Security Service; *they* threw me out...but after I sorted out my drinking problem they brought me back in and that's where I've remained until recently when I took early retirement."

"And is there a Mrs Tanner?"

"No, there is not."

"On the address I was given for you, it had OBE next to your name."

"Yes, that bit's true…but again, it was twenty years ago."

"I'm still suitably impressed."

"Thank you."

Ruth gave a faint smile and then suddenly flinched.

"What is it…have you thought of something else?" Tanner asked.

"Will you help me to find my sister?"

"What if she doesn't want to be found?"

"Do you believe in intuition?"

"Yes, I believe that particular gut feeling should never be ignored."

"That's what I've got, and I just know that she's in serious trouble!"

"How serious?"

"Marcie, she's the café owner I told you about, she hinted that Danny Dolan is involved in a prostitution racket. She was too scared to say any more, except that she had a soft spot for Becky and would hate to think of her ending up like all the others…"

"What others?"

"I don't know … she was genuinely afraid to say any more."

"Okay, I'll see what I can come up with, but I'm going to need more details from you, including an up-to-date photo…but first, why me?"

"What do you mean?" Ruth asked, puzzled.

"You went to a lot of trouble to find me, you had no idea what sort of person I was and by your own admittance you didn't even know if I was still alive, yet still you persevered to find me. I can't believe it was just to ask for help to find your sister."

"Your daughter!" She spat the correction almost with contempt that he'd forgotten.

"Yes, my daughter, but my point is still valid."

She paused in thought before answering. "When I first found the letter I was curious if you were still alive. When I found out that you were, I intended to get a glimpse of you from a distance…after all, you are my biological father."

"So what made you knock on my door?"

"The police don't seem interested in finding Becky, and mum's attitude is that whatever trouble she's in she's probably brought it all on herself."

"What about your step brother?"

"What about him? He's never had any time for either Becky or me. Anyway he was recently crippled…it was a gang related thing he was involved in…"

"Could Becky's disappearance be connected?"

"No not really. As I said, there's never been any closeness between us, so that's just coincidental. Anyway, what sort of details do you need about Becky?"

"I want to know about her personality, the type of people she mixes with, her interests, likes and dislikes. In fact anything that will help me to build up a profile of her."

As he and Ruth continued talking, Tanner noticed she was becoming slightly less intense in her mannerisms. But she still maintained an emotional distance from him, and although he knew he didn't deserve to be treated differently and this wasn't a long-lost father-daughter celebration reunion, yet a part of him wished that it was, and as they continued talking, he realised more and more that he wanted the girls, his girls, to be part of his life and even more, for them to include him in their lives.

That evening Tanner felt very restless and when he finally went to bed, his thought patterns were far too active to allow him to embrace a relaxing sleep. Both Rebecca and Ruth now occupied his thoughts and he was plainly aware that now he'd met one of them, deep down and without any doubt he wanted affection and acceptance from his daughters. Maybe even an absolution for his having never been there for them. But dreams were for the future and he was aware he needed to focus on the present and, as unpalatable though it may be, to confront the possibility that his daughter Rebecca had been coerced into the sex trade.

The following day dawned cloudy with signs of impending rain. Tanner decided to leave his car and travel on the Underground and by bus. He felt a need to get a closer feel for the area, to walk the same streets that Becky walked and visit some of the same places that Becky would have visited.

It was mid afternoon by the time he entered the Lucky Eight café. He instantly recognised Marcie from Ruth's description of her. He ordered a mug of tea and a slice of fruit cake and then sat observing her. There were only two other customers in there; they both looked like market traders and they were busy putting the world to rights … well, at least their little part of the world. After about ten minutes they tired of their conversation, fell into a brief silence, then drained the remains of their mugs and with a courtesy wave to Bob they left. Shortly afterwards Marcie collected the empty mugs from their table and gave it a cursory wipe. She made eye contact with Tanner.

"Sorry dear, can I get you something else?" The words came out like a played tape from a memory bank. The same words she had said to customers over the years, spoken without emotion or gesture.

"Yeah, I could do with some help actually," Tanner replied casually.

"Certainly dear, lost are you? Where you looking for?" She spoke cheerily as she approached his table.

"No, it's not directions I'm after; I'm actually after some local information."

"Well we've lived around here all our lives, so if I can't help, I'm sure my husband Bob will be able to."

"Thanks, that's appreciated. Tell me, what do you know about a chap called Danny Dolan?"

The sudden silence from her was deafening; she threw a nervous glance in the direction of her husband Bob. Tanner maintained his gaze, looking intently at her face, as though trying to read her thoughts.

"Sorry dear, never heard of him." She quickly avoided eye contact and turned to walk away.

"I'm trying to locate the whereabouts of a Rebecca Wilson...Becky ... and I've been told that she really looked up to you...perhaps, as the type of mother she had always wanted?" The sudden change of her facial expression told Tanner that his change of tack was spot on target direction.

"What are you...old Bill or something?" she asked suspiciously.

"No, nothing like that." Tanner spoke gently to put her at ease. "Her sister Ruth asked me to dig around to find out what's happened to her. After all, the police don't seem too bothered about her so someone's got to do something."

"Oh yeah, 'an how much are you charging her for this so-called digging around as you put it?"

"Not a penny...I'm related...albeit a distant relative...but at the end of the day, it's still blood."

"Yeah, I suppose I can see a resemblance..." Her tone relaxed a little, perhaps with an acceptance of his explanation. "So, what do you want to know?" she asked.

"I suppose without going into too much chapter and verse, just who is Danny Dolan?" Tanner spoke in a matter of fact fashion; he could almost have been enquiring about the weather.

"Well you didn't get this from me..." She leaned towards him speaking quietly, "... but he's a lowlife...total scum; he does a lot of work for Dougie Mann..."

"Who is Dougie Mann?" interrupted Tanner.

"Well, if you've never heard of him, then trust me, he's someone you need to stay well away from. Nothing happens around here without his say-so. Becky's brother Alby, he crossed him and now he's in a wheelchair." As Marcie spoke she was settling into her gossiping stride.

"Thanks for the tip..." interrupted Tanner again, "...but please tell me some more about Danny Dolan."

"Well..." Marcie lower her voice as she continued, "... of course I've got no proof of this, and I'm only going by hearsay, but they say he gets teenage girls…you know, romances them, and then sells 'em to the Slavs and Albanians…"

"You mean he's a pimp?"

"No, he does what they call grooming … you know, he gets 'em ready and turns 'em out, all ready to work…"

"What's going on here?" It was Bob, Marcie's husband, his forehead creased into worried lines.

"This chap's looking for Becky Wilson…he's family…" Marcie spoke quickly almost as though she was justifying Tanner's presence.

"Yeah, well we don't know nothing, we just run a café that's all…we don't stick our nose in where it ain't our business. Now if you've finished your drink you can go!"

Tanner looked up at the man and watched as he gently tugged Marcie's arm positioning her behind him. There was nothing threatening in his manner. He appeared frightened of a stranger's presence and protective of his wife. Tanner smiled in a friendly gesture. "I'm sorry, I didn't mean to cause offence or upset you."

"That's all right, none taken…and I take it we shan't be seeing you in here again?"

John Tanner stood up and turned as though to leave, then stopped and looked back at Marcie. "But if a young woman is being held against her will, then do you not agree that anyone who conveniently turns a blind eye is actually no different to the people holding her?"

"Look, I'm sorry, we can't help you, but if you do meet Danny Dolan then be careful…he's not someone to be crossed and like I told you, he has some very heavy connections in this area."

"Thanks for the tip…oh, and I will be coming back in here…but don't worry, as far as anyone else is concerned, I've neither been here nor met you before!" Tanner left, without looking back at either Bob or Marcie.

The morning had begun damply and by midday a heavy mist had descended from the overcast skies. As Tanner stepped outside the warmth of the café and stood under the cold grey skies, it had worsened into a persistent drizzle of rain which in turn quickly turned into a downpour around him. The late afternoon traffic was gearing up for the rush hour and was its usual chaos, with drivers trying various routes to avoid the jams, but succeeding only in creating further hold-ups. Impatient drivers in bottlenecked queues blasted their car horns, in a pathetic demand that the unknown obstruction to their journey be removed, without comprehending they were also part of the problem.

Diagonally opposite the café Tanner spotted a pub, which from the outside certainly looked at though its best days were far behind it, a chalked message on a blackboard was advertising all day food. Tanner turned up his jacket collar as a gesture to keep out the rain and crossed the road, weaving between the gridlocked traffic.

The rain continued throughout the remainder of the afternoon and into the early evening before dying out. Tanner had taken the Underground, and now walked hazily through the back streets of Kings Cross into what is commonly referred to as the red light district. He ignored the kerb crawling cars passing him slowly on their look out for girls. His feet moved him through the filthy streets, past the rent boys, the pimps, drug pushers and beggars. Groups of prostitutes stood on street corners; the girls – barely teenagers – resembled old women, their drug dependency stealing their youth with each new fix. Tanner ignored his surroundings and the multitude of languages being spoken. He stopped close to one of the many railway arches and observed a group of young girls plying their trade. His eyes focused on the back of one of them; her hair and posture partly resembled Ruth. The thought flashed across his mind that it could be Becky, but just as quickly he dismissed it. From what he'd heard of Becky, she'd escape at the first opportunity, so whoever was holding her certainly wouldn't risk putting her on the streets.

As he stood studying the woman, he sensed a movement coming towards him from across the road, and as he turned her eyes found his; she looked about forty but of course she may only have been mid twenties.

"I take it you like what you see?" She placed her hands on her hips, swaying her body provocatively. Her face was bruised; she had several missing teeth, the result of either beatings or of neglect. Her mouth was lined with what could only be described as severe cold sores; she looked like a walking disease and as she reached out towards Tanner's groin, he quickly stepped backwards.

"No, sorry love, I'm only looking tonight…"

"That's okay, we can work out a price and you can watch me do it with a punter…"

"No, I'm really not interested…"

"What the fuck's going on here?" interrupted a raised voice angrily, and at the same time the open palm of a hand caught the girl around the back of her head.

"I'm sorry Nathan…" The girl quickly apologised to her pimp and then turned to offer her services elsewhere.

Nathan was built like the proverbial brick shit house, a solid man; from his speech Tanner assumed him to be of East European origin, although wherever he was from was largely irrelevant. His face was flushed, which Tanner assumed to be from the effects of too much alcohol, but more importantly he was angry and he wanted to take that anger out on someone … and John Tanner just happened to be in front of him. This was the one thing he didn't want. Acting tough was one thing, actually delivering the goods was another, and these street guys were renown for being a very tough breed indeed.

Tanner kicked out, catching him hard on the shin, then followed up with a punch, his arm straight from the shoulder ensuring it had the full weight and force of his body behind it. This sent Nathan sprawling, and as he fell to the pavement Tanner kicked him solidly in the groin, making sure his drunken aggression was temporarily put out of action. The prostitute, on turning and seeing Nathan on the ground, screamed and immediately went to her pimp's aid. Tanner was satisfied that the man wouldn't be getting up for a while, but as he looked up he saw figures running towards the sound of the fracas. Instinct and experience threw him into autopilot and he quickly backed into the shadows and disappeared into the night.

The following morning John Tanner rose early; coffee and a couple of slices of toast sufficed for breakfast. He showered and then dressed in a dark suit with a crisp white shirt and plain tie. His agenda today was to visit Becky's ex-landlord, or at least the letting agency that had arranged her tenancy.

As he left his building and stepped outside he squinted; the early morning sun was shining with full intensity as though desperate to dry out every spot of yesterday's rain. He climbed behind the wheel of his car, started the engine, checked the rear view mirror and waited for a break in the traffic; he pulled away from the kerbside, smoothly and silently joining the flow of traffic.

The address Ruth had given him was of a local estate agency and their office was located in a small parade of shops. As Tanner entered the office he saw a smartly dressed woman in a dark mini-skirted suit. The suit showed off her long slender legs, which were lengthened by the tall stilettos she wore. She appeared to be the only staff member present. She beamed a welcoming smile as she moved towards him. Tanner smiled back, his eyes wide in appreciation of her looks. He estimated her age to be around the mid-to-late thirties. Long, golden-blonde hair hung in waves down her back. Her bright blue eyes flickered with alertness and intelligence, and complimented her clear complexion. Without intention Tanner's eyes fixed upon her white silk blouse, unbuttoned to the cleavage of her full bust. Tanner considered her to have a certain style. She was obviously used to the finer things in life, which had given her a confidence of superiority.

Tanner identified himself to her as a Special Branch officer. He didn't offer any identification and she didn't ask to see it. She informed him that the proprietor was currently away on business and wasn't expected back until the following day.

She looked him up and down as she continued talking, "But of course … if there is anything I can do for you…I'd be more than willing…" she purred her words seductively. Tanner looked hard at the woman and wondered if the whole world had now become totally obsessed with casual sex. But to get information he had to play the game, remembering that he was now just a civilian pretending to be a serving police officer, which on its own was illegal. He gave her a saucy grin.

"Mmm, I could think of quite a few things…especially if, as you say, you're willing, but I suppose we should get the boring stuff out of the way first, namely the reason for my visit." The woman giggled as though they were already sharing an illicit encounter. He passed her a piece of paper showing Becky's full name and previous address. "What can you tell me about this girl?" As he spoke, he pulled a small notebook from his pocket, adding to the illusion of his being on official business.

"There's not a lot I can tell you really…is she in a lot of trouble?" As she spoke she moved towards a filing cabinet and withdrew a folder. Opening the folder, she held up a letter. "We received this letter instructing us to terminate the tenancy. When the boss went around to see her, the flat was completely empty … well, apart from some unpaid energy bills."

Tanner read the typed letter; there was no clue as to the sender. Becky's name had been typed but no signature accompanied it. "Can I have a copy of this?" he asked.

"Yes, of course." She moved over to a small desktop photocopier and inserted the letter for copying. "You know, I actually felt sorry for her, what with her flat mate going to prison and your lot turning the place over…well, she was only a kid herself wasn't she…and you never did answer my question: is she in a lot of trouble?"

"Obviously, you understand I can't say too much at this stage, but I need to find her for her own protection." Tanner's tone was officious.

"We had another one of your lot in here asking questions about her. Mind you, that was before all that trouble with her flatmate really kicked off."

"Out of interest, what was the officer's name?" asked Tanner.

"Hang on, it should be here in the file…oh yes, here it is … a Detective Sergeant Priack, he was the one …. do you know him?" she asked innocently.

"No, we work different sections; I'm more involved in missing persons, while he's more of a crime fighter."

"Well, I don't know about that, but he seemed a bit creepy to me. I certainly wasn't comfortable being alone with him…whereas you on the other hand…" She slid her tongue over her lips, signifying pleasures to be had.

"Well, thank you very much for your help…" Tanner interrupted, "…but I've got a wife and eight kids to get back to."

"Eight kids, eh? Yes, you've got that virile look about you." Tanner grinned and turned to leave. "If you want to leave me your phone number, I could call you if I remember anything…important or otherwise." She moved towards him as she spoke.

Tanner's eyes again fell to her cleavage and, as enticing as the thought of a possible steamy session with her was, he was also aware it was a distraction he could do without.

"I'll tell you what, you give me your card and I'll call you," he said offhandedly.

"Isn't that something you're suppose to say *after* you've screwed me?" She spat out the words almost with a snarl as though he was to blame for every man who had mistreated her. Tanner gave her a puzzled look. "Well, don't all men say '*I'll call you sometime,*' even though they have no intention of doing so?"

"I really don't know," replied Tanner.

"Well they do, hence the phrase: all men are liars!" she shot back, bitterly.

"Oh that," Tanner quipped. "Yes, it's something we learn from our mothers!" Then without another word between them he turned around, opened the door and walked out.

Next on his agenda was a visit to Danny Dolan's flat. Becky had previously told Ruth where he lived during their chat, as she had believed she would be moving in with him, and in turn Ruth had given the address to Tanner, along with a photo booth picture of Becky and Dolan together. As luck had it, just as he pulled his car into a parking space opposite the flat, he caught a reflection of Dolan in his wing-mirror, ambling along with his arm around the waist of a tall blonde teenage girl. Tanner alighted quickly from his car and came up behind Dolan just as he fished his door key from his jeans pocket.

"Hello Danny, how's it going then…everything alright?" Tanner spoke casually as though he'd known him for years.

Dolan flinched slightly at seeing Tanner so close behind him on his doorstep. He quickly replaced the door key in his pocket. "I don't know you pal," he answered defensively.

"Then allow me to introduce myself. My name is Tanner, John Tanner." Tanner extended his hand and as Dolan took it, it became a bone crushing vice-like grip instead of the usual wet wimpy handshakes he was used to.

"Well now you've introduced yourself, you can piss off…okay?" Dolan expressed a cocky grin, which encouraged the teenage girl beside him to giggle.

"The thing is, Danny, I'm going to be around for quite a while and I just know our paths are going to cross…you see, I'm investigating the disappearance of Rebecca Wilson…"

"Naw, never heard of her mate," Danny quickly interrupted, albeit disinterestedly.

"Ah, and I was led to believe that you two were going to be married."

"Well I don't know who told you that but…"

"Oh so you do know her then?" Tanner replied quickly, catching him off guard.

"Um, yeah … er, I knew her as Becky, that's why the name didn't click with me at first." He was flustered, but quickly composed himself. His hesitation before answering was to Tanner almost the equivalent to having the word LIAR etched in large letters across his face.

"That's okay Danny, it's not a problem…so tell me, when did you last see her? But …. hold on… you were about to open the door when I came up to you, so why don't we all go inside and discuss it? It also saves the neighbours from knowing everything."

"Naw, it's alright mate; I can't tell you much anyway. The truth is, she dumped me…said something about wanting to experience more from life…whatever that means…anyway she pissed off and I ain't seen her since." He lit up a cigarette and took a deep drag.

"So when was this?"

"Must be a couple of months ago now…" He inhaled again, deeply, as though to calm his nerves, and then flicked the ash of his cigarette on the ground.

"Can you be a little more accurate?" Tanner fired his responses quickly, like a hungry news reporter.

"Naw, sorry." Danny shook his head.

"So, let me get this straight. The woman you love, and plan to marry, dumps you and takes off and you can't quite recall just when it was…"

"Why don't you leave him alone…everybody knows she was just a dirty slag!" the leggy teenager suddenly butted in.

"I'm sorry…" Tanner turned to face her. "…I didn't catch your name." As he spoke he pulled his notepad out of his pocket.

"Naw, and you don't need it either…if you're the filth, then show us your warrant card, otherwise fuck off!"

Tanner took a step backwards. "Okay Danny, but as I said earlier, our paths are going to cross quite a bit over the next few weeks, because I'm like a little terrier with a bone; I just don't let go!" Dolan and the girl ignored him and turned their backs. Dolan again fished out his door key, opened the front door and quickly ushered the girl in, then followed her, slamming the door behind him. Tanner stood looking at the closed door, replaying the conversation in his head. There was something about Danny Dolan that made him feel uncomfortable. He couldn't put his finger on it, apart from the fact that all his instincts told him he was dealing, just as Marcie had warned him, with a particularly nasty piece of work.

As Tanner drove back to his own flat, he realised he wasn't equipped to deal with this alone; he was aware that physically he would be no match against Dolan and, whilst he also knew some unsavoury characters he could call on for help, their way of problem solving wouldn't necessarily result in getting Becky back safely.

Moments after arriving home, Tanner flicked the switch on his kettle to make coffee, and then telephoned his ex-work colleague, Ernie Palmer.

"Hello Ernie, it's Tanner, John Tanner."

"Hello John, it's good to hear from you; how are things going?"

"So-so, but the purpose of the call is that I need a favour."

"What kind of favour?" replied Ernie suspiciously.

"Not the sort to be discussed over the phone. Can we meet?"

"Yes, tomorrow lunchtime, at our usual watering hole and as it's you that wants the favour, then lunch and the drinks are on you." Tanner could hear the humour in his voice.

"Yeah, alright … I suppose that's a fair deal."

"Okay, I'll see you then … oh, and by the way, I've got some news for you; not gossip, but to do with Maureen Dickins."

"What's that then?" probed Tanner.

"You'll just have to wait until tomorrow won't you…bye." Tanner heard only silence as Ernie ended the call. Tanner made himself a coffee and paced around his flat; his adrenalin was fired up and he wanted to keep working. He hadn't felt this restless about a job for a good many years, but this was more than a job: this was family – his family. He checked his freezer and found a pre-packed meal ready for the microwave.

Within a few minutes the meal was cooked and on a plate, only Tanner had no appetite; he picked at it and chased parts of it around his plate with a fork but he had no desire to eat it. He checked his watch: it was mid afternoon. The image of Danny Dolan kept appearing in his mind. He scraped the contents of his plate into the waste bin, grabbed his coat and went out. Earlier in the morning he had noticed a bus shelter close to Dolan's flat, which he knew would make a good observation point.

John Tanner had been standing in the bus shelter for over an hour, watching Dolan's flat. The lights were on and the curtains were drawn, but he'd seen nothing else; no movements, nothing. For all he knew they could be wrapped up together watching DVDs back to back until the following morning. He suddenly became aware of the air becoming colder as the day prepared to turn into early evening. He turned up the collar of his jacket and placed his hands into the deep side pockets. He watched with amusement as a car driver across the street bartered with a prostitute. Eventually they agreed a price and she climbed into the car next to the driver. Tanner watched as the vehicle merged with the passing traffic and became one with the rush hour. He hadn't realised until now how tired he was, but suddenly every movement was becoming an effort, and his eyelids felt like one-ton loads.

He left the bus shelter and walked slowly down a side street towards where he had parked his car and remembered just how little sleep he'd actually had since Ruth had visited him. Since her visit his mind had always been far too busy to allow him to sleep peacefully and when it did, it permitted him only a couple of hours' sleep at a time. He reached his car, unlocked the driver's door and hauled himself inside. He was going home, and this time with a determination to sleep the sleep of the dead.

The following morning Tanner awoke at eight thirty, feeling refreshed and pleased that he'd actually been able to drop into a deep sleep, knowing it was something his body needed. He thought about his meeting with Ernie Palmer at lunchtime; he felt restless and wished he'd made it a breakfast meeting. He showered, dressed and was eager to start his day. He looked at the clock for the umpteenth time; the hands had hardly moved, almost as though it was on a go-slow, whilst he was fired up and ready to go.

He decided to drive over to Dolan's flat before his meeting with Ernie. If he could just rattle him enough, he may let something slip and Tanner was desperate for something, anything which would give him a closer step towards Becky's whereabouts. Strangely the traffic was light, enabling him to make good time driving across London into the East End and luck certainly appeared to be on his side, for as he drove past the Lucky Eight Café, he saw Danny Dolan entering.

Tanner parked his car and walked back to the café. On entering, he ordered a coffee, giving no eye contact or any indication that he previously laid eyes on either Bob or Marcie. He paid for his coffee without comment and took it to the table where Dolan was sitting. "Hello Danny, d'you mind if I sit here? All the other tables seem to be occupied."

Dolan looked around at the empty tables surrounding them. "What are you playing at? I told you, I don't know anything!"

"I don't play games Danny...I told you, I'm trying to locate Becky Wilson and I'm sure you'd feel a lot better if she was found."

"What's that suppose to mean...why would I be happier?" His tone fully expressed his hostility.

"I thought she was the love of your life...I mean, you must wonder what happened to her?"

"Who the fuck are you?" he asked with a sneer.

"I told you: I'm just someone who is trying to find Becky Wilson."

"So you're not the old bill then?"

"Let's just say I'm in a related service." Tanner smiled condescendingly.

"What's that then...you're a fucking ambulance driver or something?"

"Why the aggression Danny?"

Dolan ignored the question, pointed his finger at Tanner and spat, "You keep the fuck out of my face..."

"Is that a threat Danny?" Tanner maintained the smile and his calmness seemed to unsettle Dolan, who continued pointing his finger.

"I suggest you back off now, otherwise I might start looking for you and that ain't gonna be none too healthy for yer!" He curled his lip as he spoke.

"Well, I've obviously rattled you, Danny boy. Maybe I should ask my friend the Chief Inspector to call on you and offer his apologies as well."

This seemed to agitate Dolan even more. "You're on dangerous ground pal. You've been warned, and I don't give no second warnings..." Dolan stood up, as though to leave.

"Sit down Danny and let me mark your card for you. You see...you think you are tough; you probably even think you are, in fact, the local man! But let me tell you this: until you've been in an interrogation run by the Security Services, then you have no idea of exactly how intimidating and traumatic they can be, nor of exactly how much power we have over an individual. Tell me, have you ever been really anxious Danny? You know, when your chest feels constricted, your breathing becomes shallow; your voice is tight with that high-pitched nervousness? Your stomach gurgles and you feel that at any moment you're going to shit yourself? Well, multiply it by a couple of dozen times and you get some idea what a fully-fledged Security enforcement interrogation feels like."

The colour drained from Dolan's face. He said nothing as he backed away and then walked out of the café. Tanner drained his coffee and took his cup back to the counter. Marcie was alone.

"I really could do with a couple of leads. I can't keep leaning on Dolan and I'm not sure where else to go."

"Listen, I'm not a grass and I know what 'appens to them that are..." She paused and looked around at the empty café. "Now you didn't get this from me, but 'ave a word with a Marion Perkins or a Sarah Mulden; they were involved with Becky's mate Hannah...they may be able to help you."

"Thanks, I'll add them to my list, and don't worry – as far as anybody else is concerned, you've told me nothing. In fact we don't even speak. Tanner gave her a wink and left for his luncheon appointment with Ernie Palmer.

Tanner stood outside the café, gazing at nothing in particular; his mind was filled with far too many thoughts and churning them over. Thoughts of his daughter Ruth, his joy at their reunion and concerns about his daughter Rebecca ... and just what the hell was behind her disappearance? Had she just run off in a tantrum following a lovers tiff, or had Ruth hit the nail on the head with her claims of people trafficking and sexual slavery? He thought about Danny Dolan; was he just a tuppenny-ha'penny back street pimp running a couple of girls, or was he in fact connected to something larger, something with international connections? No, Tanner shook his head as he dismissed the idea.

He looked along the street before turning towards his car, but his eyes focused on a group of men further along the road, looking back at him menacingly. One of them was a very pissed-off Danny Dolan and each of the other three looked nasty pieces of work in their own right. Tanner turned and started walking towards his car; as he glanced over his shoulder, he saw the men were now running towards him.

As Tanner approached his car, he clicked the remote unlock button on his keys, then quickly jumped in behind the steering wheel. The engine instantly fired into life as he turned on the ignition, and he sped away. He hadn't driven far when he felt a jolt at the back of his car. He looked into the rear view mirror and saw the grinning faces of Danny Dolan and his fellow thugs chasing behind him in an old-style Mercedes. He quickly increased his speed, causing the cars around him to sound their car horns and flash their headlights; other vehicles filled the roads in front of them. Tanner knew he had to avoid a frontal collision. He had to use whatever escape route that became available. At each turn he made in his attempt to lose his pursuers, the tyres screamed and he stabbed at the brake pedal to ensure the wheels didn't lock.

He saw a sign indicating a left-hand turn to an industrial area; he spun the steering wheel, turning the car and almost ploughing into a group of pedestrians who were crossing the road. His eyes flickered into the rear view mirror; the Mercedes was still following, although he had widened the gap between them. He looked ahead and the words screamed through his head, "Road block!" His eyes transfixed on the articulated vehicle that had pulled across the width of the road as it manoeuvred to reverse into one of small manufacturing units. Tanner again checked his rear view mirror.

The Mercedes was approaching at a distance behind him. He envisaged the four of them inside the car, almost rubbing their hands together with glee that their prey was now cornered. Tanner knew an evasive turn would be his only chance of escape. He braked hard and slung the gear lever into reverse; at the same time he pushed down hard on the accelerator pedal. The car reversed quickly building up speed. He swung the steering wheel into full lock whilst lifting off the accelerator pedal at the same time. The car's tyres screeched in protest, as the car's front swung round through one hundred and eighty degrees. Tanner rammed the gear lever into forward gear and stamped the accelerator pedal to the floor. The car roared away in the opposite direction. Another articulated vehicle had turned onto the industrial area, effectively blocking the Mercedes from following him.

He drove around, mingling with the busy late morning traffic, until he was sure he had lost his pursuers. Only when he was satisfied they weren't suddenly going to appear in his rear view mirror, did he feel comfortable enough to head towards his meeting.

Shortly after one o'clock in the Three Kings Public House, John Tanner looked up smiling as his friend and ex-colleague Ernie Palmer joined him at his table and sat in front of the pint of bitter that was awaiting him.

"Hello Ernie…I've ordered a couple of ploughman's for lunch."

"Yeah, that's fine …I haven't had one of those for ages." Ernie took a sip from his glass. "So, what's this favour you're after?"

"You occasionally acted as liaison officer between our lot and the police…" Tanner slid a piece of paper across the table. "I want you to have a look into these two chaps for me."

"Priack…DS Priack … I can't say the name is familiar…what do you want to know about him and more importantly, why?"

"Between you and me Ernie, I have a couple of daughters from my first marriage…well, it was my only marriage, but we divorced well over twenty years ago. I lost touch with the girls. It didn't help matters that their mother hated me, but then she remarried and changed their names. Anyway, I'm back in touch with one of them and the other one has disappeared." Tanner nodded towards the piece of paper that his friend was holding. "This chap here, DS Priack, he paid her a visit prior to her disappearance…"

"Perhaps that's why she did a runner?" Ernie injected.

"No, I don't think so…" Tanner shook his head gently.

"So, why don't you ask him?" Palmer asked, as though it was the most logical action.

"I intend to, but I want to know a bit about him first…call it a gut feeling."

"Okay, I'll see what I can find out…who is this other one, Danny Dolan?"

"That's just it, I don't know what he does; there's talk of involvement in the sex slave trade, so he could be involved up to his neck, or it might just be silly gossip."

"Do you think this DS Priack is also into smuggling girls?"

"No I don't think he's involved, but if it's going on under his nose then I can't believe he's not aware of it."

"Okay, although he may just be following the official line…"

"What's that?" asked Tanner.

"Well, basically it's make a bit of noise, turn over a few brothels belonging to the East Europeans but on the whole, just kick it under the carpet; let's just say that some of the cultures involved in this are politically sensitive."

"I suppose they'd think differently if a politician's daughter was kidnapped and forced to service up to twenty men a day!"

"Yes, but it doesn't happen John…or if it does, it gets hushed up at the highest level."

"Do you know any tame contacts in the Vice Squad that might be useful to me?"

"Give me a couple of days and I'll phone you; we'll have another meet."

"Good … uh…there is one other thing that I need you to get me."

"If I can…what is it? Ernie asked as he spread pickle onto a chunk of cheese.

Tanner looked around them, ensuring nobody was within earshot to hear.

"I want a gun. Nothing big, just a small calibre; what we used to call a handbag pistol…"

Ernie raised his eyes and looked directly at Tanner as he picked up a piece of the pickle-covered cheese with his fork and pushed it into his mouth.

"It's okay," Tanner continued, "I'm not intending to shoot anyone, but I am dealing with the lowest of the lowlifes and as I no longer have any back up…"

"Be careful John, remember you're no longer covered by the department."

"Trust me, I'm treading very carefully."

"To be honest, if anyone else had asked me that, I would have walked straight out without even acknowledging the question..." Ernie Palmer paused and studied Tanner's face before continuing, "…but I know that you're not a fool and if you believe you need a gun then that's good enough for me."

"Cheers Ernie, it's appreciated."

"No, it's nothing. Anyway, changing the subject, have you heard about Roger Dickins? "

"No."

"He's dead, it finally happened…"

"Shit! How's Maureen taking it?"

"She's on compassionate leave at the moment, but I think she's more relieved that its finally happened…anyway, the funeral is next week; I take it you'll be there?"

"Yeah, of course, let me know the place and time…poor Maureen."

"Well, she didn't have much of a marriage did she? It was more of an existence with him, although you've got to admire her for being loyal. Anyway I can't see her being alone for long; she's a fine woman."

"Ernie…are you trying to tell me something?" Tanner asked, amused.

"What? Good God no! She wouldn't look twice at me other than as a friend…but you, on the other hand … well, there's always been that little spark between you two."

"I don't think so. Anyway I've got enough on my plate at the moment with my newly discovered daughters."

The remainder of their lunch was spent with Ernie bringing Tanner up to date on office gossip. When their food had been eaten and their drinks drained the two men left the pub.

Tanner returned to his flat; he had a very important dinner appointment that evening and he wanted to ensure he was at his best for it. A number of new fashionable chic restaurants had opened along London's Whitechapel Road, and one of them, not too far from the Aldgate, had as its proprietors two friends of his daughter Ruth. She had picked the venue and Tanner was meeting her there to update her on his progress over dinner.

Her initial reaction upon seeing him again was icy, bordering on hostile, but good food and fine wine and the relief that someone was actually doing something to locate her sister eventually brought about a mellowing of her stance. After the discussions regarding Tanner's progress, she became inquisitive about his past work for the Security Services, and due to Tanner's reluctance to give too much detail, she picked up the notion that he had in fact been a shadowy James Bond type character.

Tanner was happy for her to remain under this illusion for a while as it helped with his excuses for not having been around for them as they were growing up. He also discovered the truth about his ex-wife Madge, her vile tempers and of course her continued hatred of Tanner.

Ruth talked about how she and Becky had often wondered if it was actually Madge who had stopped their father from visiting them, or maybe she had withheld his letters and cards to convince them he didn't really care about them. The thought flashed through Tanner's head that here was a golden opportunity to absolve himself in his daughter's eyes by shifting the blame for his absence onto Madge. He believed he could almost sense Ruth willing him to blame their mother to enable him to emerge as a wronged white knight returning to their lives to make amends, but as tempting and as easy as the route looked, he couldn't lie to her – he couldn't re-enter her life after twenty-odd years and lay the blame for his absence at his ex-wife's feet. Not that he felt he owed Madge anything, but he wasn't such a bastard as to tarnish his new found relationship with his daughter by lying.

By the same token, he wasn't a saint either; he decided to take the middle route, by saying it was six of one and half a dozen of the other, adding that it was also far too long ago to drag it all out and start apportioning blame. He said he was more interested in making up for all the lost time when he should have been there for them. He added that maybe, just maybe, if he'd been around then Becky wouldn't be missing now and … he trailed off as his emotions brought a genuine lump to his throat. Ruth said nothing but slid her hand across the table and squeezed his as a comforting gesture. Tanner felt an overwhelming urge to hug his daughter, and then immediately felt uncomfortable with the thought. He knew that openly showing his emotions was something he wasn't very experienced at.

Two days later Tanner received a padded envelope by registered post. He sat at his table and opened the envelope; a small black pistol fell out into his lap. He picked up the pistol and instantly recognised the model from his days as an active undercover officer. A Czechoslovakian point thirty-two semi-automatic, eight shot military model. He tipped up the envelope; a full magazine, taped to a piece of card to stop its movement during transit, dropped out onto the table. He removed it from the card and inserted the magazine. He held the pistol flat in the palm of his hand, appreciating its light weight of around one and a half pounds and, with an overall length of six inches, it was ideal for concealment.

Chapter 9

Becky

Each day and night an endless conveyor belt of faces, terrifying numbers of men brought to my bed. Young men who thought they were cool and hip; middle-aged men who probably had their own daughters of my age; older men who could be pensioners. All of them strangers, who I could only hope I never, ever saw again. A mixture of races and colour, all of them disgusting in the way they treated women and because they were paying for a prostitute they acted as though it was expected of them to degrade her as if she was devoid of feeling, just an emotionless husk for them to release their urges and perverted lusts into, and all of this in the same bed I had to sleep in at night.

Harvey had been my soulmate throughout this entire nightmare, helping me to keep my sanity. She taught me to climb into that tiny cell inside my head and switch off while my body was being violated and she was right: it was the only way to survive, the only way to block out their voices, the voices that all said the same things... *"This feels good, doesn't it?"* and *"You know that deep down this is what you really want..."* Lots of voices from lots of men and all of them pieces of shit, just scum from the cesspit and I hated them all.

But I no longer had my saviour. Four nights previously I had heard Harvey screaming. Not the usual type of scream from when a pervert has overstepped the mark; no, this was more intense. When the screams stopped I heard her begging, "No please...no, don't...please no!" and then male voices, Crestwell and Tyler's voices. I couldn't make out what was being said but it was followed by the sound of her being beaten. The sounds of her frantic struggling and continued pleading came closer until they were outside my bedroom door. I rushed to the door but as usual it was locked. I banged on the door and shouted at them to leave her alone. The sounds of her struggle became distant as she was dragged down the stairs and into the living room. I continued listening at the door but there was only silence and as my adrenalin subsided I suddenly grew very afraid of what may be happening to her. After what seemed an eternity, but was probably no more than an hour, I heard very faint male voices, several of them and then the front door slamming shut. Shortly afterwards there was the sound of a car revving up angrily and then the screech of tyres as it pulled away.

I curled up on my bed and cuddled my pillow. Tears filled my eyes and I felt wretched. I remembered Harvey telling me about the two girls who had arrived at the house with her and how they had been taken away screaming in the middle of the night, and that she hadn't heard of them again. I wondered just what Harvey did know about her destination that caused her to react in such a hysterical way and what had happened in the living room for the sudden silence.

The following morning Paul Tyler unlocked my bedroom door, stepped inside and stood leering at me. He was wearing his trademark sweat-stained tee shirt and dirty jeans; the top button and the zipper of the jeans were both undone.

"What d'you want?" I sneered, wanting to give the impression I was so sure of myself that I could brush off everything that had happened, but I couldn't and I heard my voice crack as it tailed off.

"What d'you think I fucking want? You're a slag and I've got a hard on, so you're gonna take care of it…an' I want it to feel good, d'understand…"

I looked at him with contempt, but said nothing; to him I was just a piece of meat, a commodity to be used and to be sold, it made no difference. "… and afterwards you can get yourself all scrubbed up ready for tonight," he continued. "Friday and Saturday nights we do our most lucrative business!"

"What do you mean *we*? I haven't heard the sounds of you being abused senselessly by the endless stream of moronic scum that regularly rape me and Harvey!" I spat back at him.

"You're not raped; you love it…you get the chance to completely wallow in your slutty urges…" he sneered.

"What would you know about it, you arsehole?" He moved quickly towards me, far too quickly, and as the open palm of his hand connected with the side of my face, I climbed into that little cell of sanctuary in my head while the inevitable happened. Similar words that I heard every night. Different men, different voices, same crap!

"Feels good, don't it?" he whispered. "I knew you wanted it…knew you weren't gonna resist…and this is better than that first time…" Another thing that Harvey had taught me was to listen to their breathing, to judge how long they were going to take, and by the sound of Tyler's grasps and grunts he was going to be very quick.

Afterwards he climbed off me and lit a cigarette; the end glowed brightly as he sucked on it, then he blew the smoke straight at me, and as the smoke wafted around my face I swallowed deeply to keep from coughing. "Oh thanks a lot…" I retorted, my tone heavy with disdain. "And where's Harvey?" I asked.

"Don't worry about her, you're top girl now," he answered vaguely.

"What do you mean by 'don't worry?' Of course I worry…"

"Listen, she's gonna become a famous movie star and if you play your cards right, you could as well." He spoke as though he was doing me a favour and coming from a guy who I considered to be the world's biggest lowlife, this really set the alarm bells ringing in my head.

"I don't believe you…what do you mean?" I asked, trying desperately to mask my anxiety.

"Listen to me, stupid! The man that runs this operation also makes and supplies films, and that's where your friend Harvey has gone…for fuck's sake can't you be happy for her?" He moved towards the door to leave.

"So why was she screaming when you dragged her out?"

"Let's just say she was over excited," he answered without looking back at me.

"Oh yeah, well I think I can smell bullshit," I said guardedly.

He stood in the door frame and turned around. "You still don't get it do you?"

"Get what?"

"You're a nothing...you don't exist anymore, you're the property of the boss and he can do whatever he likes with you."

"I don't know what you're talking about..." I was genuinely confused.

"The boss! Dougie Mann, he owns you, he owns me. He owns everything! He's the kingpin. Now, what fucking part of that don't you understand?" His lip curled as he spoke and hostility had crept into his tone, and knowing just how unpredictable Tyler was, this suddenly made his insinuations about Harvey and me even more terrifying. But there was something inside me; almost as though something in my genes was driving me on and, like a terrier with a bone, I couldn't let it go.

"What do you mean by he owns everything? Nobody owns me." I wanted to sound defiant but I knew the words came out passively.

"Really? Well, the wake-up news for you, little miss stuck-up is that Danny Dolan sold you to Dougie Mann for three grand. He prepares all you slags for us, it's what he does...and he's exceptionally good at it!" Tyler spat the words hurtfully.

I responded almost on autopilot, defending Danny without fully taking in the meaning of what he'd said and of how I got here or of how long I'd actually been here.

"I don't believe you...not Danny, he wouldn't...couldn't do that...no, not to me."

Tyler let out a burst of laughter. "That's what they all say.... *Ooh no, not my darling Danny*," he mimicked.

"Why are you telling me all this?" I could feel tears of hopelessness building behind my eyes.

Tyler made a poking motion with his finger towards me. "Because you're just a prossie, a tart, a street slag. The boss has more than doubled his investment from what he's earned out of you and now he's going for the big bonus payment. Becky at the movies...although you may only be making the one..." His expression had just as quickly changed into a sneer.

"I think you're just trying to wind me up." I looked away dismissively.

"Really, well if you want to know just how connected the man is, who do you think set up that slag Isaacs on her blackmailing scam and who do you think arranged for a witness to slag her off in court and who do you think paid the filth to plant evidence in your flat making sure she went away for a long time?"

"I…I don't know…" I stammered. I was stunned through to my core.

"The same person who now runs all her little scams and is the new owner of her mini cab business…and runs her massage agency, and has taken over fencing all the stolen gear that the pair of you used to do!"

I shook my head. "No, this is all beginning to sound a little bit too far-fetched."

"You got no idea how much money she was making a week have you?" he continued, "…and believe me, that sort of money draws attention…"

"If what you're saying is right, then why didn't he just move in and take over?" I countered.

"Because he had to send a clear message to everyone that he is the main man. That's why he had your brother crippled. He could easily have muscled in and taken over his club…but now he's only got to hint to someone that he wants their business and they queue up to offer it to him!"

"So why are you telling me all this now?" My voice was rising as fear, hysteria and frustration battled one another to take control of my emotions.

"Because like I said, you've been chosen along with a couple of other slags to make some very special hardcore porno movies, and just like your friend Harvey …you're gonna be a movie star…"

"And if I say no?" My voice was barely a whisper. I had previously told myself that things couldn't get any worse and they just had … tenfold!

"Listen slag, you got no fucking say in anything, alright! Now, you're top girl and you'll do what Harvey did for you and when the two new girls arrive, you'll show them the ropes, what's expected of them and importantly, if they behave then we'll be nice to them…" While his words were still ringing in my ears and my brain was still analysing the full implication of what he'd said, Tyler left, slamming the door behind him as usual, and then the sound of the bolt sliding across as he locked it seemed to echo, as though mocking me. In less than half an hour I heard the sound of the bedroom door being unlocked. This time it was Costi; I sat upright as he brought in a plate of sandwiches and a hot drink. I was allowed out of my room to go to the toilet and to freshen up ready for business.

Over the course of the rest of that day, eleven men were brought to my room. The following day business started later but by six-thirty in the evening I'd already serviced another nine men. I had no idea how much each of the men was paying, but I was most certainly earning my keep. After the last one had left, Costi came into my room and told me there would be no more business that day. He told me to freshen up, as later on we would be having visitors. I pressed him as to who they were, but he wouldn't say any more than that.

He returned later and collected my plate and mug. I asked him for a couple of painkillers, giving the excuse of having a headache but the truth was that for the past week or so I'd had very bad back pain. Of course if I'd told him that, they'd think it was an excuse not to work and Andrei's answer to anything that could stop me working was the icy bath treatment and so, in spite of how I may be feeling, every day was a working day, even during my periods, which these days were quite painful.

As I sat curled up on my bed, deep in thought, it dawned on me just how quiet it was. The entire house was in silence, which eerily seemed to add to my apprehension. I started to pace around my room. I couldn't give attention to anything; sleep was impossible even though I felt very tired. It was like the feeling you get when you suddenly awake in the middle of the night from a nightmare, only I was already awake and it was only early evening. My thoughts went to Harvey. I thought back to the time she'd told me how she had been forced to pose for pornographic photos, along with another girl. She said she'd hated it more than the prostitution, because whilst the punters quickly forget the face of the girl they've been with, a photograph remains in existence, especially with the Internet, and so even if you did manage to escape and start rebuilding a new life, it would always be there to come back and haunt you.

I lay back on the bed and rubbed my eyes, my poor tired eyes. I still felt unsettled. I may even have dozed off for a few moments, but as the evening darkness now closed in, I found myself feeling lonely. I watched the night shadows dancing across the bedroom walls. My thoughts centred on what had happened to me during the past days, who these mystery visitors were and just what did they have planned for my future, and more importantly, did I have one?

It wasn't long before I heard noises, then voices, followed by footsteps on the stairs, and quite a few footsteps at that! I recognised the voices as belonging to Crestwell, Tyler and Costi and shortly after I heard the raised voice of Andrei. They were in Harvey's old room. There were two female voices and whilst I couldn't make out what they were saying, they sounded as though they were either very immature or still in their early teens. All too soon I heard screaming followed by the familiar sounds of them being beaten and then raped. My eyes quickly filled with tears, and as my shoulders shuddered in despair, I sobbed. I sobbed for them, for me, for Harvey and for every parent's daughter subjected to this sexual slavery.

From the sounds coming through the wall, one of the girls was fighting back. Silently I found myself willing her to submit. Let him have you, I urged mentally … I knew what would be coming, I knew what hell she was about to experience. When they had finished raping one, they turned their attention to the feisty one. I could hear the first one crying out for her mum, and then for anyone to help her. Afterwards I heard the bath being filled and I knew it would be with cold water. I heard footsteps on the stairs and again I knew one of them was bringing up a large sack of ice cubes from the big freezers they kept downstairs. It wasn't too long afterwards when screams of sheer panic rang out as the feisty one experienced the icy bath punishment. I pulled my pillow over my head to drown out her screams, which is exactly what Harvey told me she did when she first heard my screams and pleas for mercy when I was also being submerged into the icy cold bath water.

The ordeal for the girl wasn't repeated as many times as it was for me; however, whatever they did to her at the end I don't know, but she gave the most blood curdling scream you could imagine. I heard the sounds of the four men going downstairs, and then just the gentle, almost whispered sobbing from the two girls in Harvey's old room. I tried to visualise them; the room was actually two large rooms knocked into one. There were two double beds, one on either side, and a curtain draped across the middle of the room divided the room. It was used for when a group of boozed up men wanted to round off their evening by sharing a couple of girls between them.

Early the following morning, I was awoken by Costi. He spoke softly and told me to wash, dress and to meet him downstairs. Although his voice was an attempt at reassurance, I was apprehensive. But I knew that in the cupboard next to the bathroom there was a selection of shampoos, various soaps, clean towels, even a hair drier…"
The skirt and top I'd previously been given, and told to wear during business hours for the punters had been taken for washing, so all I had to wear was a baggy t-shirt, which came to just below the top of my thighs; bottom skimming but only just. I eased my way down the stairs in bare feet, trying to avoid stepping on squeaky sections of the stairs. I stopped a couple of times and listened.

I had no idea what was waiting for me when I entered the living room. It was quite a large room, as though three normal rooms had been knocked into one; the scarcity of furniture added to the illusion of vastness. In one corner a large flat screen television took pride of place. In that same part of the room was a long curved sofa, with a glass coffee table in front of it. A table and four chairs occupied the corner opposite. Costi motioned to me to sit at the table, and as I sat I saw that it had been laid out ready for a meal, with two place settings. My mind tried out several permutations but before I reached any conclusion, Costi arrived with two plates containing a traditional full English breakfast. The plates were heaped and as he placed it in front of me, I tore into it before he could say so much as *bon appetit*. He sat opposite me and watched me as he ate his own breakfast. As soon as I'd stopped shovelling the food into my mouth like a savage and began eating normally, he spoke.

"Becky, now that Harvey has moved on, you are now top girl; that means you are responsible for ensuring the other girls toe the line. Whatever you may think of it, this is still a business and our customers pay for a service. Those two new girls will supply that service and your role will be to ensure they do not cause us any problems." He stopped as he forked a piece of bacon into his mouth, his eyes fixed firmly onto mine awaiting my response. I dropped my eyes down to my plate as I answered.

"What exactly do I have to do? And does it mean I no longer have to service the scum that come in?"

He finished chewing before answering. "Becky … look at me, Becky." I looked up into his eyes. "Teach them everything that you do, the way that Harvey taught you; the quicker they learn, then the quicker Andrei will stop their punishment…but if they don't learn, then you will also receive punishment alongside them…you will go into the bath Becky!" The mere thought made me want to vomit up the lovely breakfast I'd just enjoyed. Costi must have seen the colour drain from my face and my eyes fill with fear. He reached across and touched my arm.

"It's okay Becky, I know you will do a good job and those two girls will not be a problem…if they are, then tell us; that way you cannot be blamed…" He smiled as though he was my guardian angel, before carrying on, "…and as for your last question, yes, you are a very popular girl amongst our clients and so you will continue to service those who ask for you." He spoke with the same casualness as if he was discussing typing services with an office supplies company.

We finished eating and there seemed nothing else to say. We both stood up; it was an awkward moment, but as I turned away to return to my room Costi pulled me towards him and kissed me gently, his lips moving around my face. He began to nibble my ear, as his fingers ran through my hair. His lips returned and deepened the kiss to taste me more intimately, his tongue probing my mouth while his fingertips now gently trailed across my lower stomach to the top of my legs. My arms hung by my side passively, and when he saw there was no passionate response to his actions he pushed me back against the wall, sneered as he looked me up and down, and growled, "There's a tray of sandwiches in the kitchen; take them up to the girls." He walked off in the direction of the television. I didn't need telling twice. I got the tray from the kitchen and immediately returned to my room with a great sense of relief that not only had I eaten well for the first time in ages, but also that I'd managed to avoid his sexual advances, which wasn't normally an option.

I waited to make sure he wasn't going have second thoughts and come upstairs after me, then went to Harvey's old room to see the new girls. I slowly slid the bolt back on their door and went in. They were both cuddled up together on the one bed: both blondes, one of them with a cluster of freckles covering the top of her cheeks and across the bridge of her nose. They both looked up at me as I entered their room, their faces frozen with fear.

"Hello, I'm Becky. I've brought you some food; you must be ravenous." They huddled even closer together, as though by merging their bodies into one they would be safe. I placed the tray on the bedside table and sat on the edge of the bed. They really did look like kids. I gently stroked the hair of the one nearest to me and whispered softly, "It's okay, I'm not here to hurt you. I'm the same as you and I've gone through what you went through last night." I moved the tray onto the bed between them. "Eat while you can; you can never be sure when you they'll give you your next meal." One of them took a sandwich, the other one still looked at me wide-eyed, like a rabbit caught in a car's headlights. "I'll run you a hot bath, you can clean up and then we'll find you some clothes. I assume they've taken yours?"

Both girls nodded; the second one had now plucked up enough courage to take a sandwich from the tray.

"What are your names?" I continued speaking softly.

"I'm Siobhan," answered Freckles; the other one said nothing.

"Look, I'm trying to help you, the same as the girl who was previously in this room helped me when I first arrived...it's the only way we survive, helping one another."

"Lucy..." the other one said. "Are we going to die?"

Neither of them could have been more than sixteen, and I suddenly felt myself becoming very mumsy towards them. They were children, who needed protection, but I knew I couldn't protect them and I was afraid to tell them what was in store for them, afraid that they would look upon me as a judge passing sentence.

"If we stay together, Lucy, then hopefully none of us will die...all I can say to you is, be passive; whatever happens, let them have their way. If you struggle, they'll beat you." Freckles started crying and I knew she was the one crying for her mum the night before, which meant that Lucy was the feisty one, and as she pulled herself out of the bed I saw the horrific welts on her leg where an electric iron had been held against it, almost identical to the scars that Harvey had shown me on her leg. I helped her into the bathroom and bathed her leg. Then I left the pair of them while I went to the large walk-in airing cupboard at the far end of the corridor, where an assortment of clothes were kept in dustbin bags. I picked out a couple of skirts and tops in what I guessed were near enough their sizes ... not that there was much of a selection ... and returned to the bathroom. I gave them the clothes. "You will probably be kept locked in the house for at least two weeks." I spoke as though I knew it for a fact, but it was exactly what Harvey had said to me and I had still never been allowed out of the house.

Suddenly both girls froze. I honestly thought Freckles was going to wet herself. I looked around and Paul Tyler was standing there, his face glazed with hatred, as his eyes bored into me. I dropped my gaze submissively and returned to my room.

Shortly afterwards, business started and my first punter of the day was brought to my room. I was oblivious to his horny grunting on top of me. The automatic words of encouragement that I was expected to say came out like a pre recorded tape: "Oh yeah, baby. Oh, you're good baby. Oh yes, yes..." I'd said them to these losers so many times, I wasn't even aware now that I was saying them. My ears were honed to the sobs, from both Siobhan and Lucy as they were being held down and raped by hungry punters eager for the thrill of taking a virgin; that's what the girls were being passed off as, and each sick punter believed he was the first, purely because he was told he would be and because he paid a much higher rate for the privilege to be the first.

For the next two days we were really busy; it was what I called the conveyor belt syndrome and when business finished for the night and we were allowed to sleep, I really fell into a coma. I'd previously taken a packet of painkillers from the kitchen and hidden them in my room. I swallowed them a few at a time, dry; I was desperate to ease the back pain, which was now intensifying.

I woke suddenly … or was it that my consciousness had just returned? I had no idea of the time. I could see the light outside the small window trying to penetrate the thick curtain. I heard the floorboards creaking outside my door; I felt disorientated. *'Oh please no, please don't let it be another of their lowlife clients'* the voice in my head cried out to no one. The door opened and Paul Tyler's body filled the doorframe. "I thought as it's quiet and everyone's out you'd like to have a shower, then put something on and come downstairs for a while. I figured it's time we chilled out together, perhaps shoot a few lines and well, talk about you…perhaps talk about getting you back to Danny. I was naked under the duvet but I had no qualms; I leapt from under the cover and made my way to the bathroom.

I enjoyed a lengthy and well-needed shower, and as I dried my hair I could smell the fragrance of the scented soap. Outside my body was clean, spotlessly clean, but to me the inside was dirty, dirty and contaminated. I thought of the men who had abused me last night. Their faces were always a blur, but they'd had a fun night with their friends, filled up with a belly full of beer and thought they'd round the evening off with a kebab and a whore!

I went back into my room, and pulled on my skirt and top. I don't know why but a voice inside told me to put my trainers on. I hadn't touched them since my first day in the room; they were still under the bed. I quickly slipped them on and laced them; at least if the chance came I'd be able to run from them. I walked slowly downstairs, each stair creaking with the weight of every step. The foot of the stairs was mid-way along the passage. At one end of the passage was the front door; my instincts yelled at me to make a run for it, but I didn't trust them. I could see the large bolts had been slid back; it was unlocked, but this was probably a test. The house was just too quiet. If I failed the test then no doubt the four of them would stand in line to dish out a punishment beating to me.

The door to the living room was diagonally opposite the foot of the stairs. I opened the door gingerly and went in. Paul Tyler was on the sofa watching a porno movie: two women giving an American cop a blow-job. He looked up at me as I entered the room.

"Come in Becks…don't be shy; you're almost one of the family now." He waved his hand, beckoning me and giving me the full welcome, but it was an act and I could see through it. The only thing I didn't know was why! He patted the sofa, indicating I should sit next to him. As I passed by the coffee table I could see that apart from a few bottles of spirits, there was an open envelope containing pills, a number of which had spilled out onto the table. There was also a mirror, a razor blade and what I assumed to be a small bag of coke. He pulled out a joint and offered it to me. "D'you want some of this?"

I shook my head. "No, no thanks I don't smoke."

He reached down and grabbed a couple of pills from the coffee table. "I know how you're feeling. Take a couple of these…and a few swigs of booze … it'll numb the pain and suddenly you'll feel like nothing in the world matters anymore."

"Naw, no thanks, I don't do that either." I smiled as sweetly and as inoffensively as I could.

"Don't try and kid a fucking kidder…you and that Isaacs slag were well known for your booze and pills sessions."

"People change, Paul. It never messed me up and I stopped doing it exactly when I wanted to. I'm not taking any shit now, and there's no way I'm gonna turn into a fucking zombie."

"What you accusing me of?"

"I'm not accusing or saying anything…I'm a different person that's all."

"What, you think you're better than me?"

"I didn't say that. I just don't want pills and booze, that's all."

"Well, I'm offended…let's do a couple of lines each and show there's no hard feelings."

"Look, I'm not being funny Paul. I tried it once it before but it felt like it was burning my nose. To be honest, I didn't like it and I haven't touched it since." I could see he was taking my rejection angrily, and a flush of fear went through me. I couldn't allow myself to lose control and if he got me stoned then I'd be at his mercy and he could pump anything into my veins, but I wasn't handling it right; I had to keep him happy, and as much as he now repulsed me, I could only offer myself … willingly. I heard the voice in my head urging me … after all, what difference did it make? So many had abused me since I'd been here… and then I shuddered at the thought of actually contemplating, *initiating* sex with this most vile, most repulsive person imaginable…and then fear took over. I rested my hand on his thigh. "I've thought of something else we could do…" I tried to sound as though I really wanted him. He said nothing; he just stared ahead. He was scaring me. I hesitated, then started drawing little circles on the inside of his leg with my fingers.

I didn't see it coming…he moved quickly and slapped me hard with the back of his hand. In the next second he smashed his fist into my face and as it connected, I felt my mouth filling with blood. Then he grabbed my hair and yanked it, dragging me across the room, slamming me into the closed door. As I bounced off it he again dragged me by my hair back to the opposite wall and slammed me into it, only this time his fist followed and connected squarely with my kidneys, causing my legs to give way and as I slumped to the floor I felt him lifting me up by my hair, which felt as though it was being torn out by the roots.

I was aware that I was screaming but I couldn't hear any sounds. Tyler began to spin me around by my hair as if he was competing in an Olympic shot-putt. He let go and as the momentum sent me flying forward, my shoulder crashed into the doorframe, I heard the wood crack with the force of my impact. I was aware of the pain of wood splinters in the top of my arm. Excruciating pain searing all the way down. I rebounded from the collision and, as I turned to face him, I saw him reach out for me. My foot instinctively launched itself and as I kicked out, the toe of my trainer buried itself deep into his groin. He gave a sickening scream. As I pulled my foot back his hands covered his testicles as though they had magical healing power, and in the same instance his legs buckled and he fell to his knees. I grabbed the whiskey bottle from the coffee table, swung it with all the force I could muster and hit him on the head with it. The bottle didn't break, but it certainly sent him crashing face down onto the floor and for a moment he looked completely out of it.

The adrenalin was flowing through me. I felt I had the energy to take on the world; the downside was that the neck of the bottle had bruised the palm of my hand; it was now swelling and beginning to hurt like hell! I knew I had to get away, but I couldn't think rationally; I was in serious panic mode. I was swallowing blood from my bleeding mouth and began to gag.

"You fucking bitch…!" It was Tyler; with one hand still holding his crotch he was getting to his feet.

Loud voices screamed inside my head: "Stop him, he's going to kill you…! Stop Him He's Going To Kill You…!! STOP HIM HE'S GOING TO KILL YOU!!!"

The whisky bottle was on the floor but closer to him than to me; my eyes fell on the coffee table; his little bag of coke, a make-up mirror laying face down and a single razor blade. I quickly picked up the blade, holding it between my thumb and forefinger. An involuntary retch took over as my body rejected the swallowed blood and along with bile from my throat and God knew what else, heaved outwards. That same instant Tyler grabbed my wrist. I instinctively slashed out with the blade, more as a warning for him to back off, but I caught him with a long cut to the side of his neck. A long deep cut. I saw a look of real fear in his eyes as his hand frantically tried to stop the blood flow from the severed artery in his neck. I walked backwards out of the room, unable to break eye contact with him as his eyes pleaded with mine, pleaded with me to help him.

Outside the room, every part of my body hurt, as though a train had hit me full on. The adrenalin had done its job and was now in decline and as it waned it was replaced by the generated pain of a battered, beaten body. The vision of Paul Tyler's life ebbing out of him with each pump of blood came into my head. In my mind's eye it was me, drifting into oblivion as my life essence drained away. I realised that I didn't have any escape; wherever I went they would find me, they would drag me back and beat me, they would turn me into a junkie, dependent on them to spend the rest of my life allowing scum from the streets to violate me. To screw me and use me for their despicable sordid fantasies, and I would be forever willing to comply, eager to sink to the lowest depths, to guarantee my next fix, to ease just for a moment my body's dependency and craving.

I was still holding the razor blade; I looked at my wrist and then back at the blade. The voice in my head spoke softly as it tried to justify my thoughts. '*It probably won't even hurt. Paul didn't look at though he was in pain…just slide the blade along that vein in your wrist and then relax…nothing in this crapped-out world will ever bother you again…*'

I wanted to do it, I wanted to escape from this shit that I'd been dropped into…but something stronger was stopping me; something inside me wouldn't let me do it. A surge of anger, defiance, rebelliousness, call it whatever…but I wasn't ready to give in, not while I still had an ounce of fight in me. I had to escape, but I also had to think clearly. Money. I would need money. I cautiously stepped back into the living room. Tyler's body was lying face down on the floor, but more importantly there was no longer any movement from it. I saw the outline and bulge of his wallet in the back pocket of his jeans and as much as I really didn't want to have to go anywhere near his body, with an outstretched arm I reached forward and removed the wallet. I flipped it open and couldn't believe my luck. 'Bulging' wallet was an understatement – it was absolutely crammed full with notes!

I left the living room and ran upstairs. I unlocked the bolt on the girls' door. As I went into the room both girls recoiled in horror, and I realised that both my hands and one entire arm was covered in Paul Tyler's blood. They'd both heard the commotion downstairs and assumed the blood was mine. It took a while but I managed to convince them I was okay, without getting any of Tyler's blood on them. Siobhan wasn't okay though; her young mind couldn't cope with the horrors it was experiencing, and she just curled up on her bed into a ball, with her thumb in her mouth and appeared to be almost comatose.

Thankfully, Lucy had her wits about her. I told her to dress and to find me some clothes while I washed Tyler's blood from my skin. We were racing against time; Kevin, Costi or Andrei could return at any time. Lucy came up trumps and found a suitcase filled with clothes, mainly tops, jeans and shoes that probably belonged to the girls who had been in the house before us, but the important thing was that we had clothes that fitted us. Lucy and I dressed quickly. Siobhan became our problem; she refused to dress, and stated she wasn't going to leave. She shouted at me that I'd got them into trouble! She was adamant that she wasn't going to leave or do anything to upset Andrei or Costi. I looked at Lucy; we both knew that we had no time left to coax her round or even to forcibly drag her with us.

"Siobhan, listen to me, we're leaving now, but I promise I'll come back for you, do you understand?" I kissed her on the cheek and that's when I noticed the small tattoo on her shoulder of two rabbits humping. It seemed so out of character for this child-like waif to even have a tattoo, let alone one with a sexual undertone. I quickly dismissed the thought and, grabbing Lucy's hand, she and I quickly made our way downstairs. Apart from the creak of the stairs, the joint thumping of our hearts was the only sound we heard. Our anxiety was at bursting point as we approached the front door. I gently slid back the door bolt, turned the catch and took the first breath of fresh air that I'd had for what seemed almost a lifetime.

The street outside was empty. Large Victorian residential houses and each of them almost identical in their respectability. The nearby neighbours had probably not suspected any kind of unusual activity or maybe they just weren't interested in what happened behind the curtains, provided it didn't interfere with either their daily routine or the quiet order of the area.

I kept hold of Lucy's hand and, as our hearts pounded and absolute fear fired up the adrenalin inside us, we ran to the end of the street, and along the next street and then into another one, running until we came to a busy high road with a bustling parade of shops. I saw a Black Cab with its 'for hire' sign illuminated coming towards us. I hailed it and we both climbed inside. It was only then that I realised I had nowhere to go. I told the driver just to drive and as he pulled away from the kerb, we both let out a loud sigh of relief.

I asked Lucy where she wanted to go; she said she knew nobody in London, except a guy called Danny, but she wasn't even sure where he lived as she'd only been to his flat once before. I suggested she went back to Manchester. After all, she knew the place and she knew the people, but more importantly, her parents were there, and she could put this nightmare behind her and restart her life. Thankfully she agreed. I told the taxi driver to take us to Euston Station.

Intuitively I knew the Danny she was talking about was my Danny, but in the same way that a moth is drawn towards a flame, so I was drawn into asking questions.

"Tell me about this Danny; how did you meet him?" I asked casually.

"Well, that's the funny thing … he just sort of appeared and he always seemed to be at the same places that we were…"

"We?" I asked.

"My mates. We always hung out with the same crowd, and after a while Danny started talking to us. He never seemed to be short of cash. He told us he was a contractor for clients in London and Manchester."

"Wasn't he a bit old for you?"

"Do you know him?" she asked suspiciously.

"Well, let's just say I know someone like him. It may be the same guy or it could just be a coincidence with the name." I fought hard to keep my emotions in check. I knew the bastard she was talking about was my Danny, but inside I just had to know everything he did, almost like the cheated partner wanting to know all the details of an affair.

"Anyway," she continued, "whenever there was a party he'd be the one to turn up with bottles of booze and cans of beer, then after a while he was the man with the cannabis, and then he was the man giving us some freebie ecstasy. The way he used to look at me, I knew I was the one he fancied. Soon we became more than mates and I knew that at some point we'd be having sex, but I didn't mind and when we did finally do it he was fantastic, far better than my boyfriend, so at Danny's suggestion I quickly dumped him and for the next few months he and I were inseparable.

"Were you *In Love*?" I don't know why it bothered me, but I was willing her to say no.

"I don't know. He had loads of money and he liked spending it on me, the sex was good and he was an exciting guy to be around, but love…no I don't think so."

"So, why did you come to London?"

"Oh it was becoming a drag where we were and Danny told me that when he was in London it was constant parties and all the celebrities from the telly turned up. He even told me that his previous girlfriend was now married to a famous footballer. I mean, it was like talking about another world…"

"So how did you end up at the house?" I was actually becoming bored with her silly immature fantasy.

"One evening at his flat he took a phone call, then told me we'd been invited to a party at a famous rock star's house in St John's Wood. I'd heard of the area before and knew that's where they all lived…"

"Who…where who lived?"

"In the papers… when they mention rock stars, they always say they live in St John's Wood…"

"Do they? Oh, yeah, you're right…sorry…carry on." I involuntarily rolled my eyes in disbelief.

"Anyway, on the way to get a taxi, a mate of Danny's pulled up. Siobhan was in the back of the car. Mind you at that point I didn't know her from Adam. Danny told me to go with them; he said he was going to get some money from the cash point and that he'd see me there. I protested a bit but he said I had to go because the girls who got there early normally got loads of free tickets for gigs and invites for other parties, and of course when you see another girl you naturally assume you'll be safe. Besides, Siobhan acted as though she knew Danny…I never did ask her about that… but anyway, that's when they took us to the house, so we didn't even get to the party!"

I couldn't see the point in telling her that there never was any party, and thankfully at that point, we'd arrived at Euston. I paid the taxi driver and walked into the station with Lucy, who suddenly grabbed my arm and said, "D'you know, I could kill for a cigarette." The irony wasn't lost on me and for the first time in ages I burst out laughing. I pulled Paul Tyler's wallet from my pocket and gave her two hundred pounds.

"Here, get yourself a ticket to Manchester…ask if I need a platform ticket, and then get yourself some treats. God alone knows you deserve it." I waited as she wandered off, my mind preoccupied with the content of our previous semi ludicrous and yet disturbing conversation.

Eventually she returned, looking calm and relaxed, the smoke from the cigarette in her hand wafted by my nose. She exuded in full the overconfidence of a teenager and from her coolness it was as though she had completely erased her experiences in the house.

Time was against us; her train was due to leave, we made it to the correct platform, quickly hugged, kissed and promised to stay in touch, although just how that was going to happen was beyond me. I watched and waved as her train pulled out.

I now had to focus my thoughts onto me. Where did I go? My flat would surely be the first place they'd look for me. I thought of my sister Ruth, but if they did come after me, I didn't want to involve her in this mess. Madge was out of the question; right now I needed an ally, not another enemy.

No. All I had was Danny. I thought perhaps I should just confront him, especially as I really couldn't think of any alternative. As I slowly walked towards the taxi rank I started rehearsing in my head exactly what I was going to say to him. But as I approached the first taxi in the queue, suddenly the face of Siobhan and her freckles came into my head. Oh my God, how could I have forgotten her? The poor kid – what was happening to her? Then I realised that I had no idea of the house number, nor even the street where we had been held; I couldn't even alert the police to her predicament, but at that moment I vowed to myself that one way or another I would get those bastards. They were gonna pay, and pay heavily!"

I climbed into the first cab on the rank and gave Danny's address to the driver. My mind went blank; I couldn't think of anything to say to him, except, 'You bastard I want to kill you.' My eyes were heavy, and it suddenly became a struggle to keep them open. I wanted to be asleep, to sleep the sleep of the dead, but the best I could hope for was a quick nap before we reached Danny's flat.

The next thing I knew I was being shaken gently on the arm. "'Ere you go love, we're 'ere…" The taxi driver was leaning in through the rear door, yet astute enough to keep his meter running until I was fully awake.

"Oh yes, I'm sorry…what do I owe you?" I tried to act as though I was fully conscious, but in truth I could easily have slipped back into a deep slumber. I paid the driver and stood on the pavement, watching as he pulled away. Then with a great sense of foreboding, I approached Danny's front door and pressed hard on his doorbell. My ears strained for any sounds behind the door, but it was silent. I pressed the doorbell again, this time keeping my finger on it for a longer time. As I waited I could feel my anxiety building up, but there was no answer; he wasn't home. I felt conscious that people were looking at me, even though logic told me they probably weren't, but I felt uncomfortable and exposed. I waited for a break in the traffic and ran across the road, and then just a few more steps towards a bus shelter, where at least I could wait without looking conspicuous.

I'd been waiting there for exactly twenty-two minutes – that is, if the clock outside the dry cleaners, with the silly slogan on its dial was to be believed. When a mini cab pulled up outside his flat, I hoped more than anything that it would be Danny, but it wasn't. I watched as a tall, leggy blonde climbed out, laden with carrier bags from the local supermarket. She paid the driver and to my surprise she went to Danny's front door. I was curious, and expected to see her repeat what I'd done – pressing the doorbell, getting no answer, waiting a few moments and then going away, but instead she fished in her pocket and retrieved a key, a door key! My initial reaction was that Danny had moved but, glancing upwards, I recognised the same dirty patterned curtains that were hanging at the window when I was last there.

Purely on impulse, and without any logical thought in my head, I ran across the road towards her, causing a car to brake hard and swerve. I heard the angry blast on his horn, but like a sprinter with the winning post in sight, I was focused solely on reaching that front door before she could get in and close it. She unlocked the door, letting it swing open and as she bent down to pick up the carrier bags; I rushed past her, over the threshold and then turned as though I was opening the door to her. The look of shock and surprise on her face was a treat to behold.

Seeing her close-up she was certainly beautiful, although she didn't look any older than seventeen. She had rings on each of her fingers, and she was wearing a gold bracelet with the initial '**B**' etched into it, and I could certainly remember seeing that before.

"What the fuck do you think you're doing?" Her previous angelic expression had quickly transformed into a snarling savage aggression.

"You got that one wrong darling; just who the fuck are you is more like it!" I matched her aggression.

"Not that it is any of your business, but this is my boyfriend's flat..."

"I know *what* the fuck it is...I asked who *you* were?" I could sense my mouth also snarling as my tone became more violent.

"I'm Elizabeth...Danny's girlfriend. This is his flat. Now, whoever you are, why don't you just piss off?" Her eyes gave away her lack of confidence at confrontations.

"And I bet they call you ... Beth; hence the bracelet..." I said it with more than a trace of ridicule in my voice, but then snapped back to aggressive. "I think you're living in a dream world. Now, you be the good little girl and you piss off!"

"I'm still waiting for you to tell me just who you are?" She was now reduced to nothing more than a schoolgirl's defiance.

"I'm Becky...Becky Wilson...remember it and fuck off!"

"Oh yes, Danny's told me all about you; how you took him for all his money and then dumped him. You really are a class A bitch for the way you treated him!"

"Well, for your information, lady, I didn't dump him; the bastard sold me into prostitution if you must know...just like he did with his previous girlfriends and just like he's gonna do with you!" I snapped the words at her.

"Yeah, yeah, yeah ... he told me all about your off-the-wall lies...bit of an acid head as well ain't cha'? Well, he's better off without you, lady, so if anyone's gonna fuck off it's gonna be you, alright!" Her confidence had returned full blown.

"Yeah, well that's what I thought when his other girlfriend warned me. Just think about it will ya, cos I don't lie...alright!" I took her key out of the lock and slammed the door in her face. Strangely enough, the thing that seemed to have pissed me off more than anything was the fact that Danny had given her a key, which was something he'd never offered to me!

I thought back to the time I'd met Laura Walsh in the pub toilets and how frantic she was, and now I felt ashamed for being too wrapped up in myself, and too busy despising her to really listen to what she was saying, because I believed she'd hurt my precious Danny, which was exactly the reaction Beth had displayed towards me.

I started checking around his flat. I didn't really know what I was looking for: clues, evidence, I suppose anything that I felt I could confront him with, but there was nothing, not even any of my things that I'd left there, when I foolishly believed he and I were going to be a long-term couple.

It wasn't long before I heard a key in the front door. It was Danny. Beth had obviously phoned him but, surprise, surprise, he hadn't brought her in with him. I knew that if this had happened when we were together I would certainly have wanted to be present! I moved into his kitchen to wait for him. I hid a knife under a tea towel on his draining board, within easy reach. If he did decide to attack me, then he'd certainly see a side to me that he hadn't seen before. I stood with my back to the sink, my arms folded across my chest. My pulse was racing and I was bricking it!

Danny appeared and stood in the kitchen doorway, his eyes wide as though he cared, as though his concern for me, for my welfare was the only thing that mattered to him.

But it was shit! I could see through him...I could hear Laura Walsh's words of warning...

"Oh Becky, thank God you're safe! I looked everywhere for you...I repaid them the money but they wouldn't release you...I've been frantic with worry, I even considered going to the police...." He took a tentative step towards me, his arms out in front of him ready to embrace me. I held up the palms of both hands in a fending-off gesture, but then a silly seed of doubt planted itself: what if I was wrong? What if he really was genuine and all this was due to circumstances that he couldn't control? And what if... but then with the same speed that the thought entered my head, so it left.

"Oh c'mon, you have got to be joking! Do I look completely fuckin' stupid?" I spat the words at him contemptuously.

"No babe, please, you've got to hear my side of the story...I've been through hell as well."

"And I suppose the blonde bimbo was giving you therapy?"

"No, nothing like that she's just a friend..."

"Danny, before you go any further, she's told me she's your girlfriend and about *how you felt when I dumped you*...I dumped you?? That's an understatement if ever I heard one! What was it, couldn't you bring yourself to tell her that you sold me into prostitution?"

"Oh, for crying out loud, Becks, is that what you think?"

"No, it's not what I think – it's actually what I was *told*, by Paul Tyler, Kevin Crestwell, oh ... and of course Laura Walsh, who tried to warn me as well, but like a fool I was too wrapped up in you to believe her!"

He went very quiet for a few moments then spoke softly. "So what do you want?"

"Want? Yeah, I'll tell you what I want. What I want is to know just what sort of person you are...you've got to admit it takes a pretty special type of arsehole to kiss your girlfriend goodbye, knowing full well that she's about to be beaten, then gang raped and then beaten again, don't you think?" He looked down at the floor, as my torrent continued. "Night after fucking night I was raped by a succession of strangers, Danny, and if I caused any kind of fuss then I was nearly drowned in a bath of freezing cold water. Other girls had an electric iron held against their leg...we would have welcomed death sometimes! Can you even imagine what it feels like to know that you're no longer considered a human being, but that you're just a piece of meat to be abused over and over again!"

"I hear you...so either tell me what the fuck you want or else piss off." His eyes were cold, his face expressionless; he showed absolutely no emotion, and if I'd suspected it before, I realised then that he didn't care anything, not only about me, but also about anyone or anything. Danny cared only for himself.

"Danny, do you actually understand reality?"

He said nothing.

I didn't feel threatened by him. But I did realise that I had also become just as emotionless. Yeah, there was a part of me that was pissed because of what he'd done and a part of me that wanted payback, but there was no real burning desire for vengeance. I had become as cold as he was. We both stood staring at the floor, neither speaking, both deep in our own thoughts.

Eventually Danny spoke. "Look, I've got to make a couple of phone calls …it's okay, it's got nothing to do with you being here. I was due to meet some of the lads for a few drinks and a game of cards; I just need to tell them I won't be there." He fixed his eyes squarely onto mine and held my look; anyone who didn't know him would have interpreted it as a gesture of honesty, but I was long past believing in his acts of supposed sincerity. My own thoughts raced ahead. If he called Andrei and Costi I would have no chance of survival, and before the day was over I would become just another victim of an overdose of dodgy heroin, and no doubt I'd be found at a later date, with no identification, floating face down in the river.

"Yeah, well don't let me interfere with yer evening. I'm gonna clear off as well; it's time for me to get well away from here…okay?" As I spoke I gestured a move towards the door he was still blocking.

"No, don't rush off Becks. At least let me buy you a meal; you look half starved…"

"You don't have to do anything for me Danny, except stay out of my life!" It was only then that I realised my stomach was empty and now the thought of food was very appealing.

"You'll need money," he continued. "I'll go to the cash-point and draw some out…and looking at you, you'll need clothes as well." His voice had changed; now he spoke with feeling as though he cared, as though he expected me to believe he cared.

"I think you've done enough for me Danny. Memories of what you've done will stay with me for the rest of my life…and that's not something that many guys can brag about." My tone fully expressed the contempt I felt for him.

"Becks, please, let me get changed and then we'll both leave here together. I promise you you're safe. Nothing's going to happen to you." The puppy dog eyes were back and the mere fact that he'd said I was safe immediately told me that I wasn't. I smiled as though I appreciated his help, as though I was still that naive silly girl who once believed in him.

He smiled, turned around and went into the bedroom, closing the door behind him, and as I looked at the closed door my first instinct was to run out of the flat, book into a small hotel somewhere and just lay low for a few days while I decided my future. But curiosity won and I crept over towards his bedroom door and listened. He was phoning someone from his mobile phone and from what I could make out, judging by the argumentative tone of the conversation I assumed it was either Kevin Crestwell or Andrei on the other end of the call. I strained my ears, trying to hear what was being said; he was obviously at the far side of the room, but Danny was one of those people who had to walk, normally in circles while he was talking on the phone, and as his voice became clearer, I knew that was exactly what he was doing in there.

But I only caught a part of what was said: "No, it's *your* fucking problem, it was *your* end that screwed up, so now *you* put it right!"

That convinced me even more than anything that I *should* be running out of his flat just as fast and as far as my feet would carry me…. but no, for reasons I could not fathom I moved away from the bedroom door, but remained, waiting for him to emerge. He didn't take long and when he reappeared his face seemed slightly flushed. He looked at me differently … not in any way that I could describe, but just … differently.

"Have you got any money Becks?" he asked casually, avoiding eye contact with me.

"No! What did you expect? They were hardly gonna put me on a fucking wage!" I snapped back sarcastically.

"Okay, I only asked…I'm going to get you some money and I just wondered if you already had any, that's all." He spoke defensively.

My mind instantly went to Paul Tyler's wallet in my back pocket; my hand subconsciously moved to my butt and felt the outline of the wallet through the denim.

I remained assertive. "Well I don't want to have to spend another minute either in this flat or in your company…so, I just hope that in the not too distant future you get sucked down into the same hell that you put me through…"

"Ah c'mon Becks, everything you've accused me of is based on what *you* think happened, *your* assumptions. At least let me tell you my side of the story." He had that tone he used when he was irritated. When we were a couple and he'd used it, I always apologised, assuming it was because of something I'd either said or done; but that old me no longer existed.

"Do you honestly think I'm actually interested, or more to the point, gullible enough to listen to any more of your lies? You really are a detestable piece of filth so just slide back to your cess-pit and wallow in your slime!" As I spat the words at him I could feel my hatred towards him now beginning to burn its way through my veins.

I turned away and started to move towards the front door.

"Hang on a minute, why are you in such a rush?" He moved towards me as though to grab my arm.

At that very same moment the penny quickly dropped. I was the stupid one! He was stalling me and I was allowing it. I was going along with it, and I certainly didn't need too many guesses to realise just who was probably en route to us this very minute.

The instant that thought entered my head I felt a wave of fear spread throughout my body, which triggered a surge of panic. "Fuck you, Danny!" I ran to the door. I was conscious of him behind me, but I opened the door and was out in the street before he could reach me. Outside it was busy with people, cars, buses and even a passing police patrol car. I turned around and faced him, my heart beating loudly, rhythmically, like a heavy drum beat. "What were you about to say Danny?"

He looked around him before answering. "Look, come back inside… we can't leave it like this, we've got to talk." He was playing the dejected little boy act. He reached out to hold my hand. Needless to say, I quickly snatched my hand away from his.

"You never did tell me how you escaped," he said suddenly.

"It was easy. I just walked out of the door."

"And nobody said anything?" He made no attempt to disguise his cynicism.

"Pretty much, yeah."

"What about Paul Tyler?"

"He got in my way so I cut his throat, but you obviously know about Tyler so why are you asking?"

"I heard on the grapevine that Tyler was dead."

"No you didn't, you liar; you heard it a few moments ago on your mobile, and while we're on the subject just who were you talking to …. Andrei? Or was it Crestwell?"

"You've caused a lot of trouble to a lot of people Becks, and these people are unhappy, not only with you, but with me as well…"

"Oh dear, my heart bleeds for you." I started walking away; I felt relatively safe in a public place with people around.

"There's also been a man asking about you; tried to claim he was from some sort of security service, but he was more likely from the benefits agency, stupid bastard. Anyway, we chased him off so I don't think I'll be seeing him again!" He was walking quickly behind me

"Are you still bullshitting?" I scoffed, without looking back.

"No, he was actually beginning to give me some grief; thought he could lean on me and get away with it!" Dolan had now come alongside me and strutted with a sense of his own self-importance.

I felt a cold shiver across my shoulder blades and down my back and the wave of fear returned; the same intensive fear I felt in the house, and the feeling of nausea that came with it. My body stiffened as I fought to control the bile rising in my throat.

The voice in my head repeated over and over, *'Don't panic! Keep calm, stay in control.'* But my instincts told me differently, and with a take off speed that an Olympic sprinter would be proud of, I started running, accelerating as I wove between the build up of people. I could hear Danny behind me, but I was too scared to look round. The traffic was too heavy and too fast for me to risk running into the road. I was running for my life and my legs carried me like I'd never run before. I could feel my face had twisted grotesquely, I was conscious that I was panting loudly, and my mouth had dropped open drawing in air. I wove around a couple of middle-aged women and as I looked up, I looked straight into a nightmare. Coming towards me was the unmistakable face of Kevin Crestwell, with another face I hadn't seen before. Both of them were wearing hoodies, the ones with the deep side pockets; the hoods were up and they both looked very menacing. I froze with fear and I know that my heart skipped not one but several beats. The same fear that used to overwhelm me at the house whenever he came near me had now completely possessed me. It was hard to describe but for want of another word, it was a frenzied fear! I mentally reasoned with myself that surely he couldn't do anything here … not here, not with all these people around.

Crestwell had a determined expression as he moved through the people towards us. Danny obviously hadn't seen him and turned back towards me to see why I'd stopped dead in my tracks. My legs wouldn't move; somebody behind me tutted irritably at my blocking their way, causing them to step into the road to get past us, Danny frowned – he had no idea at all why I'd stopped, either that or he was a much better actor than I'd given him credit for! Crestwell was now upon us. I saw his arm move as he took his hand out of the deep pocket of his fleece…

The next thing I remember is feeling a sudden searing pain in my right side as though I had been stabbed with a red hot poker. The force of it had pushed me off balance. I don't actually remember falling, but I was suddenly aware that I was lying face down in the gutter. I could smell urine and vomit, the leftovers of the previous evening's revellers. I became aware of something sticky under my chin, probably a discarded kebab or, worse, a dog turd, but strangely I didn't feel repulsed; in fact I had hardly any feeling. I felt detached from my surroundings, detached from everything. I could hear shouting: "Come on, leg it…come on!!" the yells uttered almost in panic.

Then I heard three very loud explosions, one after another… or it could have been one large one; the sound was repeating over and over in my brain, almost deafening … then I felt the burning sensation again, but not as intense as before … it now felt like a heavy weight inside me. I could sense that people were fussing around me but I was oblivious to what they were saying … I heard the sound of a siren in the distance coming closer, but I heard them all day, so I dismissed it. I heard a loud rasping sound …. I'm sure it wasn't coming from me, but as quickly as the sound appeared…so it went away. I could feel myself becoming cold …. a chilly cold as though I'd been dropped into a freezer, but yet different; the cold was inside me, not at all like a normal cold sensation …. and then it was gone. I couldn't feel my body at all … in fact I felt completely detached from my surroundings. The noise around me had diminished into a silence … it was a strange, relaxing sensation. The pain that had previously been searing through my body had also faded … I was vaguely aware of people kneeling beside me, whispering … I couldn't make out what they were saying. I didn't care either. I knew that I was going to float into the blackness that seemed to have descended around me ... but strangely it was not at all scary ... there was nothing, just peace ....

Chapter 10

John Tanner

John Tanner's mobile phone played a soothing classical tune as its ring tone, and it was playing now. The phone was in his jacket pocket and his jacket was laid along the back seat of his car.

Tanner had just dropped his speed as he approached a speed camera, to avoid being flashed, along with the other vehicles in the convoy of congested late morning traffic. He looked in his rear view mirror; an idiot driving a small hatchback was glued to his rear bumper. His eyes flicked ahead to the endless column of vehicles in front of him and then back again to the idiot. "Oh geez…back off you wanker!" He spoke to the mirror as though his words would magically be conveyed to the driver tailgating him. He looked ahead again and saw a car waiting to pull out of a lay-by outside a mini supermarket-cum post office. He indicated, braked, allowed the other car to move out and then eased his car into the freshly vacated gap. He leaned over to the rear sear and retrieved his phone from his jacket.

"Hello," he snapped irritably into it.

"John, it's me, Ernie…I haven't disturbed you in the middle of something have I?"

"No, sorry mate, it's just me getting a bit short-tempered with some of the dick-heads on the road!"

"Well calm down and listen. I've ferreted out some interesting information on that DS character you asked me about."

"What's that then?"

"Can you get to the Three Kings pub for this lunchtime?"

Tanner glanced at his watch. "Yeah, might be a bit tight…but shouldn't be a problem."

"Okay, see you then…bye."

Tanner looked in his wing mirror to view the traffic behind him. An articulated lorry was approaching but it was slow moving. In the opposite direction a learner driver from a local driving school was also approaching cautiously. Tanner took his chance, threw the gear stick into first as his foot pressed down hard on the gas pedal; the tyres spun and sent a few stones flying upwards behind his car as it performed a u-turn and accelerated away.

Tanner made good time, despite the heavy traffic and arrived only a few minutes past the pre-arranged time. He parked the car and entered the Three Kings pub. As Tanner approached the bar, Ernie was there and had already ordered two pints of best bitter.

"You eating?" Ernie asked as he gave a sideways glance towards Tanner.

"No, I had a late breakfast and I still feel pretty full from that." Ernie paid the barman, picked up the two pint glasses and nodded towards an empty table. The two men sat in silence and in unison both drank a third of the way down their glass, almost in ritualistic tradition.

"So…" Tanner spoke first. "Thanks for the package; it was exactly what I wanted." Ernie Palmer nodded in acknowledgement. "So…what did you find out then?"

"Firstly, your Detective Sergeant Priack is a man with different faces for different folks."

"How d'you mean?" asked Tanner.

"Well, his superiors see him as a staunch upright thief catcher – he's got a good record in putting villains away – yet some of his colleagues view him differently. Innuendo, rumours, hearsay, locker room gossip, call it what you want but apparently he has been known to turn a blind eye to favoured criminals."

"But on what sort of scale?" asked Tanner.

"It actually goes a bit deeper. There have been more than a few suspicions that he's planted evidence to secure a conviction. One fellow officer even reported that Priack had lied in Court whilst on oath, although he did later withdraw the allegation."

"Withdrawn willingly…or persuaded?"

"It could be the latter. Rumours abound that he is on the payroll of a local villain who is expanding his empire at an alarming rate and, interestingly enough, the bulk of the minor criminal gangs whose territories and businesses he's taking over are also the ones your DS is securing convictions against…"

"And what's the name of this modern day Al Capone?" Tanner asked.

"Mann, Dougie Mann and by all accounts he's a very nasty piece of work!"

"So how come, if all these rumours about Priack are circulating openly, why hasn't he been investigated?"

"Because he has a high rate of successful convictions and that is something the top brass want. After all, each area is judged on conviction rates and so all the time he's hitting the targets, then nobody higher up is going to look too closely at his methods, although the top brass are not that stupid; ask yourself why a man of his age is still only a DS." Ernie gave a knowing shrug of his shoulders, before picking up his glass and draining the remainder of its contents.

"Yeah, fair comment…but, what are they doing about this Dougie Mann?"

Ernie pushed his empty glass towards Tanner, and then wiped his mouth with the back of his hand. "The whisper in the locker room is that as long as he doesn't draw too much attention to himself they're happy to let him carry on. If they take him down, he'll only be replaced by another villain that's waiting in the wings."

"Is he under surveillance?"

"Nothing more than a gestured surveillance; these things cost money and budgets are tight at the moment."

Tanner waved his empty glass, "Do you want another one of these?"

"Bloody right I do…I thought you'd gone dry on me…"

Tanner grinned as stood up. "You deserve it Ernie – you did well."

Tanner was quickly served and returned to the table with two foaming pints, he placed Ernie's in front of him. He looked around before speaking. "What about the other stuff … girls being snatched and forced to work as prostitutes?"

"Yeah, that's a can of worms and a half…"

"What do you mean?"

"It's true, it's actually happening…every day, in almost every town, we know that British born girls, aged 14 and sometimes younger are being trafficked for sex within the UK."

"What? Tell me you are joking…please?" Tanner didn't disguise his tone of disgust.

"John. Joe Public doesn't know the half of what's happening. The majority of them make the mistake of believing that all youngsters being offered as prostitutes have been brought in from other countries."

"It doesn't matter where they come from…they're still kids…for goodness sake, what sort of man…?" Tanner couldn't finish his sentence; the repugnance he felt for certain elements of his fellow man left more than a bad taste in his mouth.

Both men fell silent as a well-dressed middle-aged man hovered near their table. As he moved away Ernie continued. "It's not only in brothels where these kids are abused; there are as many forced to work long hours for no pay in sweat shops. It's a slave trade and sadly it's one that's swept under the carpet. Joe Public may have heard of isolated cases, but certainly doesn't want to be confronted with the knowledge that it's a rampant trade and it could be happening in his own street."

"So what are you saying … that the Government knows about it but ignores it?" Tanner asked incredulously.

"No, it's not like that at all. The Government are bringing out new measures to tackle the problem and they have had some successes, but it not always easy to establish the exact scale of the problem, especially with internal trafficking."

"Ernie, you're beginning to sound like a politician," scoffed Tanner.

"No John, you asked me to get you the facts and that's exactly what I'm giving you…your reaction to this is the same as someone eating their morning cornflakes and feeling uncomfortable because it's plastered across their morning paper!"

"Yeah…okay, I stand corrected," Tanner said sheepishly.

"Just how *do* you tackle it, John, when it's young men grooming and recruiting local girls in public places? When these girls trust their boyfriends; when those same boys, after having won their confidence, sexually abuse them and take them to other towns and cities for further sexual abuse by strangers in brothels...brothels that are located in nice suburban locations.... Oh, believe me John, I'm as pissed as you are, but apart from climbing on a soap box in Speakers' Corner, there's not really a lot that I can personally do!"

"I wasn't having a go at you, Ernie, it's just..."

"Yeah, I know...so you can imagine how I felt when I was researching this and digging out all the figures relating to young British girls who have been trafficked into brothels, and then a Government statement is released which states that it is something they are aware of and have concerns about but it is difficult for them to determine the actual size of the problem."

"They said that?"

"John...it's time for a reality check: no one has got spare money to fund a specialist task force to take this on full time. Oh yeah, they'll have the odd operation and smash a couple of little gangs...but it just brings us back to our earlier conversation about Dougie Mann; you shut one down and another opens up the next day." Tanner gave a long deep sigh as the full prospect of finding his daughter in the maze of the sex traffickers' seedy world – if that's where she was – fully dawned upon him. "Take this John..." Ernie Palmer passed across a memory stick, "...there's so much data on this...this epidemic, that it was easier just to download it onto this." Tanner nodded and put the memory stick into his pocket as Ernie continued. "When you start to read the data on that, you will see the name of a Detective Sergeant Keith Dudley appearing quite a few times. He's your contact. He's the liaison officer between the Vice Squad and their regional counterparts and the various organisations that help to rescue these girls and assist them in trying to rebuild their lives. What he doesn't know about people trafficking isn't worth knowing. All his contact details are there."

"What's he like...amenable?"

"He's a bit like us ... what I call the old world."

"What do you mean...the old world?"

"Oh it's just my definition. The old world, as I call it, is our generation, our standards, and our morals. The new world is today's twenty-somethings, who have completely different standards, morals and values. I'm not saying that ours is the only right way or that theirs is the only right way, but they're two different worlds."

Tanner gave a bemused shrug. "Well, I suppose if you have to give something a title then that's as good as any."

Ernie Palmer looked at his wristwatch. "Good grief, is that the time...I'd better be moving. We're not all retired gentlemen you know." He drained the remainder of his glass and stood up. "I'll see you on Friday at Roger Dickins' funeral." It was said as a matter of fact rather than a question.

Later that afternoon, back at his flat, John Tanner booted up his laptop, inserted the memory stick Ernie Palmer had given him and settled down to what became a couple of hours of depressing and at times horrifying reading on the statistics and case histories of the modern day slave trade, more commonly referred to as people trafficking. What he discovered shocked him. Like most people he was aware that it went on, but because he had no personal involvement with it, it didn't encroach on his daily life, it wasn't something that he physically saw with his eyes. He had never really given it a second thought. But now his eyes had been well and truly opened to the scale of the absolute misery being endured by his fellow human beings, in his own country, in his own town and under his very eyes and like the majority of the population he'd been too blind to see it.

At that moment he thought of a super-hero, someone who could swoop in and rescue all of them, but fantasy thoughts weren't his style and he knew that as one man alone he was pretty helpless to do anything to relieve their suffering. But that wasn't a reason to do nothing. He picked up his phone and pressed the numbers for DS Keith Dudley's direct line.

Early the following morning Tanner arrived for his appointment. DS Dudley met him at the front desk shortly after the duty sergeant informed him of Tanner's arrival. The two men shook hands; Dudley then nodded towards the main door, indicating that Tanner should follow him.

When they had stepped outside and moved away from the bustle of uniformed activity, Dudley leaned towards Tanner and said confidentially, "I thought it would be best if we had a chat over a coffee. I'm not really sure what it is you're after. Ernie Palmer wasn't very specific, other than asking me to give you whatever help I could…he also said it was to be kept under wraps."

John Tanner stood head and shoulders above the man. His eyes tried to scan him, to pick up a vibe. He was of the same stature, posture, and had the same tone of voice as Ernie; it was like being with his twin. "Yeah, something like that…" Tanner answered whilst looking around, "…but the street is not the place to discuss it. I'll wait until we get to a coffee shop."

The two men walked side by side along the pavement in silence manoeuvring their way through the throngs of people. Market traders and shops with day-glo posters were all competing to attract the attention of the mingling crowd; even at this early hour shoppers were struggling with laden bags, mums with pushchairs, the pushy types, the timid and the bewildered. Some of them were looking for that exclusive bargain, others moving at marching speed as they made their way towards their destination, ensuring they avoided eye contact with their fellow pedestrians. Some walked with a mobile phone held glue-like to their ear, the equivalent to hanging a *do not disturb* sign around their necks.

The two men arrived at one of the new breed of coffee shops and went inside. DS Dudley nudged Tanner's arm for his attention and nodded towards an empty table, the furthest from the counter. "I'll go and grab that table, you get the coffees; I'll have mine white with as many sugars as you can get...oh, and I'll also have a jam doughnut."

Tanner placed his order at the counter, waited while they were served and then paid. He placed the cellophane-wrapped doughnut in his jacket pocket then picked up the two mugs of coffee and took them to the table where Keith Dudley was sitting waiting. He placed one of the coffee mugs in front of him and handed him the doughnut. Tanner watched bemused as the man tore into the cellophane wrapping as though he hadn't eaten for days. He bit savagely into the doughnut causing a large blob of jam to drop onto the table.

With his mouth full of doughnut, Dudley spoke. "So, what exactly is it that you think I can do for you?"

"I'm looking for a girl. It's believed she's been kidnapped and is possibly being forced to work as a prostitute."

"Well...this may surprise you," Dudley spoke in a laid-back manner, "but based on our current statistics it's believed that as many as 8,000 under-age British girls have been groomed for prostitution by either older men or older youths, who become lovers or perhaps father-figures to them. They're flattered you see...flattered that older boys are taking an interest in them."

"And just what are we doing to protect them?" Tanner asked abruptly.

Dudley leaned forward before answering, like a kindly uncle about to pass on his words of wisdom. "The criminal network, and I do include local street pimps in that, receive some very significant amounts of money from prostitution. For example, an organised brothel can easily make between three to four hundred thousand pounds a year selling a sixteen-year-old girl. Now, you multiply that by the number of girls out there working and you get some idea of the sort of monies they're earning." Dudley sat up straight again as he continued. "Of course the girls don't receive a penny of it; they're trapped under the domination of their pimps, who are usually quite vicious and think nothing of regularly beating them. Some of the luckier ones who we've been able to rescue are so traumatised, they're too frightened to speak to us...convinced that their pimps will snatch 'em back."

"These kids, they're...they are all somebody's daughters. I mean, what kind of sick bastards do that sort of thing to kids?" The anger in Tanner's voice was evident.

"They're not kids in that sense; they're young women. We're a multi-cultural society and not all cultures see any wrong in it...did you know that as far back as five years ago statistics showed that one in ten British men used prostitutes, and since then the demand for what are now called sex workers has increased dramatically?"

"So that makes it all right, does it… a group of lads finish off their evening with a trip to a brothel and that's acceptable…? Don't these drunken pieces of scum ever stop and think how they would feel if it was happening to their own daughters, girlfriends or sisters?" Tanner's expression was of sheer contempt as he tried to control his rage and disgust.

"Why would they think that? They go to a brothel, and as far as they are concerned the girls are up for it…they have no inkling of the actual plight of these women. Of course there are the ones who are indifferent to it and sadly there will always be the ones who actually enjoy knowing they are humiliating the girl…and I do agree with you that it is a sickening situation." Dudley shoved the last of his doughnut into his mouth.

"Do you have any success stories where a girl's absolutely refused, perhaps told the punter that she was an unwilling participant…?"

"You're grasping at straws, John. These girls are cut off from the outside world. The only people they see are their captors and of course the punters. Their captors control them by horrific cruelty, both physical and psychological and I mean severe; some of the ones we've rescued have been covered in scars and bruises. Another common punishment is being gang raped. They also try to get them onto crack cocaine or heroin, and when the girls become dependent on it, they're put to work in the brothels which in some cases operate twenty-four hours a day, seven days a week … if the girls are good, they may get one day off a week! As far as telling the punters that they're not willing…we've already covered that. Far too many of them wouldn't want to listen, and some would even get turned on by it."

Tanner shook his head in disbelief. "This is fucking appalling!"

"You've hit the nail on the head John; there's big money in fucking." Dudley replied.

"Well thanks for your help Keith…it looks like it's going to be a needle in a haystack job."

"Look, Ernie asked me to help you any way I could…if this is a job you've taken on, then give it back because believe me the way these people pass girls from one place to another, you're just going to be chasing your arse around in circles."

"No, it's more personal than that."

"You haven't got yourself tied up with some little scrubber have you?"

"No! If you must know it's my daughter…"

"Oh shit…" Dudley closed his eyes momentarily. "Well our records indicate that a large number of these brothels are in ordinary suburban locations. We've got some of them under surveillance by officers working for…shall we say … particular operations … obviously I can't go into too much detail but you get the drift."

"What about names…faces … who are the major players?" Tanner asked.

"John, we've only touched on the plight of the British girls; there are also in the region of twenty-five thousands foreign nationals being smuggled into the UK and forced to work in prostitution, and they are bought and sold on the same scale as the second-hand car market!"

"I thought slavery had been abolished!"

"No my friend, it's just been pushed under the carpet...come on, we'll go back to the station, and you can look through my photo album. I can tell you who to stay well away from...and maybe point you in the right direction." The two men drained the remains of their coffees and stepped outside, then walked together back towards the Police Station.

Tanner spoke first. "What's the success rate of shutting these brothels down?"

"Excluding surveillance, we're hitting between ten to twelve percent of brothels, massage parlours and saunas. Where we can, we prosecute the brothel keepers, but as I said earlier, the overwhelming majority of these girls are non-British nationals. In a lot of cases they don't even know where they are; half of them can't even speak English..."

"What about all this Human Rights violation crap we're always reading about?" Tanner interrupted.

"Oh please...do have a reality check John...the main people who've benefited from that act are the criminal fraternity and until a politician has the balls to stand up and say, 'this is a load of bollocks' and chucks it out, then the bad guys will just carry on hiding behind it while laughing at us!"

They walked the remainder of the short journey in silence, passed the main entrance and turned in through the gates for vehicular access. Tanner reached forward and grabbed Dudley's arm pulling him out of the way of a speeding police van, complete with flashing blue lights as it accelerated towards the exit. Dudley nodded his appreciation. They arrived at the rear entrance where Dudley punched a series of numbers into the touch-pad on the door. Once inside, they went along a corridor and then down a flight of stairs, along a darker corridor and through two sets of double doors.

"Well, this is home," Dudley said as he clicked on the light switches, illuminating the room. Keith Dudley stopped and lit a cigarette before continuing. He looked at Tanner. "Yeah, I know I'm not supposed to, but no one ever comes down here so what the hell?"

Tanner looked around the room and whilst it was exceptionally large, it could still only be described as a dank basement office. "So...these girls...is anyone helping them after they've been rescued?"

"Yeah, there are a few charities and some project groups. They house them, feed them, give them fresh clothes and help them to rebuild their lives."

"So what do you do? I mean, you're a Vice Squad liaison officer, so what does that entail?"

"I'm only one of many liaison officers around the South of England, and I know that the bulk of my colleagues are quite actively involved in various operations, including, of course, the aftermaths, but to be honest I often feel that I'm deliberately kept out of the loop. It's almost as though because I'm a man then I'm no better than the punters who visit these girls!" The bitterness in his tone was clearly apparent.

"I can understand that…" Tanner replied, "…especially when you consider just what they've gone through. I'd imagine some of them would prefer it if they never saw a man again."

"Yeah, but we're not all like that, are we? Besides, I know just as many girls who stay with prostitution because it's easy money."

"Oh for God's sake Keith, you've just been telling me about the thousands of girls each year who are kidnapped and forced into prostitution…and now you're trying to tell me that they actually like the lifestyle? You're talking like an idiot!"

"No, maybe not those ones…but there are a lot who do."
Suddenly another voice spoke forcefully and authoritatively over the pair of them. "What exactly is going on down here Sergeant Dudley, and who is this?" The newcomer looked Tanner up and down, his eyes scanning and noting every detail.

Keith Dudley quickly dropped his cigarette on the floor and stepped on it. "Good morning sir, this is John Tanner from our Security Services Department. I've just been giving him an overview on the influx of foreign prostitutes in the Capital." Dudley turned to Tanner. "John, this is Inspector Ledbetter."

Tanner looked at this man who was staring hard at him, his expression revealing the degree of his own status. Tanner offered his hand. "Good morning sir."

The Inspector looked down at Tanner's hand and ignored it. "What exactly is your involvement? Because I certainly haven't been notified of any proposal for a joint operation."

DS Dudley looked downwards at his feet and shuffled uncomfortably.

"Well, I'm waiting!" Ledbetter snapped irritably.

Tanner decided to come clean. "The truth of the matter is that I've recently retired from the service…"

"Then why are you here?" interrupted Ledbetter.

"I'm trying to locate a girl, my daughter, who has recently gone missing and it has been suggested that she may have been kidnapped and is being forced against her will into prostitution."

"That doesn't tell me what you are doing here."

"I'm trying to locate her possible whereabouts..."

"Well you certainly don't seem to be having much success in finding her otherwise you wouldn't be here...so if that's the case then it's a matter for the Police to deal with. Have you submitted a missing persons report?"

"Yes, my other daughter reported it."

"Then I suggest you leave it to the professionals, and we would prefer it if civilians didn't interfere in Police matters, as there is the risk that they could jeopardise current operations!"

Tanner smiled wryly; he held Ledbetter's gaze and spoke slowly but firmly. "Like I said, she is my daughter and your track record isn't exactly impressive in finding missing people, so I will be continuing my own search...perhaps I could update you on what I find?" he added sarcastically.

Ledbetter ignored the jibe and answered in the same tone. "Mr Tanner, I don't want you to have any involvement other than posting some photographs of the girl around the area where she went missing. I will reiterate to you that my men are far too busy to have to go rescuing civilians who, by their own folly, get themselves involved in criminal activity, and I would also remind you that you could end up facing charges if any complaints are received against you."

"As I said, Inspector...she is my daughter!"

Ledbetter sighed irritably. "I believe your business here is completed." He turned towards the DS who was still shuffling awkwardly. "Sergeant Dudley, would you please escort Mr Tanner off our premises?"

Tanner gave Ledbetter a look of contempt and followed Dudley out of the door and along the corridor, past the duty desk and out onto the street. Tanner offered his hand. "Thanks for your help Keith. I hope I haven't dropped you in it?"

"No, that's alright, I'm used to him...but you watch your back; he's a vindictive bastard is that one."

"Thanks for the tip Keith, but I've spent my entire career working with jumped-up arseholes like that..." Before he had finished his sentence, the skies darkened and a loud rumble of thunder sounded directly above them; seconds later one of the heaviest rainfalls seen for a long time fell around them. Dudley quickly turned around and disappeared back into the station. Tanner put his hands in his jacket pockets and started to walk back to his car. Umbrellas popped up in unison all around him, and those without umbrellas ran for the sanctuary of nearby shop doorways. The rain appeared to be falling more and more heavily and quickly soaked through his jacket. By the time he arrived at his car he resembled a drowned rat. A loud clap of thunder, followed by sheet lightning greeted him as he unlocked the door and climbed inside, dripping water everywhere. He retrieved his mobile from inside his sodden jacket and phoned Ernie Palmer.

"Hello Ernie, I've just had a meeting with DS Dudley. There's something about him that made me feel that perhaps he wasn't the right man; he's certainly got some strange personal views on the subject we discussed."

"Yeah, I know what you're saying; they tend to use him more for analysis than anything else, but you wanted somebody at short notice to give you a bit of background on the sex industry, so whatever his personal views are, he is the man with the knowledge."

"You're right of course. Anyway I ended up getting thrown out by his Inspector, a chap called Ledbetter … do you know anything about him?"

"No, never heard of him, but you'd probably be as well to keep a low profile for a few days."

"I've got no reason to have any more contact with him. I was hoping to have a look at some mug shots of the local players, but Ledbetter intervened before Dudley could show them."

"Maureen was going to see what she could find out on that score, but what with the funeral and everything it was probably the last thing on her mind."

"It's only to be expected, but I don't want to bother her at this time…anyway I'll see you at the funeral?"

"Yeah, see you then…bye John."

Tanner started the car and drove home. The instant he arrived back in his flat he made straight for the bathroom, stripped off and stepped into the shower. The hot water hit him with a force, pummelling against his body as it exploded out of the showerhead at full power. In his head he re-ran the events of the morning and assessed his progress since Ruth had first contacted him; he was no further forward now in finding Becky's whereabouts than when he'd first been told she was missing and had agreed to try and find her. He decided it was probably time to pay another visit and lean heavily on Danny Dolan and if necessary he'd call in a few favours from one or two of the unscrupulous villains that he knew.

The heat of the water had penetrated him and warmed him inside, and he felt that he could have stayed under it for ages, but time had been ticking away and he still had things to do.

It was early evening when Tanner parked his car diagonally opposite Danny Dolan's flat. There were no lights on and no sign of any activity. He waited for just over an hour then decided to move on. He drove around the area slowly, his eyes scanning every young male, every mixed group, and every couple, comparing them with the mental image of Dolan. In his pocket he carried the pistol Ernie Palmer had sent him, and he was ready to use it if necessary. He spent another hour and a half cruising the streets before deciding that Dolan wasn't going to appear miraculously.

He parked his car in a side street and walked. Just as before, like a moth drawn towards a flame, he'd wandered into the red-light district.

He stopped by a shop doorway and observed the figures at the end of the road ahead of him, some standing in groups, some standing alone but all of them plying their trade, offering their wares to the vehicles that slowed down to barter a price.

Suddenly a voice broke his concentration, there was no-one beside him but as he looked downwards, he saw where the voice had come from.

"Something I can do for you darling?"

She looked as though she was in her late sixties, but was probably only in her early fifties, or possibly younger. In her younger days, she had probably been a stunner; the long blonde hair of her youth, whilst still long, had now turned to a whitish grey; parts of her scalp were showing through. Her face was aged through years of fatigue, excess alcohol, drugs, late nights and beatings. Sadly, when she was no longer able to earn enough money for her pimp, she had probably been given a final beating for old times' sake and then turned out onto the street. A homeless old dripper who now carried her few processions with her in supermarket carrier bags and who slept in whatever shop doorway or alley where she felt she could snatch a few hours of undisturbed sleep. Her voice wavered and cracked when she talked, her movements were sporadic and slow, her hair was flat, lifeless and partly plastered to her face. She sat with her hands folded in her lap and spoke quietly, choosing her words cautiously, respectfully, almost as though one wrong word would result in her receiving a beating, and yet here she was, still prepared to offer a sexual service for whatever few pounds it would bring her.

"Yeah, I want you to talk to me," Tanner answered softly.

"I can do that…" she answered as she struggled to her feet. "You want me to talk dirty to you while you wank?"

"No! I'm going to go into that café over the road and have a coffee and a snack and I'd like you to come with me and talk to me. I'll pay for your meal and for your time of course."

"Who are you?" she hunched back into the doorway.

"I'm just somebody who wants to have a snack but doesn't fancy eating alone, and we'll be in a public place so you'll be quite safe. Now, I'd bet that isn't the strangest request you heard in your time?" Tanner extended his hand to help her to her feet. "So, what's your name?"

"Yvette."

"Is that your real name?"

"Who wants to know?" she countered aggressively.

"Hey, relax…if you don't want to sit in warm surroundings and have a nice hot burger or whatever else you want, then it's fine. I'll just go down the road and ask one of those young girls…"

"No, I'll eat with you…you got to understand I normally get spat on and kicked; it's been a long time since anybody spoke decent to me…you're not taking the piss are you? You're not going to beat me up or anything?"

"No, I give you my word as a gentleman." He pulled out his wallet from his back trouser pocket and withdrew two twenties and a ten pound note and pushed them towards her. "This is for your time." She grabbed the money, almost ripping it as she tore it from his hand; she looked down at her collection of carrier bags.

"I think they will be safe enough there for a little while." Tanner spoke softly, then gently held her arm and together they crossed the road towards a late night burger bar.

Tanner ordered a regular coffee and a plate of fries. Yvette worked her way through the menu, including a couple of take-away orders. Tanner paid for their food and they found an eating counter near the window where she could keep an eye on her carrier bags in the doorway across the road. Tanner sat opposite her at the counter.

"So, what d'yer wanna talk about?" She sat with her arms resting on the table, almost circling her plate as though defending her food from any would-be plunderers. She gave Tanner no eye contact, but concentrated on shovelling food into her mouth with great gusto. Once again John Tanner experienced a close up view of another person's eating habits. "What are you…a reporter or something?" As she spoke she sprayed the air with minuscule particles of food, the bulk of which landed upon Tanner's plate of fries. As his appetite vanished instantly, he pushed the plate towards her, conceding her claim to it. He moved his coffee cup to the side of him, furthest from her and hopefully out of range.

"The truth is, I'm looking for someone … a young girl; well, early twenties actually. It's believed she's been kidnapped and is being forced to work as a prostitute…and I don't have a clue where to start looking for her."

"So what d'yer want from me?" Another delivery of food particles accompanied her words and sprayed across the table.

"I've heard and read the statistics regarding prostitution, but that's all very formal and doesn't give me any real insight into the workings of a pimp's mind."

"That's easy; they're all evil bastards…as far as they're concerned we're there for one reason only and that is to have sex with men to earn them money." For the first time she looked Tanner straight in the eyes. "If you want stories, I can give you stories: rapes, beatings, stabbings, torture! All of the women out there have stories…"

"Yet they still stay on the streets, despite knowing the consequences?" Tanner tone was one of curiosity

"In my day it was only beatings we girls had to put up with, and only by the punters. We used to take a pimp on to protect us…but that's all changed now; with the foreigners coming over, the pimps own 'em and sell 'em on if they become too much trouble…as for your girl, they'll probably turn her into a coke head. If they're dependent on something, then they're less trouble."

"How old are you Yvette?"

"Fifty three, and I've been working the streets for over twenty years. Before that I had a nice luxury flat in the West End, and my pimp used to bring the punters to me, but then one day he told me I was too old. He threw me out and I've stayed on the streets ever since."

"You must have earned some good money in your time, so why are you homeless?"

"What can we do when the pimps beat us and take our money? D'yer really think the police are gonna care if we report it? The last pimp I had found my building society book; he dragged me to the branch and made me withdraw the lot and close the account. He slapped me around, claiming it was his money and I'd cheated him. He kept all of the money; he said it was compensation for his costs; then he pulled a razor and cut me…" She paused as Tanner's eyes scanned her face. "Oh, not the face…" she continued, "…no, the bastard was sadistic; he cut my body … my tits, my stomach, my inner thighs … said it was for the grief and the aggravation I'd caused him." She raised an eyebrow and shrugged as her eyes filled with tears. "Nobody wanted to touch me after that, and who could blame them? My body was like something out of a horror movie, so I ended up having to perform with the type of punter that the other girls normally refuse."

Suddenly a burst of laughter erupted close by them; they both turned to see where the noise was coming from. A group of three youths, all in their early twenties, were looking in their direction and laughing. "Who let that fucking old dripper in here?" one of them shouted.

"Careful mate, you'll end up with a dose of something!" another one called out; this was followed by another eruption of laughter.

Tanner noticed a worried expression come over Yvette's face; she stood up to leave as the third one in the group called across to them: "Get that scabby old dog out of here before we all catch something!" More laughter followed.

Tanner placed his hand on Yvette's arm. "Stay where you are; you're not going to let scum like that drive you out." He stood up and moved across to the three youths who started to smirk as he approached them. When he arrived at their table he leaned his head low to the same level as theirs. He spoke softly, just above a whisper, but the snarl on his face remained evident.

"You just listen to me for a moment lads. You don't know me, and you know nothing about me, but trust me when I tell you that if you so much as frown in that lady's direction, I'll jump on you so fucking hard you won't know what day you're in, do you understand what I'm saying…and be very careful before you answer."

The three youths stared down at the table, none of them wanting either eye contact or to answer back.

Tanner stood up straight and looked back at his table. Yvette was gone and through the window he could see the outline of her waiting to cross the road, eager to hurry back to her carrier bags, her shop doorway and the little bit of security it afforded her.

Two days had passed since John Tanner had spoken to both DS Keith Dudley and Yvette. It was the day of Roger Dickins' funeral and the start to the day was made more depressing by the relentless drizzle of rain, which had continued into the afternoon. Tanner wore his dark suit and black raincoat. He caught sight of himself in the mirror; the impression that he resembled an insurance salesman entered his head and then just as quickly left.

At the appointed time he left the flat and stood on the pavement outside, waiting for his lift and, on the dot, Ernie Palmer's car pulled up beside him. Tanner climbed into the back seat and greeted Ernie and his wife; they exchanged the usual pleasantries on route to Maureen Dickins' house from where they would join the procession of family and friends following Roger's coffin to the city crematorium.

The funeral cortège moved slowly through the streets, the procession made even more sombre by the incessant drizzle. In the crematorium Tanner stood with Ernie and his wife. The service began with Roger's favourite hymn, followed by a close friend talking about his life, his achievements in business, his popularity and the sadness of his illness at such an early age. Tanner's eyes moved to Maureen; she was elegantly dressed in a dark blue satin skirt, teamed with a fitted matching jacket, dark heels, and clutch bag. Her skin was as white as a piece of bone china. Her features looked cold with no visible signs of emotion. Tanner had known her for a good many years and to him she was a very beautiful woman with a natural graciousness about her, a lady who conducted herself with both dignity and composure.

The service continued with many family members breaking down, except for Maureen who had on this day emotionally shut herself off, almost as though she was using her detachment as a protection from reality. Throughout the greater part of the service her eyes were closed serenely.

After the service Tanner joined the queue as people traipsed outside to view the various wreaths; he followed the normal practice of reading the messages. As he looked up Maureen was standing by his side.

"Hello John, thanks for coming." She smiled at him, her pleasure at his appearance evident.

"There's no way I wouldn't have come…it's what friends are about." He noticed what looked like the beginning of a tear glisten in the corner of her eye.

"You're right, family are okay, but sometimes it's just a friend you need…I've invited everyone back to the house; I didn't really want them but I suppose it's tradition. Anyway, Roger's sister appears to have taken over as chief mourner and organiser…do you fancy playing truant?"

"Yes, but what will the family think?" exclaimed Tanner.

"To be honest, I really couldn't give a damn what they think. Throughout my marriage I've put on an act of total devotion to my husband, while he was busy jumping from one woman's bed into another!"

Tanner looked around. People were beginning to make their way back to the cars for the journey back to Maureen's house. Amongst the waiting cars he spotted a taxi that one of the mourners had arrived in. He moved his mouth closer to Maureen's ear. "There is a taxi over there. You head towards it; I'm going to tell Ernie that I don't need a lift home..."

Within minutes Tanner had spoken to Ernie and was climbing into the back of the taxi alongside Maureen. He told the driver his address and then sat back in the seat, unsure of just what his next words would be. He needn't have worried; Maureen continued the conversation.

"I actually feel as though the door has closed on a major part of my life. It's like a big sigh of relief tinged with a touch of sadness, not for me but for Roger. He may have been a bastard with regards to his bed-hopping but nobody should have to die that way. He wasn't even Roger at the end. He was something existing within his skin. In my head I believe Roger died shortly after they confirmed he was terminal."

Tanner looked down at her hands; they were trembling, and as her eyes became watery, she leaned towards him, resting her head on his shoulders.

The taxi pulled up outside Tanner's flat; he paid the driver and gently led Maureen inside. As they entered his living room her eyes scanned her surroundings. Everything in Tanner's flat was immaculate. He stood studying her; she had quickly regained her composure. Suddenly her eyes found his.

"Er...would you like something...tea, coffee?" asked Tanner.

"I think, under the circumstances, something stronger is required."

"Whisky okay?"

"Mm, yes, with ice please."

Tanner took an ice tray from the freezer compartment of his fridge, snapped out some cubes into a couple of glasses and topped them with whisky. He moved back into his living room, passed a glass to Maureen and then sat opposite her in his armchair. She sipped at her drink, as though in thought and then looked up at him.

"Would you be shocked to know that the last time my husband made love to me was just over a year ago...? And then it was more for his gratification..." Tanner looked but said nothing. If she needed to exorcise her demons, then he was happy to be her listening board. "After that neither of us really wanted to do it, and then of course there was his illness and diagnosis, followed by his treatment and finally his lingering end..."

"I'm so sorry..." whispered Tanner.

"Oh, don't be sorry. I've already said he was a total bastard, but nobody asks to die do they?"

"Are you haunted by the past?"

"Not really. Part of me wonders what if...what if I'd divorced him years ago ... where would I be now? But of course in our circles, you marry and you stay together regardless; it's what's expected."

"So what will you do now?"

"Whatever I bloody well like. The time has come to kick off the confines of so-called expected behaviour. I want to experience some happiness and contentment … the Lord alone knows I deserve it after what I've been through."

"Are you hungry? Tanner asked suddenly.

"Yes, I think I am…I hadn't thought until you said, but I don't really want to go out."

"Don't worry, I'm okay in the kitchen. How does pork chop, pasta and green beans sound?"

"Absolutely perfect. Do you have any wine?"

"You kick your shoes off, sit and relax and I'll call you into the dining room as soon as it's ready."

Within no time Tanner had prepared and served the food as promised. Maureen was quiet during the meal. They discussed only general subjects. Neither of them mentioned Roger, although his presence seemed to hover above them. When the meal was finished they retired to the living room. They sat together and eventually cuddled as friends, in between consuming more than several glasses of brandy.

The evening wore on and the brandy had made them both drowsy. They walked hand in hand towards Tanner's bedroom as though it was the most natural thing in the world to do… Maureen was asleep even before her head had fully settled onto the pillow.

The following morning when she awoke, her eyes were bright. Tanner looked at her face, which looked relaxed and happy. "Good morning." He smiled at her then kissed her cheek gently.

"How long have you been awake?" she murmured contentedly.

"Only about twenty minutes."

"You should have woken me."

"I've been lying here looking at you."

"Oh John, you haven't…I wasn't snoring was I?"

He touched her face. His fingers traced imaginary patterns on her skin. Their eyes met. She was silent for a moment, then moved his hand away.

"I'm sorry, I didn't mean to…"

She slipped her arm around his waist and gently pulled him towards her. They kissed with a loving affection... and then kissed again, only this time it was longer. He played his fingers around her breasts and her whole body suddenly shivered from a tingling inside. Her face glowed with happiness, she rolled onto her back, pulling Tanner on top of her as her legs opened for him. Her eyes closed as she lay there in seventh heaven while he gently positioned himself above her. Their touch was gentle, she trailed her cool dry fingers across his chest, and as she felt his desire inside her, she let herself go with an unrestrained passion as she realised she had long forgotten just how wonderful true lovemaking could be.

Afterwards they showered together, had breakfast together, and spent some time wrapped in each other's arms.

"I'd better go back to the house. Hopefully the family have all left by now, but just in case there are some still hanging around, I should put in an appearance…could you phone for a taxi for me?" she asked reluctantly.

"No need, I'll drive you home."

"No, not today John, let me return alone… I haven't exactly followed the correct code of behaviour for a grieving widow."

"And are you grieving?"

"As I told you yesterday, the door has closed on that part of my life and I'm now embracing an exciting future…but I still have the feelings of my family to consider."

Tanner phoned for a mini-cab and within twenty minutes it was outside his flat, blasting its horn. He escorted her downstairs.

"Come over to the house tonight, John, and I'll cook us a meal…I still feel the need for company. I'll phone you and give you a time," Maureen said as they stepped outside. Tanner opened the rear door of the cab; she climbed in and settled back in the seat as Tanner closed the door. She wound down the door window. "John?"

"Yes?"

"Tonight…bring a toothbrush."

Momentarily Tanner appeared lost for words but the saucy smile upon Maureen's face told him he didn't need any. He returned the smile with a wink, waved her off as the mini-cab pulled away and then returned to his flat. He noticed that he had more than a spring in his step … he felt as though he'd just been told his jackpot lucky numbers had been drawn. A surge of happiness flowed through him. He decided to add to his happiness with a visit to Ruth.

He'd been back in his flat no more than fifteen to twenty minutes when he heard a loud knocking at his door. His initial thought was that Maureen had left something behind; he opened the door still smiling.

"Good morning, John; I trust I am not disturbing you?" Sebastian Toakes. Tanner's ex-section head stood before him, a bright and breezy tone to his very assured voice.

"Um…no, not at all…" Tanner replied cautiously.

"Good show…a cup of tea would go down nicely…if you've got the kettle on."

"There are plenty of cafés open at this time of the morning if that was all you were looking for." Tanner remained apprehensive.

"Yes, but then I wouldn't be able to have a little chat with you…and that is the purpose of my visit."

"You'd better come in then, only wipe your feet first." Tanner stepped back holding the door open for his visitor to enter. As Toakes entered his eyes flickered in all directions as they scanned and scrutinised the interior of Tanner's home.

"A couple of biscuits would be nice with that cup of tea, John."

"What exactly is it that you want?"

"I told you: a cup of tea and a couple of biscuits…and then perhaps a little chat."

"A chat about what?"

"Why, about you of course, dear boy."

Tanner resented somebody a lot younger than him referring to him as a *dear boy*. He stepped into his kitchen and switched on the kettle, then returned to his living room.

"Let's cut to the chase shall we? The kettle's on, you can have a cup of tea, but just what the fuck do you want with me?"

Sebastian Toakes gave a loud sigh of disappointment. "Oh, John, you never change do you? You were a good operative in your time, you know. You had a knack of delving in the right spot and getting results. You were also a damn good section head. It was only your own insubordination that got you busted down."

Tanner shrugged his shoulders. "Yeah, but it's all past tense."

Toakes ignored his comment and continued, "When I first joined the department, I have to admit I was slightly in awe of you…"

"Anything else I need to know before you leave?" Tanner interrupted him impatiently.

Toakes continued, his voice quiet but firm. "Go and pour out the tea John and then we can discuss how and why you are currently facing charges of possessing a prohibited firearm and ammunition…or perhaps you'd prefer to discuss Ernie Palmer not only losing his job but also losing his pension rights?"

"You bastard!"

"I'm hardly that John. Besides, I haven't even started to consider Maureen Dickins' involvement in all of this."

A silence fell across the room momentarily; it was broken only by what seemed the amplified sound of the automatic kettle switching itself off. Tanner remained silent as he moved into the kitchen, threw a tea-bag into each of the two cups and then poured boiling water into each of them. He added a dash of milk then placed them onto a tray. He split open a packet of biscuits that Ruth had brought on one of her visits and tipped a few onto a plate, then carried the tray back into his living room, speaking only as he passed a cup across to Toakes. "Have a biscuit…"

Toakes sipped his tea before answering.

"If I'd wanted to jump on you John, then it would be the police visiting you now and not me. The gun that Palmer supplied to you is from our disposable collection; it cannot be traced back to us, and that is my only concern…" Tanner gave no response as Toakes continued. "You're not a loose cannon John, and you're not going to shoot anyone willy-nilly so one more gun on the streets will not make an iota of difference…" Tanner breathed a sigh of relief as Toakes continued. "Ernie Palmer was prepared to lie for you, even to risk a charge of perjury if need be."

His tone changed. "We look after our own John, so stop treating your ex-colleagues as nothing less than snotty-nosed, wet-arsed juniors, because they are the people who are going to be there for you…provided you don't make a complete fuck-up of things!"

Tanner couldn't recall ever hearing Toakes swear before.

"Did Ernie tell you about my daughter?"

"Yes, and in your shoes I would probably do exactly the same, but remember you still need to follow the rules of the game you're playing; you must use the judiciary to take these people down. If you try to create a one-man Dodge City, then expect no help from me." As he finished speaking Toakes stood up to leave. "I haven't visited you today and we haven't had this conversation."

Tanner nodded his acknowledgement but gave no reply. He followed Toakes towards his front door and as the man left, he closed it behind him.

He returned to his living room and sat on his sofa. He thought about Ruth, and then about Becky … he wondered if she was still alive and if so, how was she coping? His thoughts then wandered to Ernie Palmer and how he hadn't fully realised the extent of the man's loyalty. His thoughts finally drifted to Maureen Dickins, and their early morning bedroom gymnastics. He speculated on whether she had used him or if he had used her? Finally he thought about Danny Dolan…he instantly rejected Sebastian Toakes' advice about playing by the rules. He'd tried that and got nowhere, so now it was time for Dolan to go through the experience of shitting himself while on his knees begging for his life. But the all-important first question was … just where the hell was he?

Tanner toured the familiar haunts and drove by Dolan's flat several times but without any sighting of him. He then spent the remainder of that afternoon parked up the street from his flat. Apart from a couple of girls who briefly loitered outside, all was quiet. Maureen had already phoned him during the early part of the afternoon and told him what time to arrive for dinner, so he also kept one eye on the time. It would be too easy to settle down into observation mode and completely lose track of time.

As the afternoon wore on, he decided on one last tour of the area and possibly even stopping off at the Lucky-Eight café and asking Bob and Marcie if they had seen anything of Danny Dolan. He fired the engine into life again.

His trawl was fruitless. The man was either in hibernation or else he had left the area. To add to Tanner's frustration a number of roads had been shut off due to a shooting incident that the police were dealing with. Tanner sighed despondently, as he mentally acknowledged that it was now an occurrence that was becoming far too regular in major cities and towns across the country. At the first opportunity, he changed direction and headed back towards his flat. En-route he stopped and bought flowers, and a bottle of good wine to take to his dinner with Maureen.

Tanner stood under his shower, not quite in a trance of despair, but he desperately wanted to see a glimmer of light at the end of the tunnel. He felt that his progress in finding his daughter to date had been almost non existent and without either resources or some form of back-up, he was desperately delving into his memory banks for an idea, any idea, of what to do next.

It was a little after eight o'clock when John Tanner arrived at Maureen Dickins house. He was wearing a blue Armani style suit with a crisp white shirt and complimented by highly polished shoes. Maureen opened the door to him with a beaming smile.

"You're punctual…I like that," she said as she took the flowers and wine from him.

"Not that I wasn't in a hurry to see you, but I've had a bastard sort of day. After you left this morning, Sebastian Toakes paid me a visit. Nothing serious – he was just marking my card. And I've been trying to find a particular waste of space that my daughter was involved with, but he seems to have vanished off the planet!" Maureen placed her hand on the nape of Tanner's neck. It felt good to him as her hand smoothed and squeezed away the pressure that had been building up inside of him throughout the day. Her arms softly cradled the back of his neck and then, as their faces were drawn close together, he moved her hair to one side with his hand and their lips met and engaged in a kiss full of heat and passion.

Maureen eventually broke off their kiss and took a step backwards. "Phwoarr, steady on lover, we've got a meal to eat first!" She led him into the dining room. "You pour the wine while I serve," and then she was gone, back into the kitchen from where he heard the clatter of her activity. He looked around the dining room and was impressed at the trouble she'd gone to. She'd laid the table as though she was expecting royalty and what looked like best china and glassware had been brought out for the occasion. He poured wine into two quality crystal-cut goblets as she reappeared with the meal.

During the meal, conversation was lively, energetic and sparkling. After the meal, during coffee, they talked some more, but the atmosphere between them was changing; even the odd pauses felt electrifying. Maureen began to blush slightly while Tanner became fidgety.

"If you'd like to go through to the living room, I'll clear the table and join you," she said as she rose and gathered their plates.

"I'll help you. I'm a dab hand at loading a dishwasher…" Tanner grinned.

The dining room table was quickly cleared; the dishwasher was loaded and switched on. They stood close together in the kitchen and there was awkwardness between them. Tanner moved closer to her, and put one hand on each side of her face as he leaned forward to kiss her. He gently nudged her up against the door frame as their lips locked. He parted her lips with his tongue and she appeared to relish the exploration of her mouth. She pulled him to her as closely as she could, feeling his hardness against her. Finally she broke the kiss. "I think we need to take this upstairs to the bedroom..." she panted.

In the bedroom they kissed again. Tanner's lips hovered and kissed around her face and slowly down to her neck. He took off his shirt and threw it aside as she removed her blouse. In a heartbeat her bra was also on the floor. Their breathing became heavier as he kissed and gently lapped at her earlobe with his tongue, her back arched as she ran her fingernails over his skin, up and down his back, caressing and toying with him. They tore off their remaining clothes and fell onto the bed naked with their arms and legs entangled. Maureen pulled and held Tanner tightly to her, and as she felt the heat building up inside her so she wanted him faster. She was so close to the edge, it was all she could do not to scream. She bit hard on her lip to ward it off, to delay it just for a while, but to no avail, she felt herself explode inside as the orgasm shook her body and she floated to that place called seventh heaven.

John and Maureen had spent the remainder of the evening either making love, or lying wrapped in each other's arms and had both fallen into a deep exhausted sleep. The classical tune of Tanner's mobile phone had continued ringing for a considerable time before the sounds finally penetrated his sleep. His hand fumbled on the bedside table, knocking over a picture frame and scattering his car keys and loose change in numerous directions across the bedroom floor. Eventually his hand recognised the feel of his phone and moved it under the bed covers to his ear.

Tanner lay still for what seemed an eternity. Did he really hear those words or dream them? He suddenly sat bolt upright, snapping himself out of the trance-like sleep from which he hadn't fully awoken; a sudden feeling of nausea overwhelmed him.

Maureen also woke. "John, what is it?" The concern in her voice was clearly evident.

"That was Ruth...she said that Becky's been shot...that she might die!"

"Where are they?"

"At...at the hospital...Ruth wants me to meet her there...Maureen, I might lose my daughter before I even get to know her..."

"Do you want me to drive you?" Maureen asked as she quickly pulled on and zipped up a skirt.

"No...no I think I'll be better if I'm alone, but thank you..."

"John, I'll send someone from my section to sniff around. They should be able to find out what the local police won't tell you."

Tanner finished dressing and tore out of the house to his car. He accelerated away, almost colliding with a passing taxi. The taxi sounded its horn and flashed its headlights at him. Tanner switched his headlights on as another vehicle flashed its lights at him. He looked at the digital clock on his dashboard. He punched the steering wheel, angry at there being so many cars on the road delaying his progress.

His car radio was on and the hourly news bulletin was in progress. The announcer relayed the news of the day's events and then gave a breaking news report:

" *A 25-year-old man and his 23-year-old girlfriend were victims of a shooting in London late yesterday afternoon.*

A police spokesman said the victims were not involved in gang culture, but that it was another tragic case of young people being in the wrong place at the wrong time. He added that the female is in a critical condition in hospital suffering from a single gunshot wound, while the man died instantly from three shots at close range in the chest.

A member of the public who tried to apprehend the assailants was also shot and his current condition is also described as critical."

The report continued with a statement by the Home Secretary expressing his concerns over the spiralling number of gun-related incidents now occurring on the Capital's streets.

It took Tanner a little over an hour to arrive at the hospital. He had driven there almost on automatic pilot as his mind speculated on just what Becky's condition was, and in what state Ruth might be. He quickly snapped himself out of his daydream mode as he pulled into the hospital pay-and-display car park. He ran across the tarmac and entered through the double doors of the Accident and Emergency department. He suddenly remembered he hadn't bought a parking ticket, but as quickly as the thought had entered his head so it left – somehow it wasn't so important.

The nurse at the reception desk gave him directions as to where Ruth should be. The amount of swing doors he passed through and corridors he walked along seemed endless, and then he was there, standing outside two large swing doors. He could see Ruth through the narrow oblong window in the door. Through his eyes she looked for all the world like a little girl lost. She was sitting across from the doors, in what looked like a large recess in which several padded chairs had been placed; she seemed to be in a daze, just staring across the room.

Tanner's heart was pounding; he couldn't remember ever feeling this scared. He took a deep breath, pushed open the door and made his way towards Ruth. As he approached her he could see her hands trembling, and at that moment he wanted to scoop her up in my arms and say, 'It's okay, Daddy's here, everything is going to be all right.' But he knew that in that sense, she had never been his little girl and he was never her Daddy! He quickly sat next to her and cupped her hands in his.

"How is she…have they told you anything?" It was all he could think of to say. She turned and looked at him, her eyes welling up. She was on the verge of tears; she swallowed deeply, unable to speak, just looking at him with a helpless expression.

Tanner gently squeezed her hands, trying to convey, his love, his guilt and his wanting to be there for her.

After a while she spoke. "They won't tell me anything. All they will say is that they are doing everything possible…and apparently the police are waiting to interview her before any relatives are allowed to see to her…. that is, providing she pulls through." Her eyes were filled with tears. Tanner put his arm around her and pulled her to him. He felt her body shudder as the full flood of tears left her and she finally let out her grief in the arms of the father that deep down, she had always longed for.

Tanner and Ruth had been waiting at the hospital for a little under three hours. Tanner had been unable to find out the extent of Becky's injuries; at one point, when he became insistent and stated to one of the nurses that, as Becky's father, he felt he was entitled to know the degree of her wounds, the nurse replied with a natural frostiness, in no uncertain terms, that aggressive behaviour would not be tolerated and if continued then their policy was to either have him ejected via their own security or to summon the police.

Ruth pulled him away. "Leave it Dad; that one has been a real bitch since we arrived." Tanner and Ruth looked up and down contemptuously at the nurse, then turned away and returned to their seats.

No more than ten minutes later another nurse appeared. This one spoke and treated them with compassion. "She's just been transferred from the Intensive Care Unit," the nurse informed them. "She's in a private room just off Laburnum Ward. You can go in, but if she's sleeping, don't disturb her." And then the nurse was gone.

Tanner had been aware for a while that he was being watched, by a tall man, dark haired, solidly built, probably late twenties, with a heavy stubble around his face. He was wearing a dark brown leather jacket, jeans and a patterned tee-shirt; from a distance the pattern gave the impression he had vomited down the front of it.

Ruth gripped his arm. "Dad, I'm not being funny, but let me see Becky alone. She might not be up to the shock of seeing her father just yet."

"That's okay, I agree with you. I'll wait until you say the word…I need some fresh air anyway, so I'll take a stroll outside." He kissed her on her forehead; he felt respect and a sense of pride at again being referred to as Dad. He turned towards the exit; from the corner of his eye he noticed the brown leather jacket watch Ruth until she disappeared up the stairs and then turn away and follow him.

As Tanner stepped outside the hospital he looked up at the sky; every indication showed it was it was setting itself to become the greyest of days. A sudden movement caught his eye and the brown leather jacket was beside him. "John Tanner?" asked the jacket.

"Who wants to know?" replied Tanner suspiciously.

"Maureen Dickins asked me to meet up with you…to find out discreetly what the police know and to pass it on to you." The man's face remained expressionless.

"And what have you found out?"

"Basically they don't know shit! They think it's possible the pair may have been victims of a gang-related attack."

"But on the radio it said…"

"They just tell the news people that to shut them up; it gives the media a human tragedy angle to their bulletins and they stop asking too many probing questions that the police haven't the answers to."

"What actually happened…apart from the fact that two people were shot?"

"It was three people actually; a have-a-go hero tried to grapple the gunman before he could escape, and he received a single gun shot at nigh on point blank range. His spine was shattered; his life now will be one of a paraplegic."

"Tell me about Becky."

"To be honest, the police don't know very much at all. That's why they want to question her. They believe she may be able to help them regarding the male victim's recent movements."

"Was it Dolan?"

The brown leather jacket shrugged. "The police officer I spoke to told me that whilst they believed the victim to be Danny Dolan, they couldn't definitely confirm it as such as the body needed to be formally identified."

"Anything else?"

"Only…according to the ambulance crew … if the girl makes then it will be a miracle."

"It's that bad?"

"She was face down in a pool of blood when they arrived at the scene. The male victim was pronounced dead at the scene and they thought she would be as well; they certainly didn't expect to find any signs of life. However, as they turned her over, she gave a deep sigh. At first they thought it was just the last gasp before death, but then they realised she was breathing … but only just; it wasn't regular and was very shallow. Again their experience told them she probably wouldn't survive the journey to the hospital."

Tanner extended his hand. "Thanks for your help … it's appreciated…I'm sorry, I didn't catch the name."

The brown leather jacket shook his hand. "The name's not important."

"Well you've done a first class job; those bastards in there wouldn't tell me jack shit!"

"One other thing: I did tell the investigating officer that you were still one of us, and to cut you some slack…I think you'll find they will let you in to see your daughter quite soon, even if it comes to the worst."

"Once again … it's much appreciated."

The brown leather jacket nodded in response. "I'll hang around for a bit…and keep my ear to the ground."

Chapter 11

Becky

I feel I'm being lifted from out of a black pit ..... no, not lifted: ejected, pulled upwards ... expelled from the deep black pit of which I have no memory and from the blackness, there is now a grey darkness. Before there was nothing, now there is something, but I cannot see, I cannot feel, but I know there is something around me.
Very slowly, thoughts are appearing to join the scattered memories. My childhood ... my mother hitting me. My teenage years ... my mother screaming at me. Hannah ... holding me like a baby telling me I'm okay ... only now the face has changed; it's now my sister Ruth, tears streaming down her cheeks. A sudden agonising pain engulfs me. I feel a burning in my chest, a glowing red hot meteorite has landed inside me and is slowly scorching its way out of me, but I can't move ... I can't touch it or hold it ... I just have to endure the pain until it has burned its way through and finally leaves my body. I visualise it as it blisters and erupts out through my skin ... a glowing ember of a sphere pulsating with its heat ... and the pain is gone; now there is nothing. I want to drift away. I feel peaceful and I feel myself drifting ... I know that I'm asleep, but I'm also conscious; I know that someone is near me ... I can sense them but I'm unsure if they can see me or even know that I'm here ...
The darkness is becoming a lighter grey. I want to open my eyes, but they are too heavy...I lift them fractionally, I can see through my eyelashes, I can see the silhouette of someone leaning over me, touching my hand, I can feel it! I know that it's Ruth ... Oh my God, I'm in a coffin, that's why she's leaning over me, yes, I felt a tear, she's crying! I've got to let her know I'm alive, but I can't, I can't move, not even a muscle, not a twitch, nothing...Oh God please don't let them nail on the coffin lid! Ruth's moving away ... no, come back, please, come back...! Wait, other faces now ....I can feel them prodding me, touching me, checking me...Oh God, thank you, thank you, thank you......

Chapter 12

John Tanner

John Tanner was restless as he strolled around the hospital car park. His mind focused on the trivia. There was no clear shape to the car park, bits had been added on as previous old buildings had been demolished and cleared. Almost a crude star outline but in offered in square block shapes. He shook the thoughts from his head, what the fuck did he care about the shape of a poxy car park! He pulled his mobile phone from his jacket pocket and punched in the numbers for Ernie Palmer.

"John, are you okay? Maureen told me what had happened. How is your daughter?"

"I haven't seen her yet, I…I…"

"John, just say the word and I'll come straight over."

"No, it's okay, I'm just very wound up. I want to do that piece of scum that did this to my daughter. I'm burning inside Ernie, I want to fucking kill them, like they tried to do to my daughter!"

"Try to calm down a bit John. We've both got a long history in security which means we have a closer knowledge of locating and tracking these bastards; we'll get them, I promise you."

"And what happens when they're caught? I'll tell you what'll happen Ernie, they will scream human rights and everybody will be so fucking frightened they'll shit themselves senseless and then start pussyfooting around ensuring that these scum have their every comfort catered for…compare that to my daughter…if she lives, she'll be discharged from hospital and that's it…she'll be forgotten."

"I hear what you're saying John, but the mobile phone network is not the place to say it."

"Yeah, you're right, I'm sorry…I just get so fucking angry and frustrated."

"John, I'll give you whatever help I can, and you know that Maureen feels the same…but if it goes pear shaped, you're on your own. I still have a pension to protect and I'm not sure just how lenient Sebastian Toakes will be if things hit the fan."

"Point taken Ernie…I'll ring off now and catch up with you later." Tanner clicked off his phone and walked towards his car. A fixed penalty notice had been stuck to the windscreen under the windscreen wiper; he yanked the paper off and shoved it in his pocket as he climbed in behind the wheel of his car. Turning the ignition, the engine roared into life and he pulled away with a screech of tyres.

Tanner drove aggressively and was soon on the receiving end of the wrath of his fellow drivers. He turned onto what he knew was a long dual carriageway, moved into the outside lane and accelerated. He was driving fast, much faster than usual; he was out of his comfort zone. He glanced at the speedometer: one hundred and fifteen mph. He looked back up at the road ahead. A car in the distance was changing lanes. Tanner hit the brakes but the distance between him and the car in front was closing fast. He pushed harder on the brake pedal, he felt the rear wheels lock, screaming as they scorched the road, and the smell of burning rubber wafted into the car.

Thoughts entered his head. 'So this is how I'm to die: crushed in a metal cage, squashed like an insect, just another road traffic accident statistic, with maybe a mention on the radio, one of those where the detached voice of the announcer calmly says, '*an accident is causing long tailbacks*' etc.'

Tanner waited for the impact, and then almost as though his own guardian angel was directing it, the car in front moved into a slipway in the central reservation to make a right hand turn.

Embarrassment took over, and Tanner felt as though the other drivers were all looking at him, laughing at him. The boy racer who never grew up, now a menace to all other road users. He pushed hard on the accelerator again, to distance himself from this group of drivers and hide himself amongst another group who didn't know that he'd just made a major pratt of himself. But his concentration had gone; he was now an accident just waiting to happen. He moved into the nearside lane, slowed the car and turned off onto a residential street. He felt weary and despondent. He eased the car slowly to a stop by the kerbside. His vision became blurred as tears filled his eyes, his bottom lip quivered, his shoulders sagged, he dropped his face into the open palms of his hands and he let go for the first time and cried. Heaving shoulders, loud sobs, he cried for his daughter Becky, for his daughter Ruth, for all his past mistakes and for all that was wrong in the world today.

Chapter 13

Becky

Whatever the shadowy figures and silhouettes did, it worked. I could hear noises, distant noises but I couldn't make out what they were. I think I heard a voice as well but again it was in the distance. My eyes partly opened, but I could see only a grey mist; I closed them again. My head was filled with the sounds of a twenty-one-gun salute. Again I forced my eye lids open; slowly the grey mist became a haze, which in turn became a fuzzy vision before returning to normal. I looked around at my surroundings. The windows of the room were shielded from the outside by wide vertical blinds. The gaps between them were the only points for the outside brightness to enter; yet surprisingly the room was light. I was lying in a bed, with covers across me pulled tight, almost binding me. My eyes flickered upwards and were immediately hurt by the brightness of the overhead lights. I closed them and could feel myself drifting off into a relaxing sleep.

I didn't think I'd slept for long, although I had absolutely no idea of time. I gradually opened my eyes again; my head still felt heavy but the cannonade inside it had now ceased. Somebody was sitting by the side of my bed reading a magazine; the face wasn't familiar to me. My eyes closed again, it was too much effort to keep them open. My chest felt as though it had been crushed and then padded out again, but the worst part was that I could remember everything that had happened … except for why I was in a hospital bed. No memory, no recall, my mind was just a blank, as though it was protecting me by not fully absorbing what had happened. I forced my eye lids open again and I recognised the face reading the book; my sister Ruth.

"Hello you…" I mumbled to her.

Her eyes widened with happiness, a beaming smile spreading across her face.

"Becky, you're awake! Oh, thank God, I've been so worried…" and then tears appeared in her eyes. "Oh Becky, we thought we'd lost you. I felt so helpless… isolated, that there was nothing I could do."

"What happened to me?" My words came out confused, but that was how I felt.

"Don't you remember?" she replied softly.

"If I could remember, I wouldn't ask…" I felt snappy, irritable, but I knew my words came out weakly.

"Becks…you were shot…you and that Danny Dolan." She had the expression of someone who had just told a young child that Father Christmas doesn't exist.

Shot! My mind quickly went into replay mode. I could remember everything: the beatings, the rapes, escaping from the house, talking with Danny, even the sly look on his face…then being on a crowded pavement …. we were going somewhere, but I couldn't remember where. I knew that I wanted to get it over and done with … whatever it was. I remembered a strong sensation of fear, real fear, an almost bricking it type of fear, but then nothing. I certainly didn't have any recollections of being shot.

"Shot! Are you bullshitting me or something?" My tone was disbelieving, albeit weak.

Ruth raised an eyebrow in surprise at my snappiness, then spoke softly. "Becks, they did warn me that you could react in this way. Firstly, you need to know you are not in any immediate danger, and it's perfectly natural for you to feel anxious and distressed, needing information and wanting someone to talk to; it's all part of it, it's something that they called crisis reaction."

If I'd had half a clue as to what she was talking about, I would have accused her of being condescending, but she may as well have been talking to me in Swahili for what sense she was making.

"I actually thought I'd lost you last week, just before you were moved from the Intensive Care Unit. They let me see you, but they said that while your body and your organs were all responding well, it was possible you could stay in a coma, something about the body's way of protecting itself. Suddenly all hell let loose, all the machines you were wired up to started going mad …. talk about all bells and whistles! I was quickly ushered out and the last I saw they were all huddled over you."

"What do you mean last week? It was only yesterday that I was with Danny."

"No, sorry Becks, you've been out of it…"

"Out of it? How long have I been here then?"

"You were in intensive care for a day and a bit and you've been in this room for just over five days."

"No, you're doing my head in…I can remember, I was with that arsehole Danny *yesterday*, I escaped from the house *yesterday*, I saw Kevin Crestwell *yesterday*, I…Oh my God, it was Kevin Crestwell…what's happened to me…I can remember Crestwell, but then nothing."

"It's okay, relax, you're safe now." Ruth placed the palm of her cool hand on my brow and as confused as I felt, I did feel the panic in me ease away. I looked up at her, my big sister; her eyes were filled with love as she looked down at me and stroked my hair.

"Ruth, can I ask you a question?"

"Of course you can."

"When you came to see me in the ICU, did you have tears in your eyes?"

"Every day that I've come in to see you I've had tears in my eyes…why?"

"I can remember, thinking that I was lying in my coffin, and you leaned over me and a tear dropped onto my cheek and…"

"Stop it Becky…no more talk about coffins, it's morbid."

"But, don't you see, I panicked. I didn't want to die and be buried, and I can remember seeing the faces huddle over me…I wasn't in a coma I was conscious…"

"But since then Becky, all you've done is sleep so what's the difference … coma … sleep … it's all the same when you're out of it."

"Yeah, whatever." My irritability was returning.

"The thing is Becky, you're lucky to be alive, and while we're on the subject, you should know that Danny Dolan wasn't so lucky. He was confirmed dead at the scene." She paused, waiting for my reaction.

I hated Danny, I despised him, and he deserved to die for what he did to me, so why did my eyes fill with tears?

"Good! I'm fucking glad, because if he had survived, I would have killed him myself. He was a bastard, a cold calculating bastard and I hope he's burning in hell!" I spat the words out.

"Oh, I'm sure he is," Ruth replied with conviction. "There's another thing you need to know," she continued. "The police have said they want to interview you as soon as you're conscious. They were going to stop me from seeing you until after they'd spoken to you, but dad spoke to someone who pulled some strings and they backed off…"

"Who the fuck does Victor know with that type of clout?" My bewilderment was clearly evident.

"No, I mean our real dad…he's been trying to find you."

"Well you can tell him to fuck off as well…I'm certainly not interested in some old drunk…anyway, what's he after?"

"He's nothing like Madge has told us, he's…"

"Save your breath, I'm not interested!" I retorted.

"But you don't know anything about him."

"I know he's never bothered about us…booze was obviously more important to him."

"Well maybe its not all his fault that he never saw us…" she replied softly.

I couldn't believe she was actually defending him! "…and how do you know that he didn't send letters or cards, and that we never got them? You know how wicked and vindictive Madge is. We grew up having to listen to her outbursts of hatred against him, against our real father…and just think about this: Madge, our mother, wasn't interested in coming to see you in hospital, even though we didn't know at that point whether you were going to live or die…whereas he's been here every day sitting outside praying that you'd pull through…and no, he's not a drunk, he's actually a very nice man."

"Alright, I believe you, I just don't need anyone new in my life at the moment." The cannonade in my head was starting up again and I could feel elephants jumping up and down on my chest, but Ruth wasn't giving up just yet.

"Look, why don't you give him the benefit of the doubt, and at least give him a try out. Find out what sort of guy he really is?"

"Yeah, okay. I'm reluctant, but let's just agree to disagree… would you call a nurse please? Something's wrong, I don't feel right…"

I didn't know what happened to me because I was drifting in and out of it. There wasn't any resuscitating or anything like that involved. I remember my eyelids being yanked open and a piercing white light attempt to cut into my eyes and overhearing a female voice say something about Acute Stress Reaction, but for what that meant to me she could have been talking about her own cat allergy. But they obviously did a good job of whatever it was they did to me.

I was once again conscious and aware of my surroundings. I could hear a doctor speaking to Ruth … well, I assumed it was a doctor; her voice had that tone of authority. In fact it sounded more butch than feminine, but anyway, she was telling Ruth that I was a very lucky young lady to be alive. "Yeah, right," I thought. "Like, tell me something I don't know!"

She said that an inch either way and it would have hit a vital organ affecting the central nervous system, and the situation would have become life threatening.

Ruth began sucking up to her saying, "Oh, we are so grateful to you doctor, for your skill, and the care that you and…well, everyone at the hospital has given to our Becky. We all have tremendous confidence in you and you've really given my family and me peace of mind."

I opened my eyes to look at them as the doctor continued talking about the anatomic location of the wound … blah, blah … severe disruption to tissues … blah, blah … which in turn caused it to haemorrhage … blah, blah … but they'd been able to remove the bullet and expected me to make a full recovery … blah, blah, blah.

And there was my sister Ruth coming on to the doctor! Flicking her hair, smiling sweetly at her, tilting her head, her eyes wide and checking out the doctor, who was obviously loving every minute of it, and then the doctor started twisting a strand of her own hair, almost mirroring what my sister was doing, and smiling back at her!

The first thought that ran through my head was, "No, please, not in front of me!"

In the absence of a bucket of cold water, I gave a small groan to let them know I was conscious. The doctor was immediately by my side and then I heard shots echoing through my head, the same shots as before only this time they were louder and they were originating from inside my head, ghostly sounds returning to haunt me, and then just as before I felt myself slowly drifting out of it.

I had no idea how long I'd been asleep, but when I woke I felt completely refreshed. The doctor and Ruth were present, both of them standing by the side of my bed looking down at me.

"Good morning sleepy head." Ruth's expression was a cross between relief and worry.

"How long was I out for this time?" I murmured.

"Yesterday afternoon…you gave a loud groan, fluttered your eyelashes and then you went off back to the land of nod." She looked happy now.

"I feel great…the pain's gone…can I get up?" I tried to move as I spoke, but discovered it wasn't so easy.

"Your body has undergone a traumatic experience, Rebecca. Physically the wound will eventually heal, but how you react to it can make a huge difference to the healing process." The doctor had her authoritarian voice on, but I could also see that she genuinely cared.

"My reaction is that life has to go on…" I tried to sound positive.

"There is a natural progression of emotions you may find yourself experiencing. They're all part of the healing process and considered normal in these situations, especially in the beginning so you will need to be patient and I'm sensing that patience is not one of your strong points?" She tilted her head in that questioning schoolmarm sort of way.

"Becky is going to be living with me when she leaves here, doctor, so could you put it in plain words, so we know exactly what to expect?" Ruth flashed me a look that said, 'Don't try arguing, you're in my care now!'

"You need to watch for feelings of depression, or anxiety and even anger. You will also need to ensure that you resist any temptation to lessen any pain or feelings of hurt through either alcohol or, dare I say it, illegal drugs…"

"Oh I can assure you, doctor, there will be nothing like that going on," Ruth interrupted with a very strong matter of fact tone.

The doctor carried on as though she hadn't spoken, "…finding it difficult to intermingle with other people, insomnia and a lack of appetite are also symptoms that Rebecca may experience." I was beginning to feel more than a little cheesed off being spoken about as though I wasn't there, but still she continued. "It's important that Rebecca feels comfortable with talking openly about her feelings with her family, her friends and…I don't know if she has any religious beliefs but I know that some people have found great comfort from their faith. It is also important for her to occupy her time positively which in turn gives support towards a more thorough recovery."

The doctor paused for breath and by this time I'd had enough! "For God's sake will you speak *to* me and not *about* me…I'm not a child alright, and I'm becoming more than a bit fed up at you two treating me like one, yeah?"

Ruth and the doctor looked at each other in silence for a moment, and then:

"That's good Rebecca, you must express your feelings and not allow them to harbour inside you." The doctor's tone was patronising, but I let it go over my head.

"When can I get out of here?" I asked.

"We'll continue to monitor you for a few more days and then we'll be in a better position to make that decision. Obviously you have a loving family to help and support you and that will be a factor in our decision, but you must remember your body has had a trauma and so it also needs a period of healing."

I closed my eyes and gave a deep sigh of frustration. I felt angry but it quickly subsided. My eyes became watery, in my head images of Harvey and her smiling eyes appeared, followed by images of Siobhan cuddled to a pillow, too petrified to move, her eyes wide like a small child. I had meant every word when I'd promised her I'd go back for her and the look on her face told me she believed me, but I'd let her down. I'd betrayed her trust and heaven alone knows just what those evil bastards had done to her...

As the tears ran down my cheeks I blotted out the pictures appearing in my minds eye, the horrific pictures of what-ifs; and then, for the first time in as many years as I could remember, I prayed. I prayed that Harvey was okay. I prayed that Siobhan was alive and that she was also okay and not being made to suffer for what I'd done, and during my prayers, I again heard shots echoing through my head. I had no power of resistance and without that control I drifted off into the blackness of sleep.

When I came round again and opened my eyes Ruth was yet again sitting by the side of my bed, this time with her nose engrossed in a celebrity gossip magazine.

"Don't you ever go home?" I meant it in the nicest way but the look on her face told me she'd taken it the wrong way...and I suddenly felt very guilty. "What I mean is, thanks sis, I do appreciate it and I love you for it." A smile flashed across her face and I knew everything was okay again.

"Well, did you finish checking her out? I asked saucily.

"Checking who out?"

"The doctor...I was going to throw a beaker of cold water over you at one point," I grinned.

"I'm sure I don't know what you're talking about," she answered as her cheeks blushed a nice crimson colour. "Anyway, Sandra has been kind enough to give me some leaflets to help increase my understanding of your needs. Apparently the needs of a gun victim differs greatly from the needs of other crime victims..."

"Who the hell is Sandra?" I interrupted.

"Sandra...Doctor Atkins...the doctor whose skill, along with that of the trauma team, kept you alive...hello!"

"Mm...Sandra now is it...very cosy..." I answered light-heartedly.

She chose to ignore my teasing. "Anyway! As I was saying, according to the leaflets that Sandra gave me, while a number of victims do recover from their physical injuries, many of them can suffer from the mental scars. For example, the memory of it may still haunt them, which in turn can lead to a 'psychological trauma' …. and that's where I come in with the emotional support and your special needs, which can sometimes be for quite a long time."

"Are you seeing her outside?" I interrupted again, hoping that Ruth would take the hint that I didn't give a flying fig about special needs.

"I don't think that's anybody else's business," she answered in her own particular snotty voice.

"That means you are…" I said cheerfully.

"No it doesn't!"

"Then why are you blushing?" I sensed victory.

"As you are obviously feeling so much better, perhaps we should carry on with our discussion about our father…or maybe you'd like Doctor Atkins to inform the police that you're now coherent!" She had that 'don't mess with me' look about her and I knew I'd met my match.

"Ruth, I honestly don't want to do the daddy thing, alright? We grew up without knowing who our real dad was and now this arsehole walks back into our lives and says 'hi girls' and we're supposed to go running to him as though…"

"It's not like that Becks. As far as he's concerned we didn't want anything to do with him either." She was beginning to sound argumentative.

"Then why has he suddenly turned up out of the blue?" I responded in the same tone.

"He didn't. I went and found him."

"What?! Why?"

"Because the police did sweet sod all when I first reported you missing … people just kept saying you'd moved away, but I knew you hadn't…I knew something had happened to you, but nobody was interested, nobody would listen to me."

"How on earth did you find him?" I asked curiously.

"I was desperate. I didn't know where to turn. I remembered I'd previously found an old letter of his that had his National Insurance number on it. Anyway, a girl that I knew from University – I didn't particularly like her, she wasn't exactly the most hygienic of girls if you get my meaning – but like I said, I knew she liked me and she agreed to trace his current, or at least his last known address…"

"In return for what?"

"I'd rather not discuss it…it wasn't very pleasant for me, but I knew it was nothing compared to what you could possibly be going through…"

I held my hand out to her. "Oh Ruth, I had no idea…"

"Anyway I went to the address she gave me – quite a swanky place actually – and gave him the shock of his life when I announced who I was."

"How did you feel...you know going up and knocking on his door?"

"I actually stood outside his door for quite a while before I plucked up the courage and before that I'd been standing outside the building for ages before I felt brave enough to go in."

"So what did he say?"

"Well obviously I was very frosty towards him and..."

"You gave him your snotty voice."

"I don't have a snotty voice!" she protested.

"Yes you do, but carry on. What happened next?" Ruth gave me her look, the one that said, 'I'll save that one for later!'

"Well what I was about to say before you interrupted was that, as I looked him up and down, my feelings were that I despised him. He was a piece of shite who didn't give tuppence for me and I just wanted to tell him what I thought of him and then go."

"So why didn't you?"

"I don't know, something held me back, something wasn't right; the man I was looking at wasn't the same vision of the man that Madge had instilled into us throughout our childhood. We were led to believe he was pretty much a derelict, yet I was in a classy flat in a classy area, the inside was well decorated with good quality furnishing. This man wasn't a drunkard, he was smartly dressed, casual but smart. He was well mannered, everything was the opposite of what Madge had led us to believe about him."

"So if he's got money then why didn't he spend some of it trying to find us?"

"Becks, neither of us wanted him as we were growing up. In fact we hated him because he abandoned us, but what if he was told to stay away because his daughters wanted nothing to do with him? What if Madge blocked him from having any access to us when we were tots?"

"Yeah, yeah, what if...the fact is he wasn't interested in us..."

"You mean in the same way as we had no interest in him?" she fired back at me almost immediately. I shrugged my shoulders disinterestedly as she carried on. "I discovered he worked for the Security Services. He won't discuss what he actually did but I also found out that he was awarded the OBE."

"Is that suppose to mean something to me? Because whatever dearest daddy did in the war certainly doesn't interest me!" I was being deliberately sarcastic.

"What it means, Rebecca, is that he wasn't and isn't the waster that Madge would have us believe. She's lied to us all this time about our father. You know what an evil vindictive woman she can be...she won't even come to the hospital to see you, she claims you brought it all on yourself, that you probably deserved it..."

"She never…" I couldn't finish; the words had stuck in my throat, and my throat felt like a tight knot. Being aware that my mother didn't care was one thing, but faced with undeniable proof of her lack of any maternal feeling towards me was something different. I felt numb and I felt cold and I suddenly felt very alone.

"I'm sorry Becky, I didn't mean to blurt it out this way, but are you honestly telling me that you want to believe that everything she has said about our father, that every piece of venom she has spat out about him is true?"

I knew that I wasn't crying, so why did I have tears streaming down my cheeks? Ruth was immediately at my side hugging me. "Sssh … don't let her get to you, she's not worth it. I care about you and you'll soon discover that so does our real dad." She spoke softly and reassuringly.

The door to my room opened and Dr Atkins popped her head in. "How are you feeling Rebecca?" she asked.

"I'm alright, thanks…a little emotional, but okay."

"Rebecca, the police are here and they've said they need to speak to you, they need to get a statement from you." She spoke almost apologetically.

"It's okay, let them in, I suppose I've got to get it over with sooner or later," I sighed.

She disappeared, closing the door behind her, and a few moments later, it reopened and a uniformed WPC entered, followed by Dr Atkins and two other men. The first man, in uniform, introduced himself as Inspector Ledbetter. As the second man entered, I pointed my finger and almost screamed at him. "You can get that bastard out of here, I don't want him anywhere near me!"

Detective Sergeant Priack looked down at me disdainfully. "You obviously don't understand, young lady…" his tone was raised and formal "…if need be I intend to hold you in custody until I receive satisfactory answers to all my questions."

"No! Not you…not you…" I was becoming almost hysterical. Dr Atkins pushed passed Priack and gently held my wrist, checking my pulse; she lifted my eye-lids and looked into my eyes.

"I'm sorry Inspector but my patient is becoming distressed … I cannot allow this to continue."

"This is important police business, Doctor. A man has been shot and another is in a critical state, and we believe this young lady may be able to assist us with our enquiries." The Inspector was also very formal in his manner.

"While this patient is under my care and in this hospital then her welfare is my prime concern, and not your statement." She looked at DS Priack with disdain. "Why don't you just send *him* out? I mean how many of you does it take to get a statement?"

Inspector Ledbetter nodded to Priack, who snarled at me and then reluctantly left the room. The Inspector looked at Ruth.

"I want her to stay," I blurted quickly, then continued more calmly, "In the absence of my solicitor I want my sister to stay here…otherwise I shall get hysterical and you'll get nothing!" The inspector again nodded his agreement. "And lastly, I want her to take my statement." I indicated the WPC. "In fact, I don't want a man in here."

"Now just you hold on a moment young lady…" he began.

"No! Fuck you! I've been gang raped on a daily basis while you sat with your thumb up your arse and did nothing…I don't even want to be in the same room as a man!" I felt my tears flowing, and I knew my face was twisted in distress.

Ruth spoke. "Aren't you people supposed to be sympathetic in these cases?"

Inspector Ledbetter looked at his WPC questioningly.

"It's alright Sir, I think it would probably be for the best," she answered as though she had read his mind. The Inspector looked at each one of us in turn and then without another word, he left the room, followed by Dr Atkins. The WPC smiled at me reassuringly, introduced herself and asked me to confirm my name, then she asked the same of Ruth. Her manner was very gentle and her probing questions were posed in a way that made me feel comfortable, almost as though I was discussing everything that had happened with Ruth.

I told the WPC everything she wanted to know, and she wrote every word down. I told her about my love for Danny Dolan and about how he would tell me of his dreams for our future together, and then of his plea, that he was in trouble. I described to her the journey riding in the boot of a car, of Andrei, Costi, Paul Tyler and Kevin Crestwell and how the four of them raped me. I described in detail the ice-cold bath punishment, followed by more gang rapes, of how I was forced to work as a prostitute servicing anywhere between ten and twenty men in what was sometimes a fifteen hour working day, and I told her of the beatings I'd endure from Andrei if I didn't please the punters. I also told her about Harvey and of my concerns for her. Each word was meticulously written down by the WPC with no emotion shown.

I told her about the sadistic tendencies of Andrei and the insatiable and perverted sexual urges of Costi. I told her about Paul Tyler and his attempt to get me hooked on hard drugs, of how he attacked me and of how I just couldn't take another beating. I told her of the razor blade and Paul Tyler's slashed throat. At this point she asked me to slow down as I was speaking faster than she could write.

I then told her about Lucy and Siobhan, of our escape from the house, of Lucy at Euston railway station and of how fearful I was of what they would do to Siobhan. I lowered my voice to just above a whisper when I recalled for the first time how I was drawn back to Danny, despite my own self-preservation screaming at me to get the hell out. I remembered being on a busy-ish pavement and looking up and seeing the sadistic face of Kevin Crestwell.

"Oh my God …no!" I cried out as the scene replayed vividly in my head. I described the sounds of the gun shots, the burning sensation inside me, the vile smells of the pavement as I lay face down on it, the sounds around me, the shouting, the screaming, the crying. I remembered every last detail and as my memory banks released it, so I let it all out…I had to. It was like a confession, my confession, my purging myself of the nightmare I'd endured and when I was finished, I saw for the first time that Ruth had been sobbing like a child; even the WPC had the glistening of tears behind her eyes.

I asked her, like an innocent child asking an adult, "Why are people allowed to sell other people into slavery in this country? Why don't the government do something to protect us? Why do the police acknowledge it and yet turn a blind eye to it?"

The WPC gently shook her head. "I'm sorry, I don't have any answers for you, but we will catch these men, that is something I can promise you."

She finished writing out my statement and then read it back to me. Hearing it for the second time was too much for Ruth.

"Excuse me…I have to go outside for a moment." Her voice was weak; she had heard my story and the thoughts and mental images of the atrocities endured by her younger sister were far to much for her delicate nature and the anguish showing on her face was evidence of her distress. The WPC finished reading out my statement. I confirmed it was accurate, glanced over what she had written and then signed each page accordingly.

After the WPC had left, Ruth came back into the room, her eyes still red from crying. She sat on the edge of the bed, almost in a trance. After a while she composed herself. "I am so sorry Becky. I just couldn't bear to hear again what you went through…couldn't imagine you at the mercy of such evil sadistic bastards."

I watched her do what I'd seen her do so many times before whenever she felt anxious. She began to push her open palms back and forth along her thighs and then clench them into little tight fists, her small white hands becoming whiter as her anguish intensified. I took hold of her hands in mine.

"Ruth, if you really want me meet him…to meet our real father… then I don't have a problem with it."

She lifted her head and looked at me with red-rimmed eyes. "Becky, having spent some time with him, I honestly believe that Madge…that our mother has lied to us about our father; she's deliberately poisoned our minds against him while doing everything in her power to make sure he had no contact with us, and that's why we haven't as much as received a card from him in all these years, because she's either stopped it or obstructed it!"

"But that isn't what he's specifically told you is it?" I asked sceptically.

"Not in so many words, no. In fact he hasn't said one bad word against her."

"Then what, he's suddenly become a saint?"

"I didn't say he was a saint!" Her snotty voice returned.

"Okay, I'm listening to what you're saying, it's just that at the back of my head there's a voice reminding me that he's never been there for us, we have no relationship with him and if he honestly had any feelings for us then I believe he would have found a way to get in touch with us long before now!"

"Did you know where he was living while we were growing up?" Ruth asked.

"No! And to be honest, I didn't give a monkey's either," I snapped back.

"Exactly, and he didn't know where we lived either and as far as he knew we didn't want anything to do with him…"

"Well he was certainly right there…" I scoffed.

"Well, like I've already said, I went to see him. I didn't know what to expect or what sort of welcome I'd get, and do you know what I discovered…that he's a really nice guy!"

"Ruth, I've already said that I'll meet him, and I've no doubt that whatever the truth is, we'll find it out soon enough!"

Chapter 14

John Tanner

John Tanner had spent the last few days in a restless mood. He'd visited the hospital each day for an update on Becky's progress, as well as with meeting and lunching with Ruth, and awaiting confirmation from her that Becky had relented from her stance of not wanting any contact with him. He had been sitting patiently in the waiting area when Police Inspector Ledbetter walked passed with his WPC in tow and another man, who Tanner assumed to be CID. Whether or nor Ledbetter had recognised Tanner he had no idea but the Inspector gave no sign of recollection as he passed him.

Ruth later updated him on the developments of the meeting and when she left Becky's room in tears it was into her father's arms that she ran and her head went into her fathers neck as she sobbed out each of the unpleasant episodes of Becky's statement.

Tanner had spent each evening with Maureen Palmer at her house, and although he also stayed there most nights, they hadn't made love since Becky had been shot. He had no desire to; the blood did not want to flow to engorge that part of his body, despite his attraction to Maureen and the appeal of her welcoming body. His mind was elsewhere: his daughter, his own flesh and blood had been shot! Shot on the capital streets of London. It was something that happened to other people, something that was read about in the newspaper over breakfast, something heard on the radio. But it wasn't something that happened to your own family, not to your own child...

He experienced a feeling of guilt that it had happened. It was his role as a father to protect her from these horrors of life, but it had happened; and he couldn't be with her because he hadn't been in her life before and the guilt intensified with the reality that apart from the odd recollection that he had two daughters somewhere, he had never bothered to acknowledge them in any way, shape or form. The guilt continued to build up in him as he confronted the truth that throughout the years it had never occurred to him, nor had he any inclination to locate them, to find his daughters, and at no time had he even been curious, but now.... now that he'd met one of his daughters and quickly formed a close bond with her and realised the joy of having a daughter, he wanted to repeat the experience with Becky. But Becky had been shot and as yet she hadn't expressed any desire to see him and his fear now was that his twenty-odd years absence from her life had created in her a contemptuous hatred of him.

It had been mid morning when the police had visited Becky and taken her statement. It was now noon the following day, and Tanner was sitting in the office belonging to Maureen Dickins. He sat opposite her desk; he had declined her offer of refreshment and watched her as she returned to her desk, sat down and sipped her tea.

"Quite an honour to be invited up here into the higher echelons of power." His tone carried more than a hint of contrariness.

"Perhaps if John Tanner hadn't been so bloody minded and insubordinate he would still have his office in the higher echelons, as you so eloquently put it." Maureen's tone was abrupt and Tanner felt he'd truly been put in his place.

"I'm sorry…I was being lighthearted," he replied.

"Outside of work, John, I'll even allow you to tickle me, but while I'm behind this desk then it's strictly business only." Her comment didn't require an answer and she didn't expect one. She picked up one of the three phones on her desk and spoke into it. 'You can come in now.' She replaced the received. Within moments the door to her office opened and a young woman entered. Tanner estimated her age to be no more than that of his daughters. She was of Indian origin with large brown eyes and about the most beautiful face he'd seen. He had no doubt that if she'd wanted, she could have walked away with the top prize of almost any beauty competition. Maureen studied Tanner's face and as the girl approached her desk she said, "John, this is Kamalika. She is currently on secondment to my section and she is going to monitor the activities of the Metropolitan Police during their investigation into the shooting of your daughter." Tanner stood up and extended his hand. Kamalika held it with the lightest of touches and gently shook it. Tanner sat back in his chair as Maureen continued. "Obviously this is unofficial. It has to be understood that any information given to you regarding this matter is in strict confidence and in the event of exposure will be strenuously denied by this department."

"Yes, I understand," Tanner replied formally.

Maureen gestured to Kamalika to sit and commence her report.

"Okay, firstly, from the reports I've managed to procure from the police computers, they apparently moved very quickly yesterday following the receipt of your daughter's statement. The house she had been held in was located and raided. Upon entry it was found to be completely empty. Forensic are currently sweeping it. The house was actually rented from a letting agency, which was told it was to be used by a Romanian businessman and his family. They were supplied with false names, but although they were suspicious the agency didn't ask too many questions as they received a full year's rent in advance, in cash. The woman who arranged the letting on behalf of the alleged businessman told them she was supposed to have arranged this a month earlier and would lose her job if it wasn't all completed a.s.a.p. She then offered them a cash bonus if they could fast track everything through for the next day. Unfortunately greed won the day and the agency was more interested in the bonus than completing the formal checks."

"I don't suppose they are the first, or the only ones to take a back-hander to grease the wheels as it were…" Tanner said with intended irony.

"Well it didn't do them any favours…" continued Kamalika, "…they are now under investigation on possible money laundering charges!"

"Let's move on," instructed Maureen, her face expressionless.

"All our European allies have surveillance on known people traffickers. They send our Intelligence services their detailed reports and the relevant copies come through to me for compilation. These reports, however, only contain data on the major players; there are still a large number who slip through the net on a regular basis…"

"Is anything being done to tighten the net?" interrupted Tanner.

"John, let her finish…" Maureen's tone was assertive.

"The name Dougie Mann came up quite frequently; his name is on the databank of a number of agencies. Apart from illegally moving people across borders he's involved in gun running, drug smuggling, armed robbery and counterfeit money and his name was one of those mentioned on your daughter's statement. Other names she mentioned who also appear on these reports are Andrei Siliqi and Costi Vllasl; they are also major players and both wanted in several Eastern European and Baltic States, for murder, drug dealing, people trafficking and controlling prostitution."

Maureen Dickins looked directly at Tanner. "John, I don't want you to even consider going up against these people alone. You're experienced enough to know that one man with uncontrolled vengeance can do nothing except get himself killed. We have the resources and I promise you one way or the other, we'll get them…all of them."

Their meeting continued for a further hour and then Tanner's mobile phone rang…

"Hello, Dad?" It was Ruth's voice.

"Hello, I'm with Maureen at the moment."

"Oh sorry, I not interrupting am I?" she asked apologetically.

"No, absolutely not…it's always lovely to hear from you." She could almost hear the smile in his face.

"Well, I've some good news for you…at least I hope it's good news?"

"I shall never know unless you tell me," he teased.

"Becky wants to meet you…"

"Oh my God!" Tanner's exclamation came out subconsciously.

"She's said that she wants to see you alone…one on one as it were."

"Yeah I understand…it's not a problem…when?"

"How about tea time today?"

"Okay…I have to be honest though, I'm more nervous about this than I was at meeting the Queen!"

"You're going to be alright, Dad, and I shall be in the waiting room for moral support." Ruth's happiness was also evident in her voice.

"Okay, I'll see you then…bye."

Tanner looked up at Maureen. "Is everything all right John?" she asked, concerned.

"It's Becky…my daughter…she wants to see me, today. Oh my God, I've wanted this since Ruth first visited me and now that it's about to happen I feel apprehensive."

"I think you'll find that's a natural reaction John…look, we're about wrapped up here. Kamalika will contact you with any new developments."

"Yeah, thanks, I appreciate it Kamalika."

Kamalika smiled sweetly. "Look, I've got some people to track; I'll leave you alone…it was nice meeting you Mr Tanner."

"John… call me John," he said as she moved towards the door. He looked at Maureen. "What do I say to her?" he asked almost pleadingly.

"No doubt she's going to be just as nervous as you are, and for both of you it's going to be like meeting a complete stranger. Let her know that now you've all found each other, you want to be there for her. Tell her that you understand her anger that you have not been there for her up till now. Tell her that it has been hard for you in ways that no one else knows. The important thing is to show her plenty of love and acceptance. She feels betrayed by you and that's a very big bridge to repair."

"I know that this is my one chance and I really don't want to screw it up! I've got to break the ice gently."

Maureen rose from behind her desk and moved to his side. "Once the initial introduction and awkwardness is over, just say something like, 'I'd imagine you must have a hundred and one things you'd like to ask me,' and allow her to be in the driving seat." She kissed him lightly on the cheek. "Good luck, I hope it all goes okay."

Tanner weakly smiled his acknowledgment, but his mind was elsewhere.

Later that afternoon Tanner stood outside Rebecca's hospital room, one step away from his first meeting with the youngest of his estranged daughters.

"Are you okay Dad?" Ruth asked gently as her hand touched his arm.

"I feel awkward, embarrassed and if you can believe it…tongue-tied!" he gave a discomfited smile.

"I'm sure it will be alright. I would come in with you but Becky has insisted that she sees you alone first."

"I can understand that, she needs to see for herself how her father really is."

"She's also built up an emotional barrier. She's not really the hard-faced bitch that she will try to portray…but in her mind, everyone that she's trusted has betrayed her."

"And now her father has re-appeared after being absent from her life for all these years and wants to play happy families." Tanner's tone was cynical.

"We both know it's not like that…and I don't mean to tell you what you already know but, be patient with her and please don't resent any spiteful comments that she may start off with…"

Tanner turned and kissed Ruth on her forehead. "I think that any spiteful comments that she makes will be entirely deserved, and anyway, it may just be her way of breaking the ice."

Ruth kissed him on the cheek and gently patted his shoulder as he walked into Becky's room, and before the door had fully closed she heard the sound of her sister's voice, "And who the fuck are you?" Then the door closed and Ruth could hear no more. She sat back in the waiting area with her fingers crossed and began mentally chanting, over and over. *'Please let it work, please let them get on.'*

The minutes ticked away and Ruth was desperate to know what was happening, she hadn't heard any raised voices from her sister's room so she had to assume that however Becky was handling it, at least she hadn't gone into a screaming fit! Her thoughts drifted to her mother and to all the things she'd said to them about their father; horrible things and, being so young, they had believed her. He hadn't been there for them and to their knowledge he had never tried to contact them. She tried to view it as an outsider, to analyse it factually. For whatever reasons their parents had broken up; it happens. Their mother had consistently slagged him off to them, poisoning their young minds and although he hadn't really told her his version of the events, he had never once said a bad word about their mother. Her mind again jumped back to the fact that to their knowledge he had never tried to contact them … She quickly dismissed the thoughts; after all, she reasoned, things are never in black and white, there is always a rational explanation as to why things either do, or don't happen. She so desperately wanted him to be the knight in shining armour who had been wrongly judged…

The door to Becky's room opened, breaking her thought pattern. Tanner appeared in the doorframe and left the room. Her eyes flashed up to the clock on the hospital wall: he'd been in with Becky for forty minutes. She told herself that that had to be a good sign. Apprehensively she caught his eyes, and he gave her a relieved smile as he approached her.

"How did it go?"

"Okay, it was awkward at first, neither of us really knew how to act around each other so it started off quite formally and just like you warned me, her attitude was quite frosty, but she asked questions and I answered them as honestly as I could…"

"What do you mean, as you could?" Ruth asked accusingly.

"You have to remember I've spent my entire career working for the Security Services and I'm restricted by the Official Secrets Act as well as current National Security regulations."

"Yes, of course...I'm sorry, I wasn't thinking."

"But I'm pleased to say that while it was the expected rocky relationship at first, I felt that in a small way we got to know each other and I'd like to think that as time goes on she will slowly become fond of me."

"I think she will..." Ruth's face beamed with pleasure as she spoke, "... deep down she's a good person. The most important thing for me is that we've all found each other, and I want us all to move on and look to the future."

Chapter 15

Together

John Tanner continued with his daily visits to the hospital, only now he wasn't relegated to just sitting in the waiting area. He remained selective with his answers to both the girls' questions and because Ruth had readily accepted her father and formed a close relationship, Becky slowly began to see him through her sister's eyes and warmed to him. This in turn had a positive effect upon her and her new found happiness aided her recovery. Sandra Atkins, her doctor was happy to release her from hospital and into Ruth's care for rehabilitation.

With the immediate worry of Becky's health now moved from the forefront of the girls' minds, their thoughts moved to their father, and curiosity took more of a hold. Their questions about his current life had been answered, but they wanted to meet with his friends, they wanted to see the places he frequented, but more importantly, they wanted to meet with his significant other.

Their light-hearted nagging eventually wore him down and he agreed to their meeting Maureen. Because Becky still wasn't one hundred percent fit for an evening out, he decided the initial meeting should be a pub lunch. He chose what was now his regular pub: The Three Kings. Ernie Palmer had also agreed to join them, and so the date was set, and although they would only be having a bar-meal, the lunch time trade at the Three Kings was renowned for its bustle and the constant ebb and flow of its clientele. Maureen therefore pre-booked them a table.

The day arrived and Tanner booked a taxi, collected both Ruth and Becky and took them to the pub. Maureen and Ernie arrived separately from their respective offices. Outside the pub the girls alighted from the taxi and stood on the pavement, waiting while Tanner paid the driver. Becky felt relaxed and happy and was casually glancing around looking at nothing in particular when suddenly she realised she was looking directly into the eyes of Marion Perkins whose look of hatred, burning back at her from where she sat in the front passenger seat of a passing car being driven by her spaced-out brother Pete, sent a cold shiver right through her.

"Becks? Are you okay?" Her sister Ruth snapped her out of her momentary daze.

"Yes, sorry I was just daydreaming for a moment." Becky smiled unconvincingly.

"Well, whatever you were dreaming about, it must have been a creature from hell going by the expression on your face!"

"D'you know what…sometimes you can hit the nail right on the head! But as for now, I'm feeling rather peckish." Becky turned and entered the pub.

Maureen and Ernie stood at the bar and greeted the trio as they approached them. Introductions were made, appropriate hugs and pleasantries were exchanged. Drinks were ordered from the bar and they eventually moved to a round table reserved for them. Tanner sat with his back to the bar, Maureen sat on his left and Ruth sat on his right. Ernie Palmer sat next to Ruth and Becky sat between Maureen and Ernie. Becky and Ernie were the only two facing the main bar area.

During the meal the conversation was light-hearted. Maureen and Ernie told the girls various amusing anecdotes about their father and as Ruth looked at her sister she realised that she couldn't remember when she had last seen her in such a cheerful mood; her laughter was genuine, her happiness was whole and she was thoroughly enjoying herself.

Becky excused herself for a visit to the ladies and as she left, Ernie chuckled and nodded towards the back of Tanner and said, "Hey John, turn around and look at that bloke who has just come in. The hair, the moustache, the beard – he's a dead-ringer for King Charles the First if ever I've seen one."

Tanner turned slowly in his chair and looked at the man, then he looked back at Ernie. "Well I suppose it makes a change from some of the usual lunchtime pantomime characters we get in here!" he grinned.

"He's got lovely hair though," added Ruth. "For a girl!"

"The eyes are cold, though," Maureen said guardedly. "The eyes tell me he's someone to be wary of…"

"Talking of eyes…" Ernie interrupted, "…I've been thinking of having laser surgery on mine; apparently it makes them feel as good as new."

"Oh yes, a woman in our office had her eyes corrected by laser, she said it's the best thing she's ever done," Ruth said, nodding her approval.

"Yeah, but I've also heard horror stories about it as well," put in Tanner.

"What are you talking about now?" Becky asked as she rejoined them.

"Eye surgery," answered Ruth.

"What is it about old people, that when you get together you have to talk about operations?" Becky teased.

"I'm not old!" protested Ruth.

"Maybe not, but you act like it!" Becky responded quickly.

Maureen laughed at their banter. "You two remind me of my own children when they were at home…"

Before she could finish, Becky let out a blood curdling scream and as they all looked up at her, they saw that her face had drained, and she was looking over the head of Tanner into the lunchtime swarm of customers milling around the bar area. Tanner spun around in his chair and as he did so, two deafeningly loud explosions filled the pub, followed by the sound of tables and chairs tipping over as people panicked. Drink and glasses flew in all directions, adding to the piercing high-pitched sound as women screamed. As Tanner turned, he found himself looking into the face of King Charles the First, whose arm was

outstretched and holding a hand-gun, an automatic pistol, pointing it at them ....
no, pointing it over their heads, pointing it at Becky. In that same split second
Tanner saw the man's eyes; they were eyes that had no reflection, eyes you could
not see into, but you knew someone in there could see out. He felt a cold shiver;
he was looking into the man's lifeless eyes.

The gunman's body appeared to have stopped in its movement towards
them, as though an invisible shield had stopped him in his tracks. Tanner then
saw the two red patches of bright red blood appear on the chest of the man's
white shirt, the two patches in almost a nano second merged into one and the
man's body dropped to the floor.

Tanner turned back and faced his table. There, standing behind Maureen
with gun in hand, was the dark haired, brown leather jacket he'd seen at the
hospital, only this time he was wearing a navy blue blazer. Another man beside
him in a light grey suit was talking into a mobile phone, then he leaned across
and spoke quietly to Maureen; she nodded her approval, her eyes caught
Tanner's and she gave him a reassuring smile.

Ruth had her arms around Becky, like a mother protecting her off-spring.
Tanner quickly moved to behind the two girls and placed his arms around both
their shoulders. Only moments had passed since the shooting but to Tanner time
had slowed down. In his head he had travelled back more than twenty years and
the vividness of running gun battles with Irish terrorists replayed in his memory.
He became aware of Maureen's voice talking to him and as his eyes again found
hers, she handed him a small bunch of keys.

"John, I have a car arriving any moment take the girls to my house. I'll
deal with this and meet you there later." She turned to Ernie. "You come back
with me, and I'll coordinate what statement we give to the police."

The dark blue blazer approached Tanner, his eyes indicating a rear exit.
"Leave by that door, it leads to an alley; at the end of the alley we have a car
waiting."
Tanner nodded his gratitude and with his arms still around his daughters'
shoulders he ushered them towards the exit.

"How is Becky?" Maureen Dickins had just arrived back at her house
and it was her first question.

"She was expectedly quite shaken up. There's no physical damage but
it's really screwed her up in her head," replied Tanner as he threw ice cubes into
a couple of small tumblers and topped them with whisky.

"That's understandable. The poor kid – just when she thought the
nightmare was over..." She took the tumbler from Tanner and sipped the
whisky.

"I take it that it was you who sent the Department's own doctor to look
at her?" he asked.

"No. Actually it was your old section head, Sebastian Toakes. I believe if you drill down through his layers of formality you'll find that he actually likes you."

"Well, he's certainly building up on the number of favours I owe him. Anyway, the doctor gave Becky a strong sedative and Ruth put her to bed in one of your spare rooms; I hope that was okay?"

"Good grief, yes! Take it as read."

"Your man, the one who I saw at the hospital and today at the pub – I didn't get the chance to shake his hand and thank him…"

"He thought the gunman was coming after me; those two were there for my protection," she answered candidly.

"You need protection now?" There was no hiding the surprise in his voice.

"John, you're well aware that I've been Acting Director for this past eighteen months and it's been hinted to me that I've now been earmarked for the position to be made permanent, and with our national security being at the level it is, it was deemed appropriate that I should have close protection." She held his gaze as she spoke.

"I'm pleased for you, but more pleased that your protection officer had such quick reactions."

"I've actually reported the incident as having been an attempt on my life…it meant we were able to issue a DA Notice 5, keeping it out of the media but, more importantly, it will keep Becky's name out of the news."

"Thanks Maureen." Tanner's tone was heartfelt.

"She will still need to speak to a Special Branch officer. It was obvious that it wasn't just the gun that spooked her. She also knew the man holding it."

"Have you identified him?"

"Oh yes, Tony Chandler, an extremely nasty piece of work who I believe the Metropolitan Police believe is responsible for a number of gangland shootings."

"Known associates?"

"The name at the top of the list is none other than Dougie Mann, in whom I again believe the Police have a special interest!"

"So it definitely was Becky that he was going after!" Tanner gave a deep sigh.

"Yes, and unfortunately Becky also knows it now."

"Do you have a safe house I could use until I can arrange somewhere to hide her?"

"Kamalika is already arranging it. The only thing that I can't offer you is twenty-four hour protection; she's not a national security issue so even I can't bend the rules…if you want it, I can arrange it but it will fall under police jurisdiction."

"No! I don't want that...not while one of them is possibly on Dougie Mann's payroll." Tanner's earlier conversation about DS Priack sprang into his mind.

"I can recommend a freelance from outside the department you may be able to use, but he's not cheap," suggested Maureen as she drained the remainder of her whisky.

"I appreciate the offer but I have a contact of my own who owes me a few favours."

"Who?"

"It doesn't matter."

"It does matter if you're putting him into one of my safe houses!" Maureen's tone was adamant.

"Okay, it's Gabby."

"Gabby!"

"Yes Gabby. He's nobody's fool, he's useful with a gun and he doesn't mind getting his hands dirty! If Dougie Mann decides to send a team after Becky then Gabby's the man I'd prefer to have with me."

"Okay, it's your decision, but make sure you keep him on a leash."

Chapter 16

Gabriel Bracken

Gabriel Bracken resembled the typical stereotype nightclub bouncer-cum-gangster. His thick set frame holding together his fifteen stone body of muscle gave a perpetual aura of menace. Where Bracken differed from the stereotype was that he also had a highly intelligent mind, analytical, questioning and above all, alert. Where he matched the stereotype was in muscle, violence and menace.

Known to all his friends as Gabby. Ex-paratrooper, ex-Security Service operative and now currently for hire as a close protection security and guarding specialist. In his chosen field he was considered one of the best, so much so, that his services had frequently been employed by British Embassies who found within his area of expertise an absolute discretion in all matters, however dirty, to be a most desirable forte. During the period he'd been employed by the UK Security Services, he'd worked in John Tanner's section, with Tanner as his Section Head. Bracken became a deep penetration agent, a role that Tanner himself had held many years earlier during the late eighties.

Bracken however found himself in a terrorist group on foreign soil, a group with the sole intention of destabilising a new independent state, a country freed from its previous communist shackles, still in its infancy and reaching out for political friendship with the government of the United Kingdom. The terrorist group was made up of the usual anarchists and criminals along with many foreigners and foreign paymasters. Bracken installed himself as a deep cover operative and John Tanner was his main handler. As time went on Bracken became deeply embedded within the group, and whilst from his position of trust he was able to hinder attacks on major installations, to avoid any suspicions he planned and accompanied the group on various kidnappings and occasional violent attacks. He was under instructions not to expose his undercover status under any circumstances until the group's ultimate paymaster could be identified.

Unfortunately events don't always follow the wishes of man. When the group's operational commander informed him they had been instructed to assassinate the Country's newly elected Prime Minister he knew it was time for the state police to raid and arrest the group before any plans could be set in motion.

John Tanner reported the plot to his own handlers in London and they in turn informed him to do nothing. The plot was set and both Gabby and his operational commander, known only as Petrovic, would be the triggermen.

The place would be the Prime Minister's summer residence and on the night chosen for his assassination he would be staying there on an unofficial stopover. He would be in his office alone, no wife, no children, no aides, just a couple of personal protection guards and a minimal amount of house staff. A lone police car would be stationed at the end of the drive.

On the day in question both men were smuggled into the house and hidden. Later that evening the Prime Minister arrived, and after dismissing the few members of the house staff, poured himself a drink and settled down alone in his office with a quantity of government papers to review. Gabby and Petrovic left their hiding place and moved slowly towards the Prime Minister's office; Gabby instinctively checked the magazine in his pistol was full, replaced it then slid the safety catch off and cocked it ready to fire. Petrovic gently twisted the door handle and they both burst through into the office. The Prime Minister looked up at them, his eyes wide, but he didn't utter a sound, almost as though he had accepted the inevitable. Petrovic extended his arm, his automatic pistol pointed directly towards the man's face, but before he could release a volley of bullets, Gabby placed the barrel of his own gun against Petrovic's temple and squeezed the trigger, decorating part of the Prime Minister's bookcase with Petrovic's brains.

Gabby was immediately apprehended by the PM's security men and taken to one of their interrogation blocks. He exposed himself as an undercover operative and gave a full breakdown on all the group's activities. The police subsequently arrested the group, and seized a large cache of weapons and explosives. The surrounding publicity highlighted the fact that a number of foreigners were active within the group, all of them known terrorists from Jordan, Syria, and Eastern Europe and a British National who claimed to be working for the British Security Services. Gabriel Bracken was charged with multiple counts of kidnapping, robbery and various other terrorist activities.

Her Majesty's Government remained silent; politically they had apparently changed their allegiance from the fledgling country. Tanner was recalled to London. The official line was one of damage limitation and Gabriel Bracken was deemed expendable.

John Tanner, however, viewed it differently; he wasn't prepared to allow one of his own men be hung out to dry. He hatched his plan and using the department's own resources had forged documents prepared, documents so authentic looking they would deceive officials of a foreign country, deceive them into believing that their own Prime Minister had agreed and signed authorisation for the prisoner Gabriel Bracken to be handed over the UK's government representative, a Mr John Tanner, and without any further hindrance be escorted to a nominated airport for deportation.

When Tanner and Bracken arrived back in the UK the shit truly had hit the fan within the so-called corridors of power of both the Foreign Office and the headquarters of the Security Services at Century House in Lambeth. Whilst no action was brought against Bracken, Tanner faced a disciplinary hearing, the result of which meant that he was moved from what was known as MI6 to domestic homeland security. Due to Bracken's high profile it was deemed prudent to transfer him also. Tanner now had a much smaller section and Bracken remained part of it, along with an in-depth loyalty to Tanner.

Tanner, as always, was effective and efficient in seeking, monitoring and eradicating any threat to her Majesty, her government, her subjects and the country's economic interests. Until, that is… Gabby again brought himself to their masters' attention. He had been profiling and trailing a particular suspect; he had little proof but a very big intuition that something big and bad was about to happen. He didn't know what or where or when or how, but it was causing him sleepless nights and a severe loss of appetite.

One evening he was following the suspect to a warehouse that the man used from time to time. The man wasn't his usual alert self; he was slovenly, which Bracken quickly picked up as indicating that he was in fact being led into a trap. He continued following and, as he entered into the darkened recesses of the building, two men came at him brandishing knives, their intention obvious. Bracken caught the first man in a headlock and, twisting it hard, snapped the man's neck. He allowed the body to fall and narrowly avoided having his arm dismembered as the suspect he'd been following slashed at him with what resembled a small sword. Gabby was trapped in a corner; the man came at him again, slashing. Gabby had nowhere to go, and instinctively he raised his hands to protect himself; with the weight of the momentum the small sword cut through to the bone on his forearm. He brought his knee up into the man's groin and with his good arm lashed out at the man's chin with such a force he not only dislocated the man's jaw but also rendered him instantly unconscious.

When the man regained consciousness he found he was tied to a chair. Bracken had used the man's shirt as a makeshift bandage on his own arm and as the man's eyes opened it was met with Bracken's fist from his good arm wreaking revenge. Bracken began his own vision of interrogation with his fist coming into play when the answers he required were not forthcoming.

At the end of the session the man's face was a bloody pulp and Gabriel Bracken was in possession of the location of the terrorist group's cache of weapons, explosives and, more importantly, a list of their imminent targets. That night the lives of a high court judge and a senior member of parliament was saved as the anti-terrorist arm of the Metropolitan police foiled the assassination attempt.

Unfortunately for Bracken the man was also the son of a high ranking foreign diplomat. John Tanner defended Bracken stating that he believed the end justified the means, as the lives of two men had been saved, but when it became obvious that the hierarchy were looking for a sacrificial lamb to appease the diplomat, then Tanner let rip. He accused them of being gutless, and of being more interested in pandering to a foreign diplomat and the likes of his murdering son, than protecting a hard working operative trying to protect the safety of the country and particularly its prominent citizens. In typical John Tanner style he went over the top and was subsequently charged with gross insubordination, the result of which he lost his seniority and was demoted to a desk job. Gabriel Bracken completed his recuperation from his injury, then promptly resigned and commenced work as a freelance. He and Tanner had remained friends and although they rarely met, Tanner had ensured that Gabby received his fair share of contract work.

Chapter 17

Reunion

John Tanner parked his car and walked across the hotel car park. It was a large car park and as he passed the rows of cars, their numbers gave the impression of spanning every make and model available. Vehicles and people appeared to be arriving and leaving in a constant stream. The occasional sales reps sat in their cars administering their paperwork.

He'd arrived only a few minutes before the agreed time; it was the perfect meeting place, a place so busy they would never be noticed. The hotel reception, as expected, was buzzing with activity. Tanner walked through the lobby, into the dining room and sat at an empty table in the corner; from this position he could clearly see the main entrance and across the car park.

A waitress approached him. "Excuse me sir, have you booked a table?"

"Yes, a table for two in the name of Harry Albion," replied Tanner.

"Would you like to see a menu, Mr Albion, or would you rather wait for your guest?"

"Actually I'd like a pot of tea for two." He watched her produce a small pad, scribble onto it and then move away. His eyes scanned the main entrance as he awaited the arrival of his guest. The waitress returned and brought a tray containing a pot of tea, biscuits and two cups to the table. She placed them on the table and as she left, another figure appeared by his side.

"I've been watching you since you arrived – you're becoming careless…" Tanner recognised the voice immediately and as he stood up a broad smile was already beaming across his face.

"Gabby, how the devil are you…it's bloody good to see you!" The two men hugged, a hug that only men who have faced death together would understand. They sat and Tanner poured tea into each of the two china cups; he passed a cup across to Gabby along with a plate of assorted biscuits. "Have a biscuit."

"Thanks, but I was thinking more along the lines of a good piss up and a night on the town," he said light heartedly.

"This is work…well actually, I need a favour and then it's work."

"Affirmative John, the favour's already there for you, just say what it is and I'll do it!"

Tanner nodded slowly. "Thanks, but it's a little complicated." Just then the waitress reappeared and handed a leather bound menu to each of the men; they both gave it a fleeting glance, then ordered the first item that took their eye. They both watched as she again produced her small pad, scribbled onto it, collected the menus from them and then moved away.

Tanner told Gabby about the circumstances of his reunion with his daughters, and about how Becky had been kidnapped, gang raped and forced to work as a prostitute. He told of her escape and the subsequent shooting that left her on the brink of death whilst killing Danny Dolan. He told Gabby what he knew of Dougie Mann, the rumours about DS Priack being on his payroll and the recent attempt on Becky's life in the pub. Gabby's first reaction was to offer to terminate the men involved in harming Becky, thus completely removing any future threat. Tanner could see the logic but reminded him they had to stay within the law. He suggested that Gabby should meet Becky, especially as he would be around protecting her.

They finished the meal, discussing old times and bringing each other up to date on developments since they had last met – which they realised had been almost two years ago. The meal finished, they returned to their vehicles and Gabby followed Tanner's car to the safe house where Becky was convalescing.

The house was a three bedroomed semi-detached house, identical to every other house on a housing estate that in itself was identical to every other housing estate. It had a small driveway on which Tanner parked his car. Gabby parked his car on the road outside. Becky was sitting up in bed talking to Ruth when they arrived. He kissed both his daughters on the cheek and then introduced Gabriel Bracken as someone who was going to be keeping a close eye on Becky's well-being.

"Forget all that Gabriel crap, call me Gabby…any family of John's is family of mine." Tanner could see that Becky had warmed to Gabby almost immediately and so he and Ruth left them to acquaint themselves.

Ruth and Becky were sharing the master bedroom, which left the middle sized bedroom for Gabby and the small box room for Tanner. When the girls were asleep, Tanner and Gabby sat in the kitchen sharing the last half of a bottle of whisky.

"Y'know Becky really opened up to me when we were chatting; it was like she finally had someone to confide in who wasn't a dad or a sister."

"I was hoping she would. What did you find out?" asked Tanner.

"She said that the day you all met Maureen, prior to going in the pub she saw a girl who used to run in their little gang: a Marian Perkins Apparently she and her brother were driving past and the girl looked straight at her and recognised her; the next thing a hit man is visiting you all in the pub and Becky doesn't believe in coincidences…"

"Now, that's interesting…she hasn't mentioned that to anyone else," Tanner observed.

"That's because you're family John…you're too close. This girl Marian lives with her brother; apparently they're the incest king and queen of East London. Becky used to have a close mate, a girl called Hannah who was running quite a successful – albeit illegal – little business."

"Yes, I think Ruth has mentioned her."

"Well this girl Hannah was well and truly stitched up in court. Becky also mentioned the name of that bent copper you told me about; he was also involved in the stitch-up and one of those arseholes who had her locked up in the house bragged that it had all been a set up so that a Dougie Mann could add her little operation to his own business empire."

"Yes, that ties up with what I've heard about him," concurred Tanner.

"There's one other thing about which she became quite emotional…"

"What's that?" Tanner frowned.

"There were two other girls in that house with her, one of them an Indian girl called Harvey; they became close mates and she's worried about her. There's also another girl, a young teenager who was brought down from up north. I get the impression that Becky was a bit like a mother hen towards her. Anyway, when she escaped she promised the girl she'd go back for her and now that she's heard the house was empty when the police raided it she feels she's let the girl down and because she's bottled it up inside her, she's becoming quite emotionally upset."

"D'you know something Gabby, you are absolutely incredible! You got more out of her in half an hour than me, the police, her sister…"

"I know…I've got an irresistible smile!" he grinned back.

"Maybe this girl Marian Perkins should be our first port of call?"

"Actually John, I've got a better idea. I have the keys to a medium sized industrial unit – the owners had to leave the country rather quickly on account of some fraudulent insurance claims they were involved in, and I was hired to keep an eye on the premises. It's a cold and dank place, semi secluded and just right for scaring somebody shitless."

"You've got the keys to the place?" asked Tanner.

"They're jangling in my pocket as we speak."

"Well, there's no time like the present, so let's go get the bitch; we'll take my car," said Tanner jumping up from his chair.

"Let me grab some bits out of my car and I'll be with you!" Gabby drained his whisky and followed Tanner outside.

Just under an hour had passed when Tanner eased his car onto a large concreted area, which was the allocated parking area for the surrounding block of flats and maisonettes. Along one side was a row of lock-up garages, which had long since been left to the local hooligan element. Graffiti covered every wall and garage door. The shell of a burnt-out car remained, almost as a display of ownership. Some of the garages had had their doors torn off, others remained open. A few were firmly padlocked but unused. Tanner slowed the car and parked behind a burnt-out shell of a van. He looked out through the car's side window and a feeling of deja vu sent a brief shiver through him. Gabby opened the front passenger door of the car and stepped out into the night. Tanner followed suit, the stench of dirt, dust, vomit and stale tobacco hit them hard as they breathed in the night air.

As they stood outside the door of the maisonette Gabby spoke softly to Tanner. "What do you fancy John, ringing the doorbell or a good old fashioned forced entry?" Before he had the chance to answer, the front door of the house opened. A muscular girl with short hair and mannish features stood before them. She showed no nervousness at their presence; she'd mistaken them for CID officers and looked down her nose at them as she spoke.

"I suppose you want to come in?"

"That depends, we're looking for a Marian Perkins," responded Tanner.

"Who wants to know?" she snapped back aggressively.

"Just answer the question, you inbred slag!" Gabby spat the words at her.

It was a response she wasn't expecting; the expression on her face showed her surprise, but just as quickly she regained her aggressive composure. "No, you go and fuck yourself instead. You're just a couple of flash bastards with a bit of power!"

A voice called out from inside, "Marian shut that fucking door will yer…it's cold enough in here without that being left open!"

Gabby pulled out his pistol and held it to her face with the tip of the barrel against her teeth. "You make one sound and your teeth are going to be flying out the back of your head along with your brains…now nod if you understand me."

Her eyes opened wide in fear as she nodded. Tanner quickly wrapped thick insulating tape across her mouth, and then placed a dirty sack over her head while Gabby secured her hands behind her back with plastic cable ties. They led her towards Tanner's car. Gabby was about to put her in the back seat when Tanner remembered Becky's experience of travelling in the boot of a car.

"Wait a minute, I don't want her in with me, she can ride in the boot!" The boot was opened and Marian was unceremoniously thrown in. They took the motorway route outside London to the outskirts of Luton. They turned off the motorway; Tanner followed Gabby's instructions as they drove along a series of B-roads and then stopped at a closed wooded farm gate. Gabby got out and opening the gate, beckoned to Tanner to move forward; he then closed the gate and climbed back into the front passenger seat. The vehicle moved forward and pulled up outside a red bricked industrial warehouse. Smaller, unused buildings stood opposite the warehouse, creating a courtyard effect to the cluster. The two men climbed out of the car and entered the building, leaving Marian in the boot, following the same pattern that Becky had been made to endure.

As the lights inside the building changed from a dull glow into brightness it highlighted the floating dust particles they were now breathing. "Hells bells, Gabby – when was the last time this place was used?" Tanner asked as he attempted to refrain from inhaling the dirt-contaminated air.

"Let's just say occasionally and briefly…" Gabby replied as he positioned and switched on two industrial air blowers. He set the temperature to cold. He then went across and into a far corner office and returned with two full-length padded coats; he threw one of them towards Tanner. "Here, put this on…that bitch out there is going to freeze but I don't see why we should!"

Tanner pulled on the heavy padded coat. "How are we gonna play this?"

"We'll try the good guy, bad guy routine…she doesn't come across as being the brightest spark, so with that and the cold, she'll probably tell us everything we want to know quite quickly." Gabby then went outside, and after a few moments returned with Marian. She was still tied, gagged and hooded. He positioned her at the point where the cold air from the two blowers met. He held his gun to her head, lifted the hood slightly and ripped off the insulating tape covering her mouth, causing her to yelp. "Okay, I'm now going to untie your hands and I want you to strip, down to your underwear. You are not to attempt to remove your hood, do you understand?"

Marian nodded in a positive gesture and as her hands were freed she began removing her clothes, rushing as though in the belief that the faster she stripped, the more it would please her captives. Gabby kicked her clothes away; he could see her body shiver as the blasts of cold air hit it with a ferocious impact.

"If you want sex, it's okay, I'm willing…I'll do anything you want…anything." Her tone was a cross between whimpering and pleading.

"You have got to be joking…I've put better trash in the dustbin!" Gabby spat the words at her, and then winked at Tanner as he continued, "I've had enough of this. Get down on your knees, bitch!" As she knelt he nudged her leg ensuring they were crossed at the ankles. "Hands behind your back, bitch!" he yelled, and this time as she moved her arms behind her he placed the barrel of his gun against the base of her skull. She was now positioned in the method of the traditional gangland assassination.

As the two men looked down at her, she was kneeling in a puddle of her own urine, the wet streaks still evident on her thighs where it had run down to her knees. She was sobbing, sobbing so hard that Tanner became concerned she would choke.

"Say goodbye to world, bitch!" Gabby clicked back the hammer on his pistol, looked up at Tanner and nodded: it was Tanner's signal. Tanner rushed between them and knocked Gabby's gun away; the pistol exploded still close to her head, Marian screamed and more urine joined the puddle on the floor between her knees. She appeared traumatised; the sack on her head hid the fact from her that Gabby had fired a blank.

"Let's give the kid a chance!" Tanner yelled, "Maybe she'll willingly tell us want we want to know."

"No, scum like this…they never tell…she won't tell us jack shit, let's end it now!" Gabby pushed the barrel of his gun back against Marian head.

"Let's just try it my way first..." Tanner played the good guy role, "...you go outside and wait; if she doesn't answer every question you can come back in and blow her brains out, and I'll admit you were right!" Gabby removed the gun and stepped backwards. Tanner leaned close to the sacked hood and whispered, "I want chapter and verse...I want everything you know about Dougie Mann and if what you tell me is useful, then you'll live, if not then my friend will return and I'll leave you alone with him."

"Please, I'll tell you everything...but I'm so cold..." Marian's teeth chattered as she spoke.

"Then I suggest you stand up and start talking because if my mate comes back in here you really won't have to worry about the cold!" Tanner took hold of her arm and helped pull her to her feet. Gabby produced a digital voice recorder from his pocket and began recording. Marian Perkins talked and told them everything she had ever heard relating to Dougie Mann and Kevin Crestwell. Often she had to repeat it, as they couldn't understand her words due to the chattering of her teeth.

Eventually she had no more to tell, and Tanner threw her clothes at her feet. "Get dressed!"

"What're we going to do with her...we can't let her live." Gabby was back in bad guy role.

"I don't know, she's a clever girl, maybe there could be a place for her in our organisation." Tanner spoke as though he was throwing her a lifeline.

"You must be mad...she'd have to do more than prove her loyalty before she joins our firm!" scoffed Gabby.

"How's she going to do that – can you think of a way?"

"No! Let me put a bullet in her head...then you won't have to worry about it." Gabby moved his gun close to the sacked hood and pulled back the hammer, ensuring she could hear the click.

"Wait a minute, I've just thought of something." Tanner leaned forward to the sacked hood. "If you were to go to the police and tell them everything that you've just told me...I think that would be a good sign that you could be trusted."

Marian's head inside the hooded sack nodded affirmatively.

"Of course..." Tanner continued, "...if you betrayed this trust I'm putting in you, then my friend here would find you and execute you, you do understand that don't you?"

Once again Marian's head inside the hooded sack nodded.

Tanner gave a deep sigh. "Okay, for the moment you can live...let's get you back home. You can travel in the boot again."

They made good time; it was still early morning when they arrived back in East London, close to where Marian lived. Tanner brought the car to a stop near to an alleyway. A few early morning risers were milling around. Tanner and

Gabby sat in the car and when they were comfortable that no one was close by, they jumped out of the car, released the boot lid and yanked Marian out. Tanner ran back to the car while Gabby dragged her a little way up the alley, threw her to the floor then ran back to join Tanner and as he climbed into the front passenger seat the car sped away with a screech of tyres.

They drove in silence for a while and then Tanner spoke. "D'you know, at times I was uncomfortable with that. A voice at the back of my head kept saying *this girl isn't a terrorist*, and as I saw just how pitiful she was…the thought crossed my mind, are we using a sledgehammer to crack a walnut?"

"Would you have felt better attending Becky's funeral?" Gabby replied, deliberately casually.

"What a stupid question, of course I wouldn't!" retorted Tanner.

"John, that girl has just told us how she was involved in setting up Becky's friend Hannah so that she would receive a hefty prison sentence and, not being content with that, they arranged for the kid to have her face slashed once she was in there. She told us how it was agreed that Becky would be beaten until she had no more resistance and then forced to work as a prostitute. She told us how she informed a Kevin Crestwell that she'd seen Becky outside a pub, which set the wheels in motion for a renowned hit man to pay a visit to the pub. Ask yourself what would have happened if Maureen Dickins and her protection team hadn't been there. Would he have just hit Becky, or would you and Ruth also be laying on a slab of marble beside her?" Gabby emphasized the last sentence.

"Yeah, you're right, I think it's this new daddy thing; I'm still getting to grips with it." Tanner's tone showed his recognition that the softer side of his emotions were now becoming a bigger part of his personality.

"One of the first things you said to me years ago when I first started working for you was that if you take your eye off the ball for just a minute, then you're dead! You need to be careful John – just make sure you haven't forgotten when the ball is!"

"That's why I've brought you in Gabby. You're still a first team player … I'm the old hand who has dropped into the reserve team."

"Nah! You've still got it John and believe me, when it's needed then you'll be the man to watch."

"I'm glad you still think that Gabby." But in his mind Tanner still had his doubts.

Early the following week Tanner received a call from Kamalika.

"Hello John, it's Kamalika, can you talk?"

A number of flippant comments sprang to mind but he refrained. "Yes."

"As we agreed, I've been monitoring the ongoing police investigation concerning Dougie Mann."

"Oh yes, and have they actually done anything?" Tanner's sarcasm wasn't lost on Kamalika.

"Well yes, they have…there's been rather a surprising development actually. A young woman has gone to the police and made a full statement, including detailed information regarding some of the recent activities of Dougie Mann and gang."

"Who is she?" He pretended ignorance.

"Her name is Marian Perkins. Apparently she was loosely connected to his gang."

"And how good was her information?"

"Quite thorough, and the police acted quickly. They conducted a dawn raid at all his known premises, at near-enough the same time, but unfortunately he had either anticipated their action or had been tipped off, as he appears to have gone to ground without leaving a trace."

"What about the rest of his gang…the inner circle ones?"

"No, only the foot soldiers were picked up; all the main names have disappeared along with Mann."

"Are any of them talking?" Tanner had smelled a rat.

"One or two are hoping to make a deal, but overall they're staying tight lipped!"

"This doesn't feel right…have they got anything other than the girl's statement?"

"At the moment it's the girl's statement and Becky's statement, but a good defence lawyer will rip them to shreds, which is why the police are still collecting whatever evidence they can get their hands on …but there is a more worrying aspect…"

"What's that?" The concern in his voice was all too evident.

"One of my contacts at the station told me that two of the men arrested in one of the early morning raids were questioned and released. The arresting officer claimed he was satisfied the men had no connection with the enquiry. A uniformed sergeant, who knew of the men, noticed that their names had been mis-spelled on the report – seriously mis-spelled – and when he brought it to the arresting officer's attention, there was, shall we say an angry exchange of words! The men's names appeared earlier on Becky's statement as Costi and Andrei."

"I believe I already know the answer, but who was the arresting officer?"

"A Detective Sergeant Priack."

"Yep, I was spot on!"

"You also need to be aware that DS Priack has made a formal complaint, and that in order to be able to conduct his investigation efficiently he needs to know the whereabouts of Becky Wilson."

"Have they told him where she is?"

"No, because they don't know. Maureen let it be known that you had taken her away for a couple of weeks to convalesce, but they will eventually need to know…if this is going to court than Becky is a key witness."

"I know and it also makes her a key target!"

"I've got to go now John, but I'll keep you updated."

"Yeah, thanks Kamalika…listen, I may sound a bit grumpy but I really do appreciate your help."

"You don't have to thank me John. I've read Becky's statement…I just want these monsters locked away for a long, long time!"

"I guarantee that one way or another, they will be off the streets."

"Goodbye John."

Chapter 18

Becky

I was bored, bored, bored! I was stuck in a strange house, I wasn't allowed out and I'd have run out of things to do. I'd read plenty of books and I'd used the internet on Ruth's laptop, but the boredom was getting to me. I slept quite a lot through the day but when I was up I felt like I was going stir crazy.

Ruth was like the nursemaid from hell! I knew she had my welfare at heart and everything was done with the best of intentions, but if I used the bathroom, she was outside the door; if I showered then she was standing there waiting to wrap me in a towel. Dr Atkins had said I must rest quietly and eat a sensible and healthy diet; she visited every other day, supposedly to check on me, her patient. But to be honest she just prattled on for a bit, and then cleared off to see Ruth! I followed her out into the living room once and sat with them. Ruth just stared at me icily – talk about if looks could kill – so I left them alone and wandered back into the bedroom and read another uninteresting chick-lit novel.

One of the things the doctor had also advised was that I should do some gentle exercises to keep my blood flowing and my muscles loose but most importantly some deep breathing exercises, and so every day Commandant Ruth used her snotty voice to take me through her schedule of pelvic tilts, neck circles, and leg lifts amongst others. Then another time, she'd thoroughly pamper me. She'd sit and do my makeup, my nails, my hair and once even a foot massage; she always instinctively knew when my spirits needed a lift.

My other main visitor was Gabby. He was one of Dad's friends from the Intelligence Services and he was great; he always had a humorous tale to tell me, or he'd come out with some witty comment when I was least expecting it, so I'd go into fits of giggles. If he followed it up by pulling one of his funny faces, normally aimed at Ruth, then I just fell about.

Ruth wasn't too keen on him. She'd never actually said why, but it seemed to stem from the time we noticed he was wearing a shoulder holster. I mean, he was here to protect us, so I supposed he had to have it, but Ruth didn't think anybody should have guns around me in light of what had happened. I thought it was just her being over protective again.

Dad either visited or phoned every day and for the first time in my life I had a parent that I actually loved … and I mean loved. He was my Dad. He was everything I could ever dream of in a Dad and every day as my contentment grew, my dislike of Madge intensified for keeping him from us.

Dad was trying to find somewhere else for us to stay; he was quite evasive and wouldn't go into too much detail as to why, but Gabby knew all about it and filled in the blanks for me when he came to see me one day.

Apparently Dad's ex boss – some guy called Toakes – had called at Dad's flat with the excuse that he'd heard that Dad was going to publish a book about his life and experiences in the Security Services and advised him not to! Dad apparently told him where to shove his advice; I'd often wondered from whom I'd inherited my streak of rebelliousness! Anyway this guy Toakes then revealed the real purpose of his visit, which was to tell Dad that the Security Services safe houses were provided at Government expense for matters relating to national security only, adding that his daughter did not fall into that category.

Gabby said that Dad really laid into the guy verbally, but it didn't do him any good, and Toakes finished off by saying that if he wanted a safe house then he should provide for it himself at his own personal expense. If Gabby hadn't have been there to stop him, Dad would probably have punched out Toakes's lights!

Gabby also told me that the police would want to speak to me regarding any future legal action they would take against Dougie Mann, Kevin Crestwell, or Andrei and Costi. He also warned me that DS Priack was insisting on knowing my whereabouts, but told me not to worry as anyone with any silly thoughts about me would have to go through him first. Then he gave me a hug, and something about that hug told me that I was safe and everything was going to be okay.

Ruth arrived at that point, took one look at Gabby and, adopting her snotty tone, stated that it was time for my medication. Gabby gave me a wink then pulled one of his funny faces at Ruth, which caused me to giggle and I could see it really pissed off Ruth. He left the room and as the door closed behind him: "You really shouldn't encourage him you know!" she said distastefully

"Who?" I asked in mock innocence.

"Neanderthal man…Gabby…the hired thug!" As she spoke she cracked opened a blister pack and dropped two tablets into the palm of her hand, passing them to me along with a small glass half filled with water.

"What do you think of that Maureen Dickins?" I asked.

She waited for me swallow both tablets before answering, "I think that Dad is absolutely smitten with her and that he's a bloody fool."

"Why d'you say that?" I was both surprised and curious.

"Trust me Becky, one thing I do understand is women, and as for Maureen Dickins I can read her like a book!"

"Well tell me what you're reading, because I honestly though she was alright."

"Her career is the most important thing to her. Oh, I don't doubt for one minute that she cares for Dad, but that's about as far as it goes – the way you would care about a good friend; I can virtually guarantee that she will drop Dad without a moment's hesitation when it suits her and he's the one who is going to be hurt."

"Ruth, how on earth have you worked that out after just a few meetings with the woman?"

Ruth just shrugged her shoulders. "Let's wait and see, shall we?"

Chapter 19

Heartache

John Tanner felt restless. He had a surge of energy inside him that wouldn't allow him to settle and yet mentally he felt lethargic; he had certainly lost all appetite for food and wanted only to be in Maureen's company again. He was full of expectation for their future and yet felt a discomfort in the pit of his stomach, almost a feeling of nausea. He badly wanted to see her. His thoughts centred solely on her, but she hadn't contacted him and he couldn't get through to her; each time he tried he was told she was tied up in meetings and he'd left umpteen messages for her to call him back. He was aware the discomfort inside him was making him feel snappy and irritable and his conclusion was that if this were how love felt, he'd rather be without it. But inside he was love-struck and it had been far too many years since he'd last felt this way about anyone.

He clicked the last-number-dialled button on his mobile and held it to his ear. He heard her voice as she answered, "Maureen Dickins."

"Maureen, it's John … I've been trying to contact you."

"Why, what's happened?" An edge of concern showed in her voice.

"Nothing's happened, I missed you…I wanted to see you again."

"Ah…John, this is probably something we need to discuss. Look, I know it's short notice but there's a pub on the corner of Horseferry Road… Lambeth Bridge end; can we meet…say seven this evening?"

"Yes…of course…is there anything I need to know?" The concern had now moved into his own voice.

"Sorry John, I've got to dash…at the moment it's meeting after meeting and there are just not enough hours in the day…"

"Okay I'll see you tonight…seven o'clock…" He heard the line go dead before he'd finished speaking.

That evening, dead on seven o'clock, Maureen Dickins' car pulled up outside a public house on the Horseferry Road. She instructed her driver to remain outside and then entered through the double doors and then through a single door which had the word saloon etched onto a single pane of frosted glass. John Tanner was waiting at a corner table, and a whisky and ice awaited her at the empty chair next to him. He rose and kissed her cheek as she joined him.

"You are certainly a sight for sore eyes; I've really missed you." As he spoke he cupped her hands with his. The tips of his fingers gently danced upon her skin, and at that moment he felt an uncontrollable urge to sweep her into his arms. He looked into her eyes, instantly feeling a pang of love hit his heart. They both sat down and as he moved his head towards her, she turned her head away.

"Maureen, I know it is early days still, but I can't recall feeling this way about anyone before. I'm like an empty shell when I don't see you. I can't settle,

I'm not myself…I know it's too early to use the L-word, but, I can't deny it, my feelings for you are bordering on it!" As he spoke to her he ran his index finger down her arm as though it was an innocent gesture, but the vibes from touching her drew him to her eyes; it was only her eyes that showed pleasure at his contact with her. She took his hand and held it, not with affection but as a way of stopping him from touching her.

"John, I like you and I've always been attracted to you but I'm also aware that you've role-played your way through your personal life and you've got this ingrained thing about not getting too close to people. To be honest, you're a guaranteed recipe for heartache and to be brutally honest, I'm too old for that crap."

"No, it's not crap Maureen, what I feel for you is real…you've known me a lot of years and yes, you're right I don't let people get close, but with you it's different … I honestly believe my feelings are of love, and I know that more than anything else, I want us to be together."

"Oh, don't do this John…" She paused as she mentally rehearsed her words. "John, I love you as well, but I love you as a friend, a friend I've known for many years. We were never in a relationship in that sense of the word. I care for you, yes…in fact I care a great deal about you, I have for a number of years, but at no time has the thought ever entered my head that we would be a couple, that there'd be any ownership." She had spoken the words hesitantly, treading on eggshells, trying to deliver the killer shot in a tender way.

Tanner swallowed deeply. "I thought after the funeral when we…and the times since then, and the nights I've stayed with you … it just seemed so natural, so right…and now you're telling me what…that it was all pretend? That we were role-playing? We were playing a game of what if?" Tanner spoke with emotion creeping into his voice.

Maureen maintained a pause, a longer than average pause before answering, her voice soft, and her tone gentle but unmistakably firm. "John, we are and have always been good friends. We made the mistake of allowing intimacy into that friendship. A lot of people before us have gone down that road and discovered that you cannot mix friendship and sex…"

"I wasn't looking for just sex Maureen! I was the one who mentioned the L-word," he interrupted.

"Yes, and I'm the one at fault for moving a genuine friendship into a more intimate one, and I fully accept that I'm at fault; it was something I needed at that time and I should never have used a friend to satisfy my needs. John, as cold-hearted as this may sound, I have spent the majority of my married life in a loveless marriage. I grew to resent Roger for his constant infidelities, and that resentment made me extremely cold towards him emotionally. If truth be known, I didn't give tuppence that he had cancer, I didn't give tuppence that he suffered and I certainly didn't care a shit that he died! He was a bastard to me, and my having sex with another man after his funeral was my way of saying,

'How do you like it, you bastard!' because it was something I could never bring myself to do while he was alive."

"So what you are telling me is…that I was just a…" He struggled to find the words.

"John, try to understand. At that time…at the funeral, yes I used you and I'm sorry, but afterwards it was different. I had feelings for you, I cared for you…the intimacy was special…but it was never going to go anywhere. We are friends, special friends, but now the intimacy stops, we revert back to how we were before, only now that friendship is stronger, because of what we have experienced together."

Tanner sighed irritably. "Okay Maureen, that's how you see it, but what about me? I had a friend who I had really fancied for a long, long time but she was married and I knew her husband and…well, to me it was almost taboo to go after a friend deliberately and break up their marriage, especially where there were kids involved …" Maureen gazed into Tanners eyes; she gave away no emotion other than hanging on to his every word, as he continued. "When we made love that first time, I was without doubt the happiest man alive and not just because it was good sex, but because it was meaningful love making…well, at least it was from my viewpoint; I had no idea at the time that you were using it either to punish or exorcise a ghost!"

"John, there's no need for spite…"

"Well, I'm so sorry Maureen, but can you explain just how we are to have a friendship…oops, I mean a *special* friendship, when I'm always going to be wishing for something else, and longing to move the friendship on and yet knowing that it will never happen and having to accept it? Having always to keep my distance when all I really want is to hold you in my arms again? No Maureen, I'm sorry, it will be a one-sided friendship based on your terms and assumedly for your benefit." Tanner sat back in his chair and drained the remainder of his whisky.

"I don't see it that way John. We were good friends who made the mistake of having sex. All I'm saying is that we put it behind us and continue to be friends, exactly as we were before. Now, if you are telling me that you cannot do that, I can only suggest we say goodbye now before any hurtful comments are made…you have a lot going on in your life at the moment, probably more that the average person could cope with, so I appreciate the fact that your thinking may not be the most rational…"

"Oh no! Don't you dare start being fucking condescending to me…" He spat the words at her with contempt.

"John, we've exhausted this conversation." Maureen stood up and as she turned to leave, she looked back at Tanner. "Phone me when you've cooled down; we've been friends for far too many years to leave it like this."

As she left Tanner said nothing; he just stared down at his empty glass as a gallery of previous lovers he'd lost appeared in his mind's eye.

Early the following morning Gabby arrived at Tanner's flat and immediately dropped a number of hints about breakfast; as much as Tanner wanted to ignore them, he resigned himself to the fact that, just like a hungry cat, a hungry Gabby couldn't be silenced. He prepared bacon sandwiches and coffee for them both and as they simultaneously tore into them, Gabby said:

"I've been offered a contract job with Special Branch."

"Really, what are they offering you?" asked Tanner.

"Nothing exciting, just a driving job for the protection squad…but they're offering some good money."

"Then you've got to take it…you're a freelance and I can't afford to hire you…heaven alone knows I'm more than grateful for what you've done for me so far." Tanner's tone was genuine.

"Yeah, but the thing is John…this gig isn't finished is it? And I never walk away from an unfinished job; as far as payment goes, well I reckon you paid that in advance many years ago because if you hadn't then I'd still be in the bowels of a foreign prison."

"You're a good friend Gabby." Tanner nodded and smiled.

"And so are you John and that's why I'm here…now is there any more coffee going?"

The two men then spent their time discussing the current situation regarding Becky and how best to eradicate the threat to her safety from Dougie Mann and his now little, but dangerous team. Tanner avoided mentioning Maureen and especially any reference to his meeting with her the previous evening.

They continued until late morning. They were both still in Tanner's living room and Gabby was preparing to leave, when a loud knocking on the front door seemed to vibrate throughout the flat. As Tanner opened the door he was met with the cheerless expression on the face of Sebastian Toakes…..

Two days later, Tanner had moved both Becky and Ruth into his own flat. He had a spare bedroom with a double bed that the girls could share. Gabby had stated he was happy to sleep on the couch as it meant that anyone entering the flat would have to pass him first. Tanner's bedroom was the next in line before any unwelcome visitors reached the spare bedroom, and Tanner slept with the small .32 automatic under his pillow.

Tanner had informed Inspector Ledbetter that Becky was now staying at his address and added that if they should require it, she would be available as a police witness. His request for armed police protection for Becky was denied, based on the judgement of the investigating officer who stated that they had no reason to believe that Becky's life was in any imminent danger. Tanner was also informed that the investigating officer, a Detective Sergeant Priack had again requested another formal interview with her, regarding certain elements of her earlier statement, but at that time they were unable to confirm what those elements were.

The following afternoon while Gabby was driving back towards Tanner's flat, a car ran into the back of him. Although the bump had caused minimum damage to each of the vehicles, within seconds a police car appeared and insisted on breathalysing both drivers. The other driver was – to no great surprise – an off duty policeman who, after blowing into the device, was allowed to continue his journey. Gabby however, who hadn't had any alcohol for the last two days, was found to be almost three times over the drink-drive limit after the police had breathalysed him. He was immediately arrested and taken to the police station to be formally charged. He was left in a police cell, allegedly to allow him time to sleep it off. However a little over three and a half hours later he was informed that the apparatus the police had used earlier that day to breathalyse him had malfunctioned and that his alcohol level was actually well below the legal limit. They then informed him that during a routine check of his car they had discovered a small number of rounds of ammunition and as a result he would be charged with the illegal possession of ammunition; bail was refused on the instruction of a DS Priack.

John Tanner had no idea that any of this had taken place. All he knew was that Gabby hadn't turned up at the agreed time as promised, and that was something that Gabby was not renowned for.

Early evening and Gabby still hadn't arrived. He hadn't phoned and his mobile phone had been switched off.

Late evening, and the Tanner household were getting ready for bed. Becky was worried and had convinced herself that something terrible had happened to him or that he was in a hospital bed somewhere, or even worse, a morgue! Ruth was completely unsympathetic to Becky's worries and was quite unwavering as she stated that he'd probably met up with some cheap old slag, had forgotten all about his responsibilities and was busy satisfying his carnal desires!

John Tanner said nothing; he knew Gabby too well. He knew that if the man wasn't at his post then he either had a damn good reason or he was dead. As Tanner checked again for the umpteenth time that he had locked the front door, a cold shiver ran down his spine. He decided against spending the night in the living room, as he didn't want to alarm Becky any more than she already was. He kept his bedroom door ajar to ensure he would hear any sounds likely to become problematic. He laid down fully clothed on his bed. He reached under his mattress and removed the Czechoslovakian pistol. Instinctively he checked the magazine was full then replaced it and checked the safety catch was on. He then placed the pistol under his pillow.

The flat was in darkness, but John Tanner's eyes were bright, his senses fully alert…

It had been many years since John Tanner had last worked as a field operative and since that time he had become a creature of routine: regular office hours, regular eating habits and a regular sleeping pattern. Lying on a bed in a dark room at his regular sleeping time in a silent flat, it wasn't long before he was giving out a sound of gentle snoring. He slipped deeper into his sleep, but it was a disturbed sleep, a sleep coupled with anxiety and in his sleep he heard the sound of his front door slamming followed by the sound of a man's voice, but before he could get out of bed, the bedroom door burst open and the light was switched on. His eyes were momentarily blinded by the brightness, and then he recognised the figure standing at the foot of his bed pointing a pump action shotgun at him, a face from his past.

Another man entered the room. His face wasn't familiar but Tanner's instincts told him that he knew him; he watched helplessly as the man also pointed a doubled barrelled sawn-off shotgun directly at him, and a sneer of hatred spread across both of their faces. He saw the flash from the guns before he heard the explosion as both men fired their weapons at him at nigh point blank range!

John Tanner woke suddenly. His heart was beating fast, too fast; it had only been a dream. He was in his bed, the room was dark. He wondered how long he had been sleeping.

He suddenly heard the sound of whispering coming from the main passage, by the front door. He strained his ears and heard the whispering again, then there were lots of voices whispering, then the realisation hit him: it wasn't whispering he was hearing at all – it was the crackling of flames!

He quickly leapt to his feet as the overpowering smell of burning began to fill his nostrils. Grabbing a torch from his bedside table, he switched it on and the beam illuminated the black smoke that was now filling the room; he felt the air around him becoming hotter. He heard coughing from the next room; the girls were choking on thick black smoke as they slept. He stepped outside his room.

The flat was full of smoke, at the end of the passageway there were flames, he knew if he didn't move quickly the girls would probably die from smoke inhalation. Tanner fought the natural urge to panic and crawled low to the ground where there was less smoke and the air would be cleaner. He reached their bedroom door and prayed the effects of smoke inhalation hadn't taken hold of them. He stood and kicked the door in. Dragging Becky and Ruth by their arms to the foot of the bed, he tried to sit them upright, then putting his arms around their waists, he stood up and started to help them out. He reached as far as the passageway outside their bedroom and became disorientated; it wasn't only difficult to breathe, it was becoming nigh on impossible. One continuous thought ran through his mind over and over: *'I've got to save the girls…'* He staggered forward a few more steps but, confronted by voluminous smoke and intense heat, he was forced back. He attempted to head for the bathroom but breathing difficulties weakened him; he vomited and collapsed unconscious onto the floor, along with both Becky and Ruth.

Fire crews, responding to an emergency call from a passer-by, quickly arrived on the scene; they took one look at the heavy flames and smoke that were pouring out of windows on the second floor, and quickly summoned additional units. The residents of the other flats in the building were evacuated as the firemen, wearing breathing equipment, entered the building and climbed the stairs to the second floor and to the burning flats on that level.

Flames engulfed the entrance to Tanner's flat, but the firemen had been told that residents were trapped inside and they battled through the heavy flames, arriving inside just as John Tanner and his daughters collapsed. Rescue came just in time. The three of them were quickly transported to hospital and treated for burns and smoke inhalation. Other residents on floor above Tanner's had climbed out of their windows and stood on the ledge in shock as they also waited for the fire brigade ladders to rescue them.

It was late afternoon the following day when John Tanner regained consciousness. His head was pounding; his nostrils felt as though hot embers had been pushed up them, whilst his throat felt as though he still had a glowing coal lodged in it. He wanted to swallow but couldn't. He couldn't even produce the required spittle to swallow. The feeling of nausea was strong inside him and he felt the urge to vomit but he had no energy to move. He opened his eyes, and he knew immediately he was in a private room in a hospital.

He saw the fuzzy outline of two figures sitting beside one another next to his bed. He sensed they were friends but couldn't make out exactly who they were. He closed his eyes again; the smell of burnt ashes in his nostrils was overpowering. He breathed deeply, his lungs almost struggling to fully expand, and the flow of air becoming restrictive. A strong urge to panic tried to take hold, but as before, he had no strength, no energy and so he just lay still.

His mind slowly released the memory of what had happened; he remembered the smoke, the choking, and the sensation of unbearable heat and of falling…falling. He then remembered Becky and Ruth, and falling to the floor with them, and that same instant the strength returned to his body as a surge of energy flowed through it.

He opened his eyes again and recognised the two figures beside him as Ernie Palmer and Gabby. Tanner tried to speak but emitted only a rasping sound; he was wearing a mask covering his nose and mouth, delivering a flow of oxygen through its tubes. Both the men next to him stood up, and Gabby placed his hand on Tanner's forehead.

"Steady on old son, you ain't ready for action just yet."

Tanner pulled the mask away from his mouth. "My girls…how are my girls?" His voice was no more than a hoarse whisper.

Ernie Palmer answered, "They're going to be okay John. Like you, they're being treated for smoke inhalation, but all of you are jolly lucky to be alive. A few more moments and the fire services would have been removing three corpses from the remains of your flat."

"What happened?" It caused him pain to try and speak and as he struggled, hardly any sound emerged from his lips, but his question was obvious.

Once again it was Ernie Palmer who answered. "The neighbour who lives opposite you, she couldn't sleep, and at about 2am she said she heard a noise almost like the sound of a door slamming and because your flats are normally so quiet she went to have a look and as she opened her front door her hair was instantly singed from the flames roaring up and filling the corridor. She had the sense to immediately close her door and phone the Fire Services, and it was her prompt action that probably saved your lives."

Gabby took over. "It quickly turned into a massive blaze, but thankfully all the trapped residents were rescued and most have been treated for minor smoke related problems. The bad news is that the fire has completely gutted your flat; it's just a mass of charred furnishings and shattered windows, and along with some of the other flats it's had quite a bit of water damage."

"How…how…?" Tanner again tried speaking.

Ernie Palmer and Gabby looked at each other before Ernie answered his whispered question. "It was set on fire by a suspected arsonist. In fact the police have issued a statement that they are treating this as arson with intent to endanger life!"

Gabby continued, "John, the flames from the window were going so high they felt the heat from across the street. There is no doubt it was a professional hit and if your neighbour hadn't been so inquisitive to the sudden noise as it ignited then it would have been a successful hit with quite a few fatalities."

Tanner looked directly at Gabby. "Where…were you?"

"I was arrested John; a trumped-up charge of drunken driving, enough to keep me in a cell for a few hours and then when they had to drop that, on the grounds that I was stone cold sober they then trumped up another charge and claimed to have found a few rounds of ammunition in my car. But I have Maureen Dickins to thank for my freedom. One of her assistants who has been monitoring the police computers informed her of my arrest and she promptly contacted the chief constable and whatever was said, it was enough for my immediate release. I also received a message from her that you were in this hospital."

"It was the same with me…" it was now Ernie's turn to take over, "…she phoned me and said she'd spoken to Sebastian Toakes. He then phoned me and told me to drop whatever I was working on and to give you priority."

"Toakes also phoned me John. I'm back on the job, albeit temporarily; he's engaged me on an interim contract…my role is now that of being your close protection," Gabby added.

"Why the sudden turn-around? And anyway, I'm retired…so why are they even interested in what happens to me?"

"You've got Maureen Dickens to thank for that as well; apparently yesterday, when she attended her first Cabinet Office briefing…"

"What! …Maureen's a member of COBRA?" Tanner's astonishment was evident even through his raspy voice.

"Yes, she did try and tell you she was going up in the world, John…anyway she mentioned to the Secretary of State that the daughter of a long serving officer of the security services had been shot and wounded on a London Street. She said that an attempt had been made on her own life in a London pub and then she mentioned that the terrible fire that was in the morning papers was at the home of that same long serving officer and his daughter, who was staying with him while she was convalescing. The Minister asked if there were any connotation to national security; Maureen played her trump card and told him that the incidents were related and it was their belief that an organised crime group, which had been infiltrated by foreign nationals, orchestrated the incidents.

"A slight variation of the facts!" Tanner rasped cynically.

"Yes, but it was enough for the Minister to issue a special warrant which means that particular group of lowlifes are now a legitimate target!" Gabby announced with an unashamed glee.

"Ah, Mr Tanner, you are awake at last!" The duty doctor entered the room and approached the bed. "I hope your two colleagues here didn't disturb you? I did try to keep them out of your room but the matter was taken out of my hands."

"No, it's okay…they're more than just colleagues…they're almost family."

"Oh, that's nice for you; now, if we could just pop this mask back on, it can continue to convey clean oxygen into your lungs, which is, of course, the reason we put it there in the first place!" The doctor replaced the oxygen mask over Tanner's nose and mouth and then turned towards Ernie and Gabby. "Now if you gentlemen could refrain from exciting Mr Tanner, I'm sure his recovery will come about much quicker!" The doctor then gave a loud huffing sound and left the room.

"Sarcastic fucker!" growled Gabby.

"Oh, he's only doing his job," quipped Ernie.

Shortly afterwards the door opened again and a soft voice spoke. "Well, this really is becoming a family affair. First one daughter, and now both daughters and the father." The voice belonged to Dr Sandra Atkins. "I know you're not my patient but Ruth and Becky both asked me to pop in and see how you were." Tanner made a sound from behind the mask of which none of them understood. "Just be quiet Mr Tanner and listen to what I have to say. Both of your daughters are going to be okay. They are breathing easily and normally which suggests to us that their airways are open and functioning normally. Now, in case you haven't been told, you actually fared slightly worse, in that your airways were constricted; however upon admittance you were given a bronchodilator which helped the muscles in your respiratory system to relax. Blood tests showed you had no presence of toxic substances in your blood, so you will be pleased to know you are also expected to make a full recovery."

The words, "Thank you," spoken emotionally from behind the mask were clearly audible to them all.

Sandra Atkins smiled a genuine smile, one that showed her concern and care for her patients. But the instant she had left the room, Tanner removed the mask from his mouth and nose.

"I want those bastards!" He spat the words with passion.

"Yes, and we'll get them," Ernie answered calmly.

"No, I'm not talking about going through the legal process! They're killers and if we take them through the courts and we're lucky enough that their smarmy brief doesn't get them off on some technicality, then the most they have to look forward to is about fifteen years, so you can halve that with good behaviour. Then we'll no doubt have a couple of looney labourites spouting on about how the prisons are overcrowded and how inhumane it is to lock people up, and they'll start releasing prisoners early and these bastards are suddenly back on the street after only three or four years...no I want these bastards dead!" Tanner's tone was adamant and emotional.

"Okay, but you can't be anywhere near them when it happens...it will have to be me and Gabby." Ernie Palmer stared straight into John Tanner's eyes as he spoke.

"No, I'm sorry Ern, you've got too much to lose if it goes pear shaped. It's my family there are hitting, therefore it'll be me who takes them out!"

"Well, it seems to me John, that a while ago you introduced us as 'almost family', so Ern and I have as much right to terminate these pieces of scum as you do!" Gabby's expression highlighted his gentle teasing of Tanner and his eager anticipation for some action.

"Okay you win...between us we'll get rid of this slime from the sewer once and for all...but for now, clear off and let me recover in peace!"

The two men grinned at him, and as they left the room a wave of emotion flooded over Tanner, a reaction to the loyalty of his friends and to the limits to which they were prepared to go for him.

Chapter 20

Becky

I was dreaming, although I wasn't aware it was a dream at the time. But I was surrounded by what I can only describe as huge shadow figures, but whereas shadows are flat, these were three-dimensional and the main one, the biggest of them was leaning over me as I lay in bed, his hands tight around my throat and squeezing. I told myself to get up, but I was tired, so tired, and my eyelids aching and heavy. I was powerless to stop him; I couldn't struggle. I couldn't fight back in any way shape or form. As I felt his hands tighten and my windpipe shut out any incoming air, I suddenly felt myself hanging in the air supported by the tight grasp of his hands around my neck. I knew I was about to die, but then something else grabbed me and was dragging me away, albeit with great difficulty.

The next thing, I was hearing the sound of my dad, close by and coughing like crazy. My eyes felt like they were burning and my throat felt like it was on fire. I knew then where I was, and as that realisation hit me, so I felt myself dropping … dropping into Hell's own furnace and I was about to be roasted alive. All I could think of was, *"God, please let me live."* And I chanted those words to myself over and over. Whatever happened after that I had absolutely no idea of!

I awoke and my eyes instantly took in my surroundings … the familiar sights, sounds and smells. I was back in a hospital bed, and my eyes fell upon a doctor who was looking directly at me with a look of deep sorrow in his eyes. I don't remember anything after that so I must have slipped back into unconsciousness.

When I came around again it was the same hospital room, only this time I had the stench of burning in my nostrils as though I was standing too close to a bonfire, and my throat … I wasn't sure if it had been burned from the outside in, or the inside out, but it felt as though I had a gaping wound where my tonsils should be. I tried to focus my eyes but everything was blurred. I heard a voice speaking and tried to listen. I felt my eyelids being lifted open and a light being shone, and I realised the voice was speaking to me, telling me to follow the light with my eyes. "Look up, look down, look left and look right." I realised that I was wearing a mask over my nose and mouth, but still that horrible smell of burning seemed to have consumed all of me, all of my senses as though I had been plunged head first into a giant ashtray filled with cigarette ends, only the smell was intensified ten times over! At that moment a feeling of dread hit me; an icy cold tremor through to my very soul. The faces of my sister Ruth and my dad appeared before me. I gripped the doctor's wrist, and as I looked at him, I knew my eyes were filled with despair.

"Where's my family?" I asked. Whether my words were coherent from behind the mask I don't know, but he looked at the nurse standing at the opposite side of the bed and then back at me; he gave a deep sigh and I immediately feared the worst, and as his eyes caught mine I felt a tear run down my cheek.

"Rebecca..." he paused and I just knew that I'd lost them, "...the newspapers have quoted a fireman as saying that no one should have survived the effects of that blaze. But for those people who believe in miracles – and I am one of them – I'm happy to say that a miracle occurred, because other than smoke inhalation and burns, there was not one fatality in that building. To answer your question, your family have suffered no lasting damage; you will all be leaving this hospital together." His face showed no emotion, not even a simple smile. He just nodded to me as though it was a formality and then left with the nurse following in tow. I closed my eyes and instantly the memories were uncovered and displayed inside my head. I felt my heart begin to race with intensity; panic was preparing to unleash itself. I opened my eyes again. *Calm down.* I mentally barked an order to myself.

Once again I didn't know how much time had passed, but I was suddenly aware of a familiar face looking at me and smiling. Happiness seemed to radiate from it; it was infectious, and at once I felt better in myself. Dr Atkins was certainly a sight for sore eyes.

"Is it the hospital food you like or do you have your sights set on one of our doctors?" she smiled.

I clasped her hand tightly. "How's Ruth?"

"She's going to be fine...I've just left her. In fact she ordered me to come and check on you...you have a very bossy sister!" Again her infectious smile told me that everything was going to be okay. I heard my own sigh of relief.

"How's my dad?" I asked.

"That's where I'm off to next...Ruth said you first and then Mr Tanner, but from what I've heard he's okay," she answered, her tone putting me immediately at ease.

"What actually happened Sandra...I mean, I know there was a fire, but what happened?"

She took a deep breath and bit her bottom lip before answering. "I can only repeat bits that I've overheard, so there is no guarantee about how accurate it is, but apparently it's believed the fire was started deliberately in the hallway outside your dad's flat. They also believe it was carried out by professionals and possibly by the same people who shot at you." She fell silent as soon as she'd spoken, almost as though she'd committed blasphemy and was awaiting suitable chastisement.

"And Ruth is honestly okay?" I asked again.

"Yes."

"And my dad?"

"I haven't seen him yet, but from what I've heard, yes…and he's also a bit of a hero; he was trying to carry both you and Ruth to safety and had just been overcome by the smoke when the fire rescue team broke into the flat…the neighbours had said he lived alone so if he hadn't dragged you both out of the spare room, the fire rescue team wouldn't have looked for you…he saved both your lives."

"Go and see him for me…please see that he's okay…" I spoke straight from the heart and the look on Sandra's face told me that was just how she'd received it.

She then probably broke every rule in the doctors' handbook and leaned across and kissed me on the cheek.

As she left the room I wondered if I would ever be able to escape this nightmare scenario that, not only had I been sucked into…but one that I'd drawn my family into as well! I closed my eyes and as I drifted my thoughts began to wander, previous conversations were replayed and scenarios of recent events were viewed and in between there was a sprinkling of trivia. But the more profound thoughts were of how I could see in myself just how much I had changed as a person.

The word *family* now took on a new meaning to me, as though I'd stepped from out of my old life and into a new one, but the horrors I'd had to endure during the transition would probably scar me for far too many years to come. I thought back to the old me, and now with hindsight I could see how I'd felt that a part of me, a part of my life was missing. Semi-rootless and angry with a mother who despised me as much as I despised her, and a stepfather who was nothing short of a cowardly bully, and a step brother who openly loathed me. Was it any wonder that I went off the rails?

The only time my real dad's name was mentioned was when my mother was having one of her hate filled rants about him, otherwise it was almost an unwritten law that no-one ever spoke about him.

But, young girls are naturally very curious and so, as we were growing up, Ruth and I used to have little chats away from Madge's prying ears, and we'd speculate on what he looked like, which of his features we'd inherited and then the scary bit…whether in fact he was the drunken good-for-nothing that Madge had convinced us of, and if so, then would one of us inherit that aspect of his personality?

Ruth had always nurtured a burning desire to find him, whilst I lumped him in with Madge and Victor and held him in the grossest contempt. It was something that she just couldn't seem to understand.

I thought back to that first meeting with Mr John Tanner, my natural father. I remembered being extremely nervous before he came in to see me. He was a man whom I held in contempt because he had chosen not to have me in his life and yet deep inside I was worried in case he was expecting to meet somebody different. I wasn't like Ruth; would I match his expectations, and would he sideline me in favour of Ruth the same as our own mother had done? I didn't know, and so I did what I always did and adopted my typical stance of aggression. But when he walked through the door and looked at me, it was a look that I'd never experienced before in my life. A look that only a father could give, a look of parental love. I looked earnestly for any physical resemblance to either Ruth or myself and discovered that yes; it was there in abundance.

I felt instantly relaxed in his company, although I wasn't going to let him see it and even though I had questions for him, it wasn't the aggressive questioning that I'd always visualised in my head that I would put him through if we ever met. Ruth was right in that he didn't put any blame at Madge's door; he just said that he'd believed our being brought up in a stable and happy family environment was in our best interests and he'd wanted us to have the best start possible.

The most amazing thing was that in such a short space of time, I felt that I'd known him forever, the anger had vanished and I now felt nothing but love and admiration for him. He was now in every way a very big part of my life and I really couldn't visualise myself calling him anything other than Dad.

Within a few days we had been discharged from the hospital and were busy settling into a hotel suite just off London's West End. It was quite plush and laid out like a flat on the top floor of the hotel. We had a main living area with a kitchenette and bedrooms leading off. But it wasn't anything to be excited about; it was no different to being under house arrest, as we were told not to leave our suite for at least a week until the police had apprehended the suspects believed to have been responsible for starting the fire at Dad's flat.

On the second day, Dad said he badly needed a new wardrobe of clothes and so using Gabby's laptop we logged onto a couple of the major West End stores, Dad chose for himself a pretty cool selection of clothes, then he produced his credit card and allowed me and Ruth to do the same. Wow, we certainly did some damage to his credit limit, but he didn't seem to mind. We had opted for collection and Ruth volunteered to be the one to collect. Gabby said he'd go with her; he seemed to have taken quite a shine to her, but boy was he going to be disappointed!

Dad and I were alone when his mobile rang. He answered it and told the caller he was switching it to loud-speaker and also told the caller that I was present.

"Hello Becky, my name is Kamalika. The information I am about to give you may cause you some distress, but we feel it is important that you are aware of developments."

"That's okay…please carry on," I answered nervously.

"None of this has been released to the media yet, but the police are currently investigating the deaths of four women after their bodies were found in a basement flat in Plaistow, in East London late last night. The women were aged between late teens and early twenties, and the initial results of the post-mortem examination have recorded the official cause of death as a drugs overdose of heroin and morphine. A large number of sleeping tablets were also present in their bodies. This cause of death was identical for each of them; they appear to have died only minutes apart. Forensic officers are still at the scene, so we should have more information later…"

"Is there a connection to us?" Dad interrupted her…quite irritably I thought.

"The initial assumption of a serial killer was beyond the realms in coincidence, and it was not a security issue so we had no real interest in it, but it was an off-the-cuff remark made by one of my colleagues that made me delve a little more deeply into it…"

"What was the comment?" snapped Dad again impatiently.

"Yes, I'm sorry, it was a flippant comment, she said it was as though somebody was getting rid of incriminating evidence all in one go."

"Kamalika, there's no doubt it is a horrific story, but as you said, there is no security implication so I am slightly at a loss as to why you are…"

"Well perhaps if you allowed me the courtesy to finish, then you would know!" she retorted, and I thought, yes; I like you.

"Initially I thought it was a bit far fetched…" she continued, "…but what if either Dougie Mann or one of his trusted lieutenants is making doubly sure that nobody can point a finger at them? So I checked the pathologist's report and under the section on identifying marks, I saw that one of the girls had the shape of an iron burned into her leg and her description matched that given by your daughter of a female she referred to as Harvey. Another of the bodies had a tattoo on her shoulder of a pair of rabbits copulating which also matched a description given by your daughter of another of the females she had come into contact with."

I couldn't hear myself, but I know that I cried out. I know that my face contorted as both their faces appeared inside my head and I visualised their arms reaching out to me for help…a help I couldn't give them. My eyes became filled with a watery film, which then cascaded down my cheeks as my shoulders sagged and I broke into a spasm of uncontrolled sobbing. I blurted an apology and ran into my bedroom; as I lay on my bed crying, my head was still filled with memories of both Harvey and Siobhan.

Dad's mobile was still on speakerphone so even through the closed door I was still able to hear both sides of the conversation. Kamalika had heard my distress at her news and had asked him if I was okay?

"Yes, it's understandably come as a shock as she had a close bond with one of them and felt protective towards the other…I'll leave her alone for a few moments and then check on her."

"Okay, if there is anything I can do, just let me know."

"Actually, there is something…" he added as an afterthought.

"What is it?"

"Well, we know how these sick bastards operate so can you find out if there were any other marks on the girls' bodies?"

"What sort of marks?" she asked probingly.

"It's just something that Becky said to Gabby…"

"Who's Gabby?"

"Oh that doesn't matter, but Becky told him that she'd been told that the girl we now know as Harvey was apparently going to be a movie star and we know what type of movies they were into…but what if they went that bit further?"

"You mean a snuff movie, where somebody is killed for real on camera." It was a statement rather than a question.

"It's all just supposition…I'm just throwing another thought into the hat."

"I'll see what I can find out – give me a couple of days."

"Okay, thanks."

It was then silent so I knew the conversation had ended, but it was a conversation that I wished I'd never heard; the images now running through my head were just too horrendous to contemplate and I hoped and prayed that he was wrong. I prayed that poor little Siobhan, who wouldn't escape with Lucy and me because she was too afraid of getting into trouble, was actually alive and was somewhere safe, but I knew in reality that it was just wishful thinking.

That evening room service had delivered us a sumptuous meal along with a bottle of exceptionally good wine, but I couldn't enjoy it; my spirits were still low. Harvey, little Siobhan and two other girls were dead, murdered; and I could have just as easily been one of them. I looked at the faces of Ruth, Gabby and Dad as we sat around the circular table, the three of them tucking in and enjoying their meal, while I just picked at the food on my plate. I could tell that Dad had something on his mind, something concerning me, and that he was just waiting for the right moment to mention it.

After the meal the plates were piled back onto the trolley ready for room service to collect. Ruth was standing in front of a mirror putting the final touches to her make-up. She had arranged to meet Sandra Atkins at some new art gallery that was opening and as she stood brushing her hair back away from her face she radiated happiness. When she was sure she was ready, she kissed each of us on the cheek, made a saucy comment about not waiting up for her and left for her date, although she had insisted it wasn't a date, just two friends with a mutual interest in art.

I gave a deep sigh, one that declared just how fed up I was and I sat at the table and started browsing through some of the leaflets advertising places to go in London's West End. I definitely felt I was going stir crazy. Dad and Gabby joined me at the table; Dad sat opposite me whilst Gabby sat by the side of me.

Whatever had been on Dad's mind, this was going to be the moment he disclosed it.

"Becky, I think it's time you started carrying some form of protection." His expression was stern, his tone was precise and, as down in the dumps as I felt, an offhand comment sprang to mind about condoms, but I decided against saying it.

"What are you thinking of…Gabby teaching me some form of martial arts?" I replied flippantly.

"No, I was thinking more along the lines of this…" He slid a small black pistol across the table towards me.

"Whoa! I certainly wasn't expecting that…is it real?" My shock was genuine.

"Yes, pick it up…it's light and it's comfortable, but don't worry – I'm not going to let you loose with it. Gabby will take you to the indoor range and give you some training with it."

"What indoor range?" I asked.

"Let's just say your dad still has quite a few contacts within…what you know as MI5 and some of their facilities are…shall we say unofficially open to us," Gabby answered.

I picked up the pistol. It wasn't that light, but I supposed it wasn't unduly heavy either, and it fitted nicely in the palm of my hand, as though it was made for me. "So what is it, a Dirty Harry magnum or something?" I asked in ignorance, but it made Gabby laugh.

"No, it's a girly gun, ideal for spies and handbags…but don't be fooled, it packs quite a powerful punch. It's a semi-automatic and it holds eight rounds, and if you feel up to it we can try it out on the range tomorrow." To me Gabby was like a big protective bear and it was impossible not to feel safe and comfortable in his presence, so I nodded my agreement to him.

The following morning I was awake early and, while I still carried a degree of sadness over Harvey and Siobhan, I was really excited about going to a firing range. Gabby had previously told me to dress comfortably so I wore jeans and T-shirt. We'd all decided it would be better not to mention it to Ruth who was an ardent anti-gun campaigner, and who had become even more zealous in her condemnation of them since I'd been shot and wounded.

But to me the wow factor was that I was going to be using the same range that our counter-terrorist agents used, and that I could possibly be standing next to an under-cover operative…. a spy! I didn't know what to expect, but when we arrived there everybody just looked so normal, not an ounce of suave, debonair sophistication amongst any of them, so there was no nurturing that little fantasy.

I overheard Gabby talking to someone who I assumed was the equivalent to a range manager or whatever they were called, and telling him that I was a friendly diplomat's daughter and it had been agreed higher up that I was supposed to receive personal training. He then put on this big act of being annoyed that nobody was prepared for us, and considered it nothing short of incompetence. After that the guy couldn't do enough to ensure all facilities were available to us.

Another man joined us; he was aged somewhere around his mid fifties, he carried a clipboard with him and was apparently one of the senior instructors and simulation director. I didn't catch his full name but I heard Gabby refer to him as Alan so I followed suit. Alan's life was guns, and anything to do with shooting guns, and what he didn't know about guns, according to the grapevine that Gabby had attached himself to, quite frankly wasn't worth knowing.

I soon discovered it wasn't just going to be a fun day out! It was enjoyable, yes, but also very intensive; these guys took it seriously and I was expected to do likewise. Initially they discovered that I had no natural instinct with my hand and eye coordination. I felt embarrassed but Alan was quite sweet; he kept me at ease and said that everyone had the ability to point at an object so it would come with practice, and boy did we practise; I learned quite a lot about shooting! Alan told me about the getting the correct visual picture, which is that first glance a shooter takes in of their target, so we practised that. I learned about the correct amount of pressure that should be applied to the trigger. I held the pistol one handed at arm's length, but they said I was pulling it to one side when I squeezed the trigger, although it looked all right to me. I tried again with both arms extended out in front, but then I was gripping it too tightly. "Hold it loosely," they said. "Feel comfortable with it," they said.

We eventually reached the point where they were happy with my grip, my posture and what Alan called my sight picture. I was told to take up the slack on the trigger and when I was ready, just to squeeze gently...... wow! What a thrill! I had done it properly, exactly to their instructions and they paid me the compliment of calling me a natural. I continued practising slowly, then with speed as my proficiency increased. Alan and Gabby between them taught me the techniques for engaging an enemy at close range and at five yards, at ten and at fifteen yards and each time I aimed the pistol I had a tape playing in my head of Alan's instructions and as I smoothly squeezed the trigger I hit the target, my enemy, in the chest, stopping him dead.

It was late afternoon by the time we were eventually driving back towards the hotel. Before we'd left the range I had foolishly accepted Alan's offer of a coffee, which he hadn't served in a polystyrene cup as I'd expected, but in an oversized mug. It had been a long day, a dry day and I'd surprised myself at just how quickly I drained it. In turn the coffee had drained itself through me and now my bladder was informing me it was full. I was hoping I could last until we reached the hotel but that certainly wasn't going to happen. My bladder had now stopped asking to be emptied; it was now demanding. And oh, how I regretted that mug of coffee. Every part of me was now clenched tightly. I knew I couldn't last.

"Gabby, we're going to have to stop for a comfort break otherwise there's a strong possibility you'll have a pool of pee on your front seat!" I certainly didn't need to exaggerate the urgency – I really was that desperate.

"There's a pub up ahead. It's off the road a bit and has a car park at the front. I'll pull in there; they should still be open."

I jumped out of the car very quickly, grabbed my small shoulder bag and mouthed the words, "Shan't be long." I ran across the small car park, in through the main doors and then in through another door, which had a small plate attached to it indicating it was the saloon bar. Once inside I saw the welcome sign on the far wall pointing to a door for ladies and gents toilets. As I headed towards it I paid only minor to the few customers: an elderly couple sat at a table by a window, a middle aged man sat alone at another table studying the racing page in his newspaper ... and then out of the corner of my eye I spotted Andrei propped against the bar. He was dressed in a grey oversized suit, looking more like an American gangster from the forties. He was in conversation with an attractive woman by his side. She could easily have been mistaken for a company executive. Her dress sense was smart and I guessed she was probably either in her late twenties or early thirties. I maintained my momentum, into the ladies, into a cubicle and then relief!

But as I sat there the full realisation of who I'd just seen came over me, and in my head every sadistic punishment he'd dealt out to me was replayed. I was frightened. Gabby, my protector, was outside in the car unaware of my danger. I looked in my shoulder bag for my mobile phone; it wasn't there. I remembered using it in the car to text Ruth – I must have left it on the dashboard. I controlled my breathing; I was determined not to panic. I thought back to my training with Alan that day, but shooting at cardboard figures of a man was completely different to coming up against the real thing! I removed the pistol from my shoulder bag and checked the magazine; it was full. I tucked it into the waistband of my jeans, with my T-shirt flapping over it, covering it. I just hoped that he hadn't seen me and that I'd be able leave the pub unnoticed, join Gabby and continue back to the hotel.

I left the cubicle and as I washed my hands I saw my reflection in the mirror; my face was colourless, my eyes were wide and my expression was blank. I stepped out of the ladies' toilet and back into the saloon bar. The elderly couple had left, as had the man and his racing paper, and the woman who had been talking to Andrei was also gone. There was just Andrei, leaning with his back to the bar and grinning as he looked me up and down. My eyes flickered towards the door leading to the exit. The door was closed and leaning against the door frame was none other than Costi with a sickening lustful sneer across his face as he looked at me. The place was empty. Costi walked slowly towards me and as he drew level with Andrei they approached me together.

"I've really missed you Becky...I've missed all those little things you used to do for me." Costi sounded depraved, as ever.

"Yeah, well don't get so fucking anal over it, 'cos I haven't missed you...and let's be honest, 'little' really does sum you up, doesn't it!" I spat the words at them contemptuously.

They drew nearer towards me. "I think we're going to have to teach you some discipline all over again..." As Andrei finished speaking, both of the men rushed at me. I moved my hand towards my waistband and then brought it up from under my T-shirt. I aimed the pistol and fired once. My aim was accurate; the point thirty-two bullet entered Costi's upper chest, piercing his heart and killing him instantly. I then aimed at Andrei as he was reaching inside his jacket pocket and I fired twice. The first bullet went wide of its target; the second bullet hit him in the arm causing him to recoil in pain.

I don't know what took over me, but in an instant I moved towards him, pushing the barrel of the pistol against his head. He showed no signs of resistance.

He gave a lecherous laugh. "Ah Becky, so you have killed again ... you really are no different to me..." He reached out slowly with his uninjured arm and put his hand on my breast and began gently caressing around my nipple with his fingers. "You were always the best fuck out of all my girls." His eyes remained on my breasts but I continued holding the barrel of my pistol against his head and knocked his arm away with my free hand. So much of me wanted to squeeze the trigger, but I couldn't; something inside me wouldn't allow me to kill him so coldly and as his hand returned to my breast, the realisation dawned on me, that he also knew that I couldn't kill in cold blood, that my holding the gun to his head was no more than an empty threat!

"Leave it Becky..." The voice belonged to Gabby. "Go out to the car and wait!" It wasn't a request. Gabby had barked an order and I wasn't about to argue.

As I moved away, Gabby put his hand inside Andrei's jacket and removed a pistol, similar to mine, but bigger.

I ran across the car park and climbed into the car. Shortly afterwards I heard the sound of a gun shot and what seemed no more than seconds later, Gabby came walking out of the pub and across to the car. Once he was inside behind the wheel we pulled away with a screech of tyres; luckily there were hardly any people around to look at or show any interest in us – erratic driving was now so common on the streets of London's suburbs. We were even luckier in that it was one of those rare periods where the traffic had cleared so we were able to distance ourselves from the scene very quickly.

Gabby told me I'd handled myself well and he was proud of me, but it still didn't stop my insides from shaking and gurgling. He said that he'd been on his way into the pub to see what was talking me so long when he heard the first shot.

"So what was the shot I heard, while I was waiting in the car?" I asked.

"I accused him of murdering those four girls that were found. He laughed and said not to worry, they'd already been replaced... his eyes told me of his intention even before I saw his arm move. I was too close to him; it gave him an advantage, and he took it. His arm came up with a small blade in it and caught me under my forearm. I could have pistol-whipped him but I thought, what the hell, he's already admitted murdering those young girls so I squeezed off a round and sent him off to discuss it with his god!"

"Oh my god Gabby, was anyone around? Did anyone see?" As I spoke I suddenly noticed the arm of his jacket, which was heavily soaked with his blood. "Gabby, pull over, let me look at that arm before you bleed to death!"

"We're almost at the hotel. When we've parked, go to the boot. I have a wax jacket in there; I'll carry it over my arm when we enter the reception area to cover the blood. There's also what looks like a plastic fishing box. It's actually a comprehensive first aid kit, and it'll have everything we need to disinfect and stitch the wound." He then answered my earlier question regarding possible witnesses, and said that it was more than likely one of Dougie Mann's pubs and so the landlord would have known to make himself scarce when they were conducting business; when he heard the shots, he would have assumed it was Andrei doing the shooting.

Gabby said he'd bet a pound against a penny that the pub would be cleaned up before opening time and the bodies would be stripped and left on a rubbish dump somewhere, well away from the pub.

We arrived back at the hotel without any further mishap and, more importantly, without Gabby passing out through loss of blood. The arm of his jacket was now quite saturated with his blood and as stubborn as he was, he remained adamant that he wasn't going to hospital. Luckily for us Ruth wasn't around when we entered our hotel suite, otherwise she would have been running around like a headless chicken and getting herself into a panic, which was one of the traits she'd inherited from our mother.

Dad's first question was if I was okay, and as soon as I'd confirmed that I was he took hold of Gabby and the pair of us led him into the bathroom. We stripped him to the waist and Dad cleaned away some of the blood and checked the severity of the cut to determine the best way for us to treat it. I took over the cleaning of it with antiseptic wash, and although I was considerably gentler than Dad, I could still sense through Gabby's occasional grimace that it was more than a little painful for him. He looked pale and exhausted. We pressed the wound properly to control the bleeding, applied some antiseptic cream and covered it with gauze, then wrapped the arm loosely in a bandage. I'd found a wad of sterilised strips in his fishing box-cum-first aid kit, so I volunteered to change his dressing each day and keep an eye on how it was healing. Dad was concerned about how dirty the knife had been, and thought that Gabby may need antibiotics or even a tetanus injection. Gabby, of course, would have none of it, maintaining that it had been a clean cut with a clean blade and within four or five days his arm would be as good as new. I hoped he was right and that he healed fast. He'd made a big impression upon me; I felt safe and secure whenever he was around and I viewed him as I imagined somebody would view a favourite uncle.

Dad poured each of us a tumbler of whiskey. Gabby's, I noticed, was an extra large one, and as he took it he nodded at Dad; it was almost as though they had their own secret code. They seemed to be constantly exchanging either specific looks, gestures of the eyes or distinctive nods.

Gabby drained his tumbler in one go, stood up and bid us goodnight, then retired to his room. I wasn't sure if it was the whiskey or the events of the day, but I suddenly felt very cold and hungry. Dad telephoned room service and shortly afterwards we were sitting opposite one another at the table with a tray each of hot coffee and sandwiches. It was then that he asked me about the day, about my training, and about my comfort level with and around guns. He asked tentatively about what he called the 'incident' at the pub. I told him word for word as it happened, of my fear, of the memories that came flooding back as I sat in the cubicle and then of just how confident I'd felt in using a gun, and at how I'd felt no remorse that I'd killed a man. Costi's death meant nothing to me. I told him that when I had the barrel of my gun held against Andrei's head, and being so close to him, I'd frozen and I believed that if Gabby hadn't had arrived when he did, there was more than a strong possibility that Andrei would easily have overpowered me. Dad told me my feelings were quite natural. He asked if I felt I could use a gun again, if I was threatened and my life depended on it.

My reply was an assertive, "Oh yes…bring it on!" And just like Gabby had said to me in the car, my dad told me he was proud of me and I don't think I'd ever be able to describe my emotions at hearing that. I immediately felt myself filling up with tears of sheer happiness, but I couldn't release them. My dad was a man, and a man would never understand just how wonderful those words were to me or why they would bring about tears.

I decided to go to bed myself. I moved around the table, threw my arms around my dad's neck, kissed him on the cheek, and told him how glad I was that he was now in our lives. I then went and checked on Gabby, and as I opened the door to his room it was darkened, the curtains were drawn and the sound of gentle snoring came from under the duvet. I went to my room, stripped off and enjoyed an invigorating hot shower in the en-suite, but as I was towelling myself dry afterwards I felt a gentle throbbing of the expected tension headache at the back of my head which I just knew was going to travel to the front and intensify. Knowing how organised Ruth was I looked in her bedside cabinet, and quickly found what I needed: a blister pack of painkillers. I squeezed two tablets into my hand, threw them into my mouth and washed them down with a glass of water from the bathroom. My brain had shut out the horrors of the day; I felt no more perturbed than if I'd watched a violent movie on television. I climbed into bed, switched off my bedside lamp and snuggled down to sleep.

The room had been dark for what certainly seemed no more than a few moments, when suddenly the door flew open, the light flashed on and Ruth entered with an expression as miserable as sin. A lady who was very much pissed off!

"Believe me, Becky, you don't want to have the sort of day I've had!" she said with a loud sigh.

"Why, what's happened?" I asked, my concern genuine.

"Where do I begin? One thing after another ... it's almost as though everybody I've met today has been pre-programmed to piss me off!"

"I thought you were out with Sandra."

"Huh, that slag!" She frowned.

"Whoa, slow down and start from the beginning. What's happened between you and Sandra?" I patted the empty side of the bed next to me, indicating she should join me. Ruth took a deep breath, then came and sat alongside me on the bed, sitting upright with her arms folded across her chest. She sighed and had the look of someone with something very difficult to say. Another deep breath and she started.

"Sandra and I had talked about the possibility of perhaps sharing a flat together..."

"You mean moving in together as a couple?" I blurted before she'd finished.

"No!" she retorted adamantly.

"But you're an item aren't you?"

"Not officially, no," she answered almost defensively.

"Okay, so what happened?" I was trying hard not to sound or feel like an agony aunt, a very bored agony aunt!

"It's like I said, we had talked about sharing a flat, we both have the same interests and we get on well together..."

"Ruth!" I interrupted, "Please just give me the short version."

"Oh, I'm so sorry if I'm boring you..." she said sarcastically.

"You are not boring me, but I'm also not stupid. I know you're a couple...one day when she visited us at that so called safe house, I walked through into the living room area and you two were on the settee engaged in...shall we say tongue wrestling." There was a soft intake of breath as she thought back to Sandra's visits to me at the safe house. I waited for a few seconds to see if she'd say anything, but got no response. I gently pulled her arm, attempting to uncross it but she yanked it back. I pulled it again and this time she let me take it; I covered her hand with mine and entwined our fingers. "Hey it's okay...I'm cool."

She looked up at me, her big doleful eyes watery; she had the expression of a naughty girl who'd been caught and was now embarrassed. "I'm sorry." She spoke glumly as she lowered her eyes.

"Hey, you've certainly got nothing to be sorry about!" I said, trying hard to sound reassuring and upbeat.

"How long did you stand there?" she asked suddenly, as she realised what I'd actually said.

"Oh, trust me, it wasn't long. I said a quick 'whoops, excuse me,' and backed out of the room as quickly as I could," I replied light heartedly.

"All the same, it's not on is it…I mean Sandra and I making out, while under the pretence of looking after you," she said quietly.

"You did look after me! Now will you shut up about it, and tell me why Sandra is suddenly a slag?" My mind was working overtime thinking up various scenarios.

"Oh, one minute she's all over me like a rash and then she says we're getting too heavy, too fast and she isn't ready yet for a full on relationship…" She sniffed, produced a tissue from out of thin air and gently dabbed her nose with it.

"And you were?"

"Now, in hindsight…no I'm not!"

"So why are you so pissed off with her? Surely she's done you a favour?" I offered logically.

"Because I was happy with her, we were good together…and now she's dumped me and besides, I wasn't ready for it to end, so the very least you could do is indulge me while I wallow in some self pity!" Her tone told me she was bouncing back and it was just a bit of dented pride.

I gave her a sisterly hug. "Let's not mention it to the media yet, okay?" I teased.

The following morning we all woke early. Ruth and I went downstairs to the restaurant for breakfast, while both dad and Gabby ordered themselves a full English breakfast from room service. Neither Ruth nor I had any real appetite for eating and the pair of us just sat idly stirring our cereal around the bowl. I was on a downer and had quite a strong premonition of doom. Shortly afterwards Ruth left for work and I returned to our suite.

I checked Gabby's wound; it certainly looked a lot better than it had the day before. I gave it another clean with antiseptic wipes, redressed it with sterilised strips and then covered it loosely. He was right about there being no news items about the shooting at the pub, and there was just a low key report about the bodies of two men which had been found in an abandoned shipping container just outside Dover docks. The newsreader continued to say that the men had been shot with different calibre guns and it was believed they were both connected to an East European organised crime syndicate.

Gabby suggested we went back to the shooting range; he was concerned that I might have lost my nerve after my close encounter with Andrei. Maybe he was right about my nerve, I don't really know. But to be honest, whilst it *was* fun and a novelty at the shooting range, when it came to shooting somebody for real, even in self defence, it was a whole different ball game and certainly not one that I was eager to repeat. On the other hand, however, if I hadn't have shot Costi, I could have been dead myself right now and maybe it would have been my body found in a shipping container or pumped full of drugs and left to die in a dingy alleyway! Dad had warned me that I might experience delayed shock syndrome or a severe bout of the blues; he said it was quite normal the first time you killed someone. I didn't like to ask him how many times he'd killed. I didn't think I really wanted to know the answer!

All three of us sat for a while, wrapped up in our own thoughts, then suddenly the phone rang, bringing us all abruptly back to reality. The caller was DS Priack. He told dad that he had reason to believe that my life was in danger and he wanted us to meet him to discuss the options available to us. Dad switched the call onto speakerphone so Gabby and I could both hear. Priack continued, in his usual patronising tone, to say that because there were various levels of police protection we needed to be aware of what it would actually mean to a young girl like me. He added that as it would have an impact on all of the family, it was important that all of us were present at the meeting. He hesitated and said that the phone wasn't the place to discuss these matters, so therefore he'd expect to see us in his office at eleven o'clock sharp. Without even waiting for a confirmation from us, he said that he would send a car to collect us. He paused momentarily and said that on second thoughts, to avoid the attention of a squad car he'd prefer to keep everything low key and so would send a taxi to collect us instead. He reiterated that it would probably be best if all of us came in together. The line then went dead.

Gabby looked at Dad. "What do you think?"

"We know the man is bent, but he is still a serving police officer so we can't reject everything he says to us just because we don't trust him."

"He could be setting us up for a hit en-route," replied Gabby.

"I don't think we should go...I've got a horrible feeling about it!" I blurted out.

Dad pondered for a moment before answering. "I'll phone that Inspector Ledbetter; if he knows nothing about it then we won't go."

Gabby nodded his agreement and they both looked at me. I wanted to say no, in fact I wanted to scream NO! But I didn't, I whispered softly, "Okay."

Dad phoned Inspector Ledbetter and, as before, put the call onto speakerphone. Ledbetter, who was apparently about to go into a meeting, did nothing to disguise his impatience and said quite curtly that if Detective Sergeant Priack was looking at either a temporary protection program or a new identity for me, then he would have thought that Dad would have been pleased that the police were actively pursuing avenues for his daughter's safety!

Dad again stated that all he wanted was confirmation that the meeting was genuine.

"I think you've just had that, Mr Tanner…goodbye." The pompous tones of the inspector were still echoing in the room after he slammed his phone down.

"D'you know something John, I don't think the police like us…" Gabby quipped humorously.

We all agreed that we would attend the meeting and we put our suspicions down to the fact that none of the individuals concerned actually liked one another!

Dad said that I should leave my little pistol behind and it was decided that only Gabby would be armed, as in the event of anything going pear-shaped than he at least had been authorised to carry a weapon as part of his close protection duty that Maureen Dickins had cleverly wrangled out of the Secretary of State. At the allotted time we made out way down to the hotel lobby and waited for our transport. Traditional black taxis and various mini cabs were coming and going on a continual basis and I could actually see the logic of our using a cab.

Our transport arrived, a mini-cab and ironically it was from the cab firm that Hannah used to own. The driver was none other than Lew Parker, the man Hannah had put in to run the business and who, it was later discovered, had been working the whole time exclusively for Dougie Mann; the same Dougie Mann who apparently now had sole ownership of the mini-cab company. That mere fact alone should have set off every alarm bell in my head, but it didn't; I was more concerned that he shouldn't remember me.

Thankfully Lew didn't appear to recognise me, although I did feel myself becoming a little bit paranoid when I saw him through the windscreen speaking into his radio to his base. I told myself it was routine, and that cabbies always radioed in their destination to their base in case there was another job close by after the passenger had been dropped off. Gabby sat in the front next to Lew, and Dad and I sat in the back. I made sure I was directly behind Lew so that he couldn't easily see me in the interior mirror.

Traffic was light and we appeared to be making good time. I glanced at Dad, as he looked over at me and smiled and I slowly started to feel myself relax. Gabby was up front and armed so even if Lew did have anything untoward in mind, he'd be very foolish to actually try anything. It was a relatively short journey and I was protected, nothing could possibly go wrong, so why did I have nagging doubts at the back of my head? Why did I feel on the verge of bottling it?

I closed my eyes and wished for the day when my life could go back to being normal. My thoughts flashed to Hannah, and how much I missed not having her around. I remembered the sounds of laughter that used to ring out of the 'Lucky Eight' Café and despite all of our illegal activities, of how innocent I really was in relation to the real world.

I opened my eyes and quickly scanned the outside surroundings to get my bearings. I saw a white car at a junction further up from us on the opposite side of the road and as we approached, it let us pass and then it accelerated up behind us. It pulled out and quickly overtook us; it clipped the front wing of our car, then swerved across the front of us, blocking the road. The driver jumped out of the driving seat at the same time as Gabby jumped out of the front passenger seat of the taxi. The driver turned and faced Gabby who was now in the process of scrambling over the taxi's bonnet. As I saw the contemptuous sneer on the driver's face, my blood ran cold, my legs paralysed.

Kevin Crestwell raised his hand to waist level, and then extended it. I saw Gabby's eyes open wide as he also realised for the first time that Crestwell was holding a large automatic pistol, the type the bad guys always seem to have in the movies. I tried to scream out, but I couldn't be sure if I did or not. I certainly have no memory of hearing any sound; it was like watching something in slow motion. I saw Crestwell's hand jolt with the recoil as he fired twice into Gabby's stomach. Gabby collapsed instantly over the bonnet of the car and slid off downwards towards the front grill leaving a wide smear of blood across the bonnet. Crestwell then ran to the rear door where I was sitting and tried to yank open the door, but Dad instinctively leaned across me and seized the door handle to stop him from opening it. Crestwell held the barrel of his pistol against the window and fired once, shooting Dad in the hand, then he yanked the door open, grabbed my hair with his free hand and started to drag me through the open door. Dad immediately reached out with his uninjured hand to grab him. At the same time, and without as much as giving Dad a second glance, Crestwell swung the heavy automatic pistol with velocity against Dad's temple, causing Dad to drop like a dead weight with half of his body across my legs and half along the rear foot well of the taxi.

I was convinced he'd killed him and screamed; Crestwell then brought the gun hard against the side of my head, not hard enough to render me unconscious, but hard enough to daze me and send me the message not to struggle. He wrenched me out from the car and as I staggered and stood upright on the pavement, I heard a shout: "Armed Police!"

Blood was now trickling down my face from the gash at the side of my head and my vision had become blurry. I could just make out figures in the not too far-off distance. Figures dressed in identical dark blue battle smocks with body armour and with their guns pointing at us. I suddenly felt very detached from my surroundings as the gradual realisation dawned on me that this was going to be the moment when I died.

I'd obviously been kept alive for a reason, possibly so I could meet my dad, and now I'd met him and bonded, so it was time to go on that journey, the one I should have taken that day when Danny and me were shot, and how ironic that once again it would be by the gun of Kevin Crestwell…or possibly from a hail of bullets from the array of armed police surrounding us.

Kevin Crestwell stood behind me, using my body as a shield. He had one hand clasped around my throat and his other hand held the gun, which he alternated between holding it at my head and waving it at the police. He was saying something but I couldn't make out his words; I honestly had no idea if he was yelling at me or shouting at the police.

But I didn't want to die; I wasn't ready to die, not here, not now! A voice in my head said: sing, SING! *S.I.N.G!!* and instantly my thoughts went back to Danny Dolan's flat. We were curled up together watching a DVD, one of the many that I used to shoplift. I remembered a particular scene that was so clear in my head that I could have been watching it where I stood. An undercover cop was teaching self defence to a bunch of women and showed them that when an assailant grabbed you from behind you could get out of it by…by … I couldn't remember the sequence of how to free yourself and the scene in my head had now changed anyway, to one where Danny and I were arguing.

I remembered enough, though. Instinctively I moved my hand down behind me into Crestwell's groin and grabbed his balls; I imagined the contorted expression on his piggy-featured face as I squeezed as hard as I possibly could. My other hand grabbed at his fingers clasped around my throat; from the corner of my eye I saw him raise his gun hand prior to swinging it down against the side of my head. I knew I had only seconds, so I lifted my leg and stamped down hard against his instep; at the same time I released his balls and with both hands I prised his fingers away from my throat.

As I tried to run he kicked out and knocked my leg behind the other one, causing me to fall flat on my face. It was a déjà vu moment; I knew that this was when he would finish the job he'd started when Danny Dolan was killed and I'd survived. I tensed my body, anticipating the bullet that would burst into the back of my skull.

I heard a click, and then I heard Crestwell curse and I could only assume his automatic pistol had jammed; and then I heard the sound as it fired, but it wasn't the sharp crack of a pistol round, it was I suppose more like an elongated sound … suddenly my body felt as though it had been crushed, the air was forced out of my lungs and I hurt, my ribs, my shoulders, my back, everything hurt!

The nightmare continued as Crestwell's face buried itself into the side of my neck and I felt his rancid breath as his body gave its last gasp before death. I visualised his body, as it lay prostrate on top of me almost in a macabre sexual position. I sensed a lot of movement around me, the trickle of blood from the gash in my head had now made its way into the corner of my eye, which meant I could only see when squinting through my eye lashes, but what I saw was what seemed to be a score of boots, policemen's boots, and then frenzied shouts or maybe it was a flock of seagulls, the sound was similar, but I was aware the police were pointing their guns almost at point blank range at the head of a dead man!

Kevin Crestwell's body was rolled off me and I was at last able to draw air fully into my lungs. As the police helped me to my feet, I looked down at the body below me; the entire front of Crestwell's upper body was covered in blood. I was unsteady on my feet and became aware of a young policeman holding me gently by my arms. I felt a stinging sensation in my eyes, and closed them momentarily, then I opened them and turned around, only slightly but enough for my blurry vision to fall upon Gabby, whose body had been left in the grotesque position in which he had fallen. His glazed eyes showed they were devoid of life, as did the deathly pale hue of his face. There was a pool of blood underneath him.

My eyes scanned across the bonnet of the car to the front driver's seat. A pistol was balancing precariously along the edge of the dashboard. Lew Parker was still strapped into his seat belt, his head and neck appeared to be twisted backwards, an unnatural distortion, and then I saw the single hole in his forehead, where I assumed a police marksman had removed him as a threat.

The rear door of the mini car was open and a paramedic was attending to Dad. It seemed as though the entire rear seats were covered in blood. Dad's blood! I tried to choke back a sob, but without success and as it escaped from my mouth a cloudburst of tears poured from my eyes. I moved unsteadily towards the rear of the car and looked over the medic's shoulder at my dad. His eyes were closed and his mouth was slightly open as he took shaky breaths, and almost as though he knew I was looking at him, he opened his eyes and gave me a smile, a smile that said 'I love you.' A fresh flow of tears pricked at my eyes. The medic looked up and across at me and mouthed the words, *'He's going to be okay.'* I closed my eyes as tightly as I could to ease the soreness, but more importantly I just wanted to block out the scene around me.

I was put into a separate ambulance to Dad. The young policeman came with me and I know he was speaking to me, asking me questions, but asking very gently. I didn't answer; I couldn't. I just sat in a trance and the strangest of thoughts that suddenly went through my head was, *'How do soldiers deal with this sort of thing day in and day out?'*

Gabby was pronounced dead on arrival at the hospital. They told me that the paramedics at the scene had fought tooth and nail to keep him alive but too many of his vital organs had been damaged. They said that at no time did he regain consciousness; I wasn't sure if that was a blessing or not, but they let me see him before his body was moved away. I kissed him on the forehead and said, "Thank you" and as I leaned over him, a tear dropped from my eye onto his cheek. I don't know why, but I gently rubbed it into his cold skin. He was a special man who had died trying to save me.

Dad's injury was initially stabilised at the scene. The bullet had gone completely through his hand. They lost me when they started talking about ballistics, but apparently because Kevin Crestwell's pistol was classed as a low velocity, and it wasn't as bad as if it had been a high velocity weapon. At the hospital they moved Dad straight into the intensive care unit for what they called early fracture stabilisation. Thankfully they confirmed quite quickly that they found no infection and it would not require amputation. They did some reconstructive surgery and also fitted a mini plate in his hand and he was eventually to be left with some nasty scarring and a permanent numbness in his hand. He had quite a few months of physical therapy ahead of him to look forward to.

I was okay physically but they kept me in hospital overnight for observation.
Ruth, on the other hand, took it worse than any of us; when she arrived at the hospital she was nigh on hysterical and unfortunately people kept using the word 'lucky' to her, as in we were *lucky* that the Anti-Terrorist branch of the Metropolitan Police happened to be returning from an incident at the London City airport! And we were *lucky* to have been taken to this hospital, as they are one of the leading hospitals dealing with penetrating gunshot wounds.

I could see it written all over Ruth's face: the anxiety, the stress, the fear, the shock, and she needed an outlet for it all. She needed to explode at someone, and that someone happened to be a nurse who casually remarked to her, "They're very lucky; it could have been a lot worse."

"LUCKY? You gormless fucking moron! We have a very close friend of our family lying dead in your morgue! My father has lost the use of one of his hands and my sister is currently under observation as you are unsure just how badly the events of this trauma will affect her! If your stupid fucking brain calls that *lucky*, I hate to know what you call a bad day!" Oh yes, Ruth had let rip! As the nurse stood rooted to the spot, her bottom lip quivering, a doctor and a senior nurse suddenly materialised either side of Ruth, speaking softly to her, calming her down and completely ignoring the nurse who very quickly ran off in floods of tears.

Shortly afterwards I gave my bedside statement to the police telling my view of events and when Dad was finally released from the intensive care unit they wanted his statement too, but he was too drowsy to give one so they said they would wait, and I was later told that there was an armed response unit parked outside the hospital all night.

The Press, needless to say, had a field day with it apparently and immediately badgered the Home Secretary for a statement. This was quoted in the evening papers and on the radio as *'a serious, appalling, barbaric act, which apparently is becoming more common with the increase of gang violence and the easy availability of firearms.'*

It was just after lunchtime the following day when Ruth arrived to collect me; I'd already had a check over earlier in the morning, the results of which were okay. I was given another quick check after lunch and then discharged from the hospital.

The police drove us back to our hotel suite and advised us to stay put until another of their officers had called in to see us. Needless to say, he didn't visit, nor did he telephone! It suited us though, so we ordered dinner from room service along with a couple of bottles of wine, after which we were ready for a relatively early night in bed.

The following morning I slept in late. It was unusual for me these days, but I'd had a restless night; a nightmarish sort of night, one where my head was filled with visions of Gabby's dead body and with visions of having to identify the corpses of Ruth and Dad as being of my own flesh and blood. I'd woken abruptly so many times throughout the night, with my heart beating so loud and fast that it hurt. The hotel bed also left a lot to be desired and I assumed, probably quite correctly, that it had more than passed its sell-by date! And what with the recent virtual crushing my poor body had endured, with the dead weight of Kevin Crestwell's body falling on it, this morning every part of my body ached. I pulled myself out of bed and, in a gait resembling early Neanderthal man, I made my way to the en-suite and stood under the shower. Even the hot water hitting me powerfully and cascading over my body couldn't soothe the dull pain searing from my legs to my back and shoulder muscles. I stood there almost trance-like, mulling over recent events.

A large portion of luck they all said, but I was also aware that it was only the presence of Gabby that had saved my life a couple of days earlier. I couldn't take it for granted that fate would always lend a hand. My life was going to be constantly in danger for as long as Dougie Mann and his close associates remained at liberty, but even then his vindictive evil tentacles were liable to reach out through the prison walls to get me, which left only one solution, the same solution that Gabby had suggested at the very beginning. The threat to my existence had to be terminated once and for all.

I remained in thought for quite a while before a random thought came into my head: did the wrinkly skin syndrome only occur if you spent too long soaking in a bath or could it also come about from standing too long under a shower....? I knew it was trivia but it had lodged itself in my head, so I stepped out of the shower, towel-dried my body and wrapped myself in one of those white fluffy bathrobes that all hotels seemed to supply these days.

As I entered the main room of the suite, my eyes fell upon Ruth who had draped herself across an armchair, with her nose buried into a book. The phone rang and I picked it up on its first ring. A male voice spoke:

"Hello young lady. I don't know if you remember me or not but my name is Ernie Palmer, and I'm a close friend of your dad's. You and I met –

albeit briefly – in the 'Three Kings' pub along with Maureen Dickins on that dreadful day of the shooting incident."

"Yes, I remember you…I remember everything about that day," I replied.

"Yes, I expect you do…anyway the reason for my call is that John asked me to keep an eye on you…"

"What, you've spoken to him?" I interrupted.

"No, not today I haven't. John asked me some time back that if he should find himself…put out of action…would I keep some tabs on you to ensure you don't wander into any danger." He spoke almost apologetically.

"That's very kind of you, but at the moment I'm intending to remain in the hotel."

"Okay. By the way, the Department will make all the arrangements regarding Gabriel…"

"Gabriel? Oh you mean Gabby?"

"Yes, we knew him as Gabriel Bracken … but as I say, we will take care of all arrangements, including the funeral."

"Oh, yes. I must admit I hadn't given that a thought," I said, suddenly feeling very ashamed.

"You are still in the shock stage. I don't expect you really want to think about anything, except perhaps hitting back at the person who did this." His change of tack left me at a loss for words. It was a comment I wasn't expecting and I remained silent. "So, let me ask you again Becky: what are your plans?" asked Ernie.

"I want to get the bastard who set this up and to start with, I want to report Priack for being corrupt, for having blood on his hands and for working for Dougie Mann!" I spat the words out in a mixture or anger and female emotion.

"Okay, firstly…no names over the phone! Secondly, speak to Ledbetter. Yesterday his long awaited promotion came through; he's now Chief Inspector Ledbetter. Tell him you want to submit a formal complaint against one of the officers at his station, then follow whatever course of action he suggests. Phone me after you've spoken to him and let me know his response … oh, and if you should sense a feeling that you are being followed, I believe Maureen Dickins has got one of her people shadowing you." He spoke clearly, calmly and very much in control.

"Oh…right, okay then…I'll speak soon." I replaced the receiver, wondering just what the hell was going on, and just what strings my dad was pulling from his hospital bed."

I waited for a few moments to fully compose myself and then telephoned Chief Inspector Ledbetter. My call was transferred straight through to him and the instant he answered his phone I could tell that along with his promotion, his pompous attitude had also increased. I told him of my intention to lodge a formal complaint against Detective Sergeant Priack and fully expected his patronising tone to tell me not to waste his time! But he didn't; in fact he talked me through the procedure and then advised that before I chose to go down that route I should think very carefully about it, as once the process started there was no stopping it. He requested me to go to the police station and attend a meeting along with him and two other senior officers. He followed that by using the most annoying, overused cliché that every government body these days seemed to spout: *'we take these matters very seriously.'* The mere fact that that particular cliché happened to be the standard response to everything at that time really diminished any faith I could have had in him! He finished the call by offering to send one of their armed response units to collect me and escort me to the station. My immediate concern was that it would be an unmarked car, something along the lines of Lew Parker's mini-cab, but he confirmed it would be a fully marked police unit, complete with blue flashing lights if required.

I felt confident and agreed. Ruth was insistent that she came with me and within the hour we were pulling into the rear yard of the police station, and whilst it hadn't been something I'd thought about for quite a while, I had to admit that the two officers who were taking us were rather dishy! We were taken past the main desk and up two flights of stairs, along a corridor and into an empty office. A WPC stood with us and only a short while later we were joined by Chief Inspector Ledbetter, a Detective Chief Inspector Ellis, and a Superintendent James. Both Ruth and the WPC then left the room.

All three of the men sitting in front of me were masters of condescendence. I began by telling them roughly the same as I did in my statement: of my belief that DS Priack had set us up. I then added that he was corrupt and that he was on the take from Dougie Mann. Neither of them showed any emotion; they just looked back at me, and then Detective Chief Inspector Ellis told me that if I felt strongly that an officer had acted inappropriately then I should report the matter to the Independent Police Complaints Commission. He stated that corruption was defined under various guises, such as giving, soliciting or accepting a reward, which may influence that person or person's actions and added that as far as they were concerned, I hadn't produced one shred of evidence to prove one of their officers had taken an inducement or committed any offence.

Superintendent James then offered his condolences on the death of Gabriel Bracken and the hospitalization of my father and added that it was possible I was suffering from the after effects of the trauma and suggested it could be beneficial if I contacted the local victim support group for help!

They were sceptical and disinterested. DCI Ellis stated that it was their policy always to investigate any allegations against their officers, but again reiterated that without further firm evidence then they could not consider the matter any further. I responded far too quickly and without thinking, and blurted out that Priack had planted evidence in our flat at the time when they had charged Hannah Isaacs and that he had lied in Court. They asked me to provide proof and also asked if I was prepared to confess to my own involvement relating to the charges. But I was afraid to take that extra step; terrified that I might also end up in prison, and that a psycho inmate could also slash my face. So I said nothing.

The Armed Response Police car took Ruth and me back to our hotel. The journey was made in silence as the guilt at my self-preservation ate away at me. We arrived back at the hotel and as soon as we were in our room Ruth wanted to know the full ins and outs of everything that had been said. But all I could say was that they were closing ranks and protecting their own.

I pulled my mobile out of my shoulder bag and pressed the number Ernie Palmer had given me for his direct line. It rang quite a few times before he answered it.

"Hello Ernie, it's me – Becky Wilson. I haven't long been back from a meeting with Ledbetter and his cronies."

"Ah Becky, how did it go?" he asked.

"A complete waste of time if you ask me. They're not interested in catching Priack; they'd rather sweep it under the carpet and pretend everyone is squeaky clean!"

"Tell me who was present at the meeting and exactly what was said, and by whom?" his tone was thoughtful.

I told him the names of the three muppets who were there and roughly chapter and verse on every word they had said. Of course, I did conveniently omit my little outburst…!

"You've done well Becky, I'm pleased with that."

"How on earth can you be pleased? They are not going to do anything … they've buried it!" I objected.

"Becky, this is meant in the kindest way, but you still have a lot to learn. Seeds of doubt about DS Priack have been sown for quite some time; what you have done today is to nourish them and encourage their development…"

"Look, I'm sorry but Priack is responsible for my father being maimed, for Gabby's death and God alone knows what physiological problems they have left me with, so the fact that I may have aroused their suspicions is of absolutely no interest to me at all!"

"Becky, I can understand your being angry but trust me, using a hammer to crack an egg is not going to get us the result we want."

"So what are you suggesting then?" I asked quite abruptly.

"Imagine at the moment you are in a rudderless boat, and just wait and see where the current takes you."

"Yeah, right…okay Ernie, I'll, um…I'll let you know if I run into any rocks." My sarcasm was intentional.

"Trust me, Becky, I know what I'm saying…" He paused, "…You take care of yourself…bye."

"What was all that about?" Ruth asked glumly as I put my mobile back in my bag.

"It was Dad's friend, Ernie Palmer; he was talking about plants and boats with no rudders."

"What?"

"Yeah, exactly! He means well, bless him, but he's a bit slow-lane material if you get my meaning."

"So what are we going to do?"

"I think for starters, as it's close to visiting time at the hospital, we should go and visit our dad."

It was about mid morning the following day. Ruth was out, clothes shopping, and I was bored and just dossing about when the hotel phone rang and I was informed there was a Chief Inspector Ledbetter in the foyer to see me. I asked them to send him up and then quickly tidied the place up before he arrived.

When I let him into the suite he gave a friendly smile, looked around and asked if we were alone; I told him that my sister was out shopping but could return at any time.

"Miss Wilson, I'd like to talk to you off the record regarding your allegations about Detective Sergeant Priack."

"As long as you understand that what you refer to as an allegation...I call a fact," I retorted.

"Yes, quite. The thing is, I do believe you, and my colleagues yesterday were quite correct in that, without sustainable proof, they are unable to act upon your allegations..."

"Then why are you here?" I asked aggressively.

"I am aware the Metropolitan police does have a few bad apples and in that we are no different to other constabularies. However, one of the problems with any anti-corruption investigation is that the officer or officers concerned will be fully aware of just how these crimes get investigated and as such they are practised in covering their tracks..."

"So what are you saying...are you trying to justify the fact that you have no intention of doing anything?" I folded my arms across my chest and gave him a defiant look.

"No, in fact I'm proposing the opposite. If we try gathering evidence against him, there is a very strong chance that he may somehow find out what we're doing before we've accumulated sufficient evidence to bring a successful prosecution."

"I'm sorry, you've lost me...perhaps you could tell me again exactly why are you here?" My tone fully expressed my disinterest.

"I believe that this is one of those cases where to enable a successful prosecution we need to catch the individual concerned in the act via a highly secretive and carefully planned operation, more commonly known as a sting."

"And just where do I come into this?" I asked suspiciously.

"Early this morning I had a clandestine meeting with a gentleman from the Security Service at Thames House – I believe you aquainted with him – a Mr Ernie Palmer, and he has come up with a plan not only to catch DS Priack but also to ensure he turns Queen's evidence against Dougie Mann. There is, of course, a *but*…and it is a big *but*…" He paused momentarily. "It will require you putting yourself on the line, so to speak."

"Well, I'm still listening, so feel free to carry on talking." I wanted to come across as completely confident, but my insides were more like dissolving jelly.

"The plan put forward by Mr Palmer will require a considerable amount of guile. I'm not going to give you carte blanche to go out and do whatever you want whenever you feel like it, but I have been assured that you have the particular skills and resources which will be required for this operation."

"Are you actually planning to tell me what it entails, or is that something I've got to guess?" I said, assuming an expression of boredom; the truth was, I was as curious as hell as to what Ernie Palmer had in mind.

"What I will tell you now, Miss Wilson, is that I am on your side. You wanted DS Priack to be brought to account … well I am the man who is going to help you to achieve that aim. I have also run the plan by the Metropolitan Police's anti-corruption unit, CIB3, and they are happy for me to run with it for the present. Now, to answer your … um, rather sarcastic question, the details of the plan will be explained to you by Ernie Palmer himself, who will be co-ordinating every stage of this operation." Chief Inspector Ledbetter looked at his watch. "Mr Palmer visited your father this morning prior to my arriving here; I envisage he should be arriving back here quite soon…"

The hotel phone rang cutting him off in mid-sentence. It was the front desk informing me that a Mr Ernie Palmer was in the foyer and wished to see me. As before, I asked them to send him up and after replacing the receiver I went to the door to greet him; unfortunately Ruth had arrived at the same time, laden with shopping bags.

"Hello Ernie, what are you doing here?" asked Ruth, smiling as she followed Ernie into the suite, then she caught sight of CI Ledbetter, and the smile quickly changed to a snarl. "What's more to the point, just what the hell are you doing here?" Ruth's eyes narrowed, and her body language, her tone and her expression all showed the utter contempt in which she held the Chief Inspector.

Before he could respond, I butted in. "Ruth, leave it, will yer!" I snapped at her.

She looked at me with a stunned expression that very quickly turned to one of suspicion; she slid herself into the nearest chair, looked at each of us in turn and then said quietly, "Well, isn't this lovely? Now, why don't we all sit down, and you tell me JUST WHAT THE FUCK IS GOING ON!" Despite her outburst she still sat looking completely unflustered, only now her eyes didn't just look at us, they bored their way into each of us.

Ernie frowned as he looked back at me, while CI Ledbetter looked down at his shoes. We were like three naughty schoolchildren in front of their headmistress. I sighed quietly, knowing what I was about to say to her was going to be far more difficult than I could imagine.

"Yeah, okay, you're right...you have a right to know..." I hesitated.

"I'm becoming impatient Becky;, spit it out now! I have a right to know WHAT?"

"I believe I may be about to do something ... seemingly reckless and most certainly dangerous, but I can't be any more specific at the moment..."

"And why not?" She narrowed her eyes.

"Because Ernie hasn't fully explained it to me yet...you came bursting in too early."

"Well, excuse me, but I do live here as well!"

Ernie spoke then. "Okay girls, calm down now. I can assure you that neither the Chief Inspector nor I want to sit here and listen to you two bitching at each other. Now, I have a very serious proposition to put to Becky and yes, she was correct, we said it could be dangerous. What I need to know first from Becky is whether or not she would be comfortable meeting DS Priack and ... shall we say ... spinning him a fanciful tale?"

"I think that you should get one of your police people to go undercover and do whatever it is you want Becky to do. She's already been through hell and back these last few months," Ruth said, trying to protect me.

"Unfortunately, Becky is the key to this operation being successful," replied Ernie.

"Well in that case I believe that you should at least discuss it with our father first, because I know that his first concern will be Becky's welfare rather then whether or not you catch a couple of villains." Ruth answered in a very matter of fact fashion, but it was now time for my contribution.

"Actually Ruth, they're not just villains; one of them is the man who had me beaten and forced to work as a prostitute. He's also the man who was behind Gabby being killed and dad being maimed. The other one is responsible for lying and for planting drugs in my flat, which resulted in Hannah going to prison..." As I spoke the words I actually felt myself becoming emotional.

"And to answer your other statement..." said Ernie, drawing their attention away from my watery eyes. "... I visited the hospital and spoke to your father this morning. Yes, of course he was concerned for Becky's safety, but he also realised that while these people are at liberty, then Becky will never be truly safe. He is aware of who within my department will be shadowing her and subject to Becky's agreement he gave the plan his approval."

They now all looked at me for a response.

My answer came out just above a whisper. "Tell me what it is that I have to do."

At this point Ernie seemed to become quite excited. "Firstly, let us all sit down…around the table would be preferable." We all sat, Ruth and I on one side and Ernie and Ledbetter on the other. I was sitting opposite Ernie, and after a quick glance to check we were all ready, he began.

"I intend to use an identical plan to one I used successfully a few years back. This will also require the use of some props … mainly a prosthetic body with a clean gunshot hole in its head, and a small briefcase containing marked and easily traceable banknotes. The catalyst for this will be information passed to Detective Sergeant Priack by Chief Inspector Ledbetter, and confirmation of that information along with an Oscar winning performance by Becky, the details of which I will go over with her alone…to use that old cliché it really will be a *need to know* scenario."

Ruth half held up her hand as though she were a nervous student, and Ernie responded in kind by nodding, acknowledging she could speak.

"When you say *prosthetic body*…can you explain?" Her voice came across more confident than her body language.

"Silicone, rubber and latex foam, the most realistic looking body you will ever find. It was made to a very high standard; you'd have to dissect it to discover it's a fake," answered Ernie proudly.

"You mentioned a gunshot hole…."

Chief Inspector Ledbetter held up the palm of his hand, stopping Ruth before she could finish. "I believe we've talked enough. Mr Palmer and Miss Wilson you two now need to go somewhere and discuss the assignment in finer detail, including date and time of commencement. Miss Wilson the elder, you must not breathe a word of this to anyone!" He spoke formally, his eyes showing no warmth.

"I do know that…I'm not completely stupid you know!" Ruth always had to have the last word.

Chapter 21

Becky's Payback!

It was exactly five days later when I telephoned Detective Sergeant Priack and asked him to meet me. Ernie had supplied a grotty-looking bed-sit on the second floor of what was once probably a very classy Edwardian house, and that was where I'd asked DS Priack to meet me.

He was very formal when he arrived and also very much on guard as to what he said. He held what looked like a mini remote control and while pressing one of the buttons on it he waved it around the room.

"What's that and what are you doing?" I asked curiously.

"This will tell me if you've got any bugs planted and I'm not talking about the creeping type that you're probably used to living with, I'm interested in the electronic variety which have a nasty habit of listening to conversations."

"Well feel free and if there are any I'll certainly be having a word with the letting agent," I replied.

The bed-sit was a quite a large room. A small kitchen area jutted out from an alcove, with a couple of cupboards, a small cooker and fridge. A large double bed occupied most of the room, a small two-seater sofa sat at the foot of the bed facing a TV unit complete with portable TV and video. A couple of wardrobes stood against one wall and a dressing table and chest of drawers stood against the opposite wall.

He wandered around, opening drawers and wardrobe doors, feeling and checking for himself that it was in fact my bed-sit, my clothes. He even opened and checked the small kitchen cupboard and the fridge, scrutinising that there was food and that the bed-sit was in fact lived in.

He came and stood in front of me. "So, you think you may have some information that I need to know about," he said finally.

"Yes and no," I answered, my tone noncommittal.

"What do you mean? You either have or you haven't!" He almost spat the words at me.

"I'm in a position to help you to make some money – seven and a half thousand pounds to be exact …that is, if you want it; if not I'll ask another bent policemen. After all, there are a lot of you to choose from!"

"Don't try and be clever with me, or you'll get a fucking slapping, yeah?"

I just looked at him with an expression of hatred. "Now, tell me where this money's coming from?" he asked aggressively.

"From your friend Dougie Mann. Apparently you fucked up big time, trying to set up a hit on me, and Dougie isn't too happy with you, so he sent for a Frenchman, a guy called Paul-Louis Broque, someone with a reputation for being professional … I suppose the complete opposite of you really," I sneered, as my eyes looked him up and down. I didn't see it coming but I certainly felt it as the palm of his hand slapped me squarely across the face. The force of it sent me reeling back against the wall; he followed in and clasped his hand over my mouth. His hand stank of stale tobacco; my initial instinct was to knee him in his balls, but I had to play this out, had to reel him in.

There was no flicker of emotion across his face as he moved it closer to mine, and his lips grazed my neck. "I told you to watch the fucking lip!" he whispered menacingly. His other hand reached out and unbuttoned the thin jacket I was wearing... I made no move to stop him. He moved his head back and studied my face, and then smiled. "I have been looking forward to this," he said as his hand now moved under the bottom hem of my top and began moving upwards, stroking my skin. He cupped my breast through my bra and squeezed gently. "Oh yes, very nice," he sneered lustfully as he gripped the firmness of my breast. He paused, as if for effect, and watched me closely.

I wanted to scream at him, to claw his face with my nails but I knew I couldn't. I told myself I was an actress playing a part, that it wasn't real. His eyes narrowed, his cruel thin lips curled in an inviting smile, all the time looking for a reaction from me. The smell of his hand over my mouth was revolting; I could sense nausea building up slowly inside me. I was thankful when he moved his hand from my mouth, and I instantly knocked it away. "I'm not a fucking tom and I'm not your little slapper either!" I saw the smile fade from his lips and feared the worst. I became slightly apprehensive and instinctively edged back, but I was already against the wall. I felt a sudden surge of anger: why had I allowed him to touch me in the first place? Just who did this asshole think he was? I wasn't his property; I was nobody's property. I was no longer a sex slave living in fear that if I'd hadn't pleased a customer I faced the ensuing dread of either a beating or of being submerged in an icy cold bath. I glared confidently into his eyes.

"Let's get one thing straight, Priack: there is nothing in your trousers that interests me. Now I called you here to discuss a business deal, so either you're interested in talking business or you can just clear off!"

He spoke softly, yet menacingly. "If you ever talk to me like that again, I'm going to hurt you, and believe me when I'm finished with you, you'll think the treatment you got from Andrei was just play fighting..."

"You don't scare me, you piece of shit, and if you ever lay a hand on me again, then believe me I'll fucking kill you, and I'm really getting a taste for killing!"

Whatever he had intended to do he obviously thought better of it and stepped away. "Okay, then you've just learned a valuable lesson; now tell me about this seven and a half grand and exactly what it is you want me to do?" he replied firmly and with an evidently suppressed anger.

"Okay, there is a man…"

"What man?" he demanded.

"A Frenchman, a guy called Paul-Louis Broque. He's a hit man and charges on average thirty thousand pounds for a hit. Apparently he's worth it because he's good and he always delivers. When he accepts a job he takes fifty percent up front and the remainder upon completion, so Dougie Mann duly gave him fifteen thousand quid in a small brown leather brief case..."

"So how come you know so much about his operation?" questioned Priack suspiciously.

"Because Paul and I became lovers, albeit for a short period...and he took a perverse delight in telling me about his career, and the people he's killed and the money he's made from it."

"So why didn't he kill you?" he asked warily.

"As I said, the man enjoys some perverted delights, one of which is to make love to his female targets and get them to fall in love with him, and then I assume he gets a sadistic pleasure from killing them."

"That doesn't explain why he didn't kill you?" he repeated.

"We met in a shopping centre, he asked for directions, he was a very charming man and when he invited me to dinner I accepted. I stayed with him that night at his flat, and yes, we made love and the sex was incredible. The next day, after another lengthy session, he told me he had fallen in love with me; he started to let little bits slip, about his life and his job. I quickly realised what he was and play-acted the besotted woman. He told me about the contract on me and showed me the briefcase containing the money; he said he wasn't interested in fulfilling the contract any longer and that we'd both go back to his villa on the Mediterranean, a few miles outside Marseille. While he was showering I went through his things and discovered a single one-way ticket back to France for that evening's flight. He'd also moved his gun from his suitcase to underneath his pillow, so it wasn't hard to fathom out that I wasn't long for this world!"

"What happened then?" I could tell Priack was buying into the story.

"Paul came out of the shower and was still quite horny and wanted me to finish him off with a blow job; when that was over he lay back on the bed and closed his eyes, relaxed and contented. I slipped my hand under his pillow and pulled out the gun, then quickly placed a pillow over his head, held the tip of the barrel to it and squeezed the trigger. I then tidied up everything, wiped my prints off the gun and left. It was only afterwards that I realised I'd left the briefcase containing fifteen thousand pounds in the flat with a corpse, and I haven't got the bottle to go back in there to get it!"

"Are you confessing a murder to me?" he asked.

"No! I want that briefcase and I'll split it with you fifty-fifty, and then I intend to disappear out of this country for good!"

Priack thought deeply for a while, weighing up the proposition. "Do you have a key to the flat?"

"No, but the lock is old and flimsy; slip a credit card against the catch and it'll spring open easily."

"And whereabouts in the flat is the case?"

"Under the bed…under the foot of the bed. You could be in and out in less than a minute."

"And where is the gun?"

"I took a trip on the Woolwich ferry and halfway across I accidentally dropped over the side," I grinned craftily.

"One last thing…why have you come to me for help when you obviously know of my connection with Dougie Mann?"

"I would have thought that was logical! Asking someone to break into a flat, walk past a dead body and collect a hit man's contract money from under the bed isn't something you'd ask the average person. But you're different; you're a copper and …let's be honest … you're a bent copper who's not squeamish. You are the ideal person."

"You'd better not be putting me up…if this is a set up Becky, I'll kill you myself."

"Just leave it out with the threats, okay?" I replied giving the impression of being exasperated.

He still seemed hesitant, and for a moment I thought I'd failed to convince him, but suddenly he agreed. "Okay I'll do it, what's the address?" I gave him an envelope with the address; he glanced at it, stuffed it in his pocket and turned to leave.

"Whoa, hold on a moment. If we're partners in this then we do it together!" I spat adamantly.

"Forget it, if I do this then I do it alone…"

"Yes and you'll forget to come back with my share…no, that's bollocks, I'm coming with you…I'll wait outside while you go in."

He smiled condescendingly at me. "Actually Becky, I've just had a rethink. Maybe I should take you to the station and charge you with murder, then I can visit the flat while you're safely locked away in a cell and when I don't find any briefcase…well it'll only be your word that it was ever there…if you get my drift?"

My shoulders sagged and as I sighed deeply I looked back at him with a defeated expression. "Okay, you win, you go alone…where do you want to meet, to do the split?"

"Ten o'clock this evening, you wait on the corner outside and I'll drive past and pick you up. We'll do the split in my car; that's going to be a lot of money to risk flashing in public. Besides, this is a red light district … I'm sure you could even do a bit of rough trade while you're waiting!" he said, while leering at my breasts.

"You go fuck yourself, you arsehole…" I retorted, my face screwed up in disgust.

After he'd left, I sat on the bed. I felt very low; my performance had drained me emotionally and I felt dirty, as though I'd been used and abused, and as the first tears appeared in the corners of my eyes, I dropped my head into my hands and sobbed. My body shook almost uncontrollably as if in some kind of seizure, and still the tears flooded out – tears of grief and tears of guilt, mixed in with tears of regret.

Eventually I regained my composure, and shortly afterwards the door to the bed-sit opened and Ernie entered, along with a very beautiful Indian girl. Two slim muscular guys came in behind them, took a quick glance around the room and stood outside. The Indian girl placed her arm around me and I sat with my head on her shoulder. I knew my eyes were red and puffy and the odd tear still trickled from them.

"Becky, my name is Kamalika…DS Priack has gone, you are quite safe." She spoke gently like a mother to her child.

"You did very well Rebecca; you exceeded all expectations…I'm just sorry that you had to endure being assaulted, but if it had got out of hand we were poised to intervene instantly." Ernie spoke reassuringly.

"Er, what do you mean…how do you know that he…?"

"This entire room is one huge listening and recording studio…the far wall is collapsible; to us it would be no different to bursting through a sheet of paper."

"But he scanned the room for any listening devices."

"Yes, but he was using a cheap over-the-counter scanner, searching for small individual wireless transmitters…this entire house is, as I have already said, a permanently wired specialised recording studio, virtually impossible to detect." He spoke of the room almost with pride.

Kamalika nudged me. "We have somebody following DS Priack so we'll know where he is at all times. I think for now, perhaps a shower and some rest before you meet with him tonight?" Kamalika spoke softly but in a way that you knew her suggestion wasn't debatable.

"We have another house close by, and you will have privacy. I'll also get some food sent in," she added.

On leaving the flat and climbing into the back of an unmarked security car, my thoughts had caused me to revert once more into victim mode. I snapped myself out of it but felt myself slipping back in as though it was a comfort zone, a place to hide.

A few hours later, however, I'd showered, eaten and slept; I felt refreshed and geared up ready for my next round with DS Priack. Kamalika had brought me a pair of jeans and a thick warm jumper, along with some fresh underwear.

DS Priack had been to the flat and collected the case. He'd been photographed, approaching, entering and leaving with the case. I didn't know this at the time, however, since they wouldn't tell me before I'd met him; they didn't know if he was going to admit that he'd actually got it, and if he decided to deny collecting it and I knew differently, they were worried I may inadvertently say something and give the game away.

At precisely ten minutes to ten o'clock I was sitting in a warm car with Kamalika. If DS Priack played fair and split the money fifty-fifty then it would give us a problem, as he could cry entrapment as his defence. Therefore the plan now hinged on the greed of the man. We were discussing my various options of response when Kamalika received the phone call confirming that DS Priack was on his way. I climbed out of her car and sauntered towards the corner; it was a cold and damp evening and I was soon feeling more than a little chilly. It was just a couple of minutes after ten when a dark saloon car pulled up at the kerb about forty yards away from me and flashed its lights. I was unsure whether or not to approach it. It could have been Priack or it could have been one of Dougie Mann's hit man, or maybe just a punter chancing his luck. The headlights flashed again. I hesitated momentarily and then moved slowly towards it; I could feel my heart beating faster, faster and louder.

As I approached the car I ducked down slightly to the driver's level. It was dark and I still couldn't make out who was sitting behind the steering wheel, but as I arrived alongside it, the side window was halfway down, and a derisive voice came from within the car.

"Hello bitch, how much you gonna charge to blow me?" At the same instant a car passed by from the opposite direction, its headlights fully illuminating the source of the voice in the driver's seat: Detective Sergeant Priack, complete with sneer. I opened the car door and quickly jumped into the front passenger seat of his car.

"It'll cost an arsehole like you the full fifteen K," I replied haughtily.

We drove in silence for a few miles; not that we covered any great distance overall, as he was doing lots of left turns and doubling back on himself, constantly checking his rear view mirror to check that we weren't being followed. Eventually he was satisfied and shortly afterwards he slowed and turned the car onto an empty industrial area. There were no streetlights and darkness had fully enclosed the area. He parked alongside the high wall of a disused warehouse and as he switched off the car's headlights we were plunged into a complete blackness. I felt his hand touch my outer thigh; I moved my leg slightly away, and his hand moved to the top of my leg. I slapped it hard causing him to withdraw it quickly. He switched on the car's interior light; I immediately glared at him with an expression of sheer hate.

"We're here to divvy up the money and that's all, so keep your fucking hands off me, you pile of sleaze!"

"Yeah, well, I've actually been having second thoughts about that," he drawled in a very off-hand way.

"What do you mean, second thoughts? Who the fuck are you to have second thoughts?" I sneered at him, like he was a nothing. He half turned to face me, the look on his face telling me he was going to strike out. I quickly slipped my hand into my bag, which was now resting on my lap. "Before you try anything, ask yourself one question: how many guns did Paul-Louis Broque bring with him and is it possible that I could be holding a small automatic pistol... a handbag gun, a girly gun, but it can still pack a punch and at this range will certainly stop a man dead! Now do you still want to hit me?"

He straightened up and turned back to face the steering wheel; he looked ahead, saying nothing. Suddenly he reached across and grabbed my bag, pulling it onto his own lap, and opened it. My mobile phone, my purse, a lipstick, a small travel pack of tissues, a few crumpled receipts, but definitely no gun. He gave me a sideways glance and sensing that his fist was about to swiftly make contact with my face, I asked a question.

"Tell me about this second thought you've had...we can't carry on arguing and fighting every time we meet." I kept my tone amicable.

Thankfully it worked. He didn't hit me; he adopted a smug look, obviously pleased with himself and with what he was about to tell me. "Quite simply Becky, I've decided that I'll give you enough for a single train ticket from London to Paris, plus a few pounds for you to rent a doss house in their red light quarter and that's all."

"What do you mean, that's all? We had a deal, fifty-fifty we agreed!" I protested.

"I'm actually offering you a good deal. A single ticket is about thirty pounds or so, and I'll give you a couple of hundred to rent a place. I'm sure once you start working the streets you'll be able to afford a nice place to live, or perhaps get yourself a pimp; I've heard the French ones look after their women quite well."

"Fuck you! I've told you I'm not a tom, now I just want my money." The tears in my eyes were genuine; I really felt I was being ripped off even though we knew that he would do it.

As answer Priack reached into his inside jacket pocket and produced five fifty pound notes, dropping them into my lap. "There's two hundred and fifty quid and just to prove that I'm not such a bastard I'll even drop you off at St Pancras Station..."

"No, I want a new life and that money is going to pay for it! You've got no right to rip me off...we had a deal!" I sobbed the words, this time in Oscar-winning actress mode.

"You keep using this word ... deal. I'd suggest you go and see Dougie Mann and tell him just how you feel it's unfair, or maybe you'd like to lodge a formal complaint with my superiors...because the Metropolitan Police always investigate and I'm sure they would like nothing better than to see you locked up for the next twenty years for murdering a foreign national ... and of course, this accusation of yours about money, well the Frenchman can't collaborate it and I don't think Dougie Mann will, so it appears to be just a figment of your imagination." He had a smug glow of self-congratulation about him.

"You really are a cold-hearted bastard, Priack, or as my friend Hannah Isaacs once called you, Detective Sergeant Prick!"

"Well I've heard a little rumour that I may soon become Detective Inspector Prick...and talking of pricks I'll give you another hundred in you put your lips around mine and make me a happy man." His confidence was soaring.

I threw the two hundred and fifty pounds back at him. "Here, take all of it and I hope it fucking chokes you...but tell me one thing, why did you trust me, when you despise me so much?"

"I'd already been warned that a French hit man by the name of Paul-Louis Broque had arrived in London. Our new Chief Inspector had received notice from Interpol and asked me to keep my eyes and ears open for any whispers as to his intentions, so he in fact confirmed your story before you even mentioned it to me...but let me tell you this, if you stay in London you will be dead within a week because Dougie Mann is so pissed at you that he'll throw everything he's got to ensure that you and most probably your entire bloodline are completely wiped off the face of this planet...and that's not bullshit Becky...that's fact!" As he finished talking he threw my bag back at me and then turned the ignition, firing the engine into life.

I grabbed my bag and climbed out of the car, slamming the door behind me and then watched as he accelerated away, leaving me in total darkness to the point where I didn't even know in which direction to go. I stood rooted to the spot, feeling cold, vulnerable and very, very afraid.

Suddenly a set of headlights appeared and headed towards me at speed. It wasn't Priack's car; the headlights were different and they quickly picked me up in their beam. As the car came to a halt beside me, I looked inside the car and my eyes was rewarded by the broadest of smiles and the friendly brown eyes of Kamalika.

Chapter 22

Caught bang to rights!

George 'Goby' Williams was forty-six years of age and since he had first reached that magical age of becoming a teenager, he'd amounted to nothing more than a small time member of the criminal fraternity. Petty crime and handling stolen goods were about the most he would ever aspire to. He had one particular trait that came to DS Priack's attention during his early days as a beat constable.

George Williams was short in stature and a constant worrier but the criminal fraternity considered George to be extremely reliable when trusted to carry out specific tasks and so he was frequently used as a go between for the villainous bands of thieves, including low level money laundering operations, which earned him the nickname of Goby. For several years DS Priack had used Goby Williams to bank his illicit cash. The UK's banking and accountancy regulations had been tightened considerably since Priack first started receiving back-handers and helping himself to a percentage of any stolen monies recovered. It was now impossible to pay large sums of cash of over ten thousand pounds into your account without automatically sending up a flare to the bank. Banking abroad threw up the same problems, although DS Priack did have one account with a bank in Northern Cyprus that Goby Williams had visited on his behalf twice a year. But mainly he divided his money between three accounts he held in separate banks in fictitious names.

After he had left Becky, Priack had driven home, divided the cash into three large envelopes and then telephoned Goby to arrange an early morning meeting; he gave him a pre-arranged code so that Goby knew he would be making a cash deposit, then gave him a number, so Goby also knew into which of his accounts he would be paying the money.

The following morning DS Priack drove to the North Woolwich free ferry terminal; he parked his car close by and walked on as a foot passenger. Goby Williams had boarded a few moments earlier as the few remaining foot passengers were disembarking. He made his way to the outside seating area, checked his watch then pulled his tobacco tin from his coat and began rolling himself a cigarette.

Priack caught sight of Goby sitting smoking and made his way towards him. He'd previously placed the three envelopes back into the brown briefcase, which he now carried with him. He passed by the front of Goby and without saying a word, sat next to him, with the briefcase on the deck between them. Goby flicked his cigarette over the side into the flowing Thames, and then stood up, picking the case up with him and walked towards the exit. The crew of the ferry were busy marshalling the oncoming vans, lorries and cars into a semblance of order.

Priack entwined his fingers and flexed them, stretching his arms outwards, the cold morning air had a particular chill to it as it came up off the river, but the only flicker of emotion on Priack's face was one of a smug satisfaction. He'd give Goby five hundred quid for his morning's work and the remainder of the fifteen-K was pure profit for him.

The strategically placed surveillance team and Kamalika, their team leader, had monitored and recorded every movement DS Priack had made since leaving Becky last night, and now they had two targets to follow, relentlessly and yet anonymously from a safe distance.

The team following Goby Williams were impressed with his attention to detail as he headed to the nearest branch of the first of the banks to make the deposit. He paused several times to cross and re-cross the road, enabling him to see if he was being followed, and then turned down side streets to double back on himself. A few times he stopped in front of a large shop window, as though looking at the shop's display, but in reality using the reflection of the glass to check no one was showing any unnecessary interest in him.

He eventually made his first deposit; the surveillance team recorded it and as he left the bank one of the team remained behind, producing a warrant and retrieving the money as evidence along with a full statement for the account showing all transactions since its opening date. The same procedure was followed at the bank of the second deposit and then again for the third.

The team continued to follow Goby and shortly after midday he entered a busy sandwich bar; as he walked in and joined the queue of office workers awaiting their orders DS Priack brushed against him on his way out; he mumbled an apology and carried on walking. To any onlookers who were interested it was just an everyday occurrence of the capital's ever growing pedestrian congestion. But to the surveillance team watching the Detective Sergeant, it was an exchange of paying-in slips for a rolled wad of money.

The instant DS Priack stepped outside the shop he was stopped, handcuffed, bundled into the back of an awaiting car and taken for questioning by MI5. Ten minutes later, when Goby Williams left the sandwich bar with his freshly prepared baguette he experienced the same end result.

Ernie Palmer removed his jacket and put on his comfortable cardigan. He was almost oblivious to his surroundings, whilst mentally focussed on his forthcoming performance. He knew only too well that they had nothing on DS Priack.
They had an abundance of suspicions and hearsay but absolute zero in terms of concrete proof. The dummy body and the money was blatant entrapment, and his job now was to convince Priack otherwise. The main risk he faced was that the DS was also an experienced copper and if he saw through the scam and lodged a formal complaint, then it could be Ernie himself facing a disciplinary hearing

and possibly dismissal from the service. He took a long swig from a small bottle of mineral water and then headed towards where his adversary was waiting.

"I have absolutely no intention of either saying or doing anything until my solicitor arrives and puts a stop to this fiasco!" Detective Sergeant Priack was sitting bolt upright in his chair at the oblong shaped table in the interview room.

Ernie Palmer gave him a gentle friendly smile. "Don't be too hasty to start this ball rolling. While you and I are chatting off the record we can probably accomplish much more to our mutual benefits than we will when it becomes a formal interview…and I…" Ernie stopped in mid sentence and glanced at a written report on the table in front of him.

Priack, taking advantage of the pause, tried to take the psychological advantage. "Let me advise you of this…at the very best you are inefficient and at the worst you are grossly incompetent, and I can assure you that you have absolutely nothing that can be of benefit to me!" Priack spat the words caustically.

Ernie Palmer ignored the comment as though he was absorbed in what he was reading, then looked up and acted as though he had only just become aware that Priack had been talking. "I'm sorry, what was that?" He again gave him a friendly smile.

Priack gave an impatient sign and again repeated his indignation.

Ernie nodded agreeably. "Yes, it must look that way to you…but I can assure you that you are going to be charged soon enough, and depending on your level of cooperation it could be a simple charge of theft or a number of other charges, including the murder of Paul-Louis Broque."

Priack froze momentarily, and then replied derisively, "You're just blowing threats out of your arse! You've got nothing on me and I've never even met or heard of this Paul, whatever his name is!"

A deliberately confused frown spread across Ernie's face, as he continued in the same friendly manner. "Well, that is strange, because Chief Inspector Ledbetter has confirmed that he informed you that a highly paid French hit man, by the name of Paul-Louis Broque, had arrived in London and also requested that you keep your ear to the ground as to his possible intentions. What is also strange is that a neighbour of the late Frenchman has sworn a statement that he heard the sound of a gunshot and shortly afterwards you were seen leaving the flat. He noted the registration number of your car and he later identified you from a photograph we showed him."

"That's bullshit and you know it!" Priack retorted angrily.

Ernie ignored the outburst and continued, "Because of who the murdered man was, we set up a surveillance on the flat – that was after we'd replaced all of the money in the briefcase with marked banknotes, of which every serial number had been recorded. Consequently we now have photographic evidence of you breaking into the flat and leaving with that very same briefcase of money. The time you spent in the flat was minimal, therefore based on reasoning, the conclusion has to be that you knew exactly where the case was located."

"I am saying nothing until my solicitor arrives. This is a fit-up and you know it." Traces of concern were now evident on Priack's face.

"You've got it all wrong old chap. I haven't asked you to say anything; we're just having a friendly off-the-record chat….. incidentally, a glass tumbler was found in the flat which had your fingerprints on it…" He held up a clear plastic pouch containing a glass tumbler, "…proving to us, or should I say to a jury, that you had in fact previously visited the flat."

"It's called planting evidence and it's the oldest trick in the book to get a jury to believe something…also that is probably the most commonly used style of glassware there is…they even have them at our station canteen…" Priack stopped as he realised where they had probably obtained the glass with his fingerprints, and the realisation that he'd been well and truly put in the frame as a murder suspect.

"Shall I continue?" asked Ernie.

"Providing your little fairy story ends with happily ever after, then I don't really give a rat's arse!" sneered Priack.

"You were followed home, and photographed taking the briefcase into your home. We also have a recording of you telephoning a George Williams – to whom you later refer as Goby; the purpose of that call was to initiate a meeting. Again we have photographic evidence of you leaving your house with the briefcase and taking it to the North Woolwich ferry terminal. You then met with Mr Williams on the ferry and whilst no conversation took place between you, he did in fact disembark with the briefcase in his possession before the ferry began its crossing. He then visited three different banks and deposited money in an account at each of these banks. He later met with you in a sandwich bar and passed you the paying-in slips he'd obtained in exchange for a wad of banknotes. It was later confirmed that the wad contained twenty-five notes of twenty-pound denomination to a total of five hundred pounds; these notes were part of the marked banknotes that we had placed in the briefcase. We have retrieved the money deposited at the banks and verified that it was also part of the marked banknotes we had previously placed in the briefcase. Each of the banks concerned has supplied us with a full statement showing every transaction made since the accounts were opened. All monies that have been transferred out of those accounts are currently being checked to establish the final destination, and of course who the recipient was. You should also be aware that Special Branch officers raided your house at around the same time as we apprehended you and they have discovered a pistol which they believe is the same pistol that killed Paul-Louis Broque; we're currently awaiting the ballistics report for final confirmation."

"You bastards, you've fucking set me up…you've stitched me like I was some kind of silly bollocks!" Priack's tone and body language clearly showed his aggression and frustration; he rubbed the palms of his hands down his trousers while gently shaking his head in disbelief.

Ernie Palmer allowed him his outburst and a few moments to regain his composure. "I think this may also be a good time to inform you that George Williams, upon being told that he was facing charges of accessory to murder, money laundering and of conspiracy and illegal involvement with organised crime, has agreed to turn Queen's Evidence rather than risk a possible twenty year prison sentence."

"So you have proved that you are very clever, but I've noticed that at no time have you mentioned the name of Rebecca Wilson." Smugness had returned to Priack's expression.

"Ah yes, Becky. I was quite impressed with her performance in the bed-sit, all of which we have on film, and your little meeting with her in the car … well, we'd also taken the liberty of planting a tiny microphone transmitter inside her mobile phone to ensure we'd also have a recording of your conversation with her…I actually thought it was rather gallant of you to offer to give her a lift to St Pancras…"

"So why hasn't she been arrested? snapped Priack.

"Perhaps she has, and perhaps she's giving a statement as we speak to the Serious Crimes Squad about enforced prostitution!"

"You know I didn't kill the Frenchman." Priack's tone appeared to soften.

"It's no good telling me, it's the jury you have worry about convincing."

"So what do you want?"

"Are you saying you want to negotiate…to perhaps work out a deal?" Ernie asked without giving any eye contact.

"Yeah, the deal is that you tell me what you want to know, and if I know the answer, I'll give you chapter and verse on it, and then when you've got everything you want…I walk away with full immunity."

"Mm, the problem with that is…I'm singing from a different song sheet, and on mine it says that there is no walking away; you have to face corruption charges…but it is a lesser charge for a policeman to face than murder?" Ernie suggested, although the sarcastic tone was lost on Priack.

"I must confess I am slightly disappointed in your tactics. I thought the mighty MI5 would have dreamed up something far more elaborate than a simple logic ploy."

"I'm sorry, you've lost me…"

"The simple logic ploy. It's probably used by police interrogators all over the world, and it really is simple. You've placed me in a situation that I believe is hopeless, and now you give me a choice between two bad options, knowing I will readily jump to the lesser one, and so you have what you were originally after!" Priack sat back in his chair, folded his arms and adopted a pose of self-assured confidence.

Ernie nodded his confirmation. "Well…what can I say, I've obviously made all the wrong assumptions about you." He sighed deeply, a defeated sigh. "I suppose all that's left now is to call in your solicitor and formally charge you…"

"Whoa, wait a minute, what do you mean?" protested Priack.

"Well you see, I wasn't playing any ploys; you are currently facing so many charges, apart from murder, that it's going to take a while to process them all. Your own Chief Inspector wants you charged with perjury and conspiracy to perpetrate a miscarriage of justice relating back to someone called Hannah Isaacs and I really don't know the ins and outs of that one…"

"Where's his proof?" scoffed Priack.

"I have no idea, it's not my case. But I did hear that one of the female junior detectives has also been collecting a number of testimonies in connection with some of your previous successful convictions, and once again amongst them proof of your submitting misleading evidence, misleading prosecutors and juries, and of perverting the course of justice. A detective from another station has evidence proving you have been taking bribes. Even some of your local villains have come forward with sworn statements of how you handled stolen property."

"I don't believe any of it; you're just chucking a load of lies at me in the hope I'll crumble and then you can get whatever it is you want!" Priack retorted with a sneer.

Ernie smiled, a smile which was both friendly and condescending at the same time. "Oh, you are so wrong…the vice squad have a complaint on file from a prostitute who claimed you raped her; they've now opened an investigation into it and I believe there are a couple more old toms waiting in the wings to come forward and put their six penn'orth in…I've been up-front with everything I've said to you in the hope you'd avoid the wrong assumptions."

"Yeah, well I only deal in facts, they're what keep me one step ahead!" Priack's bravado had all but crumbled.

Ernie shrugged his shoulders in a disinterested fashion. "Ponder on that over the next thirty years while you are languishing in prison...but now it's time to hand you over to the chaps whose job it is to arrest you formally and charge you. Incidentally, it has been ordained by our superiors that bail will be opposed most strongly." Ernie moved towards the door.

Priack watched him; his eyes were wide and his breathing was fast and shallow, and as Ernie Palmer's hand reached for the door handle, Priack called out to him, "Okay, you win…whatever deal you want to put to me, I'll accept…only you got to promise me that I don't end up sharing a cell with some arsehole that I've put away!"

Ernie turned around and looked at Priack, and for a brief moment the expression on his face fully showed the strong feelings of dislike he held for the man. But when Priack looked up at him he saw a friendly, warm and comforting face.

"You know full well I can't give you any promises like that! The only thing I'll do is to knock off the murder charge and the theft of the briefcase containing fifteen thousand pounds. I'll also agree that all recordings and photographic evidence relating to those previously mentioned events will be destroyed following your court appearance on the lesser charges."

"And what do you want in return?" Priack's manner was subdued as his mind fully absorbed this unfavourable outcome.

"I want everything you know, everything you've heard and every dealing you have ever had with Dougie Mann and that includes his tie in with the Eastern European crime lords."

"Wow! That is going to bring about a number of contracts on my life; you're certainly not asking for much are you?!" Priack scratched his head and thought for a few moments and then gave his answer. "Okay, I accept...I have stuff that will bury Dougie Mann so deep he'll never see the light of day! I'll give you everything you want but I want it confirmed to my solicitor that I am to be formally classified as a protected witness unit."

Ernie Palmer's answer was short and sharp: "Agreed."

Chapter 23

Farewell Old Friend

The police finally released Gabby's body and in the absence of any known family his funeral was organised by none other than Sebastian Toakes and paid for by the Security Services.

It was a cold overcast day, when the friends and colleagues of Gabriel Bracken came together at the city crematorium for his funeral. The service began with an appropriate hymn. Nobody ever knew – or had even asked – if Gabby had any religious views, as it was something that wasn't discussed.

Dad stood at the front and fought back tears to read out a poem that he felt best described the loyalty of his close friend. Colleagues and ex-clients talked about his life, and of his achievements since he'd left the Parachute Regiment. Sandra Atkins had turned up with Ruth, who was surprisingly tearful, and they comforted each other during the emotional service. It was a full congregation with more than a few, battle-hardened men standing with tear filled eyes and one or two actually looked on the verge of completely breaking down. I had somehow shut myself off emotionally; it wasn't a conscious thing and I can only assume that subconsciously I was using detachment as a form of protection from the harsh reality, and from the sadness that I knew was just waiting to engulf me. But for now I had an absence of emotional involvement.

Finally the Lord's Prayer was said as Gabby's coffin disappeared through the automatic doors, which were then covered by a curtain. Slowly we each stood and joined the queue of people slowly ambling outside to view the wreaths and messages. As I stepped outside I looked up at the sky the sun was beginning to break through the rain clouds, and I had a mental vision of Gabby up in heaven organising the weather, looking down on me and ensuring I now got only sunshine in my life.

I sensed somebody close by me and felt a gentle tap on my shoulder. I turned quickly; it was Maureen Dickins standing next to me. "Hello Becky, how are you bearing up?" She had a look in her eyes that told me she wasn't asking because it was expected, but because she actually cared.

"Yeah, I'm good," I answered, trying to sound upbeat.

"I've been hearing some good things about you. Apparently you are calm under pressure, you remain focussed on your particular task, you have a superb role playing ability even when the situation becomes personally distressful to you and to use a modern day cliché, you have certainly had a roller coaster of a journey, but whereas a lot of women who'd gone through only half of your experiences would be either quivering wrecks or in deep therapy by now, you are still standing defiantly kicking back. You are, without doubt, your father's daughter." She smiled approvingly.

"Thank you," I answered, accepting it as a compliment.

"I don't know if you've ever heard the story but years ago, when the various security departments were looking to recruit fresh blood, they looked mainly to the universities, and suitable candidates were given what was referred to as 'the tap on the shoulder' ... it was a euphemism."

"Oh...okay," I answered, a tad confused.

"The thing is, Becky, I believe that with the right training and a little polishing you could become an asset to your country. Now that this current operation is completed and after you've had a well deserved break, perhaps you'd like to think about my offer and give me a call...this is your tap on the shoulder."

"What do you mean completed?" I was now totally confused.

She placed her arm around my shoulder and gently led me away from any eavesdroppers. "You and Ernie Palmer between you had a one hundred percent success in getting that police sergeant to turn Queen's Evidence. He's one of the most valuable super-grasses we've had for a long time, so congratulations for that.

"Now, with regard to Dougie Mann, he and his inner circle were duly arrested. Unfortunately, while being taken to the police station to be formally charged, the police vehicle in which they were travelling was held up at a set of traffic lights. A motorcyclist suddenly rode up alongside and the pillion rider fired several shots through the window, scattering Dougie Mann's brains over the accompanying officer to whom he was handcuffed. In the ensuing confusion the assassins escaped. It was disappointing that we didn't get the opportunity to interrogate Mr Mann, but perhaps it was for the best; it would have tied up a lot of man hours bringing it to court."

As she finished speaking she handed me her card, gave me a genuine smile then turned and walked towards her car. Her driver opened the rear door for her as she approached and I watched as her car pulled away, but as I re-played her words in my head, I heard the chattering of birds directly above and looked upwards; large patches of blue sky were now appearing, and replacing the grey. A fresh comforting breeze gently swirled around me, I felt a wonderful surge of optimism and I just knew that everything was going to be okay.

Epilogue

Dad decided he'd had enough of London life and bought a lovely four bedroomed house in North Norfolk, just about five miles out of Cromer, and the views were stunning. He'd allocated a permanent room for me and a larger one for when Ruth and Sandra visited. The first free weekend he had, the three of us girls visited him together, and he wore a permanent grin on his face for the entire weekend. I believe some of the local lads in the village pub were also somewhat excited at the prospect of three delicious girls within their midst.

On the very first morning that I woke up in my room, Ruth rushed in and opened the curtains and I saw for the first time that the view from my bedroom was of the garden, and beyond that, to across the meadow and down to the woods, and as she threw open the bedroom window the only words she could utter were, "Ah…it's so peaceful…!"

We went down for breakfast and Dad had cooked us all a full English; everything that could be fried, was fried! I tucked in ravenously, while Ruth and Sandra picked politely at it.

After we'd all got stuck in and washed the pans and dishes we stepped out into the garden for the grand tour. I immediatley caught a faceful of a stiff wind whipped up from the fields and felt my hair being blown in all directions.

The house was set in approximately two and a half acres and I could almost hear Gabby's voice saying, *'from a security aspect it's probably the worst place he could have picked!'*

Later that same afternoon the cold wind disappeared and the sun came out; it became a glorious afternoon, and we all sat around in the garden. It was the most relaxing time that I could ever remember, and as I stretched out on the reclining chairs I thought about my Dad, and how much I loved him, and then I thought about Gabby and how I had loved him as a good friend, and one by one I thought of Ernie Palmer …. of Kamalika … and finally of Maureen Dickins. These were people who had accepted me for what I was. They were people prepared to lay their life down for me, people who treated me as an equal, and people that I knew I could also trust. I stood up.

"Can I have your attention please…I have an announcement to make." Ruth and Sandra groaned that I was disturbing their rest, but eventually I had the undivided attention of the three most important people in my life. "You three are the most important people in my life and I want you be the first to know that I've decided that Becky Wilson belongs in a past world to the one I'm in now, and so I've decided to change my name back to the one on my birth certificate: Rebecca Tanner."

My dad looked up at me with a look of fatherly love and a smile of admiration.

I pulled out the card Maureen Dickins had given me. "Yes," I said softly to myself, "I think the name Tanner may be useful for my new career..."

Apparently it is true what they say: the people who matter, don't mind and the people who mind, don't matter!

The End

Printed in the United Kingdom by
Lightning Source UK Ltd., Milton Keynes
138992UK00001B/93/P